MAGIC MOMENT

As she swam in the lagoon's warm water, big muscular hands gripped Erica and pulled her ashore. She gasped in disbelief as she gazed into the handsome face of a man who was most assuredly as naked as she.

Indignation brought her hand back and sent it flying to slap him as hard as she could. Inches from his tanned face, his strong, powerful hand slammed into her wrist. She winced in pain at the impact.

"How dare you," she said through gritted teeth.

Towering above her, he pushed her arm behind her back and reached out to grasp the other one before she swung again. She arched her back to halt the shooting pains radiating from her twisted arm. Gently but firmly he laid her against the cool ledge of the rock.

"How dare you," he countered.

She watched his mouth descend to capture hers, his lips finding hers open to protest his domineering manner. The stranger's tongue slipped into her mouth, causing her head to spin with waves of shock. The kiss lasted only seconds, but hours seemed to pass. In a moment, she, who had always prided herself on being independent and strong, had become a woman weak and obedient, clinging to this man and begging for his touch!

SEA DREAM
TERRI VALENTINE

ZEBRA BOOKS
KENSINGTON PUBLISHING CORP.

ZEBRA BOOKS

are published by

Kensington Publishing Corp.
475 Park Avenue South
New York, NY 10016

First printing: October 1987

Printed in the United States of America

DEDICATION
To Florence Case Moyer, my friend and mentor,
without whom this book would
have never been completed.
To Tom, my husband; the hero in my life.

Prologue

The Bahamas
September 10, 1832

Conception Cay. How easily the name tripped over Erica's tongue. She giggled. Only this summer, while running wild across the Jamaican landscape with Vanessa Metcalfe, had she learned just what the name meant. She had a hard time believing her parents did those things her friend described so graphically, but Vanessa had assured her she wouldn't be here if they didn't.

She lay back, scooping up a handful of hot, white sand, and watched it filter through her fingers. She grasped more and tossed it in the light breeze. Closing her eyes, she tried to picture her mother and father here together, making love. Making her. But the details remained evasive, leaving her unsure just what the act of love meant.

Disgusted with her own inability to understand, she sat up, abruptly tossing a final fistful of sand, and watched it hit the crystal clear surf in a fine spray of pellets. Two quick slaps of her open palms dusted the residue of grit from her hands as she stood up to survey her surroundings.

Glancing down at her clothes, she knocked the sand from the creases of the boy's britches she wore. The grit biting into her tender breasts itched. Pulling out the shirt still in a half-tucked position in her pants, she wiped off the particles that had worked their way to her bare skin.

Shaking like a frisky pup, she pushed the golden mane of hair from her face. Turning, she bounded across the beach to the tree line. The white sand looked like new-fallen snow, but heat radiated up from it. She dared not stop to catch her breath. When her tingling soles touched the cool blades of grass edging the sand, she groaned relief.

She glanced back to see the fire of the sun slip below the horizon, leaving only the orange rays of sunset. She didn't have long, but she didn't care. It had taken her all day to escape the ship and her parents. She hoped they wouldn't notice her absence until dinner time, giving her at least an hour alone in the lagoon.

Her lagoon, she thought jealously. She had a right to come here by herself no matter what her father told her. Her safety wasn't in question. There could be nothing here to possibly hurt her. She scoffed at her parents' orders to stay aboard the *Anna McKyle* and not venture off alone to the island. It had been easy to slip overboard when no one was looking and swim ashore. The calm bay and gentle waves made it simple enough for a babe to swim. A snap for someone of her natural abilities.

The darkness closed around her, and she stumbled,

looking for the small creek flowing from the lagoon to the sea. Twice she stubbed a bare toe on above-ground roots, both times issuing a "damn" to ease the pain. Her parents would wash her mouth out with soap to hear her talk that way, but the word was a grown-up one, and she liked the way it sounded on her lips.

The full moon broke through a patch of clouds, illuminating everything around her. The creek bed shimmered a few yards ahead of her. Stepping into the cool water soothed the throbbing in her feet. She had no trouble navigating the sandy bottom of the stream, so she relaxed and enjoyed splashing as she walked.

Just a short distance away, the pool remained too deep in shadow to see. Was that a splash she heard coming from somewhere up ahead? She paused, listening with her breath held deep in her lungs. Impossible! The drone of insects and the cries of night birds were the only sounds that intermittently cut through the darkness, joining the inviting bubble of the natural spring that fed the lagoon. She took a couple of tentative steps, and the rippling pool appeared in front of her. The air rushed out of her chest in relief.

Except for the side where the water gushed out to create the stream she stood in, flat ledges surrounded the lagoon. She marveled at nature producing such a perfect place. The Garden of Eden must have looked like this.

The pool moved in and out of shadow as the moon rose and fell like a ship in a veil-like patch of clouds, causing an eerie effect. Surrounding bushes and trees came alive as they dipped and bobbed in the light breeze swirling around her.

Like a small, wild animal watched by a predator, she approached the lagoon. Shivers traveled up her back, and her heart drummed in her ears. She shook her shoulders to rid herself of the feeling, but it lingered, refusing to listen to reason.

Piqued at her childish thoughts, she stripped the clothes from her body to leave them lying where they fell in the underbrush. Still in shadow at the edge of the pool, she glanced across to the other bank swallowed in darkness as well. She gave the lagoon's edge one last look, still unable to shake the feeling that someone waited for her on the other side. But nothing had changed. The spring bubbled noisily to her left, and the branches of the trees and bushes danced with the wind.

With a running jump she arched into the lagoon, hitting the water a good distance from the edge. The moonlight filtered through the water, illuminating everything around her. Playing a game of endurance, she stayed underwater until she reached the other bank.

The black rock of the pool's edge loomed before her. Closing her eyes to better concentrate, she reached for the barrier. Her fingers grazed the smooth stone. She pushed upward with all her strength, her eyes still closed. She shot through the surface of the water, and exhilaration engulfed her as she took a gulping breath to fill her aching lungs. She groped for the ledge to locate a steady handhold. The tips of her fingers touched something smooth, warm, and definitely alive. She lightly traced what her hand had discovered, and her eyes popped open. A moment passed before she realized what she saw. The torso of a man, a completely nude man, her hand gripping his hip. She blinked once in disbelief. Snapping her hand back, she lost her grip on the ledge to plunge back under the water with empty lungs.

Strong hands grasped her underarms and lifted her through the water. The cool air kissed her bare skin as her bottom hit the hard surface of the ledge with a thump, leaving her legs dangling over the edge. Strands of wet, matted hair covered her face, filling her mouth and nose with each gasping breath she took between coughs to expel the water from her lungs. She caught her breath and pushed back the offending mass of hair to stare into the darkest eyes she had ever seen, so dark she couldn't distinguish the irises from the pupils. The eyes, along with the attached mouth, smiled at her. Slowly the dark orbs traveled down with a concentrated stare.

She reached instinctively to the place the eyes regarded. They contemplated her bare breast and then moved lower. Her hands hugged her body to ineffectively cover her nudity.

"What a shame."

"What did you say?" she whispered, tilting her head to observe the man sitting next to her.

"I said it's a pity." His face lit up with another smile. "I was enjoying the view."

The fire of embarrassment heated her face. Her tongue lay numbly in her mouth, refusing to work as her jaw dropped, unhinged. Her gaze darted wildly and then settled on the man sitting beside her. Never had she seen a completely nude man before. Occasionally the sailors had stripped off their shirts aboard ship, but none resembled this man. Most were furred like animals or were completely hairless. He had hair on his body, but refined and patterned, circling his chest to run into a neat V at the navel, then faintly tracing his stomach in a thin line to his groin.

"Oh," she blurted. Her eyes shot back up to his friendly, open face. Black hair with blue highlights curled around his forehead and ears in an intriging way.

"Unfortunately, my clothes are over there," he said, breaking her concentration, "so I must remain as I am." Her eyes followed his pointing finger to a place not far from her own clothes. He laughed, and she caught his mischievous grin. "You have to promise not to look any more."

She blinked, not comprehending his words at first. Her lowered jaw dropped farther. He had noticed her staring at him so boldly. His eyes held amusement. His words carried a teasing note. He just sat there, completely relaxed, making no attempt to cover himself.

Indignation brought her hand back and sent it flying to slap him as hard as she could. Inches from his tanned face, his strong muscular hand slammed into her wrist. She winced in pain at the impact.

"How dare you," she said through gritted teeth.

Towering above her, he pushed her arm behind her back and reached out to grasp the other one before she swung again. She arched her back to halt the shooting pains radiating from her twisted arm. Gently but firmly he laid her against the cool ledge.

"How dare you," he countered.

She watched his mouth descend to capture hers, his lips finding hers open to protest his domineering manner. His tongue slipped into her mouth, causing her head to spin with waves of shock. The kiss lasted only seconds, but hours seemed to pass. She studied his closed eyes in amazement. The thick lashes fluttered and opened to reveal those inky depths.

Backing away, he stared at her. She lay in his arms, her mouth still open. Slowly her lips formed an O. Never had she been kissed like that before.

"My Uncle Andrew told me he caught a mermaid once. I never believed him, until now. Are you a mermaid?"

She gaped at him, unable to reply.

"You must be," he continued. "Why else would you be here? I saw you dive into the water, and you came from nowhere." His hand released hers and reached up to stroke her hair. "My God, I can't believe it."

His fingers traced the outline of her lips, settling on a tiny scar in the corner of her mouth, the remainder of a childhood accident. "A tiny flaw in such perfection," he observed. His hand followed her jaw, outlined her earlobe, and spiraled down her neck to her shoulder. He lingered there, drawing intricate patterns on the skin in the hollow of her throat. His head dipped down to replace his fingers with his lips.

Her mind reeled with indecision. No one else dared touch her as this man did, as if he had every right. A rasping filled her ears, his harsh uneven breathing. His tongue traced the curves and ridges of her ear, erasing all thoughts from her mind and leaving only the sensations his touch created.

His expert hand moved down her shoulder to caress her firm, young breast. She didn't protest. His lips followed his hand. His warm mouth circled her tender nipple, sending shock waves to the core of her being.

Bewildered, she couldn't breathe. She panted, attempting to pull air into her lungs. His weight shifted. Something hard and warm pressed against her thigh. Her mind surfaced from the pool of sensations. This was what Vanessa had described to her. His hand fluttered across her hip.

Her body tensed. Frantically she pushed at his head, still level with her breasts. "No," she gasped. "What do you think you're doing?"

He looked up, his eyes moist and sultry. "Only what any sailor would want to do to a mermaid."

"Let go of me." Her fist swung at his head. The look of determination on his face frightened her. "No, I won't let you. No-o-o-o — "

"Damn it, if you don't want me to, I won't." He grabbed her flying arms and planted them above her head. "Just stop screaming."

She ceased her struggling, her body slumping against the pressure his weight exerted on hers. Abruptly, he released her and sat up. Like a frightened foal she twisted sideways, slipped from the ledge, and hit the water with a loud splash. The lagoon offered safety. The water hid her nudity. She considered swimming away, yet the man fascinated her. If he had wanted to hurt her, he would have. Treading water a safe distance away, she watched

14

him, prepared for any sudden move he might make.

"Do mermaids have names?" he asked as he discreetly placed his hands in his lap, hiding the essence of his manhood from her view.

"Erica," she answered, not sure she should have told him, not sure why she shouldn't have. Her arms and legs moved in tempo to keep her head above the waterline. "Do sailors have names?"

"Dirk. Just Erica?" he coaxed.

She nodded silently. Caution held her tongue.

"All right, Erica, what are you doing here?"

"What am I doing here? What are you doing here in my lagoon?"

Dirk's head flew back as he laughed with delight. "I'm sorry. I didn't know mermaids were so territorial." His eyes followed her every move.

Her heart thumped an offbeat rhythm in her throat as he rose and dove into the water. With a shriek she twisted and swam for the opposite shore. His hand grasped her kicking ankle and no amount of struggling loosened his steel grip. She surfaced, sucking in the much-needed air. His hands skimmed lightly over her hips and waist as his head broke the choppy surface inches from hers.

"I think I'll take you home with me."

"No, you can't," she screamed, childish images of pirates and plundering filling her young mind. She flipped backward under the water and shot toward the bank of escape. She anticipated his grip of iron, but nothing happened. He had let her leave.

Scrambling out of the water, she grabbed her clothes. But like Lot's wife, she couldn't resist turning to glance behind her. Dirk remained in the pool where she had left him.

"No one will believe me. I had a mermaid and I let her go. I must be insane." His hand lifted dripping water in a farewell salute. "Until next time, Mermaid. Watch for me. I'll be back."

She turned on her heels, clutching her clothes to her wet body, and ran as fast as she could from the lagoon. She stopped only long enough to yank on her britches and continued her headlong dash to the beach.

"Erica," her father's voice shouted just ahead. She tucked in the tails of her shirt, her heart sinking with dread.

Given no choice, she continued toward the point where her father stood next to the ship's dinghy. Obediently, she hung her proud head at the stern look he gave her before grabbing her arm.

"This is the final straw, young lady. Your mother is right. It's time you went home and stayed there until you learn to be a lady. No more britches for you, just corsets and skirts."

"No, Papa, please," she begged. "I don't want to be a lady. I want to be just like you and captain my own ship."

"I'm sorry, princess. This is for your own good. Learn how to be a lady, and then you can take on this man's world."

She swallowed hard. He meant it. This time she had pushed him too far.

Chapter One

Baltimore, Maryland
Wednesday, April 1, 1835

The cold north wind whipped unmercifully at the black skirts circling Erica Armstrong's long, slim legs, an enemy attempting to pull her down and allow the multitude of blurred faces around her to see her weak and defeated. The same icy fingers tugged at the silken tresses of her hair, left unbound to fall to her waist like a golden cape around her stiffly held shoulders.

"Now, let us pray," boomed the voice of the reverend standing before them. She watched in stunned silence as the crowd bent their heads in unison at the command. She refused to lower her head. Like a bee droning, the preacher began a long-winded prayer that would probably make her father turn in his watery grave, wherever he lay. The man's words fell on her deaf ears.

The warm, loving hand of the elegant woman standing beside her reached out to touch Erica's arm. She turned her head to acknowledge her Aunt Constance and patted the older woman's hand reassuringly, her way of letting her aunt know she was all right.

The deep-toned voice of the reverend came to a sudden halt. In the silence, a loud crackle rent the air as the multitude of bent heads rose.

She turned to go, but Constance's hand stopped her, insisting she hold her ground. "The people will want to offer you their condolences, Erica, and you must remain to accept them."

She nodded silently. How she wished this day to be over. How she wished no need existed for this day at all. Politely she lifted her hand to accept the muffled words of sorrow the face before her offered.

"Thank you," she murmured, hoping she said the right words, not having heard the jeremiad to begin with.

The endless line marched before her until her hand grew numb, and her face quivered with the fatigue of holding the respectful, solemn look she decided was necessary.

I must be strong, she thought. *I will never weaken before these people who expect it. If nothing else, Papa, you taught me to be strong.*

The milling crowd studied her. Their eyes pricked the back of her neck like pinpoints, the undertone of shock filtering to her ears. "Not a tear, the girl has not shed a single tear for her poor mother and father."

Her chin lifted defiantly, as the coachman assisted her into the waiting carriage.

"Erica Armstrong." Her head pivoted to glance at the man whose face loomed in the window of the coach. "We must talk."

She watched as the lean hand of Edmund Bennett clutched the window ledge. Constance pushed her back to sit in the seat, leaning forward herself to take matters in hand.

"Please, Mr. Bennett, Erica is in mourning. I know you're the manager of Armstrong Shipping, but now is not the time to discuss business."

"It's all right, Aunt Connie. If Mr. Bennett feels it's important, then he's welcome to come by the house tomorrow, late morning." Erica leaned forward and caught the man's insistent glare. "Say ten o'clock?"

He stared back boldly, nodding. As the vehicle lurched forward, his brown eyes continued to follow her.

She sat back, her fingers twisting the balled piece of lace she clutched. Something about the man bothered her. She couldn't quite put her finger on the reason, but she felt uncomfortable around him. Shrugging her shoulders, she pushed the thoughts of the man out of her mind. Closing her gray eyes, she concentrated instead on forcing the tears scalding the back of her throat to remain where they were — unshed.

Erica eyed the man relaxing in the large wingback

chair across the room. A look of satisfied amusement encompassed his face. She wanted to slap the smug grin off his thin-lipped mouth.

"Mr. Bennett," she said aghast, "you can't be serious."

His long, tapered fingers set down the thick Cuban cigar to form a steeple in front of him. He tapped his fingertips in slow rhythm, ogling her slim figure.

"I assure you the papers are perfectly legal."

Her eyes moved down, staring at the offending documents gripped in her fingers. Loan papers signed by her father two months before his death. But why would he borrow money from his business manager with such inflexible terms?

"The terms are quite simple, Miss Armstrong. The—"

"Yes," she interrupted, "I'm capable of understanding them."

"—First installment was due yesterday," he continued as if she had never spoken, "and the balance is due July first. If you can't make the payments, I must insist you turn over fifty-one percent of Armstrong Shipping as your father agreed to do."

"Why would my father make an arrangement like this with you? The stocks in the shipping company are worth ten times the amount of this loan."

"Let's just say he didn't have much choice. He needed the money, and I had it to loan. I believe I'm being very lenient by giving you ten days' grace."

"Your kindness is overwhelming." Her mouth tightened with bitterness.

The parlor door opened, squelching the remark on his lips. Relief flooded over her as Aunt Constance's concerned face peered around the door.

"Am I interrupting your meeting, dear?" the older woman queried. "I thought you might be in need of refreshment."

Bennet shook his head, refusing her offer, as Erica waved her aunt into the room. His look promised he wouldn't forget her actions, but she ignored it.

"I really must be going, Miss Armstrong," he said, rising from his chair. "I need to get back to the office. However, I expect to hear from you in ten days." He walked out of the parlor door, leaving her to stare at his back.

She let out a long breath, glad to be rid of the man.

Erica hesitated in the arched doorway of her father's study, inhaling the manly smells lingering in the room, the odor of expensive Cuban cigars and the best brandy money could buy. As a child this room had been off-limits to her, and she found it hard to violate her dead father's orders. But the confrontation with Edmund Bennett the day before forced her to step through the door into the reality of her father's world. She must find out why her father had taken the loan from his business manager and what the state of affairs was at Armstrong Shipping. Her father's study was the place to begin her search.

Stepping over to the drapes hiding a row of French doors, she pulled them back. The chill from the early spring drizzle penetrated the panes, deepening the misery clutching at her heart. The dim afternoon light did nothing to brighten the dark, cheerless room.

She forced her feet to carry her the few steps to the large walnut desk dominating the room. Her fingers traced the creases and worn spots on the leather chair pushed up under the top drawer of the desk. Tentatively she pulled at the back of the chair, expecting it to resist her intrusion. Instead, it slid easily across the floor and angled to face her in an invitation she couldn't resist.

The chair squeaked with familiarity as she lowered her body onto the seat. Wiggling into a comfortable position, she placed her empty hands before her on the flat surface. Where to begin, she couldn't decide.

With a sigh she systematically searched the desk drawers, starting with the ones to the right of her. Most were a jumble of old logbooks and papers, none of which caught her attention. The last drawer she scanned rested against her stomach in the middle of the desk, filled with an assortment of pens, ink bottles, and other necessary items. When she pushed the drawer closed, frustration settled around her. Nothing about the loan. The drawer jammed and she butted up against it to force it shut. The corner of an envelope caught under the lip of the desk and flipped down. She struggled to dislodge it and discovered her name printed across the front of it in her father's neat handwriting.

Her heart thumped noisily against her chest. Why would her father leave a note to her in his desk where she would never look for it? Unless . . .

She ripped the sealed envelope open to allow the precisely creased pages to fall out. The paper crackled as she unfolded the letter to read what her father

22

had written.

Erica, my beloved daughter,
There is only one reason you would be reading this. Your mother and I are dead.

She couldn't stem the tears gathering in the corners of her eyes. She blinked to clear her vision and released the stale air she held in her aching lungs.

Every time your mother and I sail together, I have placed a letter like this in the drawer, knowing you would find it when you decided to take control of your life. I won't lecture you, I was never very good at that. I'll just give you some good fatherly advice. Trust your instincts, Princess. They won't steer you wrong. Armstrong Shipping is yours, and I'm depending on you to keep it going so you can hand it down to your children.

Erica couldn't stop the retching sob from escaping. The letter crumpled in her hand. A few moments passed before she collected her emotions to continue reading her father's last words.

Don't let anyone tell you different or try to take the business away from you. Believe me, there will be those who will try.
The only thing I ask of you is when you do decide to marry, do so for love. However, for my peace of mind, have a prenuptial agreement drawn up stating that all the Armstrong hold-

ings will remain in your control and not be forfeited to your husband.

I know this may seem harsh to you, but if the man loves you, he'll sign it. I never regretted signing one between your mother and me.

Know that I love you dearly and always will.

Eric A. Armstrong,
Your father

The tears flowed unchecked down her face. "I promise you, Papa," she whispered. "I'll make you proud of me."

What should I do? She clasped her hands in front of her and prayed as if she were a small child again. Never could she allow Edmund Bennett to gain control of Armstrong Shipping, no matter what her father's reason for borrowing money from the man.

The office door squeaked. She glanced up to see Aunt Constance's look of care. She dropped the letter still resting in her hand to reach up and wipe away any sign of her tears.

"Erica, are you all right?" Constance questioned.

"Of course, Aunt Connie, I'm fine," she sniffed, looking away to hide her tear-streaked face.

"You know, dear, I find it quite commendable that you have come here to your father's domain so soon, but it's really not necessary." Constance took a hesitant step into the room.

"No, you're wrong. This is something I need to do."

"If you're concerned about the business, I don't think you need to be. I'm sure Mr. Bennett can handle things efficiently. He always did in the past for your father."

"Perhaps, but you know how I am. I'm not one to sit back and let others do things for me." How she wanted to shout the truth to her aunt. But Constance's simple, earthy way would never understand the threat Edmund Bennett represented. The older woman would see his demands as a solution instead of a problem. *No, Aunt Connie, you could never understand,* she thought.

"I haven't forgotten how stubborn an Armstrong can be." Constance shook her head in resigned defeat. "But you're only a nineteen-year-old girl. You can't take the entire world on your shoulders."

"I promise you, there's just a few loose ends I want to tie up, and then I'll be the perfect niece you think I should be."

Constance turned to leave the room. She glanced back at her niece's unreadable look. "I came to remind you we have a meeting in the attorney's office at two this afternoon. Just don't get so involved in what you're doing that you don't have time to get ready to go."

Her eyes followed the older woman's retreating back. The attorney. The reading of the will. If anyone would know why her father had made the loan from Edmund Bennett, it would be George Hammond, her father's lawyer and life-time friend.

Erica canvassed the people filling the small room of George Hammond's office. She and Aunt Constance occupied the primary chairs directly before his desk. Several distant cousins, whose names she couldn't remember, sat behind them, and in one corner stood Edmund Bennett. He reminded her of a vulture waiting to pick over the remains of a carcass. How she hated the fact the man had been invited to share this moment. Pointedly, she ignored him and sensed his irritation.

The attorney cleared his throat to bring the attention to him. "Ladies and gentlemen, we are gathered here for the sole purpose of reading the last will and testament of Eric and Anna Armstrong. I'm glad to inform you that neither document is long and both are to the point. Shall we begin?" He directed his question to Erica.

She nodded her head in agreement, and the man began speaking in the singsongy voice of a lawyer. With effort she concentrated on the words he said, as he announced token bequests to the distant relatives.

Her head swung up as he mentioned her aunt's name.

"And to Constance McKyle, the beloved sister of my wife, I leave care and custody of my only daughter, Erica, and a lifetime stipend of ten thousand dollars a year." She glanced at her aunt, needing reassurance, and Constance patted her hand in understanding.

"To my daughter, Erica, I leave all my remaining worldly possessions including Armstrong Shipping, as well as a trust in the amount of fifty thousand dollars that I put aside for you when I made my first million. Use it wisely, Princess."

Erica's eyes widened with excitement. Fifty thousand dollars. Enough to pay Edmund Bennett the first installment on the loan her father had borrowed. She shot Bennett a smug look and watched as a sour expression tightened his mouth unattractively.

"And last, to Edmund Bennett, my business manager," Hammond continued, "I leave my sympathy." She swallowed the laughter threatening to escape her lips. "Now you will have to deal with my daughter, Erica, and I think you will find her a worthy opponent."

Bennett turned to leave the room, slamming the door behind him. Her father had anticipated the man's every move.

"Now, if the rest of you don't mind," the attorney said matter-of-factly, "the next document I have to read involves only Miss Armstrong. All others can wait outside in the reception room until I'm done so that proper arrangements can be made regarding your inheritances."

She watched in silence as the people filtered from the room. Constance waited until the relatives left before she turned and offered her outstretched hand to Erica, who gladly accepted it.

"I'll wait for you in the carriage," Constance offered, and she nodded in agreement.

The door closed quietly behind her aunt. Pivoting, she faced the attorney. Now she could get the answers she needed from him.

"Mr. Hammond, I have a few questions I would like answers to."

"I'm sure you do, Erica. But first, let's take care of the business at hand," he insisted.

She resumed her seat quietly and watched as he

27

shuffled the papers before him on the desk. Hammond handed her a document and waited until she skimmed the three pages before he began.

"As you can see, your mother's will isn't long or complicated. I won't bother to read it word for word to you unless you want me to."

"No, Mr. Hammond, that won't be necessary."

Nodding his approval, he clasped his hands over his protruding middle. "Your mother was a wealthy woman in her own right. As you know, her family's wealth is based in Jamaica. Anna maintained ownership of a large plantation of considerable acreage there. It now belongs to you."

"Didn't it belong to my father?"

Hammond studied her across the expanse of the desk. "Your father never claimed ownership of any of your mother's possessions. There was a legal agreement between them."

Her mind raced. Maybe she could pay Edmund Bennett with funds obtained from selling the Jamaican plantation. "How much do you think the property is worth?"

The attorney eyed her curiously. "I have never personally seen the plantation, but I would estimate its worth around two hundred thousand dollars."

Her shoulders edged forward. More than enough to take care of the business manager's demands. She needed to work out the details of selling it.

"Do you know who my mother's solicitor is in Jamaica?"

The attorney nodded solemnly.

She took a deep breath, expelling it only after her lungs demanded relief. "Please make the necessary arrangements to sell the property and let me know when a buyer is found."

"Are you sure that's what you want?"

Her mouth flattened into a straight slash across her face. "No, Mr. Hammond, but it's what I have to do."

The attorney lifted a pen from the holder on his desk and made a few quick notes. His eyes moved back up to her as he said, "I'll contact you as soon as I know something. Now, did you have some questions you wanted to ask me?"

She cleared her throat, not quite sure of where to begin. "Are you aware of the loan my father took from Edmund Bennett?"

"I was aware that he considered it. Quite frankly, I advised him not to take it."

"Father accepted the money. What I don't understand is why he would do such a thing. I hoped you would have the answer for me."

Hammond searched her face as if he hoped to read her mind. "I know the reason," he replied quietly, "but I'm not sure it's ethical to discuss your father's motives with you."

"Please, Mr. Hammond, I need to know. A hundred thousand dollars is a lot of money." She leaned forward across the desk as far as she could. "I have a right to know why he needed it."

The lawyer dipped his head in concurrence. "Eric was being blackmailed by a woman who claimed she carried his child. I advised him not to pay the demands as there would be no way for the woman to prove fathership, if, in fact, a child even existed." Hammond shrugged his shoulders. "But your father

29

was determined to keep any kind of scandal from touching you or your mother."

"But a hundred thousand dollars is outrageous," she gasped. "Is the child his?"

"That is something only your father could answer. As far as the money is concerned, if your father paid it, there's nothing we can legally do about it now."

She edged back in her chair, mulling over the information the attorney had given her. With the rise of one shapely eyebrow, she asked, "Why didn't my father fire Edmund Bennett a long time ago?"

Hammond looked back with amusement encompassing his face. "The man is ruthless. But then ruthlessness was something Eric understood. The man's a good business manager, and your father knew that."

"Then you're suggesting I keep the man in my employ?"

"No. I'm just saying Edmund Bennett will do a good job if you keep a tight rein on him."

She pushed up from her chair. The attorney had answered all her questions, except one. Staring down at his seated figure, she asked, "Why didn't my father go to a bank for a loan if he needed the cash?"

George Hammond sighed. "Your father was extremely wealthy, but all his money was tied up in Armstrong Shipping. Eric's assets were mortgaged to the utmost. I doubt there was a bank anywhere that would have extended him further credit."

She nodded with dignity and turned to leave the office.

"I'm sorry I had to be the one to give you such unpleasant information."

She twisted back with a slight smile on her face. "Don't worry, Mr. Hammond, you gave me the solution to my problem. A way to pay Edmund Bennett back."

"Wait a minute," he said, coming around the desk. "This is yours." He placed a bank deposit book in her delicate hand.

The carriage came to a halt in front of the single-storied, wharfside building housing Armstrong Shipping. Erica impatiently waited for the driver to step down and open the door for her before descending to the pavement. She touched Constance's hand as the other woman tried to follow her.

"Stay here, Aunt Connie. I shouldn't be long."

Constance sat back on the seat and folded her hands in front of her. Erica turned back to face the building looming before her like a weather-beaten old man disapproving of her presence. Reaching the building, she used all of her mental strength to grasp the handle of the door and open it. Several clerks and bookkeepers sitting at high stools before a counter running the length of the room were so absorbed in their work that they didn't notice her entry. She hesitated; then, squaring her shoulders, she demanded attention.

"I would like to speak with Mr. Bennett."

Heads swiveled in her direction. No one moved to answer her.

"Miss Armstrong?" a voice asked from behind her.

She swung around to face the speaker, a small, delicately-made man in his late fifties. Wire-rimmed

31

glasses too large for his face slid down his nose to stop just short of falling off. She knew the face but couldn't put a name to it.

His hand reached up to push the spectacles back in place. "Hollister Kerr," he offered.

"Of course, Mr. Kerr, you're the head bookkeeper, if I remember right."

He beamed at her and twisted to drop a heavy ledger book in front of the nearest clerk. Turning back to face her, he responded, "We're honored to have you here."

She smiled her thanks. "Could you tell Mr. Bennett I would like to see him?"

"I'm sorry, Miss Armstrong, he hasn't gotten back yet."

She raised her eyebrows in alarm. She'd had time to go to the bank and withdrew the funds to pay him before she came here. He should be here, also. His lack of responsibility irritated her.

"When he does come in, please tell him I'm waiting in my father's office." Starting toward the closed door, she recalled that her aunt waited for her in the carriage. She glanced up at the wall clock noisily ticking the seconds by. *I'll give him thirty minutes.*

"I'm sorry, Miss Armstrong," Mr. Kerr's voice intruded into her thoughts, "that's Mr. Bennett's office now."

She whirled to confront the little bookkeeper who stood blinking at her.

"But I'm sure he won't mind if you wait there."

"Edmund Bennett has taken over *my father's* office?" she choked in anger.

He nodded confirmation.

Without further words she stalked across the room, not stopping until the office door closed behind her with a bang. Her shoulders slumped forward and her chin dropped. If only Aunt Connie had come in with her, someone to express her frustration to.

"How dare he," she whispered, her face taut with resentment. "How dare he move into my father's office. He may have used this room temporarily, but no more."

With purposeful strides she approached the large desk. Without hesitation she pulled out the chair and sat down. Her eyes scanned the top sheets of paper on each of the half-dozen piles on the desk. She dug through them, trying to make sense out of what she read. Shipping orders, bills of lading, letters from agents and buyers. Would she ever be able to understand what she read? She shook her head in confusion. She sat back, nursing her mixed emotions. She didn't like Edmund Bennett, but did she need him? She honestly didn't know.

Again, she bent over, studying the papers without any thought for the privacy of the man using the desk. A name jumped out at her. A name she recognized. *Anna McKyle.* Her mother's maiden name and the name of the ship her parents had been on when they were swept overboard during a violent storm. The fast clipper had been her father's favorite, one of a kind, an experiment of a sort. How he had loved that ship. He had continued to captain it, even though financially it hadn't been necessary.

The document was a memo from the wharfmaster asking what he should do with the clipper. At the bottom of the note the handwriting read, "Sell it, not worth saving. Edmund Bennett."

She crumpled the memo in her hand, unable to believe what she had read. Bennett planned to get rid of her father's ship. She couldn't let him do that. Outrage strengthened her spine. *She* owned Armstrong Shipping. Edmund Bennett worked for her. Never would she allow the *Anna McKyle* to be sold.

The office door swung open. She glared at the man who filled the doorway.

"Get out of my chair, Erica," Bennett ordered arrogantly, one of her father's cigars clamped between his teeth.

She held her position. "This is not your chair, Mr. Bennett. It never was, and it never will be."

In a half-dozen quick strides he closed the gap between them. Circling the desk, he whirled her in the chair to face him. "Just whose do you think it is? Your father is dead," he hissed. "It's mine, honey. It always should have been."

Grabbing her arm, he pulled her from the chair, his face inches from hers. "Just like you. You should have always been mine. But your father thought I wasn't good enough for his precious daughter."

Her heart leaped to her throat as her anger catapulted into terror. A scream bubbled and burst in her chest. She held her chin up defiantly. This man had no right to dictate to her. Never would she allow him to run over her.

"Let go of me." She forced her voice to remain calm and steady.

Bennett's hand released her, and as he stepped back, his eyes fell to her heaving chest. "Who in the hell do you think you are, coming in here, ordering my employees around, and taking over my desk."

Staring up into his inflamed face, she stretched to stand as tall as she could. "I'm the owner of Armstrong Shipping. They are my employees, and this," she indicated with a sweep of her hand, "is *my* desk."

"You think you're capable of running this business?" He threw his head back and laughed out loud.

Her eyes steadily crossed swords with his.

"You're only a woman. You won't last two weeks, Erica, before you tuck your pretty tail and head back home to your needlepoint."

She exploded, tiny sparks filling her line of vision. "I wouldn't bet on that." Her hand shook so violently she had trouble reaching into her reticule to remove the bank draft made out to him for fifty thousand dollars.

"Here's your payment on the first half of the loan." She thrust the bank voucher at him. His hand snaked out to grasp the check. The greed in his eyes sickened her.

"I know you think you've beaten me, you stupid bitch, but you're wrong. I won't be so lenient on the next payment. July first. Not one day later. Now get out of here and go home to your knitting."

His barb stung like iodine in an open wound. She lifted her chin and planted her fists on her hips. "No, Mr. Bennett, you get out of here. You're fired."

His mouth snapped open in surprise. "I'll see both you and this damn shipping company on your knees before I'm through with you. You'll be sorry you didn't just turn the company over to me in the beginning."

35

She stood rigidly, his threats glancing off her like sticks and stones. She collapsed in the chair as the door closed behind him, the energy to stand and fight draining from her body.

So much had happened in the last two days. Her mind couldn't keep all the information straight. But she had halted Edmund Bennett's disastrous plans, albeit temporarily. Three months until the installment fell due would go by fast. She needed a permanent solution, and she needed it now.

Chapter Two

May 3, 1835

The *Anna McKyle* rode high in the water. To Erica, standing on the pier, her proud clipper's lines suggested a lean, sleek greyhound aching to run, but left instead to wither and die in a small kennel. The jutting figurehead, an exact carved replica of her mother, bobbed and bowed with the gently undulating water of the Patapsco River, keenly reminding her of her loss.

This ship meant everything to her: the answer to her problems, her means to get to Jamaica and the money that awaited her from the sale of the sugarcane plantation. George Hammond's note had come to the office only this morning. The sale had been finalized. She must go to Kingston to sign the papers and collect the money due her, the money to pay Edmund Bennett and get him out of her life forever. There wasn't time to wait for the papers to travel back and forth between Baltimore and Kingston. She must leave soon. July first wasn't far away.

She circled to confront Hollister Kerr, whose quiet patience remained undaunted.

"Why is she still sitting here?" she demanded. "The ship's in fine shape."

"Can't find a captain for her, Miss Armstrong." Mr. Kerr pushed his ever-lowering glasses back up his ample nose. "After your parents' accident, rumor has it she's a curse for any man who tries to captain her. He won't come back alive. Like your father."

"A curse," she snorted, mulling over the words the little man said. "How ridiculous."

"Yes, ma'am, I agree. But you know how sailors are about superstitions. In fact, we're having trouble securing a cargo for her."

"Why?"

"Same reason. Agents have heard the same rumor. They're willing to ship out, but don't want to take the risk of losing a cargo on a return voyage to Baltimore."

She carefully considered his words. "No *man*, Mr. Kerr, will come back alive?"

"Yes, ma'am, that's what I hear."

"But they don't say anything about a woman, do they?" She could sail the clipper; her father had taught her how. She could hold her own with any captain alive. She would take the *Anna McKyle* to Jamaica.

Silence met her ears. She turned to analyze the little man's reaction. Just as she thought. His mouth hung open in . . . what? Amazement? Protest? She couldn't decide which.

"That's right, Mr. Kerr." She presented her back to him as she examined the harbor. "I fully intend to

38

captain this ship myself."

"But, Miss Armstrong, the sailors will never accept a woman as captain. Besides, you'll have no cargo home."

"That's not your problem, but mine. My mind is made up. What you can worry about is who to leave in charge of the office while I'm gone."

Mr. Kerr cleared his throat. "Don't be concerned about things here. I can handle them," he said confidently. "I've run the office before, many times."

"I don't understand. I thought Edmund Bennett ran the business when my father was away."

"Frequently Mr. Bennett would leave as soon as your father was gone and leave me to take care of everything for weeks at a time."

Erica simmered. Edmund Bennett never ceased to amaze her. Never could she let him gain control of her company. Never!

"All right, Mr. Kerr. I'll leave you in charge." Her eyes skimmed over the elegant lines of the clipper. Mr. Kerr had a point. She could never handle a crew of rowdy sailors on her own. They would mutiny before the ship reached open waters, if she could get them to go with her at all. She cursed her lack of strength. She cursed fate, which had made her a woman. But most of all, she cursed men like Edmund Bennett who took advantage of a woman's weaknesses.

She needed someone to go with her whom she could trust until she proved her abilities on the sea. She needed a good first officer. The bane of the *Anna McKyle* couldn't touch a man in that position. She reached up her hands to rub her throbbing

39

temples, thinking. No solution came to mind.

The soft squeak of the pier boards bowing under the weight of heavy feet caught her attention. She spun as a large, callused hand touched her shoulder with gentleness. Familiar, deep-set blue eyes surveyed her. "Joshua," she cried, flinging her arms with the exuberance of a child around the neck of the tall, weather-beaten man. "Thank God you're back."

"I'm sorry I wasn't here sooner, kitten. I docked this morning and heard abut your parents. I came right away."

His paternal hug in return gave her courage. Her father had been good friends with Joshua Reynolds for as long as she could remember. He had trusted Joshua. She could, too. The wheels in her mind whirled. Maybe this man would be the answer to her dilemma.

The swish of taffeta skirts brought her head up. Craning her neck to see around Joshua's broad shoulders, she discovered Aunt Constance standing back discreetly. She smiled at the older woman and laughed delightedly. "Where did you find this old salt, Aunt Connie?"

Constance stepped froward, happy to be included. "Actually he found me. He showed up at the front step like a hungry wharf cat, then ate enough breakfast for three. He insisted we come down here and not wait for you to come home."

Staring up at Joshua she asked, "How long are you in port?"

"A long time, kitten." Her heart lifted. She had time to convince him.

"I've decided to retire from the sea."

Her heart immediately fell. No, he couldn't quit the sea. She needed him. "You're too young to retire," she protested.

Joshua smiled and looked past her at Constance. "Perhaps, but I promised a very special lady I would. The voyage to China was my last."

Erica glanced from Joshua to Constance. "Are you two marrying?"

"Aye, as soon as your Aunt Constance deems the time is proper. Would you mind so much calling me Uncle Joshua?"

"I'm so happy for the two of you," she declared. Despite her joy, her mind concentrated on her problem. She must convince Joshua to go with her. But how? What could she say that would make him leave her aunt and go to Jamaica with her, not as a captain, just a first officer? She would work on the problem. She must come up with a plan that wouldn't fail. She must do it soon.

Erica ran her hands down the kelly green silk of her skirt before she glided into the dining room. She glanced up at the wall clock in the foyer. Six thirty. Her arrival at the dinner table at precisely the right time brought surprise to her aunt's face. The older woman's eyes questioned her, but Erica smiled blankly, revealing none of her inner turmoil.

Guilt assaulted her for what she was about to do to her aunt, but it couldn't be helped. She needed Joshua. Her entire plan to save Armstrong Shipping hinged on him going with her. She peered at Constance from between her lowered lashes. *Forgive me,*

Aunt Connie, she thought. *I do this for all of us.*

Strolling to the table, she waited for Joshua to rise and offer her a chair. "Aunt Connie. Joshua," she acknowledged as she sat in one fluid motion in the chair he held out for her. She touched her hair self-consciously where it lay tied back with a simple ribbon at the nape of her neck.

Constance's stare bore a hole in the top of her lowered head. Joshua's chair scraped the floor as he sat down.

"The *Anna McKyle* is in fine shape, kitten. Wouldn't you say?" he commented with a flourish and a grin, giving Erica the opening she needed.

She waited until the salad bowl touched the table in front of her before she answered. "Yes, I agree, she is. In fact, she's the finest ship on the seas." She boldly smiled back at Joshua.

"Aye, I agree, kitten. Any man should be proud to captain her. I hear you're having trouble finding the right man. I've tested my memory and come up with a few possibilities for you," he offered.

"I've already found *someone* to sail her."

"Well, who is he, dear?" Constance asked. "Maybe Joshua knows him and can give you a recommendation."

"I don't think so, Aunt Connie, as this will be a first voyage as captain. What I haven't found is a good first officer," she added, giving Joshua a questioning look.

"I wouldn't worry about that, kitten. Captains generally find a first on their own."

She watched Joshua's face closely. Her eyes darted to the knowing look encompassing her aunt's face.

42

Joshua's mouth maintained the patronizing grin across it. "I'm well aware of that, Joshua. As I said, I'm looking for a good first. Can you recommend anyone?"

The smile froze on his face and turned into a look of confusion. His brows lifted in disbelief, then scrunched in a knot between his eyes. She had seen that look before on her father's face the night he'd found her alone on Conception Cay. Thunderous anger.

She heard Constance swallow hard as the other woman recognized the look, also. Erica leveled her eyes with Joshua's, giving him her best expression of innocent expectation.

"The hell you are, child," he roared as he pushed back his chair and rose to his feet.

"Joshua, your language," Constance gasped.

Erica sat still, unblinking. "Whatever kind of recommendation is that?"

"What kind of a harebrained scheme is this? I knew you were headstrong, but good God, girl, what are you thinking about?"

She worked to keep her face from falling and maintained her composure. She didn't dare turn into the demanding little girl that Joshua treated her as. Very quietly she began, "If I were a man, would you be speaking to me like this? If I were my father's *son,* wouldn't you expect me to take over?" Her voice rose in frustration. "I'm as capable as *any* man to sail that ship. I admit there's a science to sailing a clipper. It doesn't handle like other ships, but Papa taught me to sail it. You know that as well as I do. Besides, no *man* will take her on. She's cursed. All those brave captains think they're going to die. I'm not afraid, and I know I can captain her. I want to do this. I *must* do this."

"By God, girl, I think you're serious." Joshua sat down on his chair.

"You're damn right I'm serious," she challenged.

Joshua leaned back in his chair without a word. Their eyes locked and held, each trying to make the other look away.

"You know, kitten, you remind me of a lost bobcat kitten I once had the misfortune of coming across when I was a boy. It looked harmless, but I still have the scars on my wrist from reaching out to help it." He held his arm out for her to see. "I didn't mean you aren't capable. I know you have the intelligence and the know-how to sail her. What I know you don't have is the brute strength to handle a crew of uncouth, illiterate, and ill-tempered seamen. They'll tack your hide to the deck before you're twenty-four hours out to sea."

"I know that, Joshua." She looked away, breaking the eye contact. "That's why I need you to go with me."

Constance's gasp rang loudly in the silence. Joshua leaned forward to speak, but Erica held her hand up. "Please let me finish before you say no."

Joshua clamped his lips in a tight, grim line.

"I don't know how to explain this to you. I've thought a lot about this trip. I need to get to Jamaica and handle my mother's affairs down there. The *Anna McKyle* needs a captain. There's a cargo waiting to be taken to Kingston, and it needs to go right away." She lifted her shoulders in determination.

44

"This is just something I have to do—for Papa, and for myself. Papa would have understood.

"With your help, I can succeed. But even without you, I'm going. Not you or anyone else is going to stop me. I know I'm asking a lot." She moved to include Constance in her line of vision. "Of both of you. It's only for a month, six weeks at the longest." She stared beseechingly at her aunt. "Aunt Connie, please, make him understand."

With breath held, she waited for her aunt's decision. "Go, Joshua," Constance said, laying her hand on the big man's shoulder. "I think she would go without you. I've waited a long time; a few more weeks is nothing," she added with resignation.

Erica rushed from her chair and threw her arms around her aunt's neck. "Oh, Aunty, I love you. When we return we'll have the biggest wedding Baltimore has seen in ages."

She whirled to face Joshua. "You haven't given me your answer yet. What do you say? I know there will be a lot of work involved, but together I know we will be successful."

"Are you sure you know what you're getting into?"

She nodded without hesitation.

"Very well, Captain," Joshua agreed with a small smile and a half salute of his hand.

"Very good, Mr. Reynolds," she teased back.

"I guess I won't be able to call you kitten anymore, will I?"

"I guess not," she admitted with a grin. "Kitten won't do much for my image, will it?"

The meal continued in silence. The sadness and longing filling her aunt's eyes each time they touched

45

on Joshua's face nipped at her conscience.

Sensing Constance's need to be alone with the man she loved, Erica whispered, "Excuse me."

No one noticed when she slipped out of the dining room. Soft, feminine sobs floated out the door, chasing after her heart. Her aunt's claim to Joshua was evident in his comforting words, but Erica needed him more. At least now. Her entire future depended on his support. Somehow she would make it all up to her aunt, whose sacrifice deserved recognition.

She must remain strong, now, more than ever.

A week later, Erica paced the captain's cabin. At first, ten steps had crossed the short expanse; now only nine were necessary to cover the same distance. The cabin couldn't be getting smaller; therefore, she must be taking longer steps. She slowed, her knees brushing each other. The men's britches she wore rubbed roughly against the skin of her thighs, which had become accustomed to silk and satin. She shook her head in self-disgust, the long French braid she had twisted her hair into swinging like a pendulum against her back. Only a few years ago she had thought nothing about wearing men's clothing. In fact, she had preferred them. She had to get used to the freedom of movement all over again.

Her heart skipped one beat after another, anticipation accentuating the anxious feeling in the pit of her stomach. The men aboard the ship had no idea she was the captain, since Joshua had signed them aboard. Soon the *Anna McKyle* would be in the open water of the Atlantic. She planned to take over command at that time, when the sailors would have no choice but to stay aboard. She gulped and resumed her pacing.

Her booted feet stilled at the sharp rap on the door. At her command the barrier swung open before Joshua's large frame. His eyes registered surprise as they traveled up and down the length of her body. Self-consciously she reached up to button the billowing white shirt that gaped open with every move she made to reveal the close-fitting undershirt that hugged and flattened her breasts. Joshua recovered instantly to snap her a salute. "Captain, your ship awaits you." He swept his arm in a wide gesture toward the open door. She hesitated for a moment and he added, "That is, if you're ready."

Self-doubt shuddered through her and escaped from her eyes.

"Erica, if you don't want to do this, I can handle . . ."

"Good Lord, no, Joshua. I'm just rehearsing my speech in my head." She turned quickly to cover up her inner turmoil.

Picking up two pistols from the small desk, she tucked one into her waistband. The other she handed to Joshua. "Just in case my speech isn't as persuasive as I think it is," she said with a lopsided grin.

With a grim expression on his face, Joshua reached out and took the pistol from her hand. Silently he held it to his side as she stepped toward the waiting door.

Looking down the passageway, so long and narrow, she moved in slow motion. Her eyes leveled with the deck as she ascended the companionway stairs. The scene before her reminded her of a nest of ants. Crewmen scurried everywhere. Joshua, preceding her, made his way toward the wheel to take control.

Curious looks followed her. Some were friendly, but most were not. A woman aboard ship always made sailors nervous. She stepped forward boldly, as if on a stage in front of a skeptical audience. Joshua sent her an encouraging look as she inhaled deeply. Raising her chin with spirit, she skirted the rigging and ropes blocking her path and headed for Joshua.

Her hand gripped the wheel only inches from his. "Thank you, Mr. Reynolds," she said with a quick nod. He stepped back.

"Aye, Captain," he answered with a salute.

In one sweeping motion, the crew wheeled to watch her. All work ground to a halt. Half-raised sails flapped in the breeze, the ropes squeaking in protest at the interruption in motion. Several crewmen hung from masts, staring down at her. She swore she could hear the air rush from their lungs as they wondered why she held the wheel.

"Hoist that sail, seaman," she ordered. The dirty, barefoot sailor hesitated only a moment. He began the automatic hand-over-hand action, the sail rising higher and higher up the rigging.

She pointed to another man hanging like a monkey. "Tighten those ropes and be quick about it, mister." The sailor reached up to obey her command.

The crisp white sails snapped in the wind, filling up like puffed cheeks. The ship vibrated with action below her feet as the men completed their assigned tasks. The canvas cracked like whips over her head.

The buzz of disgruntled whispers filled her ears.

Joshua still stood behind her. She glanced at him. His hand tightly gripped the handle of the pistol, one finger lightly caressing the smooth butt. Tense and alert, the ship with its unpredictable crew reminded her of a rumbling volcano.

She struggled to maintain an air of relaxed confidence, though her insides quaked. The clipper would be under full sail soon, and the crew would converge against her and demand justice. She must keep them under control by taking the initiative and imposing discipline.

Upon completion of their tasks, the men gathered in small groups. The buzz rose in volume until she heard distinct voices angrily insisting they had been duped. She turned to Joshua. "I think it's time to assemble the crew."

He nodded in agreement as he stepped forward, calling to the knots of men, "To the bow, men. The captain has a few words to say."

Erica's hand clutched the wheel so tightly her fingers cramped in protest. Joshua spoke to a sandy-haired man in his thirties. Testing her memory, the name Rob Taylor came to mind: her second officer and a man Joshua felt they could trust. Rob pivoted and walked toward her, stopping a few feet away.

"What do you want, mister?"

"Mr. Reynolds thought you might want me to take the wheel," he stated. "That is if you want, Captain—ma'am."

She sought Joshua with her eyes. He answered her with a reassuring nod, so she motioned for Rob to take the wheel.

"Steady as she goes, sailor."

"Aye, sir—er—ma'am," he stuttered as he grasped the smooth wood.

Her hand remained tight on the helm as her eyes darted to the gathering crew. Contemplating the man standing next to her, their eyes leveled. "Do you have a problem with me captaining this ship, mister?"

"No, ma'am," he defended instantly. "I come from a family of strong womenfolk. My mama ran the mercantile better than any man could. My daddy was usually too drunk to be much help. Then my sister took over after Mama died. Quite frankly, Captain Armstrong, I don't see what difference it makes what you are as long as you're a good captain."

"Thank you, Mr. Taylor. That's all I can expect." Releasing control of the ship to him, she headed across the deck.

"Captain?" he called. She glanced back at him. "Rob, call me Rob."

She flashed him a quick smile. "I will, Rob."

She crossed the deck in long strides, sizing up the situation as she approached the group of crew members. Silently she thanked God for Joshua's astuteness at assembling them before a large crate of honking geese. Scrambling atop the crate, she stood at least a foot above the head of the tallest sailor. Authority would be easier to assume looking down instead of up at the men. She flashed Joshua a grateful smile.

Her hands planted firmly on her hips, she forced each man to look at her and willed him into silence. The sibilant sounds of protest faded, leaving only the crack of the sails, the creak of the swaying masts,

50

and the cackling of the geese below her feet.

"I am Captain Armstrong," she began. "I am captain of this ship." She paused to allow her words to sink in. "Each and every one of you signed on at top pay from Baltimore to Jamaica and back." A grumble reached her. "The *Anna McKyle* is the finest ship afloat, and I can sail her better than any man aboard," she boasted with a wide sweep of her arm. Placing her hand on the pistol at her waist, she challenged, "I dare any of you to deny it."

One man in the front cursed. She squatted before him, drew the pistol, and pointed it only inches from his hooked nose. She circled the barrel in his face.

"You have something you want to say?" she asked evenly. The sailor's eyes circled with the pistol's movement. He swallowed and shook his head no.

"Good. I didn't think you did," she said, giving him an unpleasant smile.

She stood and held the pistol down by her side, surveying the men who stood silently before her. "Now that *that* problem is solved, I'll make this promise to each and every one of you. I'm the best captain you've ever sailed under, and I'll prove it. If you're not in total agreement by the time we reach Jamaica, I'll release you from your contract, and you can get off my ship." Grunts of approval greeted her. "However, those of you who remain on board the duration of the voyage I'll pay triple the promised wages when we return to Baltimore."

The crew remained quiet. She had touched them where it counted, in their purses, as they calculated how much money her offer meant to them.

"In the meantime," she continued, raising the pistol for them all to see," "any man who attempts mutiny I'll personally shoot on sight. No questions asked. Is that understood?"

Without waiting for a reply, she snapped, "Now, all hands back to their posts." The seamen hesitated.

"Now," she demanded. The men scrambled to take their positions. She turned to Joshua, who gave her a hand down from the crate.

"Mr. Reynolds, I'd like to see you in my cabin at your earliest convenience," she commanded, tucking the pistol back at her waist. She headed for the companionway.

"Aye, Captain," he answered to her departing back.

She reached her cabin in a state of elation, her head swimming as the blood pounded in her temples. She'd done it. She'd convinced them. All she had to do now was prove out what she had said.

She laughed at the brazen way she had acted, and the knock on the door did nothing to decrease her amusement. Gasping for breath, the tears streaming down her face, she choked out, "Come in."

After entering, Joshua watched her helplessly, unable to understand what she found so funny. "You want to share the joke with me?"

Doubled over with glee, she clutched her middle. She pulled the pistol from her belt and flashed Joshua an impish grin as she clumsily cocked it. Like a drunken sailor she aimed the pistol at the lantern hanging above his head. As if he thought she had lost her mind, he ducked sideways to avoid the shattering glass. She continued laughing as she pulled the trigger. The gun clicked quietly. Joshua glanced up at the undisturbed lantern with disbelief written across his face.

"It's empty," she confessed between bouts of laughter, "was the whole time. I don't know how to load a pistol."

He eyed the pistol in his belt and glanced back at her. More laughter bubbled forth at the comical look crinkling his face.

"I told you, Joshua, I don't know how to load a pistol."

Angrily he looked from the gun to her and roared, "You mean we faced that mob of sailors with two empty pistols? Do you realize what they could have done to us if they hadn't listened to you?"

"I know, Joshua, I know. But it did work, didn't it? That's all that matters. They thought they were loaded."

He grabbed the pistol she held lightly in her hand. "Damn it, Erica, give me that. What would you've done if they'd pushed you?"

"I don't know, Joshua." She sobered. "I honestly don't know."

"Sit down, Captain. I think I'd better teach you how to use this thing if you plan on keeping control of this ship."

She sat back, smiling. "Thank you, Mr. Reynolds. I think that's a good idea."

His patience amazed her as he repeated the loading procedure over and over again. An hour later she loaded and cocked the gun as fast as he did. She sat cross-legged on her bed with the weapon lying casually in her lap.

Joshua leaned forward in his chair and loaded his

pistol. "If I were you, I would carry that gun with me everywhere, including to bed."

"You worry too much." She set the gun beside her and raised her arms to stretch. "Nothing's going to happen."

"Don't be so cocksure of yourself. This voyage has only begun. This ship is a powder keg. You may have won the first battle, but you've yet to win the war. Take my advice. You won't catch me again without a loaded gun."

She glanced at his face. She couldn't ignore his warning.

Chapter Three

May 19,1835

Pleased with himself, Captain Dirk Hawkyns settled back in the comfortable chair. He smiled at his old friend, Miguel de Tacòn, now Governor of Cuba.

"I hope you find my form of payment acceptable, *amigo*," the swarthy man across the desk said.

"More than acceptable, my friend. I feel like a thief. Those twelve crates of the finest Cuban cigars to be had are worth ten times the value of the cargo I brought you."

"Perhaps, Dirk, but my people can't eat cigars. The flour, cornmeal, and salt pork you delivered will feed many for a long time. I'm still indebted to you for taking the risk of coming here."

"So far there's been no risk." Dirk smiled, his even white teeth clamping one of those cigars between them. "My ship should be loaded and gone before the day's out."

"Will we see you again any time soon?"

"As soon as I can get back to the States and

unload my cargo I'm picking up in Kingston."

"What, no wife or niños to make you linger at home?"

"Not for me, Miguel. Women are nice, but once I'm sated there's no need . . ." Dirk lifted his dark slash of an eyebrow for emphasis.

"I understand." Miguel moved to the large window overlooking the bay. "Still looking for your mermaid?"

Dirk stiffened in his seat. "Damn it, man. I rue the day I told you about that incident."

"But I'm right. You haven't forgotten her, have you?" Miguel faced him, leaning back against the windowsill.

"No, damn it, I haven't." Long fingers toasted brown by the sun plowed a course through his blue-black hair, pushing it off his face.

"Forget her, *amigo*. Get married. It's what you need."

"No, Miguel, there's too many things I want from life to tie myself down." He grinned sardonically and stood. "I'll just keeping looking for my mermaid."

Ready to leave, he caught the Spaniard's outstretched hand. Their fingers clasped warmly in friendship. "Take care, Miguel. Keep away from revolutionaries."

"And you, *amigo*, stay away from fertile women."

His head flew back with laughter. "Your warning is well taken."

He headed toward the exit, his sailor's step jaunty, as his mind whirled, calculating his profits. Part of the extra money made from the private sale of the cigars would put his brig back into tip-top condition.

56

The rest? With luck, he could make a partial payment on one of those new clippers built in Baltimore. He wanted one so badly he could taste it. He refused to be patient any longer. He needed success now, at twenty-nine, while he was still young enough to enjoy it.

His jet-black eyes reflected his determination as he walked down the pier where the *Sea Hawk* swayed gently in her mooring. He moved his feet in rhythm to the clip-clop of the dray horses bringing the wagon load of crated cigars that would fit nicely in the empty provision room off his own cabin.

An ominous feeling nagged at him. The unloading had gone smoothly—in fact, too smoothly. The need to load his cargo quickly and set sail was suddenly of the utmost importance. Hurrying ahead, he gave directions to the stevedores who waited to carry the crates aboard. But his foreboding didn't end with the order.

He stepped onto the brig and a disquieting air assaulted him. He glanced around. His crew, who would normally have been relaxed and idle, nervously milled on deck. His instincts were right. The time to leave was now, before something happened.

A ping ricocheted from the mainmast. Dirk fell flat on the deck. More bullets followed in rapid fire from a direction he couldn't determine.

"Oh, hell," he grumbled. His cabin boy stood midships, confusion across his young face. He lunged across the deck, and diving, sent the lad tumbling to the boards.

"Stay down," he hissed when the boy attempted to rise.

His eyes roved over the crew, who crouched behind any available cover. A scream. His attention riveted to the left. A sailor lay slumped over one of the crates of cigars that had been hastily dumped on deck when the shooting started. Too far away to tell if the man still lived, he seethed in frustration.

Damn. He'd come so close to departing Havana without an incident. Another couple of hours and he would have been out to sea.

A terrifying din of yelling preceded the zigzag body of revolutionaries swarming toward the pier and the *Sea Hawk*. Bullets whizzed around the ship, bouncing off rigging and masts. His eyes looked for something, anything, to keep the wave of bandits that were approaching them from boarding his ship. The gangplank. If he could just remove it, he could halt them, even if only temporarily. It would give him time to devise a more permanent solution.

Staying as close to the deck as he could, he left the protection of coiled rope that he and the cabin boy had been behind. He inched his way to the bottom-up dinghy and then to an open hatch. Only a few more feet and he would reach the overhang protection of the railing. A high-pitched whine screamed by him inches from his left ear. He moved with darting speed and bated breath. The latticed shadow of the brass railing soon covered him. He released the captive air held too long in his lungs, and again fell level with the deck. Reaching safety, his confidence soared.

Side-crawling like a crab along the railing wall, he reached the section where the gangplank rested in notched grooves. He strained the muscles in his arms and neck to their limit, but the plank refused to budge.

"Give, damn it." He shoved and grunted with a last-ditch effort, feeling the vibrations of running feet on the pier through the stubborn board in his hands.

Creak. Pop. The gangplank slipped from the grooves and slid like chalk against slate down the outside of the ship. He gritted his teeth at the squeal. The plank springboarded and balanced against the pier and the bulging side of the *Sea Hawk*.

The revolutionaries stopped where the gangplank hung precariously between the dock and the ship. They eyed it. One even pressed his foot against the board, testing it for strength.

"Go ahead and try it," Dirk seethed from his crouched position.

Cuban hands began retrieving the plank. In minutes they would attempt to relaunch the board back in position.

Again the ping of gunfire, but from a distance. Uniformed figures surged toward the docks, scattering the rebels like a pack of wild dogs, some diving without thought from the pier into the bay.

"Thank God, Miguel. I was afraid you would never get here," he shouted, his arms raised in victory. "I hope you sons of bitches drown." He shook one fist at the figures bobbing harmlessly around the ship.

Not waiting to witness the capture, he turned back toward the sailor still draped over the crate. If the safety of the ship came first, then the crew came second. Gently he unfolded the slumped figure, so still and deathly white.

"Damn," he muttered. This man's death was his responsibility, one he didn't take lightly. More hands joined him to lay the slack body down on the deck. He knelt. His hand closed the eyes staring back at him in frozen surprise. "Prepare the body for a burial at sea," he ordered.

Standing up, he scanned his surroundings. It would take time to gather up the rebels and secure the dock in order to complete the loading. The loading would be delayed for hours. Hours he couldn't afford to lose. He would be late getting to Jamaica. He hoped Julian Goldberg wouldn't be too upset with him. At least the ship's hold would be empty, and he could load as soon as he reached port instead of taking precious time to unload a cargo first. He hoped Julian saw it in that same light.

Well, there was nothing he could do about it now, except grit his teeth and make the best out of the situation.

Erica lifted the spyglass to her squinted eye to study the multitude of surrounding islands. Each one was so different, yet a thread of similarity bound them into the Bahamas. The warm, sultry breeze caressed her face, stirring the short, golden hairs that had escaped the braid behind her head. She pushed at them, willing the annoyance to go away.

"Looking for anything in particular?"

Her head whipped around. Joshua stood next to her. "No, just remembering. Conception Cay can't be far from here."

The image of a man in a lagoon so many years ago

flitted through her mind. A man with blue-black hair and smoldering eyes; eyes that haunted her. And a mouth with generous lips turning up slightly in the corners. A mouth that had wreaked havoc on her senses. Flushing heat like quicksilver washed over her. Had he been real or the figment of her childish imagination? She'd never know. She only knew that no other man measured up to the image in her mind.

"Thinking about stopping?" Joshua's words filtered through her musings.

"No," she sighed, "there's no time now. Maybe on the return voyage if everything goes smoothly in Jamaica."

"Is there a reason it won't? I know you have papers to sign regarding your mother's estate. Are you expecting trouble?" He waited for her to respond. She shook her head. "There's the unloading and loading of the cargoes," he continued, "but that shouldn't take much time."

"We don't have a cargo home," she stated matter-of-factly as she continued her vigilance.

"What?" he demanded.

"I'll have to arrange something when we get to Kingston. There wasn't time before we left Baltimore. I couldn't wait weeks for the contracts to travel back and forth."

Joshua grasped her shoulders and forced her to face him. "Erica, what's your big rush? All this talk about time. Is there something going on I should know about?"

Her heart cried out to lay her plight before him, but her pride refused to allow her tongue to form the words. Armstrong Shipping and Edmund Bennett were her problems. She must handle them by herself, to remain strong.

She turned to face him. "No, Joshua, nothing I can't handle. I'm just anxious to get my parents' deaths behind me." She looked down to scrutinize her hands. "Papa would want it that way."

The lie turned to ashes in her mouth. She clamped her lips tightly to keep the truth of her charade where it belonged—deep in her heart.

Gray mist whirled around Erica's feet as little flecks of fine rain pelted down on her upturned face. The thumpity-thump filling her ears drummed out a message she couldn't quite understand. She shook her head to clear it, and the pounding moved to her temples. Her heartbeat.

Run, the booming told her. You must get away. She raised her feet to respond, but the motion didn't propel her forward. Nevertheless, she continued to run, her head pivoting over her shoulder to seek a glimpse of her pursuer.

Her hair whipped around her as eddies of wind tore at her face. Her lungs wheezed in protest. Her limbs ached to stop, yet she knew she must keep going.

As she slammed into a hard, ungiving barrier, the air rushed from her heaving chest. Her fingers explored the obstacle. Her head lifted in slow motion to stare into dark, engulfing eyes. The ground below her feet opened up to swallow her as the walls of a well flew past her unbelieving eyes. "Erica—ca—ca" echoed her name, but from where, she couldn't tell.

Bam! Bam! Bam! She must have hit the bottom. "Erica." Bam. Bam. Bam.

Her eyes flew open to discover the misty gray light of near-dawn filtering into her cabin.

"Damn it, Erica, answer me," Joshua called again in frustration and panic. His fists pounded the door. Bam. Bam. Bam.

"All right, Joshua, I'm coming." She sat up in the bed, fingers running through her disheveled hair. After rising from the bed, she grabbed a shirt on the way to the door and quickly slipped into it. Feet raced across the deck above her head. Retrieving her pants from a chair, she reached the door and unlocked it. Presenting her back to the entrance, she quickly slipped on her britches, the last button gliding into place as Joshua pushed his way into her cabin.

"We're being followed," he announced. "Whoever it is is staying back far enough in hopes that we don't see them."

The fog of sleep dissipated. No time for muddled thinking. The safety of the ship and crew was her responsibility. She jerked on her boots and grabbed a leather thong to tie her hair at the nape of her neck. Picking up the loaded pistol from the desk, she tucked it in the top of her pants.

"I figure she's been following us since we rounded Mayaguana Island," Joshua related as they sprinted down the companionway to the deck. "If she was friendly there'd be no need to hang back. Pirates is what I think. They're trying to find out just how fast we can go."

Her pulse jumped like doomed kittens in a burlap

63

sack as she leveled calm, lying eyes on him. Acknowledging her fear, she refused to allow it to take hold of her.

Taking the stairs two at a time, she scanned the deck as soon as she could see it. The crew positioned themselves to raise more sail. The ropes shrilled in protest. The unfurling canvases snapped like sheets as the wind caught them. The *Anna McKyle* bucked her defiance, then stretched like a hot-blooded mare in the last length of a race.

Erica cursed their lack of cannon or any form of defense except the clipper's ability to outrun their pursuers. The crew looked expectantly at her.

"Maintain distance," she ordered. "What do you think she is?" she asked Joshua, who joined her at the stern.

"Been watching her for some time." Joshua raised the spyglass he clutched in his hand. "Looks like a brig. Outrunning her should be no problem." He handed her the instrument. She raised it to eye level in silence.

"More than likely they have a sister ship waiting off one of these small islands," Joshua continued. "It'd be easy enough to set a trap for us."

"I agree. Once we enter Caicos Passage, we'll have no choice but to continue ahead. Most of these islands are under Jamaican jurisdiction, which is the same as saying they're no-man's-land. The authorities are too far away to have much say in what happens here." She snapped the spyglass shut and leaned forward to study the water rolling gently beneath them. Lazy dolphins surfaced and twisted in their wake, unaware of the danger following.

Looking up, she scanned the clear sky of dawn, willing dark clouds and heavy winds to appear. Bad weather would be to her advantage. The pirates would have to lower their canvas to ride out a storm, whereas the *Anna McKyle* could maintain full sail and speed. She sighed. That didn't seem likely to happen.

She wheeled toward the prow and lifted the spyglass to study the horizon. A few miles ahead the passage loomed before them. Electric currents almost tangible enough for her to reach out and touch made the air crisp and alive. Nervous energy, hers and that of the unsure crew.

She swallowed hard. This would be her test. The opportunity to prove just how good a captain she could be confronted her now. Fear and excitement gripped at her, each seeking to dominate her emotions.

Memories of running and crashing into an unexpected barrier haunted her. She raised the idle spyglass again to search the horizon ahead of the ship. She wouldn't be caught looking behind her now.

She held her breath as the clipper eased smoothly into the channel. She expelled air slowly and forced her lungs to take calm, steady breaths. Stares like pinpricks touched her. She gave the crew an encouraging smile. They must never see the fear gripping her insides with icy fingers.

"Keep a sharp eye on what's ahead of us." She handed Joshua the glass.

Joshua nodded, a frown furrowing the deep trenches between his eyes even deeper.

She stepped toward the wheel, where Rob Taylor

piloted the ship with a confident hand. He acknowledged her presence by stepping back and offering her the wheel. As soon as her hand took possession of the helm, he raced midship, ready to relay her orders to the bow.

The lookout placed on a crosstree of the mainmast threw out his arm, pointing starboard, his mouth moving rapidly; but the wind caught the words and blew them out to sea.

"Another canvas sighted starboard, Captain," Rob sprinted up and reported.

Swinging her attention to the right, she caught sight of a mast with each swell of the ship. She searched for Joshua on the bow. He held the glass to his eye as he observed the vessel attempting to cut them off.

"Raise all her canvas. Full speed ahead," she shouted in rapid-fire succession. The crew responded like a well-oiled machine.

Movement on the bow caught her attention. Her eyes shot to Joshua pointing frantically to port. She tossed her head to the left, and her heart sank to the pit of her stomach. Not more than three hundred yards off the bow, a third ship, a four-masted square-rigger, bore down on them at top speed to cut them off.

She frantically searched her mind. She had seen her father avoid collision in the past. A plan formulated. A plan she knew would work, just as it had worked for her father.

"They're going to ram us," screamed a sailor hanging from the rigging. A hum of fear washed over the clipper.

"Hold your positions, men," she yelled. Rob's frightened voice echoed her order to the other end of the ship. Bellows of terror rent the air as the panic-stricken sailors flung themselves from their positions, seeking a safe place to hide from sure death.

She pulled the pistol from her waist. The shot exploded in the air. All eyes went to her. "Damn it, I said hold your positions and hang on tight."

"We're going to die," wailed a tall, thin man as he raced around. Joshua crossed the deck in long strides. He stopped the stampede threatening to occur by pointing his pistol at the raving sailor.

"Go back to your station, mister," he demanded. "The next man who disobeys the captain is food for the sharks."

Erica dropped her pistol on the boards and gave the wheel her full attention. Knowing she needed extra muscle, she signaled Rob to her side. Fear soured her stomach and threatened to take control. She fought it down. There was no time for fear now.

The pirates' cannons roared. A whine filled the air, so close she ducked. The splash of the cannonball off the stern pelted her, soaking her to the skin. Rob stood close behind her, his fearful panting tickling her hot cheek. She kept her eyes glued straight ahead, urging the *Anna McKyle* to give her more. The pirate ship, only fifty yards away, closed the narrowing gap between them.

She examined the pirates' ship in fascination as it sailed closer and closer. The standard snapped from the mainmast, a skull and crossbones on a black background. The skull came alive as the wind slapped the flag back and forth, the red patch it sported over one eye socket making it appear even more evil. She swallowed. The saliva refused to go down.

Forty yards, thirty yards, the pirate ship edged closer. Elbowing Rob, only inches behind her, she shouted, "Help me. We've got to spin the wheel to port as hard as we can."

He stared at her as if she had lost her mind.

"Don't argue, just help me."

Rob's hand clutched the helm beside hers. Their combined strength forced the wheel almost a complete revolution around. The clipper shuddered and stalled, then keeled to the left at a sharp forty-five-degree angle to the water.

The blood pounded in Erica's ears, and her head spun dizzily with the struggling ship. "We've gone too far," she groaned and her heart plummeted.

Screams of terror ricocheted around her. Crew members clung to whatever they could find. She and Rob clutched the wheel. She thought of Joshua and hoped he was safe, but now she couldn't take the time to find out.

"I'm sorry, Papa," she whispered, shutting her eyes tightly, preparing for the collision. She waited, her heart lodged in her throat. She clung like a rag doll to the wheel as the clipper righted herself.

Prepared for the cries of death, seconds passed before the cheers engulfing her registered in her mind. Her eyes flew open to see the unprepared pirates' ship breeze past them, leaving the way open for escape. The wind caught the slackened sails of the ship, which shot forward like a bullet in flight.

The pirate ship tacked and turned, following close

in their wake. The angry faces of the buccaneers jumped out at her. One in particular displayed flaming red hair that encircled his face like a ring of fire. A red patch covered one eye.

"Surrender now before I send you to the bottom of the sea," the one-eyed pirate demanded, one fist raised in anger.

Erica shook her head in defiance. The thong slipped from her hip-length tresses, loosening them to wave about her triumphant face like sunbeams.

"Be damned if I will." She laughed and shouted back. "Catch me if you can, you stupid oaf."

The pirate's bellow of frustration melted into the roar of approval from her crew. Her heart sang. Her hands lifted in victory. She stood in top of the world, invincible, the winner.

The clipper steadily gained yardage, leaving the buccaneers far behind. Never again would she be caught off guard. Never again would she have to trust blind luck to save her. Her own inner strength washed over her.

"I *am* strong," she cried. "I can be a winner in this man's world."

Chapter Four

Kingston, Jamaica
May 24, 1835

Four days later the lookout, perched on a cross-tree, sighted Jamaica off the starboard. Erica adjusted the course for Kingston Harbor on the south side of the island. With a quick mental calculation she concluded it would be morning before they dropped anchor.

Most of the crew were on deck, many doing mundane chores such as repairing torn sails or frayed ropes. Some polished the brass fixtures, tarnished by the moist sea air. Their contentment showed on their faces as they whistled and sang. Her confidence soared with the feeling that she wouldn't lose any of them once they reached port.

A twinge of sorrow pricked at her because they had reached their destination. The trip was half over, and deep inside she didn't want it to end. Like a cradle of security, the ship protected her from the outside world. The simplicity of life at sea made her happy. The rest of the world could disappear and she would never know. Neither had she missed the companionship of other women. She heaved a sigh. Unfortunately, she couldn't escape her problems forever.

With silken fingers the cool night air caressed her face. Her eyelids, heavy with exhaustion, threatened to close. She fluttered them, and rubbed the back of her hand against the drooping lids. The gentle rolling of the ship lulled her, tempting her to give in to the need to sleep. The wheel beneath her hand tugged back as she steered it, sensing its master might lose control.

"No, never," she muttered under her breath.

"Erica?"

She snapped her head up at the sound of her name, a gasp of unpreparedness slipping from her lips.

"I didn't mean to startle you," Joshua reassured her. "Sleeping at the wheel?"

"No," she lied quickly.

"You know, that's a common failing among captains. We've all done it at least a dozen times."

She smiled sheepishly at his shadowy figure standing near her.

Silence accentuated their unmatched breathing. She waited patiently. She had no doubt he would tell her his reason for being there in his own good time.

"That was an amazing maneuver you pulled the other morning against the pirates."

"It's one my father taught me." She grinned in the darkness. "That's part of the beauty of a clipper like the *Anna McKyle*; she's so responsive."

"That may be, but the point is you've a crew that would follow you to hell and back if you asked them.

71

Quite frankly I've rested much easier knowing they're so loyal."

"So have I, Joshua, so have I."

"Did you notice the unusual flag on the pirate ship?"

"Yes, I did." She glanced in his direction. "The skull had a red patch over one eye socket just like the pirate himself. Do you know who he is?"

"Wesley Treacher," he answered, spitting the name out of clenched teeth. "He's gotten quite a reputation in the Caribbean for being as treacherous as his name implies. A couple of our sailors have had run-ins with him in the past. He's mean, Erica, and he's especially known for his vengeance. He'll be waiting for us on our way home."

She cocked her head thoughtfully. "Then I guess we'll have to figure out a way to avoid him, won't we?"

"What," Joshua lifted his eyebrow, "no more miracles up your sleeve?"

"Sorry. I'm only good for one." She smiled back.

"Shall I take over the helm now?" He slipped his hands from his pockets.

She stepped back gratefully, his hand replacing hers on the wheel. "Let me know before we reach harbor. I want to be on deck when we dock."

"Aye, Captain. Will do."

She turned and slowly made her way toward her waiting cabin. Her problems, like a multifaceted diamond, intruded into her thoughts, each bright twinkle another barrier to keep her from solving them. Her troubles began with Edmund Bennett and her need to get to Jamaica in order to pay off his loan. The name tasted sour in her mouth. Then, before she could leave the island, she must find a cargo home or the trip would cost the company money. That would be unprofessional and a sign she was too weak to handle her affairs. Now, to make matters worse, she would have to contend with a pirate before she could go home to take care of Bennett's demands. Her shoulders lifted and fell with the burden of her dilemma and her inability to find a quick solution.

"Take the problems one at a time," she mumbled when she reached her cabin. "Right now just get to Jamaica and take care of business there." She closed the door softly behind her. "Worry about the return voyage when the time comes." She would get home in time. She must. She wouldn't allow outside forces to get the best of her.

Leaning on the cool brass railing, Erica stared at the earthquake-shattered ruins of Port Royal, lair of the infamous pirate Henry Morgan. Before she left Jamaica, she hoped to find the time to explore the remains. Her curious gaze shifted to the Palisadoes, a natural breakwater, and bustling Fort Charles sitting atop it. In her opinion the fort spoiled the romance of the old deserted city. Kingston itself lay dead ahead, and she turned her attention to the harbor.

Within the hour, the *Anna McKyle* anchored at the main dock alongside two British brigs. The sailors raised the hatches, preparing for the boarding and unloading by the stevedores gathered on the dock.

Once the gangplanks were extended, she sauntered

down the nearest one and headed toward the burly wharfmaster. The man dropped his mouth in surprise at her approach. She emitted a deep groan. Back on land, she would again have to deal with opinionated landlubbers.

"See to the unloading as soon as possible," she ordered, flashing him her contract papers.

Joshua quietly joined her on the dock to lend his support. He didn't seem surprised to find she had everything and everyone under control. The wharfmaster nodded his permission to the dockworkers, and they converged on the ship like a swarm of bees.

She and Joshua stood watching the progress in silence. Sensing the unloading would go smoothly, she announced, "As long as you are here, it's time I take care of my banking business and find a cargo home."

He glanced down at her. "Don't you think you should change into something . . ." He raised his eyebrow.

"More ladylike?" she finished for him. "I'm not a lady, I'm a sea captain, remember? Would you dress up to go see an agent or a banker?"

Joshua shook his head.

"Well, I won't either."

"When will you be back?"

"As soon as I have a contract in my hands." She turned and started up the pier. At the end of the dock she whirled back around. "By the way," she called through hands cupped around her mouth, "as soon as the ship's unloaded, give everybody twenty-four hours' shore leave except those on duty for the watch."

The cheers of the crew followed her as she headed up the embankment boardwalk.

Erica clutched the letter of credit the banker had given her in exchange for her signature on the documents turning her inheritance over to a stranger, someone who didn't know or love that plantation as she and her mother had. She stared at the unimpressive envelope she held and shook her head in disbelief; its worth was the same as the hundreds of acres of land and the big, sprawling house of her childhood. She hadn't wanted to see the place again, but now she wished she had gone there first before signing it away. *No*, she thought staunchly, *it's better this way. I'd have never signed the papers if I had seen it first.*

Lifting her chin, she pushed aside thoughts of her actions. She glanced back down at the envelope and compared the name and address the banker had jotted across it — Julian Goldberg, 117 West Street — with the words printed across the front of the flat building before her: Julian Goldberg, Shipping Agent. She smiled. He looked prosperous enough.

Stepping through the door, she entered a bustling nucleus of activity. A short, shriveled man of indeterminate age shouted orders, and everyone scurried around attempting to please him. She watched him in amusement. Several pairs of eyes skimmed over her, but no one stopped to ask her what she wanted. The little man turned around, disgust on his face, and threw his hands up dramatically in the air as he noticed her.

"Yes, and vat can I do for you?" he asked impatiently.

"Captain Armstrong, Armstrong Shipping of Baltimore," she answered with a nod of her head. "I'm looking for Julian Goldberg. Thought we might do some business together."

No taller than Erica, the man brazenly eyed her up and down. "Vell, I'm Julian Goldberg. Aren't you awfully young to captain a ship?"

She burst out in easy laughter. "I've never thought about that. Most people have more trouble dealing with the fact I'm a woman."

He spread his arms out wide. "So vat if you're a voman. Most vomen are more capable than men, I've found." He raised his eyebrow suspiciously. "Vat you got you think I vant? I don't deal in contraband, deary."

"Neither do I, Mr. Goldberg." She raised her hands in protest. "I'm looking for an honest cargo back to the States."

"No, sorry. I've got nothing to offer you." He returned to his work.

"Wait, Mr. Goldberg, you've not heard me out. You've nothing to lose by listening to my proposal."

Pivoting, he smiled broadly as though he liked the way she handled herself. "I vill listen."

"My ship, the *Anna McKyle*, is one of the fastest on the seas today, no matter what the weather. I can better any delivery date you might have to the New England area by at least two days," she boasted.

Instantly his eyes lit up. "Vat guarantee would I have that vat you say is true?"

"Try me. If I don't deliver as I promise, you won't

owe me for the shipping."

The agent looked as if he had discovered a gold mine.

"But," she continued, "if I beat your deadline I expect a share of your bonus from the other end, as well as my normal shipping fee." If her gut feeling was right, he would accept her offer.

"I like your deal. It's a good von. Come vith me." He signaled her to follow him.

She sighed in relief.

Mr. Goldberg led her to his office in the back of the building. It reminded her of the agent: small, shabby, and in need of a good cleaning. His well-worn desk looked as if a hurricane had hit it. Numerous stacks of paper slid in confusion across the top. She shook her head. She would never be able to find anything on that desk even if her life depended on it.

He gave a fatalistic shrug of his shoulders. "If it's important, it's on top of a stack. If not . . . vell, who cares."

She watched as he shuffled through the tops of several piles. After finding the sheet he was looking for, he scratched a word here and a line there. He penned sentences in several places. She stretched to see across the desk, her heart jumping with excitement. A contract. He worked on a contract.

He handed the paper to her. It was a mess, almost impossible to read. "Look it over, Captain Armstrong," he urged. "If you agree to the terms I'll have an official copy sent to the docks vith the cargo for your final signature."

She carefully studied the document. The cargo

consisted of coffee and cocoa. No problem. She had exactly two weeks from the time the ship was loaded to get the cargo to Philadelphia. She took a deep breath. It would be tight, but she could do it. The terms inked in his tight scrawl were exactly as she had offered them to him. She looked up and smiled. He had missed nothing.

She reached out her hand, and he placed a pen in her palm. Quickly she wrote Erica Armstrong over the name he had scratched out, Dirk Hawkyns. Then she wrote *Anna McKyle* over *Sea Hawk* for the name of the ship. She placed her signature on the line provided to legalize the contract and handed both paper and pen to the agent for his signature.

His eyes skimmed the document, and he signed it with a flourish. Then he stuck out his hand and said, "Now, Captain Erica Armstrong, ve have a deal."

"Aye, Mr. Goldberg, we do." She clasped his fingers and shook his hand firmly.

Erica crossed the pier with long strides. The *Anna McKyle* swayed gently, an English brig flanking her on each side. There was no life on deck except for the lone sailor on watch. He looked forlorn and frustrated. She smiled and lifted her hand in a casual salute, hoping to cheer him.

"Mr. Reynolds is down in the front cargo hold, if you're looking for him," the sailor offered, returning her salute.

"Thank you." She headed toward the open hatch near the bow.

Joshua's salt-and-pepper hair emerged as she approached him. His eyes caught hers.

"Finished?" she asked, still smiling with her good mood.

"Aye, she's ready to load. Any luck finding a cargo?"

"Very lucky."

"So what are the details?" Joshua rose to stand beside her.

"I tell you what, Mr. Reynolds." She danced around him grinning. "Escort me to the finest restaurant for a steak as big as a plate, and I'll tell you anything you want," she teased.

"Are you paying or am I?"

"My treat." She whirled around in front of him, giving him a coy look. "Meet you back on deck in an hour."

The lobby of the Grand Hotel overflowed with people. Rowdy voices and intoxicating strains of calypso music sounded off to Erica's left. Her feet tapped an unconscious rhythm to the beat. To her disappointment, Joshua led her toward the restaurant in the opposite direction.

Masculine heads followed her as she glided beside Joshua. The emerald green taffeta gown suited her well with its plunging V waistline and a neckline that gracefully skimmed her collarbone and shoulders, accenting her slender yet womanly figure. She caught him watching her out of the corner of his eye. When their gazes met, he grinned down at her with fatherly pride.

The black maître d' showed them to a quiet table

for two. She sat facing the entrance, where she could watch the tide of people ebb in and out of the door.

She didn't bother to look at her menu; she knew exactly what she wanted. A juicy, rare steak, a baked potato with butter oozing over the top, and a fresh green salad. She smacked her lips in anticipation.

"Ready?" Joshua inquired as he signaled to the hovering waiter. The man hurried to their table and turned to Joshua, expecting him to order.

She spoke loudly, flustering the waiter as she placed her order. Regaining his composure, he wrote down what she said. Then he faced Joshua and took his order. Stiffly he walked away, never once uttering a word.

Her eyes covered the room, greedily drinking in the bustle and excitement. Startled, she realized Joshua stared at her expectantly.

"What?" she stammered. "Did you say something, Joshua?" Her gaze returned to the room around her.

"I asked about the cargo for the return voyage."

"Oh, yes, the cargo." Her eyes never stopped their vigilance.

Joshua waited patiently for her to continue. When she didn't, he asked, "What's the cargo and where to?"

The waiter approached and placed bowls of crisp green salad before them.

"Cocoa and coffee," she informed him, spooning dressing onto her lettuce. She wiped the edge of her bowl where a drop had fallen with her finger and stuck it in her mouth. "We have two weeks from loading to get it to Philadelphia."

Joshua choked on the piece of lettuce he had

almost swallowed. "Erica, are you crazy? What happens if we don't get it there in time?"

She smiled sweetly. "We don't get paid," she replied, taking a bite of her food. Joshua looked at her in total disbelief. "However," she continued, "if we get there before the two-week deadline, we'll get a bonus as well as our normal shipping fee." She chewed for a minute. "It seems fair to me. What do you think?"

Joshua threw his hands in the air. "You don't want to know what I think."

Heads turned at his outburst. He lowered his hands, grabbed his fork, and channeled his ire into the food before him. "But it's your ship and your decision to make."

"You're right, Joshua. This is my decision, and I've made it," she said in a miffed voice.

Silence. Uncomfortable silence. His opinion was important to her. She opened her mouth to apologize for her rudeness, but his attention riveted to something behind her.

"Erica? Erica Armstrong? Is that really you?" Two hands clasped her shoulders. She twisted in her seat to find a tall, willowy girl standing behind her.

"Don't tell me you don't recognize me! I'd know those radiant curls of yours anywhere. Don't you remember racing two fat ponies helter-skelter over the sand?" The tall girl giggled.

Erica's hands slapped the table as she rose and hugged the lovely blonde. "Vanessa Metcalfe? Is it really you? You were such a scrawny, thin-haired little thing. I can't believe it's you."

Vanessa threw back her head and laughed. "I guess

I should take that as a compliment. But you know, you were pretty straggly yourself three years ago."

Erica returned the laughter. "We were a mess, weren't we? I remember Mama Mandy puffing after us to brush our hair. Is she still with you?"

"Oh, Lord, yes. She'll probably live to be a hundred and fifty. And she still puffs after me."

Vanessa turned and introduced her escort. Her blue eyes gazed expectantly toward Joshua, who had risen to stand quietly beside the table. At Erica's introduction Vanessa raised a questioning eyebrow, and he gave her a noncommittal smile.

Returning her attention to Erica, Vanessa lifted a scolding finger. "Why didn't you let me know you were here? How long have you been in Kingston?"

"We just got here today. Honestly, I planned on sending a message to you this afternoon to let you know I was here."

"Are you staying here at the hotel or at the plantation?"

"Neither," she informed Vanessa. "I'm remaining aboard the ship. . . ."

"Then you must come stay with us," Vanessa interrupted. "Papa's the governor now, you know. It would be like old times again. We're giving a ball this evening, so bring a gown with you."

"Vanessa, I don't think I should . . ."

"What nonsense. I'll send a carriage to the wharf this afternoon. What ship are you on?"

"I don't think I'll be able to come." She shook her head firmly.

"Go, kitten." Joshua reached out to pat her palm-up hand with his. "It will be good for you. I can handle the ship and the crew."

Erica looked from Joshua to Vanessa's insistent face. "Sure, Vanessa, I'll come stay. I'm on the *Anna McKyle*."

"Good." With a swish Vanessa moved off, followed by her escort. "The carriage will be there around four o'clock."

Erica raised her hand and waved as her friend left the restaurant. She turned back to the table to find Joshua devouring his steak, and her own sitting temptingly in front of her. She stuck her fork into the perfectly grilled meat, then changed her mind and set her utensils down beside the plate. She no longer had an appetite.

In fact, she no longer desired anything except to get her ship loaded and be on her way home. She wished she had collected her money at the bank and headed back to Baltimore with an empty hold. She would have been home sooner to take care of Edmund Bennett. She glanced at Joshua. Maybe he was right. Her agreement with Julian Goldberg was too risky. Why had she made it? Only to prove how strong and capable she was. But to whom? To herself. She sighed with the realization.

Vanessa complicated things even further. She would be required to stay at least two days with her friend. She cursed her unladylike appetite. She should have stayed aboard the *Anna McKyle* and eaten cold biscuits and hardtack. She watched the creamy butter from her potato congeal on her plate.

"Erica, you haven't eaten a bite."

Her head flew up at Joshua's comment to find him watching her with concern on his face.

She smiled radiantly and cut a bite from the meat in front of her. "Just thinking, Joshua. That's all."

Erica plopped the satchel containing her clothing down on the pier next to the gangplank. She had packed only the bare essentials, hoping to use the lack of changes to leave Vanessa's as soon as it was deemed proper. She placed the box containing the one ball gown she had brought with her on the trip to appease Aunt Constance next to her carpetbag. She was glad her aunt had insisted.

The sound of feet running across the dock caught her attention. A young boy stopped near her and glanced at the empty deck of the clipper with concern.

"Can I help you, boy?" she asked.

"Lookin' for Captain Armstrong. Got contract papers from Julian Goldberg."

"I'm Captain Armstrong." She stuck out her hand.

The boy blinked, startled, but laid the rolled document in her hand. The neatly printed contract was exactly as they had agreed. She hesitated when the messenger handed her a pen for her signature. Maybe she shouldn't accept the cargo. No. She had made an agreement and she would keep it. She signed her name against the lapdesk he held up for her, rolled the agent's copy back up, and slipped it into the boy's hand. Her copy she folded and was about to place it into her pocket when Joshua joined her on the pier.

"Contract?" he asked as she handed it to him.

She nodded. "Loading is tomorrow at three. I'll be

here."

"Don't worry. I can handle the loading. Just enjoy yourself and your friend. There's no need to rush."

A regal carriage moved across their view to stop at the end of the wharf. A stiff-mannered Negro footman stepped down from the rear and made his way toward where they stood.

"Miss Armstrong, please," he said with a rigid bow. "We are here to take her to the governor's mansion."

She pointed to her baggage, which he retrieved. She gave Joshua and the *Anna McKyle* a final looking over. He smiled and snapped her a salute. With the enthusiasm of a convict facing the gallows, she walked up the pier, the footman following meekly behind.

The *Sea Hawk* rounded the Palisadoes. Dirk Hawkyns took in every detail of the harbor, which was unusually empty for this time of year. Passing the first wharf, he noted two British brigs, one just lifting anchor. Between them bobbed a proud American clipper that made his mouth water. She was exactly what he would buy when he got back to the States.

He craned his neck as he passed to catch her name, *Anna McKyle*. He watched as a familiar coach pulled away from the dock, the emblem on the side proclaiming it belonged to the governor. Vanessa Metcalfe. He smiled to himself. No doubt the little minx planned on entertaining the clipper's captain. He threw his head back with laughter. It would serve her right if he showed up and demanded attention from her. He would enjoy watching how she handled the situation. He had no doubt she would, quite capably.

As soon as the brig reached the dock and the gangplank was extended, he ordered the ship prepared for loading. Then, with a jaunty sailor's stride unused to land, he headed down Harbour Street to Julian Goldberg's to let him know he was here and ready to load.

Dirk's firm jaw clamped tightly shut to keep the angry words from spilling forth as the undersized agent waved his arms dramatically in explanation. He didn't give a damn how valid Goldberg's reasons were; the fact remained that the agent had underhandedly given his cargo to another captain.

"Damn it, man, we have a contract." Dirk wished he had brought his copy along so he could wave it under the other man's nose. Actually he was glad he didn't, as he would have crammed it down the little man's throat.

"Ve *had* a contract, Captain," Goldberg patiently explained, "but you broke it ven you didn't show yesterday." The agent gave a fatalistic shrug of his shoulders. "I have deadlines, too, you know."

"Good God, Julian, you could have given me twenty-four hours." The thunderous look on his face blackened even more.

"It vas a business decision, Captain. Nothing personal. I have an opportunity to make port ahead of schedule, and you know vat that means."

Dirk's anger reached the point of boiling. "That

means you gave my cargo away before yesterday. You'd have had to in order to beat the deadline." His face glowered over the smaller man.

"No, Captain," Goldberg said, sounding weary of the argument, "ve load tomorrow afternoon. A clipper ship, and her captain is confident they can make Philadelphia in two veeks on the outside."

"The *Anna McKyle?*" he asked incredulously.

"I didn't say that."

"You didn't have to. There aren't that many clippers around, and I saw her in port on my way in." Dirk clenched his hands in frustration. He would like to slam his fist into the agent's face. The man deserved it. Instead, he turned and walked away.

"Captain Hawkyns, vat are you planning on doing?" Goldberg asked fearfully.

"Quite frankly, it's none of your business. But if you must know, I plan on getting my cargo back."

"I think you'll find that unlikely vonce you meet Captain Armstrong."

Goldberg's snicker followed him through the warehouse. Outside he stopped to take a deep breath and gather his thoughts. He might be willing to share Vanessa Metcalfe with the bastard, but no way would he allow this Captain Armstrong to have his cargo. He'd waste no more time in confronting the man, and he knew just where to find him. The Governor's Mansion.

Chapter Five

Erica leaned back against the headboard of the bed with closed eyes. She had been talking for over an hour, and her dry throat made swallowing almost impossible. Vanessa sat beside her with eyes wide in amazement. She had told her things she had shared with no one else, about Edmund Bennett, her parents' deaths, and even the incident in the lagoon on Conception Cay so long ago. How complicated her life had become.

Vanessa rose from the bed and turned to face her. Bringing one slim finger to her lips, she declared, "That's quite an account, but you know, I believe you're telling the truth. Nobody could make up a story like that. What I do find hard to believe is that you told the man at the lagoon no."

"Well, believe it or not, I did," she protested her innocence, flying from the bed.

"Good Lord, Erica, I'm not questioning your integrity. I'm sure you did say no. But for the life of me I can't figure out why. There's a first time for every girl, and I can't imagine a more exciting way to begin." Vanessa waved her hand vaguely in the air. "I would love for something like that to happen to me. Your old-fashioned morals are so boring and so . . ."

"You chil'ren better start gettin' ready." Mama Mandy waddled into the room with her mouth going faster than her short, chubby legs. In one hand she held Erica's ball gown, starched and pressed, and in the other, a piece of white linen paper. The dress she draped on the mussed bed with a shake of her scarf-wrapped head. The paper she laid in Vanessa's out-stretched hand with an exaggerated slap. "Probably from one of dem no 'count men," the Negress said to no one in particular.

Vanessa ignored her, opened the note and squealed with unabashed delight. "Hurry, Mandy, get me one of those leftover invitations I put in the hallseat drawer."

"I's knowed it. One of dem no 'count men," she echoed and puffed out of the room.

"Someone special?" Erica asked curiously.

Vanessa grinned like a satisfied cat. "No, just someone I wouldn't mind meeting on a deserted island."

Erica shook her head. She'd never get used to Vanessa's casual attitude toward men. She had always felt that way, even when they were younger.

Mama Mandy shuffled back into the bedroom with the invitation. The blonde snatched it from the plump black fingers and carried it to the dainty secretary by the window. She scribbled a few lines on the stiff paper and slipped it into the envelope, then addressed and sealed it.

Poking the paper at the maid, she ordered, "See to it that this gets delivered right away."

Mandy mumbled something under her breath and continued puttering around the room.

"*Now*, Mandy," Vanessa emphasized and pointed a finger at the door.

Mandy's feet slapped the parquet floor with anger. At the door she turned an accusing, fat finger at Vanessa. "One day, girlie, I's gonna tell yor daddy what yor up to." She slammed the door before Vanessa had a chance to answer.

Vanessa shrugged uncaringly at Erica, who smiled understandingly back. "Mama Mandy hasn't changed one bit, has she?"

The blonde giggled. "Heaven help me, she probably never will, and with my luck, she'll most likely outlive me."

A giddy feeling of childishness washed over Erica, reminiscent of three years ago when the two of them were constantly in trouble for an entire summer. It felt good to act young again.

With a deep breath and a lifted chin, Erica placed her foot on the first step of the wide circular staircase that unfolded like an accordion to connect the upstairs to the main floor below. The pale lavender satin of her gown swished against her hips and around her legs as she glided down to the foyer below. The plunging neckline of the tight bodice was bolder than she remembered it to be, but Vanessa had assured her the gown looked perfect.

Several couples and a group of a half-dozen young men spilled from the ballroom into the austere, marbled antechamber as her foot touched the last step. Masculine eyes swung abruptly in her direction to assess her. Self-consciously, she picked at the billowing satin sleeves that were starched and well padded, making her ministrations unnecessary. Nervousness blocked her throat, but she forced her feet to carry her toward the music that issued gaily from the ballroom.

As she entered through the door, tiny butterflies flitted in her stomach, leaving discomfort in their wake. Her eyes darted wildly around the room, crowded with so many people, none of whom she knew except Vanessa and her father. The blonde lifted her hand in recognition, and crossing the room, joined Erica where she stood. With practiced elegance and no words Vanessa led her to the receiving line and slipped her in beside her, introducing her to each person passing as her special guest. Friendly faces welcomed Erica, and she smiled in gratitude.

Within minutes the receiving line filled with young men eager to meet her and sign her dance card before she had a chance to think about it. Vanessa waved gaily as a boyish-faced officer led Erica onto the dance floor.

Time swirled by in a kaleidoscope of colors and faces, and she gave up trying to remember who was who. People patiently reintroduced themselves a dozen times and smiled at her confusion. A heady feeling of popularity overwhelmed her, much to her delight. Her feet ached with exhaustion, but she didn't care. The desire to dance until she dropped kept her feet moving in endless circles.

Dirk entered the outside foyer door and slipped his invitation into one of the dusky hands of the butler, his valise into the other.

"Your usual room, sir?" the servant asked.

"Yes, Clark, that will be fine."

With an easiness that betrayed his knowledge of the house, he sauntered into the ballroom. Grimacing down at his stiff formal wear, he envied the military men their more comfortable uniforms. He stuck two fingers under his collar to loosen his casually tied cravat, which felt like a tight noose around his neck. God how he hated formal wear.

His eyes traveled the room, seeking Vanessa. He found her standing by the punch bowl, surrounded by a tight group of admirers. Catching her attention across the room, he acknowledged her seductive smile with a ravishing stare of his own. As usual, she looked as tasty as a freshly picked plum in her wine-colored gown. He stationed himself in the doorway, waiting as she sifted her way to him through the undulating crowd. Within minutes she stood by his side, clasping his arm possessively, and turned her cheek up to him for a chaste peck of a kiss.

"I'm glad you're here," she whispered as she gave his thickly muscled arm a squeeze, her eyes devouring him like a starving feline.

"How soon can you get away?" he murmured huskily in her pink shell of an ear.

Playfully, she tapped his wrist with her closed fan and giggled. "Honestly, Dirk, don't you think about anything else but that?"

"Not when you're around, sweetheart."

A young officer cleared his throat behind Vanessa

and touched her on the shoulder. Dirk glared at him, but the younger man didn't take notice.

"Miss Metcalfe, I believe this is my dance," the officer reminded politely. With a carefree shrug of her shoulders, she allowed the uniformed man to lead her onto the dance floor.

"Until later," she mouthed over his shoulder to Dirk, offering a coy smile.

Left on his own, he perused the masculine faces in the crowded room in hopes of picking out the Captain Armstrong he wished to confront. But no one fit the image in his mind. Most were either too young or had the fatted-calf looks of successful planters. His eyes continued their vigilance on the whirling dancers. A glimpse of golden tresses flashed into his line of vision and quickly swirled back into the swaying tide of dancers. The glorious hair reminded him of something, of someone, but . . . He strained to catch another look at the evasive curls, but no sign of them. They must have been his vivid imagination.

The dance floor emptied as the musicians stopped their playing. Across the room, by the French doors leading to a balcony, Vanessa waved one slender hand at him. He started across the room.

The music began. The empty floor filled to capacity, swallowing him in a sea of dancers. He lost sight of Vanessa as he sidestepped and slipped between the waltzing couples. As he reached the other side, pale blonde curls popped into view. At the edge of the crowd he stopped, the blood pounding in his temples. Several couples bumped into him where he stood anchored to the floor. Next to Vanessa he saw a face and figure he would never forget as long as he lived. His Mermaid. A few years older and more womanly, but there could be no doubt.

"And so I told him, don't bother to try and see me again. You're just not man enough for me," Vanessa explained with a lift of her shoulders.

Erica threw her head back with laughter at her friend's outrageous remark.

Again Vanessa lifted her hand to wave at someone across the dance floor, as she had a few moments ago. Erica glanced into the crowd to see if she could find who had captured her friend's attention. A face floated in the sea of people swaying with the music, a man whose presence shattered the rhythm of the waltzers and the regularity of her beating heart, which threatened to jump from the cage of her ribs. Her mysterious sailor. Impossible! Her throat refused to swallow the disbelief sticking to the roof of her mouth.

Dark, fathomless eyes she could never forget stared at her as frowning people bumped into him. Yet he didn't move; but then, she couldn't either. A name floated teasingly just out of her reach. Why couldn't she remember his name?

Vanessa stepped between them as she linked her arm possessively with his and led him toward where Erica stood.

Her mind denied the joy swelling in her heart as each step he took brought him closer. He held a power over her, one she wanted no man to have. Vanessa's chatter echoed in her ears, but she couldn't understand a word the other girl said.

His hypnotic look held hers until the room blurred. Beads of cold sweat outlined the fine, wispy hairs of her forehead. Yet she didn't blink, in fear he would disappear if she did.

The room spun dizzily. No, she spun around the room. She honestly couldn't tell. She didn't care which was spinning as long as his strong, bronzed arms continued to hold her up.

"How did you get here?" she asked, her frozen jaws finally agreeing to work.

"Funny," his familiar voice full of amusement replied, "I was just going to ask you that."

Yes, she was spinning, she decided. Her feet followed his lead without protest. His arm circled her waist like a band of liquid fire. His hand clasping hers sent waves of shock down her arm to jolt the very core of her.

She closed her eyes in fear she would faint. They snapped back open, but too late. She had broken the eye contact without meaning to.

No longer in motion, the stuffy, candlelit ballroom became cool and dark. She looked around her to discover they were alone on the balcony overlooking the lush green gardens.

Stormy gray eyes met coal black ones. She rested her head against his chest, unable to resist the magnetic attraction he emitted. His arm tightened about her, protecting her.

"I never thought I'd see you again, Mermaid," he murmured against her soft hair.

She peered up at him and smiled shyly. "I was never sure I had seen you in the first place," she whispered back.

He chuckled softly as his finger traced the faint scar at the side of her mouth. The same little flaw that had intrigued him three years ago. Tucking her head back under his chin, he admitted, "There were times I thought you had to be a figment of my imagination, too."

Vanessa's tinkling voice filtered through the French doors. They stepped back from the embrace.

"Erica, dear, here you are. I've had a dozen men ask me where you were." Vanessa stepped through the doorway. She didn't seem to see Dirk, who stood in the shadows. Linking arms with Erica, she pulled her back inside. Erica glanced over her shoulder. His eyes asked her a million questions. He didn't want to let her go. She didn't want to leave.

Vanessa's drumming voice pounded in her ears as they entered the stifling room. A name lingered on the edge of her mind, just out of reach. His name. She must remember. Vanessa looked at her as if she waited for an answer. *Oh God, she's asked me a question,* she thought, *and I have no idea what it is.*

"Erica, you haven't heard a word I've been saying, have you?"

"No, I'm sorry, Vanessa. I'm feeling a little funny." She touched her forehead with the tips of her fingers. Vanessa led her to one of the chairs shoved up against the far wall.

"Sit down, dear." Vanessa gave her shoulders a firm push down. She didn't resist. "I'll get you a glass of punch." The blonde turned to go. Changing her mind, she spun to face her again. "How do you know Dirk?" she asked curiously.

"I'm sorry," she mumbled between fingers pressed

against her face. "I don't know anyone . . ." she trailed off. *Of course, how could she forget his name?*

"Well, I could have sworn you two knew each other. When you started dancing you both looked as if you'd seen a ghost." Vanessa's voice faded away.

Her head flew up to make sure she had heard her friend correctly, but the blonde had walked away and blended into the mass of milling people.

"Dirk," she mouthed his name. Warning bells went off inside her head. Why should she be so alarmed? She couldn't remember.

Dirk watched as Vanessa crossed the room, leaving his mermaid sitting in a chair, her head lowered. He searched his mind for her name. A voice so young and innocent stirred his memory. "Erica," it had answered. "Do sailors have names?" The memory awoke delight deep inside of him. If she lived here in Jamaica, why had he never seen her before on his many trips here? A mystery he must solve.

That made two mysteries. He couldn't forget his original reason for coming here tonight. The captain of the clipper. The man who had dared to steal his cargo.

Determination turned him away from the golden image across the room. Find Captain Armstrong and settle that affair. Then he could turn his full attention to the lovely girl that had filled his dreams night after night for three years.

With a sigh of regret he crossed the room to join Vanessa as she waited for a cup of punch. Removing

97

the filled crystal glass from her hand, he gallantly led her out on the dance floor. Vanessa laid her long elegant hand on his shoulder with a possessiveness that weighed heavily on him.

"I came here looking for someone, Vanessa."

"Someone besides me?" She gave him a pretty pout.

"Business, sweetheart." His dark brow lifted in amusement.

"So, who is it you're looking for?" she sighed.

"The captain of the *Anna McKyle*."

"Captain Armstrong?" Vanessa burst out in peals of amused laughter. "Oh, this is too much," she bubbled.

"What did I say that you find so amusing?" Her laughter grated against his ears.

"You honestly don't know, do you?" She pulled back to look at him. "Captain Armstrong? Dirk, darling, you were just dancing with her. I could have sworn you knew each other when . . ."

"She can't be the captain," he insisted. Vanessa nodded assurance. "She's a woman. . . ."

He released his hold on the blonde. He pivoted and walked away, leaving her in the middle of the dance. "But, that's no more incredible than being a mermaid," he fumed.

From her seated position Erica drew her head back to see him when he stopped only a few feet from her. The muscles in her neck tensed and strained with the effort of her actions. The rigidity of his stance bore evidence of his anger. No longer the sultry stranger from the lagoon, but the enemy. But why? She should know the answer, but she didn't. Her eyes drew level with his.

"Dirk?" she whispered, testing his name with dry lips. The events of the day raced through her head. Where had she seen that unusual name before? Her eyes widened in disbelief. On the shipping contract Julian Goldberg had given her to sign. Dirk Hawkyns. No, he couldn't be the same person. The look of pure disgust in his eyes confirmed her suspicion.

"Captain Armstrong?" he observed with a sneer. Clasping her slender wrist in his ironlike grip, he jerked her from her seat. She swayed, her head still thrown back, her eyes inches from his face. "I've a few things I'd like to say to you," he spoke through clenched teeth, "in private."

Her eyes darted around the room, seeking a means of escape. She had taken his cargo. The crowd ignored them. Alone in the overflowing room, no one would help her.

"Let go of me," she demanded, pulling at his fingers handcuffing her to him. His grip tightened, threatening to cut off the circulation to her hand.

"Look, lady, we can discuss this here in front of all these people, or we can step outside where we can have a little privacy." His mouth clamped shut in an angry slash across his face. "Personally, I don't care which." His smoldering eyes shot fiery arrows of danger. "You make a decision, but make it quick." His hand released her wrist, which fell lifelessly to her side.

She jumped with the intensity of his last word.

How dare he try to intimidate me! I'm not afraid of this man. Her convictions fueled the fire in her mind. Giving him as haughty a look as she could, she whirled on her heels and headed toward the French doors leading outside. She didn't look back to see if he followed.

On the balcony his hand brushed her shoulder as if to stop her mad dash. Indignantly she shook him off and continued down the curved balcony stairs leading to the garden and a small gazebo.

Rotating, she faced him. He had halted in the arched doorway of the summerhouse, where he leaned nonchalantly against the frame. The anger still tainted his features, but it was tempered with mocking amusement.

"You're quite a little fireball, aren't you?" he sneered.

The desire to wipe the look from his face rekindled her resentment of his high-handed way. Holding her ground, her nose high in the air, she refused to answer him.

"Damn it, woman, don't you know you don't go around stealing other people's cargoes?" His black brows knitted together to form a solid line.

"I didn't steal it, sir. You forfeited it by being late in port."

"And what in the hell are you doing," he continued as if she hadn't spoken, "running around attempting to captain a ship? What kind of woman are you? An entire ship full of lusty men; you must be one hell of a piece of . . ."

Her simmering anger exploded. She rushed at him with fingers curled into talons to shred his face to ribbons. The growl in her throat rumbled like thunder in her ears.

Her fingernails struck their target. Skin gave way under the pressure of her claws, leaving a bloody trail behind them. Retreating a step, she held her ground, her fingers still curved weapons.

Gingerly he touched the gash along his cheek. Looking down at the red smear on his hand, the smug look turned deadly. With the grace of a panther he stalked her, his steady gaze wooing her, mesmerizing her, casting a spell of calmness she knew couldn't exist.

Her breath caught in her throat. The anger pounding in her temples ebbed, the redirected blood rushed to her heart to beat an erratic tempo against her chest. Her curved talons flattened into defensive barriers as she backed away from him, the enormity of her actions ramming home. He cornered her against a bench, giving her no route of escape. But she'd be damned if she'd act like a frightened rabbit. Bravely she lowered her hands and lifted her chin, preparing for the impact of his hand across her face. She closed her eyes and willed her mouth and chin to remain firm and taut.

Seconds ticked by like hours. Warm breath ticked her cheek as he edged closer, yet he didn't touch her. Anxiously she waited as her stubborn pride threatened to buckle under to her fear. "I wish you would just get it over with," she choked.

She could hear his calm, even breathing and the shuffle of his feet. He could only be inches away from her, yet he still didn't strike. Was he waiting for her to open her eyes to see the blow coming? Damn him for torturing her!

She swept her lashes up and gasped. His eyes, only inches from her, glittered with an emotion stronger than anger. Soft, moist lips covered hers with a tenderness that sent her confused mind swirling. Strong arms encircled her, and she pressed against the long, lean body so close to her. Her arms worked their way up to wind around his neck of their own accord. The fingers that had moments before scratched him twisted shyly in the soft wisps of hair on his neckline.

"Oh, Mermaid, you little fool," his husky voice shattered the silence, "don't you know another man might have killed you for what you did to me?"

She moaned softly and pulled his face back down to hers, pressing her open lips against his. His tongue slipped eagerly into her waiting mouth, teasing hers into action. His arms clutched her tighter, and he raised his head with reluctance, his breath hard and uneven.

"Come with me."

She pushed back to read his face, understanding fully the question he asked. "No, I can't."

Strong arms reached behind the back of her knees. She stumbled as she pushed away from him.

"No, you ask too much," she cried as she turned and raced from the gazebo as if Satan himself pursued her.

Chapter Six

Erica pressed her face against the cool pink satin of the chair she had thrown herself on. She glanced around the dark room that offered security and solitude from the world outside her guest bedroom door.

The weakness she had shown disgusted her. She had almost succumbed to the urges of her body, and his, and agreed to go with him. Did he think she would go because he asked her to? Did he think her so weak?

She had escaped him, and she breathed relief. *Is that what you want?* her heart asked. Yes, of course, her mind answered. No, her heart responded candidly, you wanted him to carry you off and make wild, passionate love to you. Then you could blame your weakness on your frail body, not your feeble volition.

"But I resisted," she mumbled into the fabric of the chair's arm, slamming her clenched fist into the softness. "I am strong. I told him no."

Beads of perspiration trickled down her hairline. *Oh, heart, you're right. If only he had taken the* decision away from me.

Music and laughter from the ballroom below her feet filtered into the room. A night bird whistled a lonely tune from a tree outside her window. His soft call tore at her heart.

Seek Dirk out, her heart whispered. Find him before he leaves forever. There won't be a next time.

No, answered her cool mind. Don't be a fool. You have enough complications in your life without adding Dirk Hawkyns. Stay away from him.

"Stay away from him," she echoed, reinforcing the logic of her mind. "I can't allow the feelings he evokes to weaken me."

She blinked in the semidarkness. The moon had risen, but when? The music from the festivities had ended. How much time had passed? The crunch of feet on gravel floated through the open window. She rose from her fetal curl on the chair and crossed the room to investigate. Carriages lined the front of the mansion, the guests departing in little groups. Dirk would be leaving, also.

A fist hammered on the door. Her heart surged with mixed emotions. Don't let it be him. Don't let him have left without her.

"Are you in there, Erica?" Vanessa's musical voice sifted through the door. The pounding of her heart eased.

"Just a minute."

Releasing the lock, she opened the door to reveal her friend's concerned face.

"I'm surprised to find you here," Vanessa said, stepping into the room. "When I informed Dirk you were Captain Armstrong, he looked ready to kill. I'm glad to see you're safe." She paused. "You are, aren't you?"

Erica nodded.

"He knew you, yet he didn't know your name."

She twisted away, avoiding the questions on Vanessa's face.

"How do you know him?" The blonde turned her squarely to confront her.

"The lagoon," she whispered. "He's the man in the lagoon."

Vanessa's insistent fingers dropped to her side as her face lit with astonishment. "Look, Erica, I've known Dirk awhile." She floundered, watching Erica's face closely. "He's not the kind of man to fall in love with."

"I'm not in love with him. How could I be? I hardly know him." She stepped toward the window, and the breeze cooled her heated face. "I admit I find him attractive," she said, her hand circling aimlessly in the air, "but who wouldn't?" Taking a deep breath, she pivoted. "You seem to know him fairly well."

Vanessa hesitated before answering. "Yes, in fact, I know him very well."

"Vanessa, please." Her hand lifted to touch her temple. She didn't want to think about Dirk Hawkyns. "I don't want to discuss it anymore. I won't interfere with your relationship with him. He's yours. You can have him. I don't need a man in my life right now."

"When you change your mind," Vanessa threw over her shoulder as she stepped from the room, "don't worry about me. In fact, I think it will be fun to watch the two of you battle it out." Her laughter echoed down the hallway before the door clicked closed.

Erica swept to the window and examined the landscape below her. All sounds had ceased except the constant whir of crickets. The drive stood empty of carriages. The guests were gone.

In the distance a soft rhythm began, rivaling the crickets, as steady as a heartbeat yet more pulsating and sensuous. She swayed with the familiar beat of the native goatskin drums, relieved that something filled her thoughts besides Dirk Hawkyns's sultry eyes and demanding lips.

"Gombay," she whispered, the name implying the mysticism she remembering from her childhood. She yearned to be a young girl again. Then, she hadn't hesitated to join the slaves as they did their shuffling dance called rushin or bent to the urgings of the crowd to dance under the limbo stick. At fifteen she had been good at the game. But now would she be able to bend with the limberness required to slip under the long pole only a few feet from the ground? The desire to try stirred within her.

She arched backward with the tempo and moved with the slow steps necessary to pass under the pole, amazed how lithe she remained. Why not go? The servants would remember and welcome her as they had a few years ago. She could forget her problems and enjoy life for a little while.

Should she ask Vanessa to join her? No, she didn't want to be reminded of Dirk. Not now. Not ever.

With the thrill of adventure, she slipped from her window dressed in shirt and britches to slide down the trellis covering the side of the mansion. She could have left the conventional way, but somehow it wouldn't be the same. On the ground she retucked her shirt and removed stray ivy leaves clinging to her hair from her descent.

The drumbeat flowed and ebbed with undeniable excitement. Her feet responded as she ran in search of the music, easily remembering the route to the slave quarters. The sound of the Negroes laughing and singing native songs joined the rhythm as she grew closer. It was customary for them to celebrate after the master's guests had left. A servants' party in honor of the white men and women who had danced so gaily only hours before.

At the edge of the shantytown, she hesitated. What if they didn't welcome her presence in their midst? She had spun around to return to the mansion when a familiar voice called, "Is that you, Miz Erica? What you doin' down here, girl?"

She whirled to face Mandy's imposing figure. The Negress's hands were perched on her abundant hips, but her smile conveyed friendliness.

"Oh, Mandy, I just couldn't resist. Do you think they'll allow me to join them?"

"Honest, child, I's figured you too grown up for dat, now."

She shook her head.

"Come on," Mandy said, waving her on with a hand.

She followed gladly. She could hear the cheering encouragements of the watchers as the dancers passed under the stick.

Smiling faces greeted her, urging her to join the festivities. She slipped among them as the men and

107

women called her name, remembering her. Had she changed so little on the outside, even though the inner person had altered from little girl to woman?

Hands grabbed her and pressed her to compete. The drums, momentarily silent, resumed the magic beat as she approached the swaying pole, bending to go under it. As she inched forward in the backward-curved position, she carefully slipped under the stick, not even her shoulders touching the smooth bar.

Cheers surrounded her as she rose on the other side. She circled the judges, who held the pole, to join the other dancers in line waiting to again slide under the limbo stick.

An audible gasp ripped through the crowd as the staff was lowered to barely a foot and a half from the ground.

One of the native judges laughed as he said, "We will see how well you remember." He pointed a long finger in her direction.

She welcomed the challenge and stood proudly in the line. She would win as she had in the past.

Dancer after dancer attempted to ease under the pole, but one after another either lost his balance or knocked the stick from the hands that held it. All except one. A tall, supple Negro waited on the other side for her attempt, his face flushed with success.

She took a deep breath and forced her shoulders to relax.

"Erica. Er-i-ça," chanted the crowd.

Stretching her arms to balance herself, she waited for the drums to begin. The beat started slowly, softly. She approached the staff as if to embrace it, her back only inches from the ground. Her pulse jumped in her throat. She wouldn't fall. She couldn't hit the stick and knock it out of the black hands holding it so lightly. First her bent knees cleared the obstacle, then her hips. Confidence fluttered in her stomach. The drums beat frantically as her abdomen and jutting breasts skimmed under the pole. As her neck reached the point of crossing, she eased her head back to clear her chin. The drums and the chanting abruptly halted. The crowd stiffened, as if it held its breath as one single body.

Shiny black boots pressed the sand inches from her face. Tight, tan britches encircled the taut calves and thighs, hiding nothing. She collapsed in the sand, the game forgotten, when her eyes fell on Dirk's face smiling down at her.

"Enjoying yourself?" Dirk's words broke the spell his eyes created.

No one moved or spoke. Fervently she wished the crowd would swallow her up. She pushed up from the demeaning position on the ground at his feet. How dare he stand over her like a master above a slave.

She spun to face him the moment she stood. "What are you doing here?" She bit her lip at the stupid question, one she seemed to ask him every time she saw him.

"It does seem you always get places before me, doesn't it? And you always seem to leave before I'm finished with you." His hand circled her wrist and pulled her hard up against his chest.

"Let me go," she murmured.

"Not this time, Erica. You've run from me for the last time."

With one sweeping motion, he lifted her in the air and hugged her to his chest.

Her heart's desire had been granted. He had taken the decision away from her.

Dirk dropped his face to scan the soft, golden hair of the enigma nestled in his arms. He'd never met a woman quite like her before. One minute she lunged at him, clawing and spitting like a cornered cat. The next she reminded him of a lost little girl, so unsure of herself, as if innocent and virginal. But no, that couldn't be possible. One woman aboard a ship filled with lusty men; there had to be at least one with whom she had been. She played an interesting game, nothing more.

He shrugged his wide shoulders and grinned in the darkness as he took the steps of the mansion two at a time. Gentle lover would be a new role for him. The thought titillated his vivid imagination.

At the bottom of the curved staircase, she lifted her chin to look at him with wide-eyed innocence. *Damn*, he thought, *she's almost convincing.* He covered her soft, pouty lips with his and kissed her with rising passion. She molded against him, reaffirming her nature in his mind.

Roughly he pulled his mouth away and covered the stairs in long, quick strides. He wanted this woman more than any other. He had wanted her for longer than he could remember. If he took her this once, he would be able to wipe her image from his mind, forever.

The top of the stairs came too soon for Erica. She hoped they would never reach their destination, but the bedroom door, silent as a sentry, blocked their way. Once he carried her over the threshold, there would be no turning back. Her heart won the raging battle over her mind as he pushed the barrier out of his way with a determination she knew she wouldn't fight. He would possess her as no other man had.

She buried her face as deeply into his neck as she could. Licking her lips, dry from anxiety, her tongue flicked innocently over the deep hollow of his throat.

He reacted instantaneously. Swinging her feet to the floor, he whirled her to face him. Experienced fingers worked down the front of her shirt, dislodging the buttons in their path one at a time. The shirt gaped, revealing the soft mounds of her breasts rising and falling with each breath she took. Only once did his gaze sweep up to meet hers; then it dropped back down to savor the display of womanly flesh he uncovered. As he glided his hands over her shoulders, the shirt slipped down to fall in a heap at her feet.

With a moan deep from his throat, he buried his face in the sensitive contour of her neck. The soft, wavy hair of his head tickled her nose and mouth. She inhaled deeply, taking in a smell new and wondrous to her. A manly smell, a mixture of so many individual odors she couldn't put a name to any one in particular. She liked it. Her head swam drunkenly, and she swayed against him, reveling in a pool of unfamiliar sensations.

He pulled back, his eyes drinking in the beauty of

111

her firm, round breast. Her hands slid between their bodies, covering her nudity from his gaze. He pushed her hands away, but they slid back to fan across her chest in embarrassment.

A frown creased his face as if he expected her to act differently. She couldn't imagine what he wanted and remained still, her eyes unable to meet his.

He placed his hand firmly under her lowered chin and lifted her face to meet his. A question filled his black velvet eyes as he raised one eyebrow. She had no answer because she had no idea what he asked. His somber eyes traveled the length of her quivering body. His look returned to her face, still questioning. Proudly she raised her chin and stared back, her only movement the sharp, quick breaths of anticipation.

His fingers dug into the waistband of her pants, releasing the fasteners he found there. Kneeling, he brought the britches with him to join her shirt on the floor before she had a chance to protest. His hot breath caressed her stomach in an intimate way, and with a quick intake of air, she stepped away from the pool of material, coming closer to his magnetic warmth.

He rose, his eyes never leaving hers as he removed his clothes and dropped them to cover the pile hers made at their feet. Curiosity kept her eyes boldly watching each move he made. Proudly he stood before her, so strong, and lean, and masculine. Closing the small gap between them, he pressed her backward against the bed. She collapsed on the downy comfort of the mattress without resistance, but did nothing to encourage him.

Nipping her ear, he whispered, "The time for

games is over now, sweetheart. Make love to me."

Unsure what he wanted, she circled his neck with her willowy arms and pulled his face to hers. She kissed him with all the passion he brought out in her, mouth open in invitation. His tongue plunged deeply, exploring every recess, challenging her tongue to a duel she gladly accepted.

The kiss lingered as his circling hand captured her upthrust breast and molded it to his palm. As if a lifeline extended from her heart to her groin, each time his fingers drew her nipple between them there was an undeniable tug of sensation she had never experienced before. Her hand covered his, stilling it momentarily, but the feelings he ignited in her overrode her modesty, and soon she was willing him to continue. His eyes glistened like pools of ink in the moonlight, burning wherever they touched. His hand fluttered across her stomach, leaving a trail of sparks as his fingers traced her tender skin. The moist warmth of his mouth followed in the fiery path his hand left, enveloping her aching breasts, first one and then the other until she thought her sanity would desert her. Rolling with each new sensation he created, she floated on heavenly clouds.

His other hand traveled down to the triangle between her legs. With a gasp she clamped her knees tight against the invasion. His tongue's warmth lifted from her swollen nipple, halting the figure-eight pattern he traced there. She arched her back, following his rising mouth. Confusion assaulted her; she wanted him to continue, yet she struggled to stop his domination of her as his gestures grew more and more intimate.

Pushing against her taut knees, he murmured into her navel. "Relax, sweetheart. You'll enjoy this as much as I will."

She relented, allowing her legs to obey his command as his tongue drew a torrid path down her abdomen. Eddies of sensation swirled around her, drowning the urge to resist that lingered in her mind. Lightning flashed behind her closed eyelids as his tongue ignited her womanhood. Little shrieks and moans filled her ears. She made them but could do nothing to keep them from escaping her parted lips.

Cool air rushed around her as he rose above her. Her hands reached to bring him back. He laughed deep in his throat and laid his full length upon her. The strength of his manhood sought its mate. Her eyes flew open to find his only inches away, watching her reaction with curiosity and fascination. Swiftly he plunged into her innocently opened body. His eyes widened with perplexed disbelief. Gasping with the searing pain tearing through her, she twisted underneath him, but his weight held her captive and gave her no path of escape.

Dirk held himself in check as his heart echoed the pounding of hers where they touched. His body pulsated with desire, a desire she shared and wanted to explore. She pushed against him, embedding his staff deep inside her. Undone, he responded with a slow, tentative rhythm she willingly matched. The pain receded to be replaced with an ache she couldn't understand, a need only he could assuage.

The waves and crests of love engulfed her, washing over her with an unbearable intensity. His groan of release filled her ears, and he collapsed against her with fulfillment.

An unfamiliar weakness traveled down her limbs, leaving her helpless to lift her hands that so wanted to trace the contours of his back and thighs. He continued to nip and lick selected places on her neck and face. Finalizing the shared pleasure, he kissed her with renewed passion as deep as if they only began. A strength of desire and need surged through her, and she clung to him, fearing he would leave. Tears streamed into her hair to soak the bedding beneath her. Why did she cry? The emotions of relief, fear, happiness, and sorrow blended together in a jumble of confusion.

He smoothed the wet, clinging curls away from her face and chastely kissed her forehead. "I'm sorry, Mermaid, I didn't know. Why didn't you tell me this was your first time?"

How did he know? Had she been so inept? "I'm sorry if I disappointed you."

"Oh, no, Erica. I could never be disappointed by you. Surprised, yes. Awed that you would give yourself to me so willingly, and so bravely." He kissed the corner of her eyelid still wet with her tears. "I have dreamed of this night for three years. It was everything I expected and more."

Rolling to his side, he brought her with him. Nestled in the crook of his arm felt natural and right.

Throwing her strength to the wind, she cradled her weakness of desire for him as if it were a child.

Silently, Erica slipped into her britches and shirt, and barefooted, she tiptoed across the soft carpet,

115

her boots clutched in one hand. Giving the figure lying on the bed one long, final caress with her eyes, she opened the door to leave.

"Don't leave me, Mermaid," Dirk mumbled against the pillow where his face rested.

She stopped, her heart responding to his words, and glanced back at him. Moonlight fell over the bed, spilling across his face relaxed in sleep. He spoke from a dream, a dream of her. How she wanted to return to him and stay pressed against him until time ceased to exist, but she couldn't.

She needed to be alone and think about the changes in her life. The changes Dirk Hawkyns had brought about, some of which could never be reversed.

The door clicked softly behind her back. Adjusting her vision to the unlit corridor, she walked toward her own room. She paused at the snap of another door opening just ahead. A figure in a filmy negligee swirled out into the hallway. Embarrassment held her back as the other woman preceded her down the hall.

Behind her another door rattled. She gasped in the darkness as a masculine voice whispered intimate words, followed by soft, feminine laughter.

Had she lost her mind? The entire house stirred with lovers. She was just one of many who had found pleasure in another guest's arms. Somehow the thought cheapened what had transpired between Dirk and her.

Reaching the safety of her room, she sought the solace of the bed, so wide and lonely and cold.

She should never have allowed him to seduce her. How could she have been so weak? She only made excuses for her behavior when she denied that he had given her a choice. He had. She couldn't change the fact that she had lost her innocence. Amazingly, the thought didn't upset her as much as it should.

She could see that he never touched her again. She must not permit her defenses to weaken before him or any man. Never! She would leave and go back to the ship tomorrow morning, where she belonged.

Erica stuffed the last of her clothing into the satchel. She scanned the room, making sure she had forgotten nothing, and caught sight of the note propped on the dresser for Vanessa. It would be better this way. The note explained her need to return to the *Anna McKyle*. It didn't elucidate her desire to leave so early in order to avoid a confrontation with Dirk, a meeting she didn't feel strong enough to handle. Heat flushed her cheeks as she remembered the intimate things he had done and said to her in the semidarkness of his bedroom. She couldn't face the knowledge she would see in his eyes.

Her hand touched the door handle at the same moment a knock pattered against it. *No, please, don't let it be him.*

She lightly traced the knob, considering not answering the summons, but she wasn't that much of a coward. Her mouth a grim line, she pulled the protective barrier toward her, revealing Vanessa's startled face.

"I didn't think you'd be up already. Lord, you must have been standing right next to the door." Vanessa's eyes traveled down to take in the bag in her hand.

"Oh, Erica, you're not planning on leaving, are you?"

"I'm sorry, but I have to. . . ."

"I thought we'd go riding together this morning. Like old times."

Erica stood stiffly, unyielding.

"Don't you remember how we used to go down to the flat rock at the stream and go swimming? This may be our last chance." Vanessa stuck her bottom lip out in a pout. "Don't old friends count for something?"

She slumped her shoulders. A last ride for old times' sake. She studied her friend's beseeching face. Chances were they'd never see each other again. "All right, but I have to leave by noontime."

The stable aroma brought a smile to Erica's face. The smells of clean straw, new hay, and freshly oiled leather were ones she always found to her liking. Even the salty scent of the ocean couldn't compare with this.

The mare that Hastings, the groom, led out for her stood patiently as he pushed the bridle bit into its mouth. "You still want a regular saddle, Miss Erica? Or would you prefer a sidesaddle now that you're all grown up?"

"Never, Hastings," she answered. "I want to ride, not hang on for dear life."

The groom's laughter echoed through the barn. Several soft nickers answered his familiar voice. Tossing the saddle on the roan's back, he cinched it to his satisfaction. He clasped his hands together and offered them to her as a step-up onto the horse.

118

Placing her boot in his outstretched palms, she mounted, the divided skirt Vanessa had lent her allowing her to settle gracefully in the saddle. Her friend joined her on a dapple gray, and together they trotted out of the well-trod stable yard.

As soon as they cleared the last paddock, both girls urged their mounts to charge ahead. Adjusting to the stride of her mare, Erica relaxed and flung her head back to allow the wind to fan her unbound hair about her. The warmth of the sun on her upturned face thawed the chill surrounding her heart. If only she could be carefree for the rest of her life. If only there was no Dirk Hawkyns or Edmund Bennett. If only she could ride on endlessly.

Their headlong dash took them over a far hill and down into a small valley lined with oaks and sporting a sparkling brook running through it like a ribbon.

Slowing to a trot, the horses aligned themselves, and the girls occasionally brushed knees. The winded animals slowed to a walk, and she looked to Vanessa with her youth glowing in her eyes. "Brings back memories, doesn't it?"

Vanessa smiled brightly. "It does." The horses continued down the path without directions. "You remember Lonny James, the shy stableboy we both went crazy over?"

Erica laughed. "Of course. We agreed that the one who got him to kiss her first, won him. And if I remember right, you kissed him before the day was out. I never had a chance."

"I saw you come out of Dirk's room last night."

"Vanessa, I'm sorry. I didn't mean to . . ."

"Don't be silly." The blonde tossed her head back

and giggled. "Just like the stableboy, he kissed you first, he's yours. I think that's only fair, don't you?"

She looked away, unable to face the knowing look on Vanessa's face. "It's not what you think."

"Look, Erica. What does it matter? I decided a long time ago, I'll make the best out of any situation. Papa and I have come to a mutual agreement. He won't interfere with my life. I can see who I want, when I want, and how I want. But when he finds the right man, a duke or earl, someone with a title, I'll marry him without protest. If I want enjoyment, I'd better take it while I can."

"Don't be so skeptical. Just because a man has a title doesn't make him a monster."

"When was the last time you met a duke? Every one I've seen was old, bald, and not my idea of a lover." Vanessa wrinkled her upturned nose.

Erica reached out and placed her hand over her friend's. "You never know, Vanessa, maybe there really is such a thing as Prince Charming."

"Maybe." The horse beneath her pricked its ears and snorted. A rider stood on a hill before them. Vanessa lifted her hand in recognition. "But for now, excuse me. I have a rendezvous to make." Urging the animal forward, she shot away before Erica had a chance to reply.

Damn it, I should have known better. Vanessa had pulled the same trick on her before, long ago. Alone, she lifted her hand to cover her eyes as she explored the surrounding landscape. The two riders met and leaned forward in a kiss before they rode down the other side of the hill, out of her line of vision.

With a sigh, she reined the mare's head around to

return to the stable. The horse willingly accepted her decision and picked up its feet and ears in anticipation. She let the animal have its head, knowing it would find its way home without any trouble.

The mare had more sense than she did. The time to go home faced her. The ship would be loaded this afternoon, and she could leave on the evening tide.

The mount slowed, tossing its head, and whinnied as if it had sensed something. She tightened her grip on the reins and lifted in the saddle, looking for what had caught the roan's attention.

A lone rider hurried down the path toward where she had stopped. Should she wait for him? He would expect her to. He sat the horse well enough, but could he outride her? She would find out.

She jerked the horse's head toward the way she had just come. It reared in surprise. With a teeth-jarring thump the animal's feet hit the ground. Urging it into a run, she flattened against its neck. She'd be damned if she'd sit there and wait for Dirk Hawkyns to ride up to her as if she danced attendance on him. He would never take control of her again.

Chapter Seven

Dirk watched, bemused, as the spirited mare dashed across the green valley, taking Erica farther away from him. He had followed the two women at a discreet distance to the stables and had seen them ride out together. Preferring not to face them in the crowded stable yard, he had decided to confront them once they left the barn. Not that he cared if Vanessa knew what had transpired between him and Erica last night, but he wished to preserve decorum.

But why did she run from him? Perhaps she hadn't seen him. No. She had looked in his direction with her hand lifted to block the sun's glare. She had seen him and decided she didn't want to wait. He must catch up to her and explain he hadn't meant to hurt her last night.

Touching his heels against the flanks of the horse beneath him, he pursued the fleeing figure that had reached the winding stream that slashed across the narrow valley. He rode with efficiency, but not expertise. He had spent his years at sea, not learning the

122

finesse of horsemanship. At this rate, he would never catch up with her.

Pushing his mount as hard as he dared, he glanced down to adjust his grip on the reins. Throwing his gaze forward, he caught sight of the roan twisting and falling to its knees, and the woman flying over the animal's head to land face down in the brook rushing around her still figure.

Forgetting his own safety, he urged his horse to top speed. Fear that she was injured—or, God forbid, dead—glued him to the saddle beneath him.

"Erica," he shouted, seeking a response that didn't come.

A hundred yards from where she lay, he slid from the back of the heaving mount and covered the distance between them on foot. She rose to her hands and knees, water pouring from her in rivulets. She sat back with a thump in the stream swirling around her.

He reached her the same time she threw her wet hair out of her face, sputtering, "I'm so damn stupid. . . ."

Their eyes met and held. "Go away and leave me alone," she ordered from her watery throne.

Anger nipped at him, but she looked so funny sprawled haughtily in the stream that he threw his head back and laughed. She was shaken and probably bruised, but as far as he could see, unharmed.

"All right, if that's what you want." He stepped back from the edge of the water and presented his back to her.

Splash! "Damn." Splash! "Ouch." The sounds coming from behind him had a rhythm of their own.

He continued toward his horse, which was patiently munching green grass. Her horse was nowhere to be seen.

"Stop," she called.

He stopped but didn't turn around.

Splash! He took a stride away from her.

"I want your help. Wait."

He pivoted and noted the look of exasperation on her face. Planting his hands on his hips, he did what she asked. He waited.

She stuck out her hand. "My skirt is caught on something underneath me. I can't get it loose. Do something."

Again he responded to her demand. He did something. He crossed his arms over his chest. She could say please, or she could sit there forever. He had all the time in the world. Besides, it was her britches filling up with itchy grit, not his.

"What's wrong with you? Just don't stand there, help me get loose."

"Why don't you slip out of your pants. Then it would be easy to uncatch them."

"Why won't you help me?" She glared at him.

"Why don't you ask nicely and say please?"

She struggled like a trapped animal. Splash! R-r-r-ip! "Now look what you made me do." She pushed to her knees; the back of her divided skirt gaped open, revealing a tempting sight. He looked openly and longingly, enjoying the display of her exposed bottom. She gasped and twisted to cover the immodest display of skin.

"Go away."

"You know, Erica, if you say that to me again, I

124

might just oblige you and leave you here alone, no horse and with your derriere exposed for the entire world to see. Don't tempt me. It might be fun to see how you handle this situation on your own." With purposeful strides he approached his horse.

"No, wait. Please. Don't leave me like this."

"At last, a 'please.' " He faced her with a smile. "I'd be happy to help you."

The water came up to his calves as he reached where she stood in the middle of the stream. Embarrassment shaded her face as she twisted, presenting him with a front view only. Seeing her discomfort, he smiled crookedly. Watching her face, he slipped the buttons of his shirt from the soft cambric fabric. Her eyes widened and he read her thoughts. For a moment he debated with himself. Maybe he should give her what she expected as she watched his every move, her tongue flicking out to moisten her lips.

Slowly she backed away as the cloth slid down his broad shoulders to reveal his chest. Her hands shook with a desire he recognized. He chuckled when she clasped her hands behind her back to control them. The realization that he read her thoughts brought her head up sharply, defiantly. She backed up two steps farther, and he stretched his arm, offering her the shirt.

"Tie it around your waist. It will give you some protection from prying eyes. Including mine." He lifted an eyebrow in amusement.

She trembled like a wary doe. He remained perfectly still, not wanting to send her flying away. Her small hand reached out and accepted his offer.

"Thank you," she whispered as she wrapped the

125

long sleeves around her tiny waist to tie them in front of her.

Their eyes met as they waded from the water. He smiled and was delighted when she returned the gesture.

"Good morning," he said softly as he placed his hand over hers curling around his arm. "I was disappointed to find you gone this morning."

She looked away, but not before he caught the flush tinging her cheeks.

"Shall we look for your horse?" he suggested, changing the subject.

Silently she shook her head. "It's probably back at the stables by now."

"Would you like me to take you back, as well?"

She halted and looked up at him. "Would you take me back?"

"If that's what you want." Disappointment coursed through him. He led her toward the horse.

"No, please. I'd rather stay with you awhile."

"If you would like." He led her toward a fallen tree a few yards ahead of them. A large old oak threw a shadow across it. A lovely spot to sit and . . .

Talk, he reminded himself. How he wanted to wrap his arms around her and pull her so close that the heat from their bodies fused them together. Last night had only whet his appetite for her. Desire consumed him, leaving no room for other thoughts.

Control yourself, Dirk Hawkyns. Don't send her running away again. He stepped back from her and swept out his arm, offering her a seat on the log. She accepted and lowered her body to sit on the rough bark.

He settled on the ground at her feet, inches from her knee—close, but not touching. Her knee brushed the hair on the nape of his neck. Without hesitation he leaned back to rest against her offered leg.

A warmth radiated from the back of Dirk's head resting against Erica's knee. Her fingers itched to explore the dark hair inches from her hand resting in her lap. No. He would think her too forward. She wove her fingers together in order to maintain discipline.

"Dirk Hawkyns." She savored the name on her tongue. "I know nothing about you."

"What would you like to know?"

What *did* she want to know? There was something about the man at her feet that frightened her in a way no other man could, in a way she found hard to understand. But why? If he were like Edmund Bennett, she could understand her fear. But Dirk had never harmed her, not even when she had attacked him so viciously last night in the gazebo. What was it about him that left her feeling weak and unsure of herself? There was power about him she couldn't deny. But her father had been a powerful man, and she had never been afraid of him.

"Where do you come from?" she asked.

"That's a woeful tale. You sure you want to hear it?"

"Yes, please."

"My parents died when I was seven," he began with a lift of his shoulders. "I was raised by my Uncle Andrew. He was quite an old salt." He chuckled.

"He'd sign me aboard as a cabin boy on every ship he took until I was old enough to be seaman. I worked my way up to Mate and finally managed to buy the *Sea Hawk* a few years ago. The sea's been my whole life, and I guess it always will be."

Her gaze skimmed the strong back and shoulders. Again she felt the need to touch him. This time she didn't resist, but let her hand travel the short distance between them as she brushed the inky curls away from his ear and neck. Electrifying shocks surged up her arm. This man could take control of her life if she weakened even for a moment. She snatched back her hand with determination.

If he sensed the battle raging inside her, he gave no indication. Like a tamed lion she had once seen in a circus when she was a little girl, he rubbed his face against her leg. She had seen that same lion minutes later maul its master over a small slight. She must never let her guard down around him.

"I'm sorry, Mermaid. I never meant to hurt you last night."

The sound of his voice invaded her musing, and she jumped.

He spun around to face her, an earnest look of concern on his strong face. How she wanted to touch the corners of his mouth where it turned down slightly and make it lift into a smile. Instead, she stared at his mouth, refusing to meet his eyes.

"You must understand. I've never known a woman quite like you before."

Her eyes met his with curiosity. Instinct told her he had known plenty of women.

"I don't deny there have been women in my life,

but they were different."

"Like Vanessa?" she asked softly.

The corners of his mouth lifted in the slight smile she yearned for. "Vanessa and I are friends. There could never be anything but a few friendly rolls in the hay. That was understood in the beginning between us." Openly he watched her for a reaction.

"I know that. Vanessa said the same thing." Like a little girl told the facts of life, she studied her hands in embarrassment.

Rising to stand before her, he lifted her face in his cupped hand. "It's not the same with you." Slowly he raised her up until their mouths met. He kissed her gently, yet she felt the passion struggling to escape his composure. What did he mean? Was he saying he loved her? The thought overwhelmed her, leaving her breathless. No, his kiss left her feeling as if she couldn't catch her breath. She swayed against him, demanding he kiss her again. His arms gathered her up, crushing her with the desire emitting from him, warmer than the sunbeams caressing her back. Her arms wound around his neck as she relished the pulsating heat rising from her loins. His response equaled hers as his manhood pressed against the tight cloth encompassing his hips and thighs.

A heady feeling of power swelled through her. The power to make him desire her so. Whether love or lust at the moment she didn't care. She wanted him as much as she knew he wanted her.

"Oh, Mermaid, your image drove me crazy for the last three years. Now your living flesh has a power over me I can't deny."

He pressed his lips against the hollow in her neck.

Her pulse jumped up to meet his kiss as she dropped her head back to bare her throat to his questing mouth.

The pound of horses' hoofs brought her senses swirling back to the surface.

"Damn," he whispered against her throat, his warm breath nearly resubmerging her senses. Lifting her away from him, he turned to face the oncoming riders.

A group of stablehands, Hastings in the lead, bore down on them, Erica's horse in tow. She blushed, realizing that even from the distance the riders were from them, they had to have seen the embrace. She stepped farther away from Dirk, leaving him to confront the rescuers.

"Miss Erica, you all right?" Hastings scrutinized her disheveled appearance.

"Yes, of course. The mare stumbled in the stream, and I lost my seat." She could see the distrust on the groom's face as he eyed Dirk. "Captain Hawkyns was kind enough to stop and help me."

"Captain Hawkyns's kindness is a well-known fact." Hastings's mouth curled in a sneer.

She ignored the sarcasm in the groom's voice. "The mare, is she injured?"

Hastings shook his head as he continued to inspect Dirk. "Where'd you leave Miss Vanessa?"

Unsure if the groom directed his question at her or Dirk, she quickly answered to squelch the tension sparking between the two men. "Vanessa rode ahead to meet a friend. I appreciate your concern for me."

Hastings gave his attention to her. He dismounted and brought the mare around for her. Clasping his hands into a stirrup so she could mount, he offered, "I'll be glad to see you back to the stables, Miss Erica."

She peered at Dirk to see his jaw tighten in anger. He must have quite a reputation if the grooms felt the need to protect her from him. "No need, Hastings. I think I'll finish my ride first." She placed her foot in his offered palms and mounted the horse. She reined the animal around as if to leave.

"Miss Armstrong," Dirk's voice rang out, "I believe you're wearing my shirt."

She reddened, and the heat of embarrassment traveled all the way to her toes.

Mischief sparkled in Dirk's eyes. "I'll see her back to the stables, Hastings," he commanded. "Thank you for bringing her mount back." His words left no room for argument from either her or the stablehands. He mounted his horse and joined her.

Maybe she should give the mare its head and begin the race all over again.

As if he read her thoughts, his hand reached out and grabbed the halter strap at the side of her horse's mouth. "Don't even consider it, Erica. I'd like my shirt back in one piece, if you don't mind." He urged his mount to a trot, pulling her along with him until they left the group of would-be rescuers behind.

Her heart raced with the thrill of being carried away by a lover. But where was he taking her? The need to take control of her destiny focused on the desire to regain command of the animal beneath her, now blindly following the rider ahead of them. What right did he have to make decisions for her? Gathering the dangling reins in her hands, she sawed with all her strength on the horse's mouth. Unprepared for her action, the animal tossed its head to fight the two opposing forces demanding obedience from it.

The leather strap Dirk held twisted from his hand with a snap. The mare responded with a wild-eyed snort and a sideways prance, taking all of her attention to keep it under control.

"That was stupid, Erica."

"No more stupid than the way you've tried to dominate me."

"Now what in the hell do you mean by that?"

She clamped her mouth shut. What was she trying to do? Her heart and mind were in the throes of conflict again. Her logic demanded she run and keep running until she was so far away he'd never find her. Life with Dirk Hawkyns wouldn't fit into her plans. He would take charge, and she would submit, her inner strength and independence destroyed. It could be no other way.

But her emotions cried to reach out and cling to him. Her life would be an empty shell of an existence without him. What good was her strength if it gave her no joy? Only he could give her that delicious feeling of well-being when he touched her.

Independence or well-being, which did she want? As far as she could see, she couldn't have both. Not with Dirk Hawkyns.

She needed time to make their decision. Time away from his commanding presence.

"Damn it, Erica. Answer me!"

Her mare edged back from the irritation in his voice. "Look, Dirk, I need some time. I'm just not ready for you to take control of my life. My ship's leaving tomorrow on the morning tide. From Philadelphia I'll head home. I'd like to see you again, but I'm just not ready for a man like you in my life."

"Whether you're ready or not, Mermaid, I've found you. I won't let you slip through my fingers again," he said with an intensity nearly shattering her resolve. "Where can I find you once I'm back in the States?"

"Baltimore," she whispered. "I'll leave an address with your shirt when I return it."

Forcing the mare's head around, she dug her heels into its sides and sped away before he had a chance to stop her.

Erica waited on the wide verandah for the coach to be brought around. She would be glad to get back to the *Anna McKyle* and a world she understood and controlled. Impatiently her foot tapped the tiles beneath it as she rocked the wicker chair she sat on with a zeal that was anything but genteel. The air of carelessness of the islanders began to get on her nerves. What she wouldn't give to stand up, start cracking orders, and push these people to a faster pace.

She didn't want to see Dirk. If she did, there was a good possibility he might convince her not to leave. And leaving was the best thing she could do.

"Erica." Vanessa's voice floated from the house. She wished she could curl up and melt into the chair she sat on so her friend couldn't see her. "You aren't going so soon, are you?"

She rose from the chair continuing to rock wildly

from her departure to face her friend. "I have a ship to run. I must get back."

"Without saying good-bye to Dirk?"

"We said our good-byes."

"Still miffed at me because I used you this morning?"

"No, Vanessa." The corners of her mouth lifted in a small smile. "I should have been prepared for that. I need to leave here. I need some time to think."

The blonde slipped her hand reassuringly into hers. "I think I understand. He's quite a temptation, isn't he? I'll miss you. In fact, the entire island will. The meeting of Captain Hawkyns and Captain Armstrong has become legendary. The word is, the invincible Dirk Hawkyns has finally met his match. Whatever will the gossips say when you leave so suddenly?"

"The gossips will realize they are wrong."

The coach pulled around from the carriage house. Erica sighed with relief. She stepped into the waiting vehicle and put her hand out the open window. Vanessa clasped it. "Take care, Erica. Please write me sometimes. Let me know how things turn out between the two of you."

"I will, I promise." The coach pulled away, and she sat back on the seat, glad to be headed to the ship and, most of all, to be headed home.

The curtain slipped from Dirk's fingers as the dust in the driveway settled and the governor's carriage taking Erica back to the docks vanished from his view. In his hand he held the piece of linen paper on which she had jotted down her address in Baltimore. He crushed it into a ball with his strong, brown fingers and considered tossing it onto the fire grate. Instead, he shoved the paper into his pocket.

He paced until the carpet beneath his feet showed a dim trail. Approaching the door, he stopped, slammed his fist back into his pocket, and continued his pacing. What should he do? Let the chit go and be damned with her, or drag her off that clipper of hers and hold her prisoner until she realized how foolish she acted? Like a tide his emotions ebbed back and forth without coming to any decision. His passion insisted he go and get her. But his pride held him back. She had run from him time after time, and like a naïve pup, he'd followed her. But not again.

He wheeled about and hastily stuffed his clothing into his valise. He didn't need her. A woman was a woman, and nothing more. He'd lived twenty-nine years with that philosophy, and he'd do just fine without changing it.

As far as he was concerned, she and her damned cargo could rot in hell.

Chapter Eight

Legs braced wide apart, Erica clutched the helm of the *Anna McKyle* as Kingston Harbor faded behind her. The early morning sun sent out hazy, golden rays over the mountains to the east, reminding her what she left behind. A man who had thought of her, dreamed of her, for three years. A man whose very presence jeopardized her self-reliance and strength. Everywhere she went men tried to control her. Edmund Bennett in Baltimore. Dirk Hawkyns in Jamaica. Everywhere except here, aboard the *Anna McKyle*. Only here could no man threaten to take control of her life. Well, she had shown Dirk she wouldn't allow him to dominate her, and she would take care of Edmund Bennett as soon as she got home. Then she would be totally free and independent, which was exactly what she wanted.

Joshua approached her. As he swaggered across the deck, she swallowed hard, fearful he would read in her eyes that she was a different person than she had been yesterday. No longer an innocent girl, but a woman who knew the pleasures of a man's body.

"Erica, are you all right?" he asked, eyeing her

curiously.

"Of course." She gave him a half-hearted, crooked smile. "Everything is just the same. Nothing's different."

He shot her a strange look. "Have you thought about what route you want to take back to the States?"

She nodded. "I studied the charts, and I think we'll go a little north to Crooked Island Passage. It should cut some time off our trip, and see to it we avoid pirates." She looked at him for approval.

"I agree. Rob and I discussed the same route over dinner in a tavern last night. It seems the best bet."

"We're headed home, Joshua." Her lips curved into a wistful smile. "I think I'm glad."

"Aye, girl, I'm glad, too." His hand covered hers, gripping the wheel.

"Even though you're headed for the bondage of marriage and being landlocked?" she teased.

"I'm looking forward to that part best of all," he replied thoughtfully. "I imagine your Aunt Constance is having the time of her life planning every little detail."

She chuckled. "Be prepared for half of Baltimore to be at the wedding."

"Knowing your aunt, I'm sure you're right," he sighed. "I must admit, I wish that part was behind me already."

Images of Dirk and her exchanging marriage vows clouded her mind. With a frown she shook her head until those pictures blurred into nothingness. *No*, she thought, *that will never happen.*

In his cabin, Dirk roughly dried the water out of his freshly washed hair. It had taken some scrubbing, but he no longer smelled of the strong, acid odor of the stable he had slept in the night before. The bath had cleared most of the alcohol cobwebs clogging his mind, but his head still ached as if someone had trampled on it, and his eyes throbbed as if hammers behind them beat a steady rhythm.

He couldn't remember much of what had happened after the first bottle of rum he had consumed trying to erase images of Erica Armstrong. He vaguely pictured a plump seaman's doxy sternly demanding her pay after his unsuccessful attempt to bed her. He had awoken this morning in a none-too-clean stable, sharing a stall with a fat, swaybacked old nag.

Slamming his clenched fist into his open palm, he couldn't believe Erica had sailed. This morning on his way to his brig, he had discovered the clipper's empty berth. He damned her for being so proud, and he damned himself for being a fool. Then, he damned fate.

Women, good women that is, had never played a major role in his life. He could never remember a motherly bosom to cry on. In fact, he hadn't known a woman's touch except the whores who had taught him he was a man at the early age of thirteen.

He vaguely remembered his family succumbing to an epidemic of measles that had swept like wildfire through the small settlement of Du Bois in the northwestern part of Pennsylvania. His pa had proudly owned a few rocky acres of dirt. His ma had seemed old even then as she worked side by side with his pa to make the land support them. He had been left pretty much on his own, too young to be of much help. Most summer nights he had preferred to sleep in the barn. Maybe that was why he had been spared their horrible deaths. He'd never forget the devastating morning he had gone into the house to find them dead.

He had thought they were sleeping and had waited as patiently as a seven-year-old boy could for someone to feed him. His mother had always managed to rouse herself no matter how bad she felt. But she had always insisted he go back to the barn so he'd stay well.

The only clear memory he had of that long-ago morning was reaching out to wake his parents and finding them cold and lifeless.

He didn't remember much of the half-dozen families who had taken him in out of Christian charity. None had been cruel, but none had loved him.

He could still see the day his Uncle Andrew had shown up to claim him. The old man had lived at sea his whole life and couldn't remain on land any longer than necessary to sign on to another ship. Lovingly Uncle Andrew had taken Dirk with him. He had grown up without female influence other than the multitude of wharfside doxies his uncle would visit when in port.

Dirk smiled inwardly. But then, there was Dolly. Dolly Monet. She was the closest he could come to a motherly image. A woman in fine satin and silk, she was a matriarch to many, including the houseful of girls she kept a watchful eye on. He had always been special to her from the first time he had entered the velvet-hung parlor of her gaming house, wide-eyed and innocent at the age of nine.

He grimaced when he thought of what Dolly would say if she could see him now. She'd ruffle his hair with one of her elegant hands and shake her lovely head. "Letting life get the best of you again?" she would ask. Then she'd cluck her tongue with disapproval. "Feeling sorry for yourself and your circumstances will get you nowhere. No matter what cards are dealt you, it's up to you to make a winning hand of them—only you."

"You're right, as usual, Dolly," Dirk mumbled under his breath at her mental image, "but damn, it seems the chit has the deck stacked in her favor."

Was playing against a stacked deck so new to him? Hell, no. He'd spent his whole life pitting himself against the biggest cardsharp of them all, fate. It was up to him to take control of his life again.

At a point of seeing a dream come true by expanding his holdings to include a second vessel, he had run into Erica Armstrong, who had taken the wind out of his sails. Just before his uncle had died, when Dirk was fifteen, he had left him with some good advice that had always served him well. A man's life got all screwed up when women became a part of it. The old man had been right. He must forget this woman and go on as if she'd never existed.

What was important now was that he replace his lost cargo, and he would get one no matter how he had to do it. If he joined the early luncheon crowd of planters that filled the Grand Hotel, he might find the answer to his need. He dressed quickly, left his cabin, and headed for the dock.

At the end of the pier he strolled up the street, debating whether to look for a cab or continue walking. The exercise would clear his head. Besides, he wanted to stop at one of the wharfside taverns for one quick drink of the same native rum he had had last night. The saying "a hair of the dog that bit you" rang true. The drink would rid him of his lingering headache.

The tavern he chose looked like all the rest on the east side of Harbour Street, with a shabby front and a sign faded to the point he had no idea what it said. The inside, dark and hazy with smoke, possessed furniture looking as if it had survived a hundred brawls. The bartender and serving wench looked like the furniture. The room was empty except for a few drowsing sailors and a mangy, flop-eared hound in one corner.

He sat as far away from the others as possible at a corner table facing the doorway. Without a word, the sagging, used woman brought him a rum and remained in front of him until he paid her. Then she slouched back to the bar to nurse a drink of her own.

The outside door swung open, allowing the startling sunshine to pour in. A crusty, ageless sailor wearing a knit hat paused there, adjusting his vision to the dark room. The man eyed him, then looked away. Nonchalantly the sailor sauntered to a table next to him and sat down.

His somber eyes watched as the other man leaned his chair back against the wall and gave him a toothless smile. "Afternoon, Cap'n," the seaman began, touching his fingers to his forehead.

141

He drank his rum and silently stared back at the other man.

"Word has it you have an interest in the captain and the cargo of the *Anna McKyle*."

He lifted his eyebrow. *What the hell could this man have to do with Erica?* "How would you know what my interests are?"

The sailor grinned. "Why, Cap'n, you two are the talk of the island. The gossips have had a field day with your little affair."

"I don't care what the gossips are saying."

The seaman laughed. "Didn't figure you would. But I have some information that might interest you."

He waited, expressionlessly, for the man to continue.

The sailor cleared his throat and scratched his nose. "I figured you might be generous if I gave you information that could save your lady's life."

He considered telling the man to leave him alone. He had no interest in anything that had to do with Erica Armstrong. His lady. He almost laughed. What fool stunt had the chit pulled now? He reached into his coat pocket and pulled out a thin roll of bills. The sailor's hand darted out greedily. He laid one bill in the man's palm and demanded, "Now, you tell me what you know, and I'll decide if the information is worth more."

The sailor looked disappointed at the money in his hand, but slipped it, nonetheless, into his pocket. "Word's out Wesley Treacher's lookin' for her, and he wants her bad." He stuck his hand out again. Dirk begrudgingly laid another bill in the grimy palm.

"Treacher knows she's headed back to the States. Last night one of his spies heard some of her crew discussin' their route home. Word has it he has one hell of a trap waitin' for her in Crooked Island Passage." The grimy face grinned. "He's got plans for her that don't include ransom."

Dirk rose so quickly his chair fell over backward. He pushed another bill in the outstretched fingers and headed for the door.

He didn't consider what he had to do. Erica was in trouble, and he couldn't allow scum like Treacher to hurt her. His lady was in danger. He had no choice but to save her if he could.

He stopped in the middle of the street. What was he saying? He acted as if he were in love with her. Dirk Hawkyns in love? How ridiculous. But what other reason would make him want to rush off and rescue her? His reasons weren't important. The only thing that mattered was that Treacher never had a chance to touch her.

The wharf loomed in front of him. Leaving wouldn't be that simple. First, he had to round up his absent crew and make sure they had sufficient supplies aboard to sail. He laughed at the ironic twist of fate. The fact that the brig's hold was empty would be in his favor now. An empty ship went faster than a loaded one. She would have a day's lead, but he hoped he could catch up with her before she reached the passage.

He trampled his dream of expansion in the dust below his feet without second thoughts. Erica's life held more importance than financial success. But damn her beautiful hide for getting into so much trouble.

The *Anna McKyle* skimmed over the aquamarine water with the grace of a great white swan. Her billowing sails reminded Erica of a multitude of outstretched wings grasping the strong, steady wind possessively. Four days out of Kingston Harbor, they made good time. This morning Jumento Cays had been sighted, warning that Crooked Island Passage lay only hours ahead.

If they kept up their present speed, they would make Philadelphia within the two-week deadline, easily.

The entire future of Armstrong Shipping rode on her ability to make this deadline. Word would spread among shipping agents, and her ships would be in demand. Edmund Bennett would get his money on time and get out of her life. The company would be back on its feet and in her hands. With success so close she could taste it, she couldn't let it slip through her fingers.

She spent day and night at the wheel of the clipper, taking full advantage of the available wind to keep the ship moving at top speed. Joshua patiently let her have her way, relieving her only when she looked ready to drop from exhaustion. He chided her for the way she pushed herself, insisting he could handle matters as well as she could. She refused to listen, as she was driven by demons he knew nothing about. Demons who wouldn't allow her to sleep unless she became so tired her brain couldn't possibly think about anything.

144

She screwed her eyes tight as the late afternoon sun poured directly into her face through the skylight in her cabin. Sleepily she tried to escape the annoying brilliance as she threw a pillow over her face. The hot, stuffy cabin made it impossible to remain buried under the soft down for long.

She dreaded this time between sleeping and waking, when images of Dirk would crowd into her thoughts. The only way to make the pictures go away was to get up and busy her mind with other thoughts. Accepting the inevitable, she rose with an unsuppressed yawn. She splashed drops of room-temperature water in her face to erase the sleep tugging at her brain.

As she pushed loose strands of golden tresses out of her eyes, a hopeless tangle of knots greeted her fingers. At times like this she wished she had had the foresight to cut it all off before leaving Baltimore. With resignation, she combed out the tangles and braided her hair neatly behind her head.

On deck Joshua greeted her with a warm smile and caught her up on their present location. He handed her the spyglass, and the mouth of the passage became visible as she peered through the eyepiece. She ordered lookouts placed to watch all four directions. She wouldn't be caught off guard by pirates again.

"Passage sighted," the forward lookout announced a half an hour later.

The feeling that something wasn't right nagged at her. She lifted the spyglass again. Nothing but the great expanse of ocean and ghostly islands came into view as they passed the tip of Long Island. Nervously she scanned the horizon with the instincts of a hunted animal.

Joshua went from lookout to lookout demanding, "What do you see, mister?" Tension snapped in the air like crisp, white sheets. A tension every man aboard could feel.

"Sail off the stern," shouted the rear lookout.

She turned with a sense of relief that the danger no longer was an unknown.

"Raise all sail," she ordered. She wanted speed even though she took a risk in the narrow passage. The clipper lurched ahead, proudly outpacing their pursuer with ease.

"Canvas on the starboard."

"Sail off the port."

She glanced from side to side, catching a glimpse of the two reported ships. "Damn," she mumbled, "how did they know where to find us?"

When the forward lookout indicated something ahead of them, her heart sank. Rob raced up and confirmed the report. "Two ships dead ahead and coming fast."

The *Anna McKyle* plowed on at full speed with the unrestrained passion of a racer. Indecision burned a fiery path through her insides. With the ferocity of a cornered lioness, she refused to accept defeat or another man making demands on her.

Rob waited for her to say something, his chest rising and falling with fear. She had nothing to offer but a grimace. "Pray for a miracle. I think it's our only chance."

"Is that all, Captain?" His question held surprise.

"We've done all we can except that."

Cannons boomed behind then as a warning, but she ignored them and the fear gripping her heart with icy fingers. Never would she lower her sails in defeat. If the pirates wanted her, they would have to catch her.

Joshua dashed across the deck to where she stood. "What are your plans, Captain?" he inquired.

She concentrated on the ships bearing down on them. "I don't have any except to keep going like we are. I hoped you would think of something." She glanced at him out of the corner of her eye. His face creased with worry, silence his only answer.

She canvassed the deck, checking each member of the crew. Gallantly they held their positions. Their confidence in her kept her hand steady as she guided the ship.

Like a wild rabbit harried by a pack of wolves, the clipper continued her futile race before the wind. Erica's heart leaped to her throat as cannonballs whined closer and closer. The splashes they made drenched the deck until seawater ran in trickles from her face and clothing. Each roar of the big guns would be the one to strike its target. But missiles pelted the sea around them almost as if on purpose.

Then she understood. The pirates had no intention of damaging a prize clipper, a ship capable of catching any merchant afloat. The knowledge didn't reassure her.

Seeking an opening, she tacked the clipper back and forth several times. Ahead of her the pirate ships held their positions as their companions slowly tied a neat knot around the clipper.

I can't let them take us. She frantically studied the

box of ships closing around them. "Maybe if we ram that smaller brig in front, we can break the trap."

"Erica, I don't think it will work," Joshua bellowed over the scream of cannon.

"I have no other choice. Steady as she goes, men. Hold your positions." She pointed the graceful bow at the smaller of the two ships ahead.

Timbers squealed and snapped as the clipper rammed the ship. With the prow wedged tightly into the crushed side of the brig, her attempts to pull the *Anna McKyle* from the wreckage were in vain. The small brig, with only a skeleton crew aboard, was a decoy, one the pirates were willing to sacrifice to take the clipper. Erica's courage turned to mush in her mouth with the realization.

Grappling hooks hit the sides of the wounded vessel with thumps like spears driven into Erica's heart. She had let her crew down and would lose the *Anna McKyle*, and most likely her and her officers' lives.

Bodies swarmed over the clipper like maddened wasps. She pulled the pistol from her belt. A pirate's face straight from a childhood nightmare bore down on her, and she blasted it to nothing but a bloody mass of gray and red.

Joshua threw himself between her and the onrush of men, overpowering a dozen pirates before falling in a heap at her feet, blood seeping from the side of his head.

"Joshua," she screamed. With courage born only of anger, she twisted to club the nearest pirate with the butt of the empty gun.

Strong, smelly arms lifted her from the deck,

jerking the weapon from her hand. She landed with an excruciating crunch on her knees in the middle of her captors.

Greedy fingers pinched her. A hand forced her head back so hard her neck cracked with a shooting pain. Another pulled her hair with a vicious tug. Sweaty, grimy fingers groped her front, ripping her shirt to shreds. Bile rose in her throat as a blur of faces leered at her and laughed. Swallowing hard to force the bad taste back down, she stared defiantly at the cruel faces above her. Fear gripped her as a cold sweat trickled down her face, but she refused to let the pirates see it.

To her left Joshua groaned, followed by a soft thud as someone turned him over with a boot toe.

Thank God, he's alive. "Aunt Connie, what have I done to you?" she moaned under her breath.

The surrounding faces broke apart, and a cool breeze brushed her bare skin. Her proud, upthrust nipples grew taut with the chill. Her breasts quivered with each frightened breath she took. Lusting eyes focused on her exposed bosom, but she could do nothing with her arms pinned behind her. Humiliation heated her face, stoking the courage lying dormant in her heart.

Flaming red hair flew wildly about the face above her, a blood red patch crossing over the left eye. Wesley Treacher planted a booted foot on each side of her thighs as he stared down his long, thin nose at her. The smell of urine and sweat overwhelmed her, and nausea rose in her throat again.

As if at a silent command, hands pushed her flat on her back there on the deck of her beloved clipper.

Treacher still straddled her hips. She wouldn't give him the pleasure of seeing her grovel or beg. Stubbornly she gave him glare for glare, her only movement her rapid breathing. If he raped her she would fight him until her last breath.

Their eyes locked and fenced. She read the vile thoughts surfacing on his face. Every muscle in her body was held tensed and ready. Ready for the pirate to thrust his weight against her unwilling body.

Treacher threw his head back with a roar of laughter. "She's quite a wildcat, isn't she, boys?" Snickers surrounded her. "Let her up, men, she's not for you." Protests filled the air. "At least, not yet," the pirate finished.

A groan of relief escaped her lips as the hands released her. Treacher stepped back to allow her to rise. Scrambling to her feet, she covered her nudity with her torn shirt as best as she could. Pushing her way to Joshua lying unconscious on his back with his arms thrown wide, she knelt beside him. "Joshua," she called softly. Her fingers touched the side of his neck. A strong pulse throbbed there. Gently she pushed the blood-matted hair away from his head. A bullet had only grazed his temple. "Thank you, God," she whispered.

Turning her attention to the scene on deck, she saw that several bodies lay motionless, but most were members of the pirate's crew. She saw Rob, firmly bound hand and foot, propped against a crate and uninjured except for scratches and bruises. He gingerly rubbed his fettered hands against his forehead where a large, purple bump formed. He nodded encouragingly, and she gave her attention back to

150

Joshua.

He moaned aloud and brought his hand up to touch his blood-soaked head. Weakly he rolled to his side. A dozen pairs of hands grabbed him, tying his hands and feet tightly.

"Don't hurt him," she choked, but no one listened to her. Strong arms gripped her from the rear and deftly bound her arms behind her so tight the blood circulation beat frantically to reach her hands.

She twisted to study the man holding her. Wesley Treacher's cold, colorless eyes offered no clue to what he thought. His thin-lipped mouth curved into a hard, cruel grin.

Lost and alone, how could she cope with the disaster that had befallen her? Her exhausted mind refused to think. Resist. Never give in, the pounding of her heart insisted. With a strength from deep inside of her, she lifted her chin and crossed the gangplank between the two ships.

The name on the side of the pirate ship jumped out to mock her. The *Freedom*. She would never give up until she recovered her freedom and the *Anna McKyle*.

Dirk paced the deck of the *Sea Hawk* like a caged black panther. A jumble of details crowded his mind, each as important as the next. He had set out from Kingston Harbor less than twenty-four hours behind the *Anna McKyle*. Taking every risk offered him, he pushed the empty brig as hard as he could. With luck, he would catch up with Erica before she reached Crooked Island Passage. He laughed inwardly. Who did he think he kidded? Only a miracle could see to it he reached her in time to stop her from falling into the hands of the pirates. Refusing to succumb to the futility of the situation, he pushed on.

The whipping breeze grew in strength, but he didn't dare lower any canvas. His nervous crew, unused to him acting so irresponsible, watched him out of wary eyes. The sturdy brig groaned and shuddered with the excess sail, but flew ahead willingly. Ignoring the problems surrounding him like irritating gnats, he kept a sharp watch on the expanse of ocean ahead of him with the spyglass in his hand.

His right eye twitched violently in protest to the abuse and lack of sleep. Lowering the telescope, he rubbed the socket impatiently with the back of his hand. He placed the viewing instrument back against his face and scanned the endless ocean before him.

Spinning around, he searched the view behind the ship. The naval brig he had coerced from Governor Metcalfe skimmed the water not far behind him, making good time.

He removed the badly chewed Cuban cigar clenched between his teeth and carelessly tossed it over the rail to watch it crest away on the wake of the ship. Like everything else, it had lost its appeal to him. Nothing tasted right since he had left Jamaica. He forced himself to eat, as food tasted like mush. His insides were so knotted with anxiety that everything he tried to swallow stuck in his throat, refusing to go down. Sleep had been just as hard to manage, as thoughts of Erica hounded him relentlessly. If only he had been gentler with her, she might not have dashed off so recklessly. If only, if only, he chided himself. His self-incrimination wouldn't change a damned thing!

A light tap touched his broad shoulder. He swung around, prepared to snap of the head of whoever dared to disturb him. The clean, shining face of his cabin boy holding forth a large, steaming mug met his angry growl.

"Your coffee, sir," the boy beamed.

He took the brown cup from the smooth, pudgy fingers. The boy flashed him a radiant grin and sprinted away.

He sipped the scalding liquid and ran his long, tanned fingers through his disheveled hair. "What the hell's the matter with me?" he mumbled under his breath. Images flashed behind his closed eyelids of himself not much older than his cabin boy. Painful memories of a captain who had beat him and unsuccessfully tried to rape him, then had beat him again for his unwillingness to cooperate. He pushed the ugly past away to concentrate on a similar future Erica might face.

By damned, if Treacher harmed one hair on her precious head, he'd kill him an inch at a time.

High above his head a lookout shouted and pointed ahead. Swiftly he raised the telescope back to his eye and searched the horizon. *God, let it be the* Anna McKyle.

The outermost island of Jumento Cays jumped into his view. Frustrated, he slammed down the spyglass. He was only hours from the passage, and still no sign of Erica. He renewed his vigilance. There was still a chance, always a chance.

In helpless frustration Erica observed from the deck of the pirate ship as the dead, both hers and theirs, were tossed overboard unceremoniously. Familiar faces stilled in death, who had trusted her to get them home safely, would haunt her for years to come. When they lifted the small, slight body of her cabinboy and flung it overboard, twin tears rolled down her hot cheeks to darken the shredded remains of her shirt. Treacher would pay for what he had done. Somehow, some way, she would see to that.

Joshua had been carried aboard and down into the hold to a fate she could only imagine. The rest of her crew remained on the clipper.

Treacher huddled with several of his men. Crossing over the swaying gangplank, they approached Rob Taylor, still tied to a crate. Roughly Treacher jerked him to his feet. She couldn't hear what the pirate said, but she understood what he wanted. "It's all right, Rob. Do what they tell you to do," she shouted to the wind whipping around her.

Staunchly he refused to cooperate. A beady-eyed pirate placed a longknife menacingly to his bobbing Adam's apple, and Rob nodded his head in agreement to their demands. Erica slumped in relief.

Cutting his hands and feet loose, the pirates surrounded Rob and herded him toward the helm of the clipper.

With a squeal the grappling hooks dropped from the battered sides of the *Anna McKyle*. Pirates lifted the gangplank after their red-haired captain crossed back over it to his ship.

She watched from her powerless position as the clipper separated from the sinking ship she had rammed. Pride filled her as Rob did an excellent job of maneuvering her ship away from the wreckage.

"Be strong. I must be strong," she chanted over and over in an inaudible whisper when the clipper shrank into a blur on the horizon as the pirate ship left her behind.

Treacher swung his attention back to her. Her body tensed when he strolled to where he had left her lashed to a mast chain. Her heart hammered against her chest as vengefulness swelled to replace fear.

His fingers were like ice as they released her to roughly push her along in front of him with her arms twisted high against her back. Her hands and wrists throbbed with a numbing pain from the tight rope around them. She moved along, unresisting, though her mind devised ways to retaliate against his cruelty. As if he sensed her unbroken spirit, he shoved her so hard she fell to her knees. Proudly she regained her stance, pulling away from his hand as he urged her on.

As he thrust her down the companionway, his laughter gurgled deep from his throat and his stare scorched the back of her neck. "Now, my little wildcat," he growled in her ear, "we have a debt to settle."

"You'll pay, Treacher. I promise, you'll pay for what you've done," she vowed.

Chapter Nine

Dirk's heart pumped excitement through his body. The *Anna McKyle* rode the swells halfway through the channel with the remnants of a sinking ship a short distance away. His emotions soared. *She's safe, thank you, God, she's safe.*

He lowered the spyglass to hang idly by his side. Maybe he should turn the *Sea Hawk* about and avoid a confrontation with Erica. Chances were she would be annoyed by his attempt to interfere. No. He must see her and make sure she had come to no harm.

A half mile from the clipper an uncomfortable feeling nagged at him. Like a bird with a broken wing, the *Anna McKyle* floundered and twisted. Raising the spyglass that had become a living part of his hand, he skimmed the faraway deck for a sign of the problem. From what he could see, the damage looked minimal, not enough to account for the strange actions he witnessed. Still too far away for him to be certain, the activity on the clipper's deck remained a blurred mystery.

His captain's instincts kept him in check while his lover's desire urged him to dash ahead without regard. Nervously he paced the deck as the *Sea Hawk* held her position, waiting for the naval brig to catch up with him. Fortunately, the *Anna McKyle* remained motionless, her sails furled tightly. But how long would she stay that way?

With mind-maddening slowness the gun-laded naval brig joined the *Sea Hawk*. Communicating the situation as he saw it to the naval captain, he unwillingly followed instructions.

The military ship lurched ahead. Taking the helm, he glided the brig to follow close behind, the slowness of their approach leaving his mouth dry and bitter. He lifted the telescope to his eye every few minutes, seeking a glimpse of Erica aboard the clipper. But nothing. Visions of her injured and dying filled his mind. He swore under his breath. The urge to lash out at something or someone surged through him. Venting his frustrations the only way open to him, he slammed his clenched fist against the wheel with a power threatening to snap the spokes.

As they drew near, the deck of the *Anna McKyle* swarmed with frantic activity. Sails lifted to grasp the breeze, and the clipper came alive.

"Heave to and prepare for boarding," the naval captain's voice boomed through the megaphone.

More canvas shinned up the clipper's masts to spread like wings in the wind.

The naval brig sent a warning shot from one of its cannons across the bow of the *Anna McKyle*, but the preparations to sail continued.

"What are you doing, Erica?" he seethed.

The clipper lurched forward, trembled twice, and careened to the left. The excessive canvas ballooned with the captured wind, and he feared she had capsized. *Erica wouldn't be so stupid,* he decided. *If she didn't control the wheel, then who did?*

"I don't care what Captain Johnson said, I'm going to stop her," he mumbled.

Lighter and faster without the added weight of the gunnery the naval ship carried, he pushed the *Sea Hawk* ahead to cut off the clipper's forward progress. He circled her as she floundered for position, and together with the naval ship, trapped the *Anna McKyle* between them.

The scrape of timbers echoed as the brig pulled alongside the clipper. Disregarding the whine of bullets around him, he urged his crew to follow him aboard.

"Where are you, Erica?" he bellowed.

The loyal crew of the *Anna McKyle,* held back at gunpoint on the bow, sought an escape. He took careful aim at the bald pirate guarding them, and his bullet sent the man crashing to the deck.

The seamen serried in a wave. Unarmed, they massed an attack on the pirates, diverting their attention long enough for his crew to take charge. The pirates tossed down their weapons and surrendered, having no stomach to continue the fight.

He grabbed the first pirate he reached. "Where is the woman?" Unable to comprehend the rapid Spanish babble, he flung the sailor aside with superhuman strength.

The next man he seized swallowed hard. "You speak English?" he demanded. The sailor nodded.

Twisting long, lean fingers into the pirate's shirt front, he nearly lifted the frightened man off his feet. "Where is she? Where's the captain of this ship?"

The man shook his head rapidly. "She ain't here no more," he choked, his fingers pulling frantically at the ones strangling him.

Dirk's fist entwined tighter into the pirate's clothing. "Where the hell is she?" he thundered. The man's hands clawed at his, little gurgles escaping from his mouth.

The flat of his hand snapped the pirate's head on his spindly neck. Side to side the face swung with a rag doll motion. "Answer me, damn it." The sailor sagged unconscious against him. Dropping the useless man, he reached for the next one, who whimpered in fear.

Strong arms grabbed him from the rear. "Stop it, man," Captain Johnson's sympathetic voice commanded. "Killing them isn't going to bring her back."

"Perhaps not, Captain," he groaned as Johnson released him, "but it will make me feel better."

A sandy-haired man stepped forward from the clipper's crew and cleared his throat. He turned to the man in expectation.

"Rob Taylor, Second Officer of the *Anna McKyle,*" the light-haired man offered. "I'm not sure what your connection is with Captain Armstrong, but I can tell you Treacher took her and Mr. Reynolds, the First, aboard his ship."

His dark eyes held hope. "How was she the last time you saw her?"

"A bit battered, but her chin was high in the air."

He sighed with audible relief. *At least she's alive.*

Erica examined the cabin Wesley Treacher pushed her into. Her heart beat an erratic rhythm, but she forced herself to swallow her fear. Glancing back at the hard figure of a man towering over her, she had no doubt he would do with her exactly as he wanted.

Vile pictures of him raping her dominated her thoughts. What would rape feel like? The idea of Treacher touching her intimately as Dirk had was unthinkable. More frightened of the unknown than of the man ready to pounce on her, the need to survive whatever he would do welled up inside of her. He had stolen her ship and killed or injured many of her crew, including Joshua. He had stopped her from returning home. The first of July edged closer and closer. Every disaster that befell her was caused by interfering men. Treacher was another damned, interfering man. Yes, she would survive, if only to get even with him.

Her vow of revenge gave her strength. She waited with her breath held tightly in her lungs.

As if sensing what she expected, the pirate approached her at a slow, steady pace. She stepped backward each time he took a stride forward, her breath coming in short pants. The look of cruel amusement on his face made evident his enjoyment of her fearful reaction.

The back of her thighs brushed the cover on the bed, and she held her ground. With a defiant lift of her chin she prepared for Treacher to reach her.

He placed his long arms on either side of her head and across the narrowness of the bunk and rested his weight against his hands, planted firmly on the wall behind her. She swayed backward to avoid his touch, her spine stretched to its limit. He pressed his thighs hard against hers and leaned closer. She didn't move, afraid she would fall onto the mattress. Holding her ground, she stared at his cold eye, inches from her face.

"Now, my little wildcat, I would like to give you what you're expecting." His rasp pierced the silence. She jumped. "But that can wait until later." Roughly he forced her to bend farther back until she collapsed in a heap on the hard bunk. Reaching down he flipped her legs onto the bed and taking a rope, deftly tied them together so tightly that in no time her feet would feel as numb as her hands.

"Joshua," she protested. "I have to know how he is."

"If you mean the fool who tried to stop me from getting you," he chuckled as he tested the knots binding her arms and legs, "you don't have to worry. He'll live if the ship's rats don't devour him between here and where we're headed."

He crossed the small cabin in three long strides. She shivered at the humorless grin he shot her from the door. "Until later, my dear." The door closed with a fatalistic click behind him.

Her courage crumped into despair as the key grated in the lock. The cat-and-mouse game he played was far worse than anything he had planned for her.

The line of mismatched pirates pressed their backs

against the railing of the *Anna McKyle*. Dirk eyed each, deciding which one to direct his questions to. Holding his anger in check, he remained calm, at least on the surface.

Aware that a dozen pairs of nervous eyes followed his every move, he paced before them. Without warning he stopped before a small, shriveled apple of a man and snapped, "Where did Treacher take her?"

The little man stared blankly at him, refusing to answer.

Continuing his nerve-shattering sweep of the deck, he questioned each man, but their loyalty to their pirate captain remained unflinching. Frustration built inside of him, threatening to explode. The urge to knock heads together again swelled, but he fought the desire down. What did it take to get their cooperation? Maybe the bastards could be bribed.

Captain Johnson, watching from a distance, stepped forward and lightly tapped his broad shoulder. The naval man's hand beckoned him to step away from the prisoners. He eyed the man unhappily but followed nonetheless.

The military man studied him for a moment in silence as if deciding what to say. Dirk's impatience threatened to burst through the thin veneer of control he maintained, as he drummed his fingers against the mast next to which the other man stopped.

"Captain," Johnson began, "you aren't dealing with loyalty here. Those men are more afraid of what Wesley Treacher will do to them if he finds out they ratted on him than what we'll do if they don't. He wouldn't hesitate to hack them to pieces an inch at a time, laughing while he did it. Those men figure they're dead anyway, so they have nothing to gain by talking."

The tattoo of his fingers stopped as he considered the other man's advice. Maybe if he could get one man alone and offer him freedom instead of threats . . . He could try.

"Do you have the power to grant amnesty?" he inquired. "Freedom for the information where Treacher has gone?"

Captain Johnson considered his words. "It's highly irregular," he answered, "but I imagine if you took one of the prisoners under American jurisdiction, there wouldn't be much I could do about it." He gave him a conspiratory smile.

Black eyes skimmed over the pirates, touching on each man. Which one should he choose? Their eyes refused to meet his, except one. Following his instincts, he jerked the pirate roughly away from the rail. The man's pale, sunken eyes pleaded with the black ones boring into him. He opened an almost toothless mouth and a high, careening wail escaped, his hot breath striking Dirk's face. The other pirates sighed in relief, glad they had not been chosen by the wild-eyed, dark-haired demon.

He dragged the screaming man across the deck and behind the lifeboat, away from his companions. Shoving the pirate up against the boat, he held him there as the man kicked and swung his arms in an attempt to escape.

"Hold on, man. Quit whining and listen to what I have to say. I can save your wretched neck if you'll cooperate with me."

The sailor's mouth clamped shut.

"If you guide me to Treacher's base, I'll see to it you're turned loose anywhere on the American coast you want." His intense stare pinned the man against the boat.

The pirate swallowed hard. "I'd like to help you, mate, but if Treacher got a hold of me, well, it wouldn't be pretty."

"I promise you, he won't touch you."

"If you try to get into his stronghold, you'll never get out alive. And if you make me go with you, I'm worse than dead," the man pleaded. "But I can tell you how to get there. I ain't got no love of that bastard. All I ask is you let me off at the nearest port to here. I don't care where it is, as long as I can catch another ship."

He gripped the front of the sailor's shirt. "How do I know I can trust you?"

The man's pale eyes bulged in their sockets and rolled wildly. "I ain't gonna cheat you. I promise. You gotta believe me."

His hand released the sailor's shirt. Should he trust him? He had no choice but to take the man at his word. "All right. I want detailed directions to Treacher's base." He pressed the smaller man up against the lifeboat. "I swear to God, if you try to deceive me, I'll find you and cut you into so many pieces it will be hard to count them."

He signaled his men, and they led the pirate over the gangplank between the clipper and the *Sea Hawk*. He stepped from behind the lifeboat to discover Rob Taylor. The sandy-haired man hesitated as he scrutinized him. He flashed Rob a perfunctory smile, and the man stepped forward.

Sorting the details of the situation, he put tasks to be done in an order of importance. First he must find Erica and get her back. His eyes surveyed the deck of the *Anna McKyle.* What a beauty! In her hold was his cargo. Her cargo, he truthfully admitted. She had fought for it, so it must be as important to her as it would have been to him. He would see to it that the clipper got to Philadelphia on time. He owed Erica that much.

Critically he inspected the approaching man. The clipper had been handled ineptly when they chased her. Had this man been at the helm? If so, he couldn't turn her over to someone so incapable of sailing her.

"Excuse me, sir," Rob interjected.

"Dirk Hawkyns." He offered his hand in a friendly manner.

"Captain Hawkyns." Rob grasped the outstretched palm firmly. "I'd like to thank you for what you did earlier."

"What happened, Mr. Taylor?" Dirk's smile remained friendly.

"They were waiting for us. They had five ships and boxed us in from every direction. Captain Armstrong took the only available opening and rammed that brig." Rob's finger pointed toward the sinking pirate ship. "But it was a decoy. Captain Armstrong is a good captain. One of the best. We never had a chance."

He silently studied the other man. Erica had an admirer in Rob Taylor, and she probably didn't realize it. "Were you at the wheel when we stopped you?"

"I was at first, but the pirates realized I stalled for

time. They pushed me out of the way. The sailor that took the wheel from me didn't know what he was doing. It was a good thing he didn't. If I had been at the helm, Captain, you wouldn't have gotten in front of me."

"Good, Mr. Taylor. That's exactly what I wanted to hear." He clapped the man on the back. "I want you to take the *Anna McKyle* on to Philadelphia for Captain Armstrong."

"Are you sure that's what she'd want me to do?" Rob abruptly faced him. "I feel I should go after her."

"Don't worry about your captain. I'll find her and bring her home safe. That cargo is important to her. I know the *Anna McKyle* is in capable hands with you. Finish the job your captain can't complete for herself."

Rob nodded in consent.

Making a quick inspection of the ship, he asked, "What is the extent of the clipper's damage?"

"A few cracked planks on the hull from the impact of the collision, but it's caulked from the inside and should hold. Also the jibboom was cracked near the bowsprit, but we made a temporary repair to it as well. I think it'll hold."

"Very good, Mr. Taylor. It sounds like you have everything under control." He walked away confident the young officer would get the clipper to Philadelphia.

"Captain Hawkyns," Rob called after his retreating figure. "What do I once I deliver the cargo?"

"Wait in Baltimore. I'll bring your captain to you." *Or I'll die trying,* he promised himself.

Late afternoon shadows lengthened and darkened across Erica, bound on the hard bunk. The airless room contained one small porthole in the wall high above her head. It was closed. She had studied in detail each item and piece of furniture the crowded cabin held. In fact, she had memorized everything within the span of her vision, seeking a means to escape her bondage, something to use to cut the ropes cruelly biting into her tender flesh.

Her arms and legs hung like dead weight, and a constant pain throbbed between her tightly strained shoulder blades. Squirming her body to get more comfortable, she succeeded in making her suffering worse.

Hunger and extreme thirst turned her mouth to cotton. Did the pirate plan to starve her to death? She groaned. If she didn't relieve herself soon, she wouldn't be responsible for her bodily functions. Torture came in many guises.

Time moved by at a snail's pace as the day stretched endlessly. Over and over she relived the capture of her ship. Could she have done something different to avoid the pirates? No, she had done everything possible. Images of Joshua, bleeding, as the pirates dragged him away, and Treacher's laugh as she pleaded for them to handle him with care, raised her frustration to a high pitch. How she'd like to claw his one good eye out.

As if someone had snuffed out a candle, total darkness engulfed her, the sound of her breathing her only company.

Unable to move on the ungiving bunk, she groaned. God must have had this cabin in mind when he created hell. She clamped her jaws shut to keep her fear in check. Silent, twin tears slid down her face. "Please God," she prayed in a childish whisper, "if you'll only get me out of here, I'll be a good girl. If you'll just see I get home to Aunt Connie, I'll never leave there again. Oh, God, please," she choked between sobs, "listen to me!"

She stopped her supplication to concentrate on the silence, expecting God to answer her. The ominous quiet remained unchanged. She wept noisily with nose and eyes running unchecked.

The click of the key turning in the rusty lock brought her tears to an abrupt halt. She sniffed and wiped her wet face against the rough cotton cover. She must not allow the pirates to see her so weak. Expecting Satan himself, she riveted her eyes on the opening door.

Hinges squealed in protest. Booted feet crossed the planking on the cabin floor. Light flared, and the sharp clink of the lantern glass being lowered on a bright flame broke the rhythmic rush of her breathing.

Wesley Treacher's face danced in the halo of yellow light the lantern cast. The same mocking sneer he had worn earlier curled his thin-lipped mouth. What she had dreaded all day would happen now.

The icy, pale eye not covered by the flaming red patch considered her from head to foot, then moved back up to watch her face. Had she seen his features soften for a moment? She couldn't be sure. She stared back with vengeance clearly on her face.

168

Reaching down toward his booted leg, the pirate broke their eye contact. As if by magic, a long, lethal-looking knife rested in his hand. Carefully he touched the thin tip of the sharp blade to the first finger of his other hand. The metal glistened as the light caught it. A look of pure delight filled his eye as he stealthily advanced toward her. She swallowed painfully, her eyes glued to the gleaming blade.

Too soon he reached her, and she watched in fearful fascination as he lowered the thin, shining blade to rest against her throat. Her eyes widened in fear. She had never met anyone like this man before. He would murder her in calculated cold blood and never blink. With slow deliberation he pressed the tip of the blade into her pulsating flesh. Blood tricked down her neck to mingle with perspiration. She didn't move, not even to draw air into her screaming lungs, afraid it would cause the knife to sink deeper. His expression remained unchanged; the knife pressed harder against her throat. She closed her eyes, not wanting to see the moment he decided to end her life.

With lightning speed he drew the blade away from her neck and flipped her over on her stomach. Two quick slices of the knife, and her numb arms and legs fell free. Lying perfectly still, she anticipated the plunge of the weapon between her shoulder blades.

Minutes passed. The familiar needles of blood rushed to deaden limbs and subsided. She flexed her fingers and then her toes as a groan of relief escaped her clenched teeth.

Angry at her cowardly reaction, she lifted her face from the mattress to glance in his direction. Calmly he sat in the room's one chair, tipped back against the wall, one shiny black boot resting on the table between them. A look of amusement encompassed his chiseled features.

In humiliation and rage, she pushed up from the bunk, but her shaky legs didn't hold her weight, and she collapsed in a heap on the floor. Curled on the planks, she rubbed life back into her stinging feet.

Deep laughter rumbled from his direction. She glowered at his insolent face as he drew back with amusement. Her eyes widened in disbelief. The knife quivered point down in the table beside his leg, beckoning her.

Taking the only chance she might get, she lunged across the room and clasped the handle with both hands. With a strength she didn't know she possessed, she jerked the blade from its resting place. Lifting it above her head, she aimed the razor-sharp point toward the pirate's exposed chest. She would kill him and send him straight to the hell in which he belonged.

With catlike grace he jumped to his feet, the chair clattering to the floor. Grabbing her uplifted arms, he bent her backward like a tightly strung bow.

Desperately she clung to the weapon as his large thumbs squeezed the pulse point in her wrists. Her bloodless hands refused to obey her command. Her stomach convulsed painfully as the knife clattered to the floor.

Their heavy, unmatched breathing permeated the room. His harsh, raspy voice cracked inches from her ear. "Don't ever try that again, wildcat, or I'll slit your pretty throat before you have a chance to blink your eyes."

"Why don't you do just that, and get it over with?"

"Because, my dear, I have plans for you that don't include you dying," he answered; "at least, not yet." He grabbed a fistful of her golden hair. "Now you listen to me, and you listen to me good. I came here out of the kindness of my heart—"

"Your black heart has about as much kindness as a snake's," she hissed, knowing her hair was about to be pulled out by the roots.

"Nonetheless, I thought you might like to stretch your limbs. Toby should be here in a few minutes with something for you to eat." Roughly he shoved her back on the bed. "But if you continue to act this way, I'll have no qualms about trussing you back up, and to hell with you. You're just as good to me stiff and hungry."

A knock on the door stilled her retort. A giant of a man ducked his head and entered the cabin. His arms carried a tray stacked with several bowls and dishes. Treacher pointed to the table, and Toby set the tray down.

Toby reminded her of a gentle ox. His bovine eyes held no malice. He cast his eyes at Treacher with slavelike adoration; he eyed her with simple curiosity.

"Toby?" Treacher said gently.

The big man swung his gaze back toward the pirate.

"I want her to stay here. Don't let her leave. Do you understand?"

A simpleton's smile lit the big face. "Don't worry, Wesley, I won't let her leave."

Treacher bent down, retrieved the fallen knife from

the floor, and saluted her with the tip stained with her blood. "Until later, my dear."

She shot his retreating back as cold a look as she could muster. The door closed with a bang. Toby lowered himself into a squat before the door, guarding it.

Treacher's final words echoed in her mind as she stepped toward the covered tray. *Until later.* What did he have planned for her? She shivered uncontrollably.

She must find a way to escape. Peering at Toby through lowered lashes, she lifted the covers from the plates. Righting the chair from the floor, she sat down before the food. Her hunger deserted her.

She ventured a smile, hoping to put the big man at ease. If he was as simple as he appeared, maybe she could use that to her advantage.

Her heart lifted when Toby smiled back at her.

Dirk held the ship's helm as the evening sun, a bright red ball of fire, dipped one final time below the undulating horizon before him. A fine salt mist left small pearl-drops of moisture on everything it touched, including his hair and eyelashes. With the back of his hand he cleared his watery vision.

The *Sea Hawk* strained before the wind billowing the sails as taut as drum skins. The familiar snapping they made soothed him just as the rhythmic groans of the wooden masts and planking did. These sounds were the lullabies of his childhood, as reassuring as a mother's voice to him.

The white sails of the naval ship disappeared with the sun. The Royal Navy had no jurisdiction in

American waters, and Captain Johnson would return to Jamaica. On his own in the vast expanse of ocean, he brought his attention back around as he ruthlessly pushed the brig in the opposite direction, toward Erica and Treacher's stronghold, only a few days away, located on one of the multitude of small islands fanning from the tip of the Florida Territory peninsula. But first, he must keep his promise to drop the cooperative sailor at Nassau, the most convenient port between here and the Florida Keys.

Fragments of rescue plans formulated in his mind to be just as quickly rejected as the flaw in each one became apparent. Damn it, there had to be a simple solution he'd overlooked.

Thoughtfully he rubbed his hand over his beard-roughened face up to his eye puffed from lack of sleep. Had it only been a week ago he had held Erica's warm, yielding body next to him? Seven days that had aged him by ten years. His mind screamed for sleep, and his heart pushed him on, demanding he find her. She was in his blood like no woman he had met before. He would find her. One way, and only one way, could he reach her. His own safety was unimportant; his life meant nothing without her.

The darkness folded around Erica like a warm, protective cloak, amplifying the moans and groans of the *Freedom*. After she had sated her hunger and thirst, Toby had shown her the chamber pot. Her need had been stronger than her delicacy, and she had been grateful for his concern.

She was again on the bunk bound hand and foot, but Toby had made her as comfortable as he could.

His big, powerful paw had patted her soft hair as he had apologized for tying her up again. He had given the rope as much slack as he could, and she could lie on her back or side with minimal pain. A small gain, but at least she had taken a step in the right direction. She was bodily exhausted, but her active mind gave her no peace. Guilt pressed against her, weighing heavily on her delicate shoulders. Guilt for making a bad decision and losing her ship. Guilt for the deaths of her men and for Joshua's injury.

Wesley Treacher puzzled her. If he intended to rape her he would have already done so. His plans for her must be much worse.

Unbidden, images of Dirk's caring face probed her thoughts. Why would she think of him now? She sighed, accepting the comfort that thoughts of him gave her. If he were here now, he would wrap his strong arms around her and make this nightmare end.

Her feelings surprised her. Just what did she feel for him? He was arrogant and conceited, but at the same time warm and giving. She could never remember feeling this way about any man. She wished she could close her eyes and allow him to shield her from the outside world. Her closing eyes flew open. She had never desired any man's protection to this extend; not even her father's.

Dirk Hawkyn's probably didn't remember her name. He would do nothing for her. She had no one to rely on but herself. She would get out of this difficulty on her own. She wouldn't give up. Never would she give in to fate—or Wesley Treacher.

Determination gave way to exhaustion. Demanding lids lowered over her eyes.

The sound of a deep-chested cough woke her. Her throat burned as if she had swallowed hot coals. Her head pounded viciously as she jackknifed with a coughing spell. Consumed by a dry, fiery heat, she shook with weakness. She opened her mouth to call for help, but little squeaks passed her swollen lips. Helplessly she waited for someone to find her.

She drifted in and out of a thick fog; occasionally someone placed a cool hand or cloth, she wasn't sure which, against her hot, dry forehead. Dark, deep eyes stared down at her, and she hoarsely called, "Dirk." With lightning speed they changed into the cold, colorless eyes of a snake. Her screams of despair echoed over and over in her ears, and the snake disappeared.

Clutching the hand she found, she cried, "Aunt Connie, I'm sorry. I didn't mean for Joshua to suffer. I promise I'll bring him home." The hand she clung to was unfamiliar, so large and calloused. "No, Aunt Connie, come back. Don't leave me here."

The air turned cool, then freezing. Snow engulfed her. She wound the blankets tightly around her and shivered so hard her teeth crashed against each other. The flakes of snow turned to tongues of fire burning everywhere they touched. She shoved the covers away and prayed the icy cold would return. When it did, she cried for the fiery flames.

The pain in her chest pressed down, suffocating her. No matter how hard she tried she couldn't get enough air in her tortured lungs. Her strength crumbled around her like ashes of a fire as she frantically gasped for breath. She must escape and find the

Anna McKyle. She had to get to Baltimore before Edmund Bennett's deadline. She couldn't lie here and lose everything she valued. She must do something.

Had the sailor's superstitions been right? Would she die on a ship from hell, headed God knew where? Please, not here, alone, with her life in ruins.

Her puffy eyelids lifted and throbbed with the monumental task of keeping them open. Toby's sad cow eyes met hers. He smiled and babbled, "Miss Erica?" His cool hand grazed her forehead. She tried without success to lift the corners of her cracked mouth to smile, but her sore lungs rose and fell with ease. She prayed the nightmare had ended as she plunged down into the dark oblivion of sleep.

Reality rushed in as she slowly breathed in and out. Refusing to open her eyes and face what she would see, she screwed her lids tight.

How long did she think she could hide behind closed eyes? Not facing the truth wouldn't make it go away. With a sigh she lifted her lids and blinked twice. She had no idea where she was. The small, sparsely furnished room contained crude, handmade chairs and a table. The lumpy bed she lay on smelled of freshly cut hay. What was different? There was no movement underneath her. She was on land. But where? How did she get here? No matter how hard she tried, she couldn't remember.

The rustic reed door squeaked as it swung open. The broad, familiar back of Toby pushed its way in. He faced her with his arms laden down with a stack of freshly washed and mended clothing. Her clothing! Her hands flew under the light covering over her. Just as she suspected; she had nothing on. Her face twisted with surprise.

Toby's gentle face responded with adoration. "It's all right, Miss Erica. Ain't nothing wrong happened."

"Did you . . . ?"

"Aw, no, Miss Angela seen to it."

Relieved, she had no idea who Angela was, but at least a woman had undressed her. The little bit of movement exhausted her, and her eyes fluttered shut. A thousand questions swirled in her head. *Where am I? What day is it? And Joshua?* She forced her heavy lids open.

"Toby," she mumbled. "Joshua. How is he?"

He studied her for a moment. "He ain't gonna die, if that's what you mean."

Her chest rose and fell with relief. "Where is he?"

He scratched his head. "I reckon he's down in the pens with the rest of the prisoners. Last time I saw him he was pacing like a caged bear."

"Other prisoners, Toby? What other prisoners?"

"Well, there's a real pretty lady in silk and satin, and a man all dressed as pretty as the lady. They're a real lord and lady, I think. There's another man, a captain like you, only he's old and ugly, not pretty like you." Toby's face lit up. "And a couple of other men. Ship's officers, I think."

"And my ship and crew, are they here, too?" Her words slurred.

"Oh, no, Miss Erica. They ain't never showed up. Wesley's mad enough to eat nails 'cause he thinks his men pulled a double cross and took off on their own. He'll have to punish them real bad when he finds them."

Her heart plummeted. Where was her ship? It was her only means of escape. July first. Edmund Bennett's face leered at her. He wouldn't give her any grace on this payment. With her ship went her letter of credit. She would lose everything. No, she wouldn't accept that. Her head spun, and her eyelids closed over her eyes as she fought the unconsciousness sweeping over her.

Chapter Ten

The Florida Keys
June 6, 1835

Erica lifted her lashes to stare into a lifeless pair of water blue eyes. A harsh but feminine voice spoke and stopped. The eyes held a question, but she blinked back, uncomprehending.

"Can't you hear me?" the voice grated against her eardrums.

"Yes, I can hear you."

"Then answer my question. Can you stand up?" The woman's speech had a familiar ring to it.

She studied the face before her and didn't recognize it. Though premature age lines creased the face, she couldn't be more than twenty-five. The once-pretty mouth turned down in a perpetual frown, and the dirty blonde hair couldn't have seen a brush in months. Why did the voice sound familiar? The accent. It sounded like home and the Chesapeake Bay.

"Angela," she said, more to herself than to the

other woman.

"How do you know my name?" The lined forehead furled into a tight frown.

"Toby mentioned you." She offered the woman a tentitive smile.

"That big dolt has got to learn to keep his mouth shut." Angela swore under her breath, the frown still pasted on her face.

"He didn't mean any harm. He just mentioned you had been the one to undress me earlier."

"Yeah, and I'm the one who's gonna have to dress you back if you don't stand up and do it yourself."

She struggled to a sitting position. Her head spun, and the bed rose up to meet her. Falling back against the mattress, body twisted awkwardly, she waited for the spinning feeling to pass.

Angela roughly pulled her limp arms above her head. "Come on, at least sit up, so I can get this damn shirt on you. I've never seen clothes like these before on a woman. Is this what they're wearing these days in the States?"

Forcing herself back up, it took all of her strength to maintain her balance. Angela jerked the form-fitting top over her wobby head to cover her chest. Poking rubberlike arms at the sleeves held out to her, she managed to get into her shirt.

Angela held a pair of lace drawers out in front of her. "I've never seen anything like those, but I like them."

"I had them especially designed to wear under pants."

Angela looked at her over the bit of lace in her

hands. "Just what I'd expect from a woman like you. Especially designed," she muttered. Her mouth drawn tight, she guided Erica's legs over the side of the bed and slipped the drawers over her feet. "Now, honey, if you plan on wearin' these, you're gonna have to stand up."

Using Angela's shoulders as a support, she rose to a teetering stance. The woman pulled the lace garment impatiently up around her hips.

Her eyes flew up as the reed door creaked. She swayed as Angela twisted to glare at the men entering the room.

"Get out of here, Wesley. Haven't you got any decency?"

The pirate watched their awkward attempt to dress her.

Angela regarded him as she pushed Erica down on the bed to slip the britches over her feet. He folded his arms and leaned back against the rough, unfinished wall behind him. He had no intention of leaving.

Dizzy and weak, Erica concentrated on remaining upright. Angela urged her to a standing position as she worked the pants up over her hips.

With a grunt the woman buttoned up the front of the pants and shoved her back on the mattress. Whirling on Treacher she hissed, "The show is over. Get out of here."

He approached the bedraggled blonde and savagely circled his arm around her. Gripping a handful of matted hair, he jerked her head back so she stared into his one good eye. "Don't push me, Angela, or by damn, I'll throw you to the alligators in the swamp."

Angela gave him as vicious a smile as he held on his lips. "Try it, you son of a bitch, and I'll drag you in with me."

He tossed his head back with a loud guffaw. "Your fire is the only reason I let you stay around. But don't push me too far, my dear," he said between his teeth, shoving her as hard as he could. She landed in a heap in the corner of the room.

He eyed Erica ruefully as she lay sprawled across the rumpled bed. The need for revenge welled up inside her. He inspected her from head to foot. "It seems to me you'll survive. That's all I wanted to know," he grunted and headed out the door, banging it behind his retreating back.

Soft weeping floated from the corner where Angela huddled. The crying, tugging at Erica's heart, expressed the self-pitying sorrow of a woman in love with a man who didn't return the feeling.

"Angela?" she called across the short span between them. "Did he hurt you?"

The blonde sniffed and wiped her face with the back of her hand. "No, I'm all right." She gathered her feet underneath her and stood. Her hands reached down to smooth the permanent wrinkles in her faded skirt. Dirty, work-roughened fingers dug a path through her matted hair. Unable to contain herself any longer, Angela burst out into fresh tears.

Erica considered the situation as she chewed her bottom lip. If she could gain the woman's trust, maybe she could use that to her advantage. "Angela, I think I understand. I'm sorry."

"What do you understand? What could you know about what I feel?" Angela snapped.

"I know you love him, don't you?" she answered softly.

Angela's eyes locked with hers across the room, analyzing her. Lowering her head to rest in her reddened hands, the woman shook her head in agreement. "He's not as awful as he seems. You'd have to know all that's happened to him," she explained between sobs. Distrust lit her lined face. "But why should I tell you? Just why in the hell would you care?"

"I don't know why." Pity rose in her heart. "But I do. If you want to talk about it, I'll be glad to listen."

Her words affected the older woman. Slowly Angela rose, crossed the room, and sank on the bed beside her prone body. "Yes, I would like to talk about it." She glanced down for reassurance.

An encouraging smile curved her lips as she nodded, urging the woman to speak.

The blonde took a deep breath as if organizing her thoughts. "You'd have to have known Wesley like I did ten years ago." Angela's mouth lifted in remembrance. "We was young with foolish dreams. My papa owned a small tavern in Cambridge, Maryland, on the Chesapeake Bay."

She nodded her head. She knew the town.

"It was a nice tavern. Clean and reputable. Wesley was a young sailor then and always came by when he was in port. Sometimes I think he made a point of comin' to Cambridge, 'cause it's not that big." She smiled, and it softened her harsh face. "I think he

183

cared about me then.

"He was up for Mate that summer, and we celebrated by gettin' married." She glanced down at her rough hands, nervously lacing and unlacing her fingers. "When the promotion didn't come, I don't know, he wasn't the same." She wiped a wayward tear from the corner of her eye.

"First Wesley turned to drink and then to highway robbery. One night there was an ambush. That's when he lost his eye as well as his manhood." Angela covered her mouth as if to stuff the words back into it. "I shouldn't have told you that."

Erica raised her head, alerted. "What do you mean, he lost his manhood?"

Angela contemplated her. Shrugging her thin shoulders, she answered. "There was a fight, and he was stabbed twice. In the eye and here." She pointed to her groin. "He can't—well, you know what I mean. He's never been the same since. I sometimes think he blames me for his problem. I don't know, maybe he's right. If I was prettier, like you, then . . ." A sob escaped her lips.

Erica struggled to a sitting position and brought the dirty blonde head to rest on her shoulder. "You can't blame yourself for his failures, Angela." Gently she pushed the sooty face back to look at it. "You know, if you washed away the grime and brushed your hair, you would be pretty."

Angela straightened and lifted from the bed. "It's not gonna make any difference. He don't see me anymore. Only you." The woman turned accusing eyes on her.

"I'm not here by choice. I would gladly leave if I could."

"Then I guess we're both prisoners, aren't we? You, your body, and me," she paused, struggling with emotion, "my heart."

Angela headed toward the door, and she held out her hand to stop the woman. "Wait, there's so many questions I need answers to. Please don't leave."

Angela hesitated at the door.

"Where am I, and how long have I been here?"

The blonde mulled over her answer. "Wesley showed up with you three days ago. You're somewhere nobody's gonna find you." Abruptly she turned.

"Angela?"

"No," she snapped. "I've told you too much already." She slipped out of the door.

Frustrated, Erica leaned back against the thin feather pillow. Now she understood why the pirate had never touched her. Relief flooded over her to know he never would.

She maintained a façade of calm as she sorted out the facts she had. Treacher had kidnapped her over a week ago. The pirates had taken control of her ship, but it hadn't shown up. There was always a chance her crew had gained control of the clipper again and had followed the pirates. But where was she? She could be anywhere in the Caribbean. She might even be in South America. She sighed in frustration. There was only a thin chance of being rescued.

Joshua was here somewhere. If she could find him, maybe together they could work out a plan of escape.

Her gaze darted up. The door squeaked open, admitting the big, lumbering body of Toby. He held a deep, wooden bowl emitting an unsavory smell.

Finding her awake and dressed, his face radiated with pleasure as he offered her the bowl with child-like zeal.

Quietly she took it, and though she wanted to push it away, she dipped the spoon into the watery stew. He towered above her, waiting for her to eat. Easing the spoon into her mouth, the stew tasted as bad as she imagined it would. But she kept the grimace from her face and swallowed. She needed time to decide how to convince him to take her to Joshua.

Dropping the spoon in the offending stew, she licked her bottom lip, forming the exact words in her mind to say. Toby's eyes questioned her.

"Toby, I'm feeling better now. I could use some fresh air and sunshine." She smiled sweetly at him.

He gaped back at her as if what she asked took a few minutes to penetrate his simple mind.

"Please, Toby," she whispered when he didn't respond.

"Wesley didn't say nothing about letting you go outside, so I guess it's all right." He walked to the door and pushed it open, waiting for her to join him.

Valiantly she pushed up to a sitting position. She struggled to clear her spinning head. She must get up and find Joshua. She had to know where she was and what was going on. She must escape. The vulnerability of being like a leaf in the wind with no control over her life was unbearable. Willing her strength to hold, she stood. Wobbling and swaying, she maintained her balance.

Concentrating on placing one foot in front of the other, she reached the door he held open. He took her upper arm into his big, gentle grip and led her out into the sunshine.

The glorious sunshine. She lifted her face to absorb the warmth and strength radiating down on her. With a deep breath she explored her surroundings. Windswept palms and clean white sand greeted her. Across the expanse of water, lapping at the beach, an island rose in line with where she stood. Straining her eyes, she glimpsed another island off in the distance. Following the shoreline as far as she could see gave her the impression they were on another island or a narrow peninsula, but she wasn't sure which.

Canvassing the landscape, she studied every detail and stored the information away like a squirrel. The crude hut made of palm tree wood and thatch they had left looked like a half-dozen others dotting the cleared area. A tangle of jungle surrounded the buildings. Crammed into the remaining cleared ground were tents and lean-tos of every description. There was no order to the buildings, and it looked as if someone had picked them up and tossed them into the air, leaving them where they fell. Worn footpaths snaked between the structures and crisscrossed each other a dozen times. They lent an air of permanency to an otherwise temporary-looking settlement.

Toby led her toward a large outcrop of black rock, out of place in the pure white sand. She resisted his urgings to sit and rest. "Oh, please, Toby, walking makes me feel so much better. I've been sitting or lying down for so long. . . ."

He shrugged his massive shoulders and led her down one of the numerous footpaths. Attempting to appear nonchalant, she inspected every structure they passed, seeking the "pens" he had spoken of earlier.

She paused and made a quick survey of their surroundings. Pointing in one direction, she asked, "What's over in that direction?"

"Well," he replied, "on the other side of that grove of trees is the harbor and warehouse that Wesley uses to store his supplies and goods."

"And in that direction?" She swung her finger around forty-five degrees.

"There ain't much there except a livestock barn and the pens."

The pens. Her pulse raced, hearing the word she waited for. "What kind of livestock?"

"Oh, the usual. A few goats and chickens. There's a dried-up milk cow that ain't good for nothing." His face lit up. "Wesley has a pretty Arabian mare he took from a Spanish duke once."

She jumped at the opportunity to get closer to Joshua. "Could I see her?"

His love of animals registered on his broad face. "Would you really like to?"

She nodded enthusiastically as her heart beat in anticipation. She would find Joshua. She couldn't wait to see him. He had to be as concerned about her as she was about him. She tried to concentrate on Toby's words as he described the horse as they headed down the path. She must have nodded and smiled at the right moments, for he never noticed her lack of attention.

The inescapable smell of animal manure, trampled and mixed with the native soil, wafted out to meet them as they approached a large, swaybacked building leaning precariously to one side. The interior of the barn was dark and humid. He led her to a large stall in the back near a rear exit. The small, delicate mare whinnied expectantly as he headed toward the stall. Absentmindedly she reached out her hand to rub the soft velvet nose pushing out between the old, broken boards of the stable door.

Straining her eyes and ears to discover what was behind the barn, she picked up the sound of human voices. Toby's soft cooing to the horse became an irritant, and she fought down the urge to tell him to hush.

As he tended to the little mare, his hand slipped away from her arm, which he had held tightly the entire time they walked. She eased her way toward the open door only a few feet away with the silent stealth of a fox.

A small outbuilding squatted in the middle of a mixture of different kinds of fencing. The pens. It must be the pens.

Glancing back at Toby, still absorbed in talking to the horse, she inched toward the barrier and craned her neck to see inside.

Joshua hunched on an old, rickety bench leaning back against the weatherworn boards of the building, his head nodding in slumber. She wanted to call his name, but her voice would attrack Toby's attention.

She stared at Joshua, willing him to look at her, but his eyes remained closed.

She searched the ground and located several small pebbles, which she scooped up and stored in her left hand. Taking one, she drew her hand back and tossed it at her friend. Maddeningly it landed a few feet in front of his boots, and he didn't move.

Reaching into her fistful of stones, she grasped another and drew back sharply to give it all she had.

A steel-like grip stopped her hand in midmotion. Her head snapped around to find Wesley Treacher's snake eye glaring down at her. With nothing to lose, she screamed, "Joshua."

The tall, silver-haired man reacted instantly. Jumping up from the bench, it clattered to the ground. "Erica?" he called back.

The pirate twisted her arm behind her back. Sharp pains tore through her limb, but the exhilaration of finding Joshua overrode the excruciation. Joshua was here and unharmed.

"Over here, Joshua," she managed to get out before Treacher clamped a damp, rough hand over her mouth and nose. Unable to breathe, she struggled to escape his grip. He pushed her arm as far up her back as it would go without breaking. She fell limp against his hard chest.

Joshua hit the boards of the fencing with a hunched shoulder. The structure shuddered and creaked but refused to crumble as he battered it over and over. "Goddamn you, Treacher, if you hurt her, I'll kill you."

The pirate laughed and pulled her slumped form

away from the enclosure.

Lifting her up off the ground, he swung her around to walk in front of him as he pushed her back toward the way she had come. Away from Joshua and freedom. But if she had found Joshua once, she'd get to him again. Somehow, she would get back to her friend.

Erica hit the dirt with a hard thump, knocking the air from her lungs. Grit filled her mouth and nose. Struggling to catch her breath, she spit it out. Treacher's shuffling boots stirred the loose sand threatening to get into her eyes as well, and she shut them tightly.

Several women stood or squatted, doing mundane chores around the community campfire where he had pushed her. She recognized Angela, whose eyes grew large with surprise when he shoved her toward them.

"By damn it, if she's strong enough to go snooping around the compound, then she's strong enough to earn her keep. See to it she keeps busy, Angela. If I find her where she doesn't belong again, I'll hold you responsible." Anger stiffened his voice.

At the sound of his retreating steps, she opened one eye. A toe tapped her shoulder, and she rolled over on her back.

Angela towered above her, a disgusted look encompassing her features. "You heard Wesley," she said, all trace of their earlier camaraderie gone.

Pushing up from the ground, she dusted the grit and sand from her clothing with wide, dignified sweeps of her hands. Angela thrust a large wooden spoon at her, slapping Erica's palm with it as her hand reached out to accept it. Not sure what she should do with it, she looked askance at the other woman. Angela pointed to a large steaming pot hanging from a tripod over the fire. "Stir it," she ordered.

Sticking the utensil into the caldron, she stirred without enthusiasm. She wiped away the sweat beading on her face with the back of her hand.

Anger boiled up inside of her as the pot of uninteresting stew bubbled. She had no intention of spending the rest of her life churning stew or doing what Wesley Treacher, or any man for that matter, told her to do. The spoon swirled the hot liquid faster and faster until it splashed up, scalding her wrist. Tears of pain and frustration welled in her turbulent gray eyes. She wiped them away along with the sweat trickling down her face, refusing to make a spectacle of herself in front of the pirates ga ering in small groups around the campfire. Her bottom lip jutted out in resolution. She would escape. She would get back to Joshua, and together they would think of a plan.

Wooden bowls and metal spoons clacked on the rickety table near the fire. A grimy hand thrust an empty bowl at her. Realty rushed in as she looked up, recognizing the pirate's face. A leering face she had seen standing over her on the *Anna McKyle* when she had been captured. A face she would much rather coat with the hot soup. A face she would like to . . . She hunched her shoulders and poured the stew into

192

the bowl in front of her, casting her angry glare at the ground.

The line of empty bowls stretched unendingly. Her hand shook from exhaustion, and many men later she spilled more stew on the ground than she got in the bowls. Angela roughly grabbed the spoon from her fist and pushed her aside.

"Damn it, Erica. Why did you have to pull a fool stunt like that?" she growled.

She glanced up, unsure what the other woman meant.

"Why couldn't you stay put in the hut. You're not well enough to be out here."

Angela's concern for her sparked interest. Maybe the woman would help her escape.

"I didn't spend my time carin' for you to have you get sick again. Besides," Angela gave her a lopsided grin, "I never had nobody care about me before. I owe you."

Filling the last trencher, Angela wiped her dirty hands on the front of her skirt. Another line formed as the sated men returned the empty bowls for the women to wash. One girl took spoons from the dishes and stacked them behind her. Out-of-place and useless, Erica bumped into the workers, who cursed under their breath at her awkwardness.

Angela stepped to the growing pile of dirty plates and signaled for her to join them. Crossing over, Erica bent to help.

After an hour of tedious work, the campfire area looked neat and tidy. As she straightened from her bowed position, little needles of pain stabbed at her lower back. These women spent the majority of their days preparing, serving, and cleaning up after meals. She couldn't imagine her entire life centered around that one task. She had been lucky to be raised in a genteel manner, never having to deal with mundane chores of that nature. More determined than every to escape, she clamped her mouth firmly shut. She refused to accept that she would spend the rest of her life here.

Shoulders slumped in exhaustion, she could barely place one leaden foot in front of the other as Angela led her back toward the crude hut where she stayed. The darkness closed around them, and a multitude of small campfires cropped up before the many structures and tents they passed on their way. Relieved, the small shack she considered home in the compound came into view.

Surprised as Angela followed her through the door, she looked at the woman questioningly.

"Believe it or not, honey, this is *my* cabin, and I'm sharing it with you."

"Oh. I guess I figured you'd stay with your husband."

"Yeah, well, it's been a long time since we shared much of anything."

Her heart sank. How would she get to Joshua if Angela stayed with her all night? She would never escape if she was watched day and night.

Erica's heart hammered with a ferocity she thought for sure would give her away. For three days she had waited for an opportunity like this to present itself. Three long, frustrating days of working with the other women, serving the men of the island. Even the few children she had noticed took second place to sating the bellies of the male population.

But yesterday the crowd had thinned to a couple dozen men, mostly older or injured ones. That could only mean one thing. Treacher was on the prowl again and had taken the best of his followers as crew. Who knew how long he would be gone. It didn't matter. What mattered was that she got to Joshua and they took advantage of the situation.

Her feet padded lightly on the path before her. The darkness was so black she had trouble making her way, even though a couple of noteworthy landmarks pointed her down the right path. She shouldn't be far from the pens and Joshua.

Familiar barnyard smells floated out to greet her on the light breeze touching her sweaty brow. The startled "maa" of a goat stilled her feet as she sucked air into her lungs in alarm. The animal had heard her movements. She must be cautious. She couldn't be caught again. She had planned too long and laboriously for something so stupid to happen again.

The restless movements of the livestock disturbed from their sleep were the only sounds she could hear. Slowly she resumed her breathing as she skirted the rickety barn and made her way to the building behind.

An air of foreboding settled around her shoulders when she caught sight of her goal. So quiet and still and dark. *Of course, silly,* she thought, *the prisoners are asleep.*

How would she get Joshua's attention? Damn, she hadn't thought of that.

Like a staunch sentry the fencing rose up to meet her. Feeling her way with fingertips, she edged along the boards and wire constituting the barrier. Her groping hand found the gate and the heavy chain holding it clamped tightly shut. Fearing noise, she avoided shaking it.

Cupping her hands around her mouth, she pressed her face against the gate. "Joshua," she whispered, hoping beyond reason he might hear.

Her heart enumerated the seconds passing. Nothing. Silence. What had she expected? Should she risk calling again? She glanced around in the darkness. She had no choice but to try.

"Josh-u-a," she enunciated slowly.

Thumpity-thump. Thumpity-thump. Her heart pounded in her dry throat and straining ears. Surveying her surroundings again, she waited until she knew there was no chance he had heard her.

The lock. Maybe she could pick the lock with something she found in the barn. Excitement carried her fingers along the chain, seeking the lock to judge the size of the keyhole.

The chain slithered through her fingers like a cold snake to land with a thud on the ground. There was no lock. Why would the prisoners' pen be left unlocked? Why didn't matter, the point being that she was inside.

Pushing the gate open enough to allow her body to slink through, she crossed the yard in long strides.

The door must be locked, she reasoned, keeping the prisoners inside at night. Why didn't she think of that earlier?

Her hand touched the door latch, expecting to find it immovable. As the catch slipped down, so did her confidence. No, it couldn't be unlocked.

No longer caring if anyone heard, she shoved the squealing door open. Lingering human odors filled her nostrils. The room was empty.

"He's not here no more.

She whirled to face Angela, standing in the doorway. "Where is he?"

"With Wesley. He figured you might try something like this with him gone."

She gasped. Somehow knowing Joshua was close by had given her the strength to be brave and coolheaded. Now she was alone, absolutely alone, for the first time. "When will they be back?"

Angela stepped toward her. "A week, a month, however long it takes to get a prize worth bringing home. But it won't make no difference to you. Accept it. You're here to stay for as long as Wesley wants you." Angela's hand encompassed her wrist, and she dragged her from the building.

She followed without resistance. There was no longer any point in fighting.

The next morning broke the horizon as if the night before had never occurred. "Oh, Joshua," she moaned, "where are you?"

If Angela heard her words, she ignored them as she

shuffled around the hut, preparing to face the day. *The endless days,* thought Erica, *almost as bad as the endless nights.* She eyed the woman. She must convince her to help her escape. Escape, escape; the thought never left her.

Wordlessly Angela headed out of the door. She followed, knowing full well they were going to the compound and another day of drudgery.

Skirting the familiar footpath, she didn't bother to lift her head, just watched her feet as they stepped in front of each other.

Angela veered away from the compound.

"Angela, where are we going?" She stopped and glanced in the direction they went.

The blonde grunted. "It's Saturday mornin'. We can take a bath." She swung around. "Believe it or not, Miss High-and-mighty, even you look like hell with grime on your face." She started back down the path. "Personally I could care less what you look like, the worse the better, but Wesley could come home any day, and if he found you lookin' like you do, I'd catch hell."

"But what about the morning meal?"

"I didn't know you cared so much. One of the advantages of bein' the leader's woman. At least when he's gone. Nobody will know the difference."

Erica's hand reached up to inspect her face. Did she resemble the rest of the women in camp? Did they each have a story similar to hers? Were they someone's loving wife or daughter? *I have become just like them,* she brooded; *helpless, hopeless, and forgotten by the outside world. No, I won't give in to despair. I must have hope, always.*

The cool, brackish water of the pool they approached looked heavenly. Throwing off her depression along with her soiled clothes, she splashed childlike in the water as Angela watched, unamused. Slapping with water playfully, a spray pelted the other woman, and she turned gleefully to escape the gleam that finally came to rest in Angela's eyes. Water rolled down the blonde's face, leaving clean white streaks, and Erica laughed at the zebra effect.

Caught up in the play, Angela grabbed her flying hair, and the moisture closed around her as the woman pushed her unwilling head deep into the water. Erica gasped as she hit the surface; Angela greeted her with a squeal of pleasure and paddled in the opposite direction. She pursued, but by the time they reached the sandy edge of the pond, they were both too exhausted to continue the game. Heaving, they fell in the sand like two young girls and laughed at each other's sodden appearance.

Erica slipped back in the water, and dousing her head, groaned, "What I wouldn't give for a bar of lavender soap and five minutes with a brush and comb."

Angela grinned and reached into a sack she had dropped at the side of the pool. She pulled out an object wrapped in tissue paper, waved it under her nose, and sniffed noisily. "Rose scent, I think. Will that do?"

The soap hit the water inches from her face. Her hand fanned the water and grasped the bar as it sank. With a moan of pleasure, she vigorously lathered her hair and every part of her body. Never again would she take for granted the simple pleasure of bathing.

"Don't be so wasteful," Angela called. "That has to last me for a long time. Wesley don't often give me things. When he does," she shrugged, "I make them last as long as I can."

She tossed the bar back to Angela and dipped the back of her head in the water, allowing her hair to fan around her as the suds bobbed away in little clusters.

Shyly Angela slipped into the water to join her and mimicked her actions. "Do you think you could make my hair pretty like yours?"

She touched the matted but clean tresses on the older woman's head. It would be a chore just getting the knots out. She smiled brightly. "I think there's hope."

After scrubbing the dirt from their clothing, they laid them on rocks to dry. Again Angela reached into her bag and this time pulled out a fine boar-bristle brush and matching comb, with mother-of-pearl inlays on the handles. *The spoils of piracy,* Erica thought, wondering what had happened to the woman they had belonged to.

Feeling as if a heavy weight had been lifted from her head, she ran the brush through her tawny hair. With practiced fingers she braided the tresses behind her in hopes the tangles wouldn't accumulate again.

Angela kneeled in the sand, watching each stroke of her hand. With a brisk motion Erica turned the other woman around and worked the comb through the blonde tangles. Eventually the comb slid unhindered through the hair waving gently down Angela's back.

Work-worn hands reached up to discover the success she had made. Beaming, Angela turned. Forcing the head back around, Erica asked as she ran the brush through the blonde tresses, "Shall I braid it?"

Angela's head bobbed up and down in answer. In a few moments the braid lay neatly between her shoulders. "Do you think Wesley will like it?"

"Wesley will think you're lovely." She handed the older woman the brush and comb and reached over to test the drying clothes. *In time,* she thought, *Angela will help me escape. I have to just be patient. God, help me be patient.*

The bath buoyed her spirits for only a few short hours. Fear of the future, fear of no future except as a slave to the pirates, crushed the hope she struggled to maintain. In a daze, not caring what happened around her, she followed instructions with stiff, mechanical movements as the women prepared the last meal of the day.

She didn't bother to look up at the faces in line she could now put names to. She didn't care who pushed the empty bowl in front of her. It was just her job to fill it. Lift the ladle, put it in the pot, pull it out, and dump the contents in the bowl before her. The procedure became a mindless rhythm she repeated over and over.

Lift the ladle, put it in the pot, pull it out, and . . . What was the next step? Her wrist froze, stew sloshing over the sides of the ladle. Her gaze studied the hands holding the bowl out to her. Did they shake, too?

Her eyes traveled up the arms, across the chest rising and falling, to the pulse jumping in the hollow of his neck. Warm, moist, coal black eyes stared out of a familiar face covered with dirt and a week's growth of beard. Did her eyes play tricks on her? Dirk? Could he really be here?

"Erica?" he whispered.

She tilted her wrist, and the hot liquid hit the ground with a loud sizzle.

Chapter Eleven

Erica crossed the compound, watching every rock and bush, silently praying no one followed her.

Lying beside Angela until she was sure the woman slept soundly had been the hardest thing she had ever done. But it was essential to be sure she wasn't followed this time. She couldn't afford another mistake.

Dirk had found her. He was here. Her spirits soared. Her feet wanted to fly across the sand. Instead, she huddled in the old shawl thrown around her head in disguise and made her steps slow and purposeful while she concentrated on her surroundings, both visual and aural.

She stopped as a rustle behind her set the pulse in her throat jumping. Did someone follow her? Her eyes scanned the empty compound, seeking movement. Nothing but the ripple of the breeze in dry palm leaves. She waited to be sure. Her pulse quieted.

The grove of trees between the compound and the harbor: Dirk had said he would meet her there. The feeling that someone watched stilled her feet again. Her gaze circled, seeking an explanation. Nothing, not even the wind moved.

Reaching the edge of the trees, she threw the shawl from her head. The darkness of the forest offered plenty of protection, and she hastened her steps to melt into the long shadows the trees cast in the faint moonlight. Would Dirk be here as he had promised? How would she find him?

A warm hand touched her shoulder from behind. A scream welled in her throat. Another hand reached around to cover her opening mouth and stifled the shriek on her lips.

Spinning her in one swift motion, Dirk smoothly replaced his hand with lips demanding a response. Willingly she merged against his solid form. His arms tightened to pull her as close to him as he could. *Oh, to remain here for the rest of my life*, she dreamed. His face lifted to end the kiss, and she placed both hands behind his head and held him down. As if sensing her need, he renewed his passion. Their first frantic embrace fused into a flaming desire she couldn't deny.

Raising his mouth from hers, he placed small, tender caresses with his lips from her chin to her ear and back to her waiting mouth.

"Ah, my little Mermaid, must you always lead me on such a merry chase?" Waves of shock sizzled down her spine as his warm breath filled her ear.

Leaning back to see his face, she asked, "How did you find me?"

"How doesn't matter. The point is I did."

Silently she nodded as he pushed her head back to rest on his chest. She savored the erratic thumps his heart made against her ear.

"The important thing is to get you out of here." Engulfing her slim shoulders with his hands, he leaned her back to study her face. "Did Treacher hurt you?" His grip tightened into her flesh as if anticipating her reaction to his question.

The pain in her shoulders gave her comfort, and she closed her eyes, swaying against his clutching fingers. He joggled her, none too gently, demanding an answer.

She shook her head in response, grateful when he pulled her back against the security of his chest.

"Thank God," he whispered, releasing her shoulders to hold her against him.

"Erica?" His hand lifted her chin to gaze up at him. "We need to leave right now. My ship is a couple of days away on the Florida mainland. With Treacher gone, we couldn't have a better opportunity."

She nodded agreement, but her head circled to turn into a no. "Joshua. I can't leave Joshua."

"Going back into the compound is too risky."

Emphatically she continued shaking her head back and forth. "I don't care. I can't leave Joshua here."

"I understand how you feel. But it won't do any of us any good to get caught."

She pulled her face from his fingers. "No, I won't leave without him."

"All right," he sighed. "Where is he? We'll figure out a way to get him out."

Her eyes widened with realization. She had no idea where he was. He wasn't on the island, but with Treacher. "I don't know," she choked.

He raised one dark eyebrow in question. "Erica, we don't have time for games."

"When I tried to find him, he wasn't in the pens. One of the women told me Treacher took him with him when he sailed. I don't think she lied."

"You've got to be reasonable. We don't know where he is or even if he'll be back to this island. We have to go without him. There's no other choice."

She vacillated. "I can't leave him behind," she repeated.

"Should I ask why he means so much to you?" He frowned.

Her head snapped up, eyes flashing. "He's like a father to me."

"Then I can tell you, he would want you to go on. I promise you, we won't give up until we find him. But staying here, waiting for him to show up, won't help any of us."

She studied his piercing eyes, shining with sincerity. His reasoning made sense. She had no choice but to trust him. Lowering her head in resignation, she didn't resist as he grabbed her hand and led her away from the pirate stronghold into the depths of the forest.

Long, shiny leaves whipped at their faces. The tangle of vines on the ground reached out as if alive to grasp their ankles, trying to trip them and slow them down. Her breathing turned into a rasp as her lungs clung to the air she drew in with a pain racking her chest.

His pace never faltered. Unable to lift another foot, she stopped and rested her head against the rough bark of a tree.

"Dawn is only a few hours away. We need to be off the island before the camp awakens and discovers you're gone."

She nodded, understanding, as she leaned against the tree, taking deep, gulping breaths. She pushed from the tree and stumbled behind him. She must keep going. The thought that her feminine weakness might slow them down tore at her.

If she were caught, her fate would be much as it had been. But Dirk . . . Her eyes lifted to take in his broad shoulders forcing a way through the underbrush. If Treacher found him—she shivered with fear. What would the pirate do to the man who had risked his life to rescue her?

"Erica, we need to keep going," he urged her lagging form.

Saving her energy, she nodded her head. His grip on her wrist shot pain through her arm. A pain she concentrated on instead of the suffocating agony in her chest. Take ten steps. Now ten more. One foot in front of the other. She kept up with the demanding pace he set.

"Do you need to rest?"

His words destroyed her concentration, and she lost count of her steps. "No," she panted. His nod of approval added strength to her stumbling feet.

The screech of a catbird brought her head up. Moisture dripped from leaf to leaf. *Dew*, she thought. *Morning dew.* The small patch of sky she could see through the foliage glowed orange. The sun would be up soon. Angela would be waking, and she would discover her disappearance. How much longer before they reached their destination?

"Dirk, I . . ."

"Shh. Save your strength. We're almost to the

dinghy I left hidden on the back side of the island."

Her legs twitched, and the calf muscles tingled on the verge of cramping. She couldn't take another step.

The wall of vegetation whipped behind her. The soothing whoosh of the ocean surf surrounded her. Her knees buckled; sharp pieces of sand cut into her hands as they hit the ground. Her face touched the coolness of the beach. She lay there, her heart roaring in her ears.

Dirk worked his way down the tree line, pushing back the bushes and vines. What did he seek? She should know. He had told her earlier. A rowboat. He'd said something about a rowboat.

She watched in fascination as he tossed wilted brush and foliage behind him to expose the bow of the small dinghy. She glanced across the expanse of ocean, seeking their destination. Another island, maybe a mile and a half away, topped with swaying palm trees, danced in her line of vision.

Dirk's grunts and groans brought her attention back to the beach. The taut muscles in his arms and shoulders bulged as he pulled the boat out of hiding onto the sand to a point where the surf threatened to carry it out to sea.

"Get up, Erica. Come on." His arm swung in a forceful motion, urging her to join him. Reluctantly she rose and limped to the spot where he held the boat.

Stepping into the small, vulnerable craft, she refused to think about being in the ocean with so little protection. She concentrated instead on rubbing her throbbing legs, willing them to relax.

With her added weight, the boat sank deeper in the surf, the bottom scraping the sand. Dirk leaned his shoulder into the side of the craft, inching it forward until it caught in the rolling surf. The swirling, briny water reached his thighs before he lifted himself up. The dinghy shot toward the open sea, then seesawed back toward the beach as he swung his legs over the side.

Water dripped from his britches and boots as he sat down opposite her, facing the beach. He slipped the long oars into the slots on the sides of the boat, then leaned his weight into them and began the long, laborious task of rowing the boat to the point beyond where the waves broke the surface so that the sea would no longer pull them back to land. Little, pearl-like beads of sweat collected over his brow and in his hairline to trickle down the sides of his face, disappearing into the dark shadow of beard on his face, only to reappear and drip off his chin. But he never lost his rhythm. His efforts were soon rewarded when the swaying of the water pulled them out to sea instead of back toward the pirates' island.

Her hands loosened their grip on the edge of the seat, and she released the air she held in her lungs. Dirk slumped forward, his tired muscles twitching under the fabric of his shirt. He wiped his face on the back of his sleeve, and his eyes, triumph shining clearly from them, touched her face. Infected by his confidence, she smiled, and he returned the gesture. "We've got a good chance," he offered. "If we're lucky the tide will cover over our tracks on the beach before anyone finds them."

He turned to adjust the oars. She explored the

coils of muscles rippling down his shoulder and neck. He risked so much coming after her. Why had he done it?

She cocked her head to one side. "Why?"

He whirled at the sound of her voice, dropping the oars back into their slots.

"Why did you come after me?"

His eyes skimmed over her. "Perhaps I felt I owed you that much after what I took from you." His voice remained light and noncommittal.

"No, you owe me nothing." She bent forward and placed one outstretched finger on his lips. "I owe you for what you gave me. I regret nothing we have done so far, just the foolish habit I have of running from you."

She slipped back on her seat, cheeks flushed, eyes cast down. She'd said more than she'd meant to say.

His long, brown fingers reached out and lifted her chin to look at him. "Do you mean that, Mermaid?"

She nodded.

"Straightforwardness and honesty between us from now on?" His eyes shined with love.

She nodded again.

"Good. Trust me, Erica. I promise I'll never hurt you. And I will get us out of this mess and home."

She smiled brightly and threw her arms out to hug his neck. The precarious craft rocked, throwing her back into her seat. He clutched the oars nearly dropping from their slots into the water. "I appreciate your enthusiasm, sweetheart, but let's save it for later." The oars firmly in his hands, he set the boat back into gliding motion.

She counted each stroke he took, losing track of

the number around two hundred. Her chin drifted to her chest as she swayed with the cradle rhythm of the boat in a light, easy sleep.

She woke with a jolt. Her body lifted and flew through the air. Throwing her glance over the side of the rowboat, she saw the ocean shimmering several feet below her. With lightning speed, the boat dipped, leaving her stomach in her throat. Just as quickly, it rose to another exhilarating peak. Struggling to clear the haze of sleep from her brain, she opened her mouth to speak. The roar of the pounding surf drowned the sounds she made, as a spray of water washed over her. Sputtering, she clung to the rim of the dinghy, praying they wouldn't capsize. He battled with the oars to keep the boat upright. He had his hands full; she would have to handle her fear on her own.

She closed her eyes to block out the terrifying view, but the up-and-down motion intensified. Her eyes flew open again. His face drawn in concentration, he continued to fight to keep them upright.

The boat trembled twice as it ascended high in the air and then crashed down into a trough. Glancing behind her, she raised her hands in a defensive action as the wave curled to engulf them. But like a bullet, the craft shot forth on the wave's crest, carrying them forward until the bow of the boat jammed into the sand of the beach.

Fear and exhilaration battled inside her. Now she was almost sorry the wild ride had ended.

Dirk jumped from the boat as it bobbed with the tide and tried to shoot forward again. Holding it tight, he guided the dinghy toward the beach until it sank with the ebb and wedged in the sand of the shore.

His hand encircled her wrist as he helped her out. The water, covering her knees, tugged and sucked at her feet, trying to pull them out from underneath her. She grabbed the side of the boat, and together they pulled it up to the safety of the land.

With the craft secure, they sat down, side by side, to remove their saturated boots. With a sucking sound, the black leather slid from her foot. Water gushed out, tossing a coin-size crab onto its back in the sand. It waved its spindly legs in the air. Chuckling, she righted the creature, which began a drunken side-crawl away from her.

Dirk's hand reached down to touch hers. The crab turned ferociously and waved its tiny pincers in the air at his invading hand. Laughing, they fell back in the wet sand. Their tension eased. They had managed to escape the pirates' island. He curled his arm around her and hugged her to him. Like a soothing balm, the warm, wet sand molded around them. The pounding surf sang a sweet lullaby. Her eyes drifted closed as she nestled in the crook of security his arm offered.

Salty water filled her nose and mouth, and Erica pushed up sputtering as the water seeped into her lungs. How long had they slept? Shading her eyes, she glanced at the afternoon sun. An hour, maybe more. Enough time for the tide to rise. The boat. She spun and caught sight of the dinghy teetering in the surf.

"Dirk," she screamed.

He sat up, then scrambled to his feet as his eyes followed her pointing finger. Throwing himself across the beach, he shouldered the floundering skiff. She followed him, and together they pulled it up into the safety of the vegetation edging the sand.

Leaning against the boat, she glanced around, taking in their surroundings. Coconut palms shimmered in the strong breeze. The ocean surf had reached high tide, and the water lapped at the thin remaining strip of beach. Lush greenery halted abruptly a few feet from the water's edge, so thick and dense it was like a barrier refusing them entrance.

His arm encircled her waist, and she pressed her head into the hollow between his collarbone and shoulder.

"We need to find shelter for the night."

She lifted her chin to view the sun, her hand raised to shade her eyes from the glare. "It's early to stop, isn't it? Shouldn't we go on? What if someone followed us?"

"We wouldn't have time to reach the next island before dark. I don't want to get caught out in the open water tonight. The wind is stirring. We could be in for a storm. Besides, if we'd been followed, we'd see some sign of pursuit.

"We'll hide the boat well. There's nothing more we can do now. We'll leave early in the morning, if the weather clears. We should reach the *Sea Hawk* where I left her on the Florida mainland tomorrow."

She studied the clear, blue skies. Her gaze shifted to the tall man standing beside her. A seaman to the core. His ability to predict foul weather on such a gorgeous day amazed her. So like Joshua. *Joshua.* Her chin lowered. *I haven't forgotten you.*

She accepted his decision, and her eyes followed the shoreline, seeking a place of shelter open enough to allow them to set up camp comfortably.

Dirk bent over the boat and reached up under the seat. He pulled out a small canvas bag and a cork-stoppered jug. Holding the jug up for her to see, he explained, "Fresh water. I wasn't sure we'd find any." Lifting up the bag, he continued, "And something to eat."

Tossing them to her, he took a knife and hacked at the limbs and leaves around him, laying them over the rowboat until the craft blended into the surroundings. Facing her, he slipped the knife back into its sheath. "There. We're as safe as we can possibly be."

Crossing the short strip of sand, they followed the line of vegetation, searching for a campsite. Three hundred yards from the boat, they discovered an outcrop of rocks forming a U at the edge of the sand. There they would be sheltered from the tangle of plant life behind it, as well as from the steady wind blowing in off the ocean.

He scouted the grove of windswept coconut palms, one of which bent so low its leaves fanned the ground. He chopped away an armful of large leaves and the two fruits from the tree and hauled his findings back to the campsite.

She scavenged the beach, filling her arms with bits of driftwood. Wood stacked clear to her chin, she headed back to the shelter and piled the wood for a fire later when the evening air cooled.

Dropping his armload in the middle of the rocks, he set about laying the palm leaves in an intricate pattern covering the sand until he formed a temporary bed. Though she was touched by his domestic attitude, her stubborn pride saw only that he took for granted they would sleep together. She wasn't ready for their relationship to take on an air of assumption.

He never glanced up from his work. He even whistled as he laid the finishing touches to the bed.

She turned her back and spied the canvas bag he had placed in one corner. Searching through it, she discovered a small burlap sack of dried, white beans, some beef jerky, and a dozen hard biscuits packed in a small cook pot. She emptied the pot and filled it from a trapped pool of seawater near the shelter. Sitting the pot on a rock beside the stack of driftwood, she poured several handfuls of beans into it to soak.

Sensing he watched her every move, she didn't bring her eyes up to meet his. With exaggerated movements she continued her task, much like an actor performing on a stage.

As she brushed by him, he reached out, grabbed her arm, and spun her around to face him. His dark eyes scanned hers. Refusing to acknowledge the question she read in his eyes, she contemplated the small hollow at the base of his throat. The pulse there twitched, holding her fascinated.

He lifted her chin and placed a small, sweet kiss on her soft lips. His mouth rose from hers. Eyes tightly closed, she held her face tilted up, waiting for him to kiss her again.

The seconds ticked by slowly. Her tongue darted out to moisten her lips, dry with anticipation. Yet he didn't kiss her. Her eyes fluttered open to discover why. A roguish smile bowed his mouth. "Taking a lot for granted, aren't you?"

"Perhaps," she said, turning her head and gesturing toward the makeshift bed, "but then so are you." She quirked one eyebrow at him.

He whipped her back around to face him. With slow deliberation his hand released the top two buttons on the front of her shirt from their fastenings. Playfulness gleamed in his eyes.

"Dirk, it's still daylight." Her hands flew up in protest.

His fingers ceased, and his mouth curved in a smile. "Who do you think is going to see us? A few sea gulls or maybe a pelican, or, if we're lucky, a curious crocodile?"

"I know you're right. It's just that I . . ."

"Erica, don't ever be ashamed of what you are. You are beautiful, every soft, vivacious inch of you." His fingers slipped the remaining buttons from the slits in her shirt. Reaching the last one, he stopped to examine her face, seeking signs of her surrender.

She leaned into him, and he pushed the material down her arms, the shirt falling in a heap at her feet.

His gaze never left her. Taking her reluctant fingers, he led them up to the buttons on his shirt. He guided her hands as she released the top button. His arms dropped to his sides as he encouraged her on with her eyes.

She hesitated for a moment. Then her fingers

worked eagerly down his front. A tingle of anticipation built inside her as each small disk slipped out, revealing more and more of his strong, muscled chest with its fine pelt of fur covering it. She pushed the shirt down his well-proportioned shoulders, and her hands fluttered to her sides as the shirt floated down to join hers in the sand.

"No fair," he said teasingly, indicating the tight-fitting undershirt molding to her bosom.

Beginning to enjoy the game, she raised her arms skyward and gave him a provocative smile. He didn't hesitate, and within seconds the top dropped on the ground.

His eyes turned to dark, passionate pools of ink. Expecting him to reach out and caress her bare breasts, she lowered her lashes. Instead, his hands slipped into her waistband and began the slow, sensuous task of unbuttoning her britches. Her eyes flew open and locked with his. He knelt to push the material over her hips and down her legs. She stepped out of them, and he added then to the growing pile.

Rising back up to face her, he lifted his hands away from his body and challenged, "Your turn."

Reaching out for the front of his pants, she released the fasteners awkwardly. She followed his actions and pushed the britches down his thighs. She gasped. Nothing covered the evidence of his excitement. He chuckled mischievously as he kicked his trousers on top of the other clothing in the sand.

She rose to meet the glint in his eyes and grinned. "I know, not fair, again." Slowly she pushed the thin lace of her underpants down and stepped out of them. She straightened to face him bravely, his gaze devouring every curve and hill of her flawless body.

He reached out and began drawing a slow, intricate spiral around her breasts until his fingers lightly fanned the rose-colored tips. As if the imaginary strings running through the core of her body were those of a musical instrument, he strummed her willing flesh with expertise. Knees threatening to buckle under her, she leaned toward him.

With one swift motion he scooped her up and carried her to the love haven he had created earlier. Encircling his neck, she rested her head upon his shoulder, now willing to let him take control.

He placed her gently on the palm leaves and knelt beside her waist. Again, his eyes traveled her figure, a look of pure amazement splashed across his features. Her gaze caressed his body, as well, finding it beautiful and exciting.

His fingers danced lightly along the sensitive line between her jaw and ear. Little shivers swept over her as his hand moved down, kneading the pliant swells of her bosom until they stood like twin peaks, rosy and erect with desire. She stretched her arms up to pull him to her.

"No, Erica," he insisted as he firmly pushed her questing hands back down to lie at her sides. "I want to know all of you. I want to memorize every hollow and hill of your body." His fingers continued their exploration, drawing a searing path across her ribs.

Overwhelming passion engulfed her as his touch skimmed over her fluttering stomach. She closed her eyes, intensifying the sensations his hands created. He grazed a trail to the moist triangle between her thighs and lingered there, stirring her desire to a demanding need that left her whimpering. Then, as if he knew the limit of her endurance, he moved lower, tracing the contours of her inner thigh, sliding over the back of her knee, and ending as he reached the tips of her toes. Arching her inflamed body, she sought his departed warmth.

"Be patient, you little minx, I've only just begun. Now, I want to taste every inch of you," he whispered. His warm breath caressed her ear. The fire of his tongue touched the same pulsating point on her neck that his hand had begun with, and the flame ignited again, only stronger.

How much more of his sweet torture could she take? She couldn't imagine, but she prayed he would never stop. Forgetting his command, her arms reached out, searching the darkness for him, and grasped his tense shoulders. Adamantly he pushed her limbs back down as his mouth glided slowly over each taut, aching breast, lower to dip into the crevice on her stomach, and then further still to savor the sweetness of her womanhood. Her hands tangled in his hair and urged him to continue his tender assault.

A throaty laugh escaped his lips, and he gave her what she asked for, but just long enough to send her mind swirling to the brink of fulfillment. His mouth traveled down the inside of her leg to end with a playful nip on the tips of her toes.

Breathless and bewildered, she groaned when he rose up away from her. His full length crushed against her aching body, and she arched to receive him.

"Oh, yes," she purled, overwhelmed with the sensation of completeness as he filled her.

His lips stifled her words as he began the slow dance of love. She pushed up eagerly to meet him halfway. The building crescendo sent crashing waves of ecstasy racing over her until they peaked. Her body shuddered as the electric shocks washed over her.

"Erica, my Erica," he moaned with unguarded emotion.

Trembling in the aftermath of love, she could feel Dirk's release as he joined her in ecstasy.

He lifted his weight from her, but she held him tightly. "No, stay where you are forever," she pleaded.

Cradling her waist, he rolled them over, still united, to lie side by side. She rested her head on the pillow of his shoulder until sleep overtook her sated body and mind.

They slept as only new lovers can in a tangle of arms and legs.

Erica woke to the sensation someone watched her. Her lids lifted to find Dirk smiling at her. "I love you, sweetheart," he said lightly, "but my arm has been numb for over an hour, and I don't think I can take much more."

"Oh, I'm sorry," she mumbled, still half asleep. She raised her head and rolled to her knees.

"Don't be sorry. I'd gladly suffer a stiff arm in exchange for such a lovely afternoon."

A blush heated her face as the details of their lovemaking washed over her. Grabbing her shirt and pants, she slipped them on, aware he watched her every move. She began restacking the driftwood so the fire could be lit. Anything so she didn't have to face his dancing eyes. Without looking in his direction, she asked over her shoulder, "Are you hungry?"

"Starving."

She stepped across to the pot of soaking beans. He crossed to the fire, dressed in his britches.

She sighed, both disappointed and glad he had covered himself. She waited patiently as he lit the fire.

The roll of far-off thunder brought her head up. A whipping breeze whirled around the shelter, setting the palms clacking and bobbing. Glancing down to where he knelt fanning the flames into a noteworthy blaze, she offered, "Looks like you were right about a storm."

"You've got to learn to trust me, sweetheart. My instincts rarely fail me." He skirted the rocks of their shelter and headed for the boat.

She put the pot of beans over the fire to cook.

He returned with a large oilskin. Wedging it between the rock formations, he created a makeshift roof over their heads. He left enough room so the smoke from the fire could escape.

Pleased with the results, she smiled as he ducked his head to enter the man-made cave to join her beside the fire. In his hand he held a pistol, which he stowed in one corner, a grim reminder of the danger threatening still. As cozy as the shelter was, they had not yet escaped.

He slipped his arm protectively around her waist. Darkness enveloped them, whether from the storm or the setting of the sun, she didn't know. The flames from the fire grew brighter and licked hungrily at the dry driftwood, devouring it, destroying it. How like the driftwood they would be if the pirates found them.

He reached out to add another piece of wood to the fire. His movement invaded her thoughts, and she shook her head to be rid of them. The pot of beans sizzled and boiled over the rim. She leaned forward and brought them to the edge of the fire to simmer.

The wind snapped the oilskin over their heads back and forth, then raced around the outside of the rocks, seeking entrance into the shelter, shrieking like a banshee. The rain came with no warning, but fell from the sky in a solid sheet, the forerunner of the enemy, seeking their hiding place. She shivered. *Don't let them find us.* The fire hissed and sputtered as the rain found the opening Dirk had left for the smoke. She barely had time to remove the pot of partially cooked beans before the fire turned into a pile of smoking kindling.

In the darkness, they ate the tough, chewy beans, cold jerky, and hard biscuits. How had her life been reduced to this? Misery weighted her spirits. They would never escape. They would die on some lonely stretch of beach without . . .

"Erica?"

She glanced up to find him offering her a large chunk of coconut meat on the tip of his knife.

"It's not much, but it's sweet and juicy. A bit easier to swallow than the dinner."

A tongue of lightning blazed the sky. She studied his face in the few seconds of light. Lined and tired, it still offered an encouraging smile. She couldn't let her strength flag. Not when he gave so much. Not when hope and confidence sparkled in his eyes.

The coconut was all he promised and more. Her spirits lifted, and the darkness became complete, to be broken only by an occasional searing brightness as lightning cracked across the sky.

Her courage swelled in the obscurity of the night; a courage inflamed by desire for the man next to her. Boldly she reached through the blackness to explore his warm, masculine body, something she had wanted to do from the moment she had met him so long ago.

Her hand traced the outline of his neck and ear, trickled down his collarbone, then gingerly worked its way through the neat covering of hair on his chest. Did he enjoy her brazen gestures, or did he find them repulsive? His maddening silence told her nothing. She pulled her hand back, unsure of herself.

His hand captured hers before it barely lifted from his skin. He placed it back where it had been and murmured, "Why did you stop?"

Laying the flat of her hand against his heart, the rough thumpity-thump against her palm indicated his desire and reinforced her spirited actions. Remembering how he had drawn a response from her shy body earlier, she took one finger and spiraled it across his chest, tantalizing the peaks nestled in the dark, soft fur. Did it feel the same to him? His nipples puckered in response.

Running her fingers across his rib cage, then down the flat of his stomach, she hit the barrier of his pants. Again she hesitated, unsure she should continue her bold exploration. His hands joined hers as they stilled, and he lifted his weight and bent. Her palms grazed his warm thighs as together they slid the rough fabric down and off to be tossed in a corner of the shelter. His britches no longer blocked her way, and the thin patina of courage deserted her.

His hand, again, took charge of hers and guided it down to rest on his virility, her fingers curling instinctively around his warm flesh, stroking and teasing it at the pace he demanded. Then, with a nearly unnoticeable shiver, he yielded to her even tempo as he stretched out, leaving her to experiment on her own. Learning the delights and intimate secrets of his body was an aphrodisiac that stirred her rising desire to the point of no return.

With an insuppressible groan, he rolled and pulled her beneath him. As ready as he, she met him in the dance of love. Familiar flames of need shot through her as she responded uninhibitedly to his every move.

"Erica," he shuddered at the same moment fireworks exploded behind her closed eyes.

Their pulses racing in unison, he lifted her chin and kissed her passionately. Working his way to her ear, he whispered, "Damn it, Mermaid, you've bewitched me."

His warm breath filled her ears as his words dominated her mind. Not wanting to break the magic, she didn't move, though her heart beat furiously. She prayed he would say what she needed to hear, fearing he wouldn't.

"I love you." The words echoed softly. Did she imagine it, or had he said them? "God, I love you, Erica," he repeated.

She threw her arms around his neck as tears of joy and fulfillment tumbled from her eyes. "I love you, too," she choked. "God help me, you threaten all I stand for, but I can't escape how I feel about you."

He rolled on his back, bringing her with him, and fitted her into the warm, familiar hollow between his collarbone and shoulder as the storm slowed to a steady rat-a-tat-tat to mimic the rhythm of their united hearts.

The beach, scattered with newly washed-up driftwood from the tide and the night's storm, looked untouched and abandoned. Trickles of moisture dripped from leaves and stems; Erica shivered in the coolness of the early morning air as dawn broke on the horizon with fingers of orange haze. The boat's covering had been blown away during the night, leaving it exposed to the storm. It was filled with rainwater, and Dirk struggled to flip it over.

Together they worked to pull the boat back into the sand, where the swirling water caught and lifted it free from the beach. He tossed their supplies, wrapped in the oilskin, into the bottom and held her arm back when she attempted to get into the craft.

"Let's walk the boat around to the other side of the island. The surf will be calmer there." He slipped their boots into the dinghy. Together they waded barefoot in the shallow water, the boat swinging back and forth behind them in the waves.

A sound she couldn't identify rang out over and over. She scanned the beach, seeking the animal making it.

"A blue heron," he answered her unvoiced question. "Lonely sounding, isn't it."

"He sounds like he's looking for his mate."

"Perhaps. More likely he's disturbed by our invasion." He placed a gentle kiss on her willing mouth as they stopped in the swirling sea. "I guess we'll never know." With a sigh of regret he pulled her along. "We can reach the ship today if we keep going."

Over his shoulder her eyes skimmed the blue-green ocean they left behind. Like the fin of a threatening shark, the stark white sails of a ship crested as a wave smashed in the breakers.

"Oh, God, no," she whispered.

He turned at the distress in her voice. "Damn," he hissed. "It must be Treacher." He pulled her at a neck-breaking speed, and they rounded the island. The water there lapped calmly against the beach just as he had predicted. "If we're lucky, they're still too far away to have seen us."

At his urging, she fell into the boat as he pushed it as far into the undulating surf as he could. As soon as he settled into the seat opposite her, he rowed, pumping and dipping the oars until sweat coursed down his face and chest.

Remembering the pistol she had seen last night, she dug through the oilskin until the cool, smooth handle of the gun grazed her fingers. Bringing it to her lap, she checked it over, finding it loaded and primed.

"Do you know how to use it?"

"Well enough," she replied, remembering the hours Joshua had spent teaching her.

"Good. Keep it handy. Hopefully we won't have to use it." He turned his concentration back to his rowing.

She studied the pistol resting on her knee. Had it been Treacher they had seen? Was he seeking them or only returning to his stronghold, unaware of her escape? Was Joshua on the ship with him? "Maybe they don't know we're here." She voiced her hopes aloud.

"Maybe," he grunted. "I hope you're right. I'll feel a lot better when we reach the *Sea Hawk*."

As they skirted the two small islands, the ribbon of beach on the mainland grew closer and closer. She watched the sea around them as they skimmed through the aquamarine water, so vulnerable, so exposed for anyone pursuing them to see. But there was nothing to be done about it.

Dirk rowed relentlessly, up and down, up and down, his rhythm rarely broken, his eyes watching where they were headed.

The horizon remained clear. No sign of the ship she had spotted earlier that morning. Had she seen it, or had her mind played tricks on her? No, they had both seen it clearly. It was more reasonable to hope they had lost their pursuers.

With a minimal surf, the boat quivered to a halt in the thin strip of sand on the beach. A thick tangle of trees crowded down to the edge of the sand, towering darkly and uninvitingly over them. Eerie and frightening sounds echoed from its depths. She prayed he wouldn't want to enter the forest.

"Our best chance is to drag the boat up into the foliage and head on foot up the beach."

Her head snapped up as he spoke.

"The *Sea Hawk* isn't more than five miles up the coast. If we keep in the edge of the tree line, we'll be invisible to anyone following us. Come on," he insisted.

The boat slid across the sand as they bent their weight, pulling, feet slipping in the loose sand. They reached the vegetation, and limbs and roots squeaked in protest as the vessel bumped and snagged in the foliage. Frantically they pulled up small trees and vines clinging loosely in the sand, covering the boat as best as they could.

Retrieving the water jug and the pistol he had set on the ground, Dirk entered the edge of the forest, setting a fast pace. She hesitated, dreading what would be in the foliage, but he didn't stop to wait for her, and she scampered to catch up with him.

A low drone filled her ears. She didn't feel light-headed, so why did her ears buzz? The whine reached a high pitch as little needles of pain pricked at her skin. She slapped once, and then again. Lifting her hand, she discovered blood smeared on her palm. What had she cut herself on? The stinging intensified. Mosquitoes. Hundreds of them fought for space to land on exposed skin. The swinging of her frantic hands did nothing to keep them away.

Aware of nothing but her suffering, her shawl descending down over her head brought a shriek tumbling over her lips. She fought the trap of material.

"Calm down, Erica. I'm only trying to help you." She slumped against Dirk's comforting chest.

"Cover as much of your head and face as you can.

It should keep the mosquitoes at bay."

She hugged the shawl to her, grateful for the relief. Nothing but her eyes peeked out. The buzzing persisted and increased as the thwarted insects circled her, seeking entrance into the protective barrier she held around her.

A swarm, so thick it looked like a black cloud around his head, followed Dirk. Silently he slapped at them, his stride never faltering. His only source of relief was a group of blue-and-green dragonflies snatching the pests out of the air.

The ribbon of beach and greenery stretched endlessly. A familiar dull ache of cramped muscles invaded her legs. How much farther? She glanced across the expanse of ocean. No sign of the pirates, but then no sign of the *Sea Hawk,* either.

He stopped, and she nearly bumped into his broad back. What did he look for? She waited patiently, glad for the chance to halt and catch her breath.

"This is the spot," he grumbled. "This is where I came ashore from the *Sea Hawk.*"

She blinked, uncomprehending. Again her eyes scanned the empty horizon. Nothing. "I don't understand. Where are they, then?"

"I'm not sure. They wouldn't have left unless they had no other choice."

"Do you think they ran into Treacher?"

"I don't know. Maybe." He pointed to a spot beside him as he slid to the ground. "Sit down. I've got to think this through."

Willingly she dropped in the sand beside him and propped her head and shoulders against the rough bark of a tree. Her eyes drooped in exhaustion.

"I don't know if I should light a signal fire or not. It could attract Treacher as likely as my—"

The whiz of a bullet skimmed inches above her. He slammed her down hard against the sand as it hit the tree she had been leaning against with a muffled thump. He pushed her farther into the woods. Another shot ran out as the bullet ripped through leaves and twigs just in front of her. The shawl slipped to her shoulders, the insects forgotten, as her throat contracted in fear.

Dirk crawled next to her and thrust the pistol into her unwilling hand. "Listen. Head straight for that clump of brush." His finger pointed to a spot ten yards ahead. "Get in there. Lie still. I'll divert their attention."

She opened her mouth to protest. His hand covered it with a rough gesture. "Damn it. Don't argue. Stay there until I come back." His brows knitted into a frown. "Understand?"

She nodded, her eyes wild with fear. What did he plan? He removed his hand and pushed her forward. She glanced back, and he gave her a quick, reassuring smile as he rose to his hands and knees and loped away in the opposite direction.

Her fingers gripped the dirt as she inched toward the brush. *God protect him,* she prayed. She reached the brush and concealed herself as clinging vines and briers ripped at her face and hands. Her heart drummed in her ears; her breathing rasped so loud she feared someone would hear.

She pushed aside a swinging vine blocking her view. Thorns ripped at the back of her hand, and tiny beads of blood welled up on her skin. She strained her eyes in the direction Dirk had taken. Where was he? Brush swayed in the distance. *There,* she thought, *he's there.* Shots exploded, snapping leaves and twigs around the movement she had seen.

"Please, God," she breathed. Her eyes searched the foliage, seeking another sign of him.

The seconds ticked by slowly. Two more shots pattered in the trees near the spot she had last seen evidence of Dirk. As if from nowhere a multitude of men appeared to surround where she knew he crouched. Like a pack of hungry wolves, they closed in on him. Frustrated with her inability to help him, she clamped her jaws tight, trapping her lower lip between her teeth. Blood oozed into her mouth.

The circle closed tighter and tighter, but still no sign of Dirk. Fear coursed through her. What if he was dead? She rose to her hands and knees, determined to run after him. The pistol bit into her palm. If she shot one of the pirates, maybe Dirk would have a chance to escape. She fumbled with the gun.

A crash and a yell brought her head up. Dirk reared out of the brush, tumbling toward the closest of the men. Unprepared for his aggressive attack, the sailor toppled like a felled tree as Dirk slammed into him. *He's going to make it,* she silently cheered. The group of men converged on him in unison, and he crumped underneath the pile. Her heart screamed in protest. With the strength of a maddened lion, he rose once more, but the pirates clung to him like bulldogs. Unable to shake free he crashed once more to the ground, the sailors pinning him down. Their shouts of triumph rent the air.

Lifting up as high as she dared, she could see no

sign of Dirk. She waited breathlessly for him to rear up, but the trampled brush where he lay didn't move. He wouldn't rise again. She gasped and ducked back down to lie as flat as she could against the ground. The men were looking for her.

The swish of a stick skimming over the brush edged closer and closer. She held her breath, fearing she would be heard. The crunch of boots on the stiff grass and briers vibrated the ground next to her ear. Fear gripped her insides, twisting and squeezing her stomach until she thought she would retch. She pressed her lips tight and watched one of the pirates walk toward her. He would step on her if he didn't change direction. She gripped the pistol and aimed it at the approaching man. If they caught her, she would send one of them to hell. Her hand trembled, and she curled her other fist around the weapon to steady it.

"Jenkins," a demon voice called out. Treacher stood over Dirk's prone body, signaling to the man nearing where she lay. The man turned a few yards in front of her and headed back to his leader.

She dropped her hands still clutching the pistol against the ground, her breath coming in short squeaks. She was safe for the moment.

As the beaters, one by one, returned to where Treacher waited, she could see the frustration twisting the pirate's features into an ugly sneer. He spun and stared down at the ground.

She edged closer to the group of men. *Dirk, please be alive.* She reached a position where she had a clear view of the knot of pirates.

Her temples pounded in rage at the scene before

her. Dirk lay in a heap on the ground, blood running down his hairline. He curled, his knees drawn to his chest, protecting his stomach and groin from Wesley Treacher's foot pounding relentlessly into his body.

"Where is she, damn you? I know the bitch was with you." Treacher's voice rose in high-pitched fury.

Dirk's silence brought the pirate's foot crashing into his exposed back. He arched to protect his kidney, and an agonizing groan filtered to where she crouched watching. He lay, unnaturally twisted, his face and body unmoving.

No, I can't let this happen to him. He sacrificed so much to help me, I can't let him give his life as well. Damn you, Treacher, I won't let you hurt him any more.

She rose to her full height and carefully aimed the pistol still clutched in her hands at Treacher. With calculated accuracy she pulled the trigger.

The pistol jerked in her palms with a deafening explosion. Treacher turned in slow motion in her direction, a look of hate and surprise encompassing his features as he bent forward, stumbling.

Closing her eyes, she whispered, "My God, what have I done?"

Chapter Twelve

The shriek of a mortally wounded man echoed through the trees. Erica stood in the same stance she had taken to fire the pistol, feet wide apart and both arms extended, her hands gripping the handle of the smoking weapon.

"I've killed him," she whispered, relief and horror battling for supremacy.

A grip of iron closed around her wrists. Her eyes flew open, fear searing her insides, as the pistol clattered to the ground. A hand filled her vision. Then exploding pain sent her mind reeling. The ground rose up to meet her. The world swung crazily. Flaming red hair and a matching eye patch swirled above her. No, it couldn't be Treacher. She'd killed him. She'd seen him stumble as the gun fired in her hands.

Her eyelids fluttered, and her vision blurred, leaving nothing but a watery mist before her. A hard, pointed boot toe nudged her in the ribs.

"She'll live," growled a faraway voice. "But she'll

234

wish to God she hadn't by the time I'm done with her."

Bright sparks danced in her sight as she blinked to clear her vision. Wesley Treacher straddled her, his mouth an angry slash.

"No, I killed you," she mumbled, her words sounding foolish as she stared at the uninjured man above her.

"You stupid bitch, you missed me. But I'm sick and tired of you shooting my men." Treacher reached down and pulled her up by the front of her shirt. "By damn, you won't do it again. I should shoot you where you lie, like the she-wolf you are, but I have better plans for you and your lover," he snarled.

She hung from his cold grip like a broken rag doll, her long palomino hair dragging in the dirt. He dropped her with a grunt of disgust, and she hit the back of her head on a small, protruding rock, sending more sparks shooting through her head. Sweat trickled between her shoulder blades and breasts as she conjured up images of his plans, twisted plans including Dirk. She made an effort to push up from the ground. Treacher stepped back over her as he planted his foot on her breastbone, shoving her back down. Unsuppressed hate welled up inside of her. "I wish my aim had been true," she hurled at the pirate's retreating back.

Toby's puppy-eyed face bent over her. "You shouldn't of done it. I seen you leave. I had to tell Wesley, 'cause you done wrong," the big man babbled.

She closed her eyes, not comprehending the meaning of his words. "Please, Toby, where is Dirk?"

"You understand why I had to tell him, don't you?"

She opened her eyes and focused on Toby's beseeching face. Her hand patted his big paw. "It's all right, Toby," she said to calm him down, "I understand. But Dirk, you must tell me about Dirk."

Toby shook his head sadly. "Nobody crosses Wesley. He had to hurt him real bad." He stood up and turned to walk away, his head swinging back and forth as he muttered, "Real bad, real bad."

"No, Toby, come back. I have to know," she cried.

Dirk lay in twisted agony, surprised he still lived. The memory of a pistol shot still rang in his ears. The sound had exploded just as he had lost consciousness. He had assumed the bullet had been meant for him. Who had fired the gun, and why? It didn't matter. He only knew Treacher's attention and torturous boot had been diverted away from him for a while. The sharp, stabbing pains subsided, to be replaced with a dull ache. His thoughts turned to Erica. She had looked so frightened when he had left her in the brush. He hoped she had the sense to remain hidden there.

One by one he relaxed his tense muscles and slipped his hip underneath his body. He sucked air into his lungs, and the soreness in his ribs throbbed. His hand skimmed lightly over his chest and groin, discovering multiple bruises, but nothing more. He groaned, then wished he could draw the sound back into his throat.

Hands converged on him. Taking a quick survey of

his surroundings before a body blocked his vision, he saw little more than the beginnings of a campsite being set up. Sand bit into the side of his face as the pirates pushed him on his stomach, deftly tying his hands and feet behind his back.

Quietly he lay there, each breath he drew into his lungs a test of his willpower. His hands sawed furiously at the rope binding his wrists. Back and forth he worked his arms, until the muscles between his shoulder blades cried for relief. He slumped forward. Had the knot loosened slightly? His hands were so numb he couldn't be sure. He must get loose. Erica depended on him. His promise to get her home safely echoed in his mind. He couldn't let her down. He jerked his hands in renewed determination.

The soft hoot of a night owl stilled his actions. Dusk settled around him. Had he worked that long on the ropes, and still he wasn't free? His shoulders sagged in frustration, yet his hands continued their frantic struggle for freedom. He would never give up; not as long as Erica needed him.

A fire crackled, and smoke drifted in his direction. Lifting his head to peer over the log blocking his view of the pirates' camp, he saw long flames of fire shoot into the air. Laughter filtered to where he lay as the large bonfire glowed in the dying light of sunset. His stomach lurched. That was to have been his signal to the *Sea Hawk* that they were back and ready to be taken aboard. He hoped to God his crew didn't see the fire and answer it, unaware of the pirates.

Darkness covered him like a blanket. Forgetting caution, he worked with all his might pulling at the ropes. *Stay where I left you, Erica,* he willed mentally.

Discovering several sharp stones beneath him, he rolled to his back, hoping no one would notice the sounds he made. As he scraped the ropes over the stones, a trickle of wetness ran down his wrists into his curled palms. Blood or sweat, he didn't stop to decide. Up and down he sawed his arms, unmindful that he tore the flesh from his wrists. His only concern was Erica, alone and scared in the dark forest.

The fire burned down to glowing embers, yet his hands remained tightly bound. He rested his head back against the ground. His throat constricted around a painful knot. Mindlessly his numb arms pumped against the stones. He would work all night at the ropes if he had to. He must get back to Erica. "I swear to God I won't let you down."

Erica curled on the ground, the glowing remains of the bonfire between her and the spot where she knew Dirk lay. Relief and fear battled inside her. Relief from when she had seen Dirk bound. He had been alive. Thank God. She feared what Treacher had planned for them. His twisted mind was capable of inventing a revenge against Dirk more horrid than anything she could imagine.

She glanced around at the men sprawled on the ground around her. Most snored softly, deep in sleep. Treacher was nowhere to be seen.

Wrists tied in front of her, she put the rope to her mouth and gnawed at the knots drawn tightly. Every few minutes she stopped to see if anyone stirred. She

238

had to get to Dirk. Together they could escape in the darkness and lose themselves in the woods. Her teeth ached from her effort to untie the ropes. An ache she ignored. The first in the series of knots pulled free. Her courage and determination doubled with her success. She renewed her effort, and the second knot fell away. One more twist of the rope dug viciously into her slender wrists. Each time she tugged at it, the raw hemp pinched the skin beneath it. Even if her teeth were pulled from her gums, she couldn't give up her struggle. So close. The pressure on her wrists released with a sudden jerk; the rope hung limply around them. She took precious seconds to rub the red, raw ring indented into her flesh.

She picked at the knots at her ankles with her fingernails, but they refused to give. One of the pirates, a few feet from her, stirred and turned with a snort. Her breath caught in her throat. She placed her hands in her lap to conceal them. Seconds ticked by. The man snored with little humphs. She attacked the ropes again, and finally freed her legs.

Pushing up to a squat, she inched around the fire and over to the fallen log separating her from Dirk. Darkness encompassed her as she slipped over the barrier and continued her crawl.

Falling across his prone figure, she squeaked, "Dirk?"

"Erica? What in the hell are you—"

"Ssh," she hissed between her teeth. She reached down to release his bound wrists; he winced as she touched him. Wetness smeared on her hands. Blood. She untied the knots pulled taut by his struggling. Without waiting, she picked the rope loose from his ankles. They were free.

"Can you stand?" she whispered.

Bushes rustled behind her. She jumped at the sound. Cold, hard steel touched the back of her neck. She froze, unspoken words trapped in her throat.

"Touching sight we have here." Treacher's cruel words pierced the darkness. The pirate pressed the barrel of the gun hard against her flesh, sending chill bumps down her back. "Now, get up slowly," he commanded.

She rose in obedience. Stepping back from Dirk, she heard the pirate stumble and fall as Dirk's hand slapped around his ankle.

"Move, Erica," Dirk demanded.

She threw her hands up at the deafening roar of the gunshot inches from the side of her face.

Treacher crashed to the ground with a bellow. Dirk reared up beside her and grabbed her hand with a jerk. Limbs and leaves whipped at her face as he guided her through the darkness. Not caring where they went, her heart lifted with each step they took toward freedom.

He pushed her hard to the side. Two angry faces, illuminated by the faint moonlight, blocked their way.

"Run," he shouted.

She spun around at his command in confusion. A familiar iron grip grabbed her flying tresses, and she fell to her knees, sure that her hair had been pulled out by the roots. The crash of bodies and grunts of pain, followed by the smack of fists pounding into flesh, brought a scream to her lips.

Treacher swung her around and pushed his face into hers. "I'm tired of your antics, my dear. Don't ever try to escape me again," he said with slow, deadly sincerity. He whipped her back around and tied her hands tightly behind her body.

"Take that son of a bitch and see to it he makes no more attempts to escape."

"Dirk," she choked in the darkness.

Silence was her only answer.

"Get up," a distant voice demanded.

A hand clutched her upper arm and pulled her to her feet. She blinked, her tired mind refusing to function. A bright sun blinded her, and she squinted in defense. She couldn't believe she had slept. Glancing out over the beach seeking signs of Dirk, she saw the pirate ship, the *Freedom,* rolling gently on the water, a small dinghy headed toward land. Milling around her were a half-dozen men and Treacher. Frantically she continued her search.

"Where's Dirk?" she demanded, her eyes flashing anger.

"Don't worry about your lover. I've taken good care of him." Treacher gave her a skeletal smile with no merriment in it.

"Damn you, Treacher, if you've hurt him . . ."

"Ah, my dear, your protectiveness is commendable." His hand cupped her jaws in a manacle grip. "But quite useless."

Her head flew around as he released her, and she jerked back to glare at him.

"Take her aboard."

Hands grabbed her from the rear, lifting her up, and carried her to the ship's dinghy.

"Let go of me." She struggled as the sailors thumped her on the seat. One man remained with her, his hand embedded in the bindings around her wrists.

She scanned the rail of the ship as the small boat crashed through the waves, heading toward the *Freedom*. The *Freedom*. Treacher's streak of cruelty ran even to the name of his ship. How many prisoners had he taken aboard who had felt the same way?

The ropes were removed from her wrists. Given no choice, she climbed the swinging ladder up the side of the ship, shadowed by her guard. Glancing down at the swirling water below beckoning to her, daring her to toss her body into its briny depths to escape what life held for her, she considered the option. A prod against her backside sent her eyes back up the ladder. With a sigh, she continued pulling herself up the side of the ship. Dirk was somewhere aboard. As long as he lived there was hope. As long as there was hope, she must seek a means to escape.

Retied and dragged unceremoniously down the companionway, her captors tossed her on the familiar bed in Treacher's cabin. The pain in her twisted arms echoed the emotions she had felt not so long ago when she had been in the cabin the first time. Then she had worried about Joshua. Now Dirk's life was in danger as well.

Frustration wove a knot in her throat so large she couldn't swallow. Tears welled in her eyes, and she dashed them away on the coverlet. A convulsive sob racked her. She placed her face against the blanket and allowed the blur of tears to roll down her face. She didn't care who heard her, and when the key turned softly in the locked door, she didn't care who saw her.

Toby's face bent over her, and he patted her hair with his clumsy paw much like he would if she were a wounded, wild animal. "Aw, Miss Erica, please don't cry," he cooed. "Wesley, he don't mean to hurt you. He's just so full of pain hisself, he can't help it."

"He's a monster, Toby. Why can't you see that?"

"He's been good to me," he explained. "He found me beat by my pa when I couldn't do everything I was suppose to. He saved me and took me with him. He ain't never been nothing but kind. Don't you see?"

She swallowed her agitation. Maybe she could use his loyalty to her advantage. "I do understand. That's how I feel about Dirk. He rescued me from harm. I need to know he's all right." Her eyes pleaded. "Please, Toby."

"He's not hurt bad. Wesley put him in the hold, but he didn't hurt him no more."

She lay back with relief. Somehow she'd find Dirk. Somehow they would manage to escape.

The sound of bare feet pattered over her head. The masts squealed with the lowering sails. They must have reached the harbor of the pirate stronghold. She and Dirk had struggled two days to reach the mainland. The pirates had taken only a few hours to drag them back. She cursed the God that had allowed them to get so close to escaping only to thwart their actions at the last possible moment. It wasn't fair!

She laughed bitterly. How many times had she said

those exact words as a child? Her father had chuckled at her tantrum and told her, "If life was fair, it would be boring."

"Perhaps, Papa," she whispered, "but at least it would be safe." And safe was what she wanted more than anything. Safe and secure with Dirk.

Toby's hand lifted her to stand beside him. He guided her out the door in front of him. The big man gripped her gently as he forced her down the companionway and up onto the deck.

The familiar sight of the pirate stronghold greeted her. Toby urged her to the edge of the railing. She glanced down at the ocean far below as the dinghy moved toward the island. A dark figure hunched on one of the seats. Dirk. She could see him.

"Dirk," she cried. Her voice carried in the light breeze. His dark head turned in her direction.

He struggled to stand, the boat swaying with his redistributed weight. "Erica!" he called back. The pirates in the boat pushed him back down, blocking her view of him.

Behind her, a lone pair of hands clapped. Treacher's grating voice reached her. "A touching performance, my dear."

She ignored him and watched Dirk's retreating figure.

"In fact," he continued, "I enjoyed it so much, I have another little performance I want you to give."

She narrowed her eyes. "The only performance I'll ever give *you* is when I do a dance of joy on your grave."

Treacher grabbed her around the waist, tearing her gaze from Dirk as he was forced from the boat and pushed up the beach. The pirate crushed her against his body, tense with anger. "We'll see about that, my dear. Perhaps when the life of your precious Dirk is at stake, you'll change your mind."

Her hands fisted in the binding behind her back. If only they were free, she would claw his one good eye out. She struggled to escape his loathsome touch. His laughter echoed in her ears.

"You impotent bastard, I know you couldn't do anything if you wanted to," she spat viciously at his face, inches from hers. Her chest heaved with the need to injure him the only way she could. With words.

Treacher's face contorted in surprised rage. "There are things much worse than rape, my dear." Roughly he pushed her at Toby. "Take her down to the hut and see to it she stays put." The pirate walked away, his back rigid.

"Damn you, Treacher," she choked as Toby swung her over his broad shoulder. "Hell isn't rotten enough for the likes of you."

Erica paced the dark, airless room until she knew exactly how many steps it took to go all the way around it. Raucous laughter filtered through the locked door now and again, as if a large crowd gathered in the compound.

In horror she hoped whatever Treacher had planned for her wouldn't include a public display. He was right; she could imagine all kinds of things much worse than simple rape. She would kill herself before she would submit to being thrown to his crew like a bone to a pack of starving dogs.

Her head dipped in despair. Treacher's threat against Dirk resounded in her thoughts. She would submit to anything to protect him, including walking through the fires of hell.

"Damn it, Treacher," she blurted to the four blank walls around her. "Just do what you're going to do and get it over with."

She whirled to face the door squealing in answer. Treacher leaned on the frame watching her with a gleam in his one good eye.

She backed slowly away from him, until she pressed against the far wall, nowhere else to go. His enjoyment of her fear glistened in his eye.

"Now, my dear, we have a little play to rehearse."

She shivered at the venom in his voice. With slow, calculated movements he approached her. An arm's length away, he stopped, eased his large, cruel hands onto his hips, and studied every aspect of her body.

Gathering up her shattered courage, she straightened and lifted her chin in defiance, though her heart pounded hard against her rib cage.

His hand snaked out and clasped her wrist. He pulled her up against him. "Your lover has created a spectacle, and there doesn't seem to be a limit to his energy. He's a madman throwing himself against the barrier, threatening to do all kinds of interesting things to me. He's becoming a nuisance." The pirate's finger reached out and traced the outline of her clenched jaw. "In a few minutes he's going to be brought up to view an interesting scene. How well you play your part will decide just how long he lives."

Fear turned her insides icy. "What do you mean?"

she rasped.

"Why, a little love scene is what I had in mind." He smiled humorlessly.

"I won't do it."

"Ah, you will do it, my dear," he snarled as he yanked a handful of her hair. "Or I'll cut him into so many pieces you'll have trouble finding them all, and I'll start with the part of him that makes him a man."

He thrust her down on the bed. "Now, may I suggest you put the most seductive smile you have on your pretty face."

Battered and bruised, Dirk threw himself against the fence, hoping to find a weak point. All he succeeded in doing was entertaining the group of pirates gathering around to watch. He didn't care. "Damn you, son of a bitch," he bellowed.

Laughter engulfed him as his fists pounded the unmoving barrier.

"Take it easy, my friend. Beating your head against the fence isn't going to do you any good."

Dirk whirled to face a tall, gray-haired man who had joined him in the enclosed yard. He could only be one man. "Joshua," he said aloud. "You must be Joshua."

"Aye, sir, I am. Who might you be?"

"Dirk Hawkyns."

"Do I know you?"

"No, but we both know Erica Armstrong."

Joshua studied him, sizing him up. "Is that so? What does Erica mean to you?"

He scrutinized the older man, deciding how much

to tell him. "A lot," he answered. "Enough to get me in this mess I'm in now."

Booted feet approaching the pen cut short their conversation. The voice of the big, simple giant, Toby, rang out through the barrier gate. "You wanna see Miss Erica?"

Dirk slammed his body against the barrier as he reached out through a break in the boards to grab the big man, but Toby stood back far enough to be out of reach.

"I'll take you to her, if you want."

"Why would you do that?" he asked suspiciously.

Toby's face held honesty. "Wesley told me I could, if you promise to shut up and quite bellowing like a wounded bull."

Joshua touched his shoulder. "Be careful, Dirk. From what I know of Treacher this isn't his style."

His eyes jumped from the older man's face to Toby. "Do I have a choice? I have to take the chance to see her. I've got to know she's unharmed."

"Aye, I know," Joshua responded. "I'd not hesitate to go either. Just be on your guard for one of Treacher's nasty tricks."

"I appreciate your warning."

Dirk nodded at Toby. The lock rattled, and the gate swung open. Toby's large frame filled the entrance, blocking his way. The big man stepped behind his back and tied his hands securely. Toby gave him a shove, and he started forward.

"Tell Erica I said to keep that stubborn little chin of hers up for me," Joshua called from behind the barricade.

"I'll do that," he answered, glancing back at the

faint outline the older man's body made behind the fencing.

His eyes skimmed over every aspect of the camp, storing away any details that might come in handy later.

Toby reached out to grasp his arm and stop him. They stood before one of the several small, crude huts dotting the compound. The big man's hand pushed at the door.

If Treacher has harmed her in any way, he thought, *I'll find him and pay him back injury for injury, no matter how long it takes me.*

Footsteps crunched in the gravel pathway leading up to the small, dark hut. Dirk was here. *God help me for what I'm about to do,* Erica prayed. *Make him understand.*

Treacher heard the sounds, too, as he pushed her down on the hard, crude bed. "Now, my dear," he hissed in her ear, "I expect a performance worth remembering."

With vicious delight on his face his hand tore at the tiny buttons on the front of her shirt. Her hands reached up to clutch the material over her, and he slapped them away. "I'll not warn you again, Erica. It would give me great pleasure to present you with a token of Hawkyn's manhood as a souvenir."

Her hand fell limply to her side. A cold numbness crept over her. Treacher's icy touch pushed the shirt from her shoulders and down to leave her arms in a helpless tangle of material. Like a greedy street urchin pawing stolen candy, he ripped her undershirt down to her waist. Her stomach lurched at his unwanted invasion. She threw her head to the side so she didn't have to watch his disgusting face. His roaming hand flashed up and jerked her head back around. His threatening silence gave her warning to cooperate.

Sweet memories welled up inside her of the last time she had been undressed by a man, by her beloved Dirk. Feeling dirty and used as the pirate cupped her breast, there was no rush of desire. Only the rush of a sour taste filling her mouth.

The door swayed on its frame, then swung open with the muted crash of reed against reed as the barrier smashed against the side of the hut. Thunder rolled in the background in answer to the bang of the door. Eerie sunshine poured through the frame, blinding her. The two men's bodies filled the opening, blocking the light. She could see Dirk's face distinctly.

His expression changed from one of the momentary blind innocence fused with concern to one of raging hatred. "Damn you, Treacher, I'll kill you for this," he growled from deep in his throat, his words as ominous as the thunder rumbling behind him.

With insolent arrogance, Treacher lifted his weight from her body. Lazily his hand kneaded and flicked her breasts, quivering with each rasping breath she took. Dirk's eyes followed the movement of the other man's hand in disbelief. His dark eyes swept up to her face for her reaction.

Before their eyes contacted, she glanced at Treacher. His hard look promised he'd follow through with his threats. With dread in her heart, she swung

250

her gray eyes back to meet Dirk's, a brazen stare etching her features. She held her gaze steady as his expression changed from doubt to a plea she react with horror at the other man's touch, then twisted into undisguised disgust. She swiveled her face toward Treacher's chest. She couldn't watch Dirk's love die.

The pirate took advantage of her move and buried her face in his shoulder, stroking her hair. Like a fatal bullet, Treacher's words shot through the air. "Now, Hawkyns, you've seen her. She's where she wants to be."

Bile rose in her throat. She wanted to scream the truth at Dirk, make him realize she had done this only to save him.

"You whore," Dirk hissed. Lightning seared the sky behind him.

Her heart withered and died in her chest at his words. His retreating steps were arrows of pain through her chest. The door slammed like the lid of a coffin.

With the strength she didn't know she had, she pushed Treacher from her. Rising from the bed, she stumbled to the door swinging crazily on its hinges. She lowered her face until the top of her head rested on the frame. "Oh, Dirk," she whispered.

Her state of undress forgotten, she whirled to face her enemy. "You'll pay for this," she choked. "Somehow, some way, I swear to God, you'll be sorry you were ever born."

Treacher rose from the bed and approached her, grinning. "When I get to hell, Satan will compliment me for my cunning." The look on his face turned solemn. He raised a finger and traced it slowly down the side of her jaw. He lowered his head, his mouth reaching toward her.

She gasped. He was going to try to kiss her. His reptilian touch sent chills of revulsion down her spine. Gathering saliva in her mouth, she sent it hurtling upward at his smug face. With satisfaction she watched the spittle roll down his forehead into his eyebrow.

Where it went from there she didn't know, as the side of her head exploded with the fireworks of pain. The floor came up to meet her.

Chapter Thirteen

Dirk watched the rain splash from leaf to leaf, then plunge in little rivulets to the sand below the lone palm tree in the pen. Drops of the same rain trickled from the damp locks of black hair wisping around his temples and ears. Oblivious to the moisture running down his face to soak the front of his shirt, he relived the scene he had witnessed minutes before. Erica lying easily in the arms of Wesley Treacher, her look defying him, daring him to make something of it.

"Whore," he groaned. Like every woman he had ever known, seeking to feather her own nest.

The patter of the rain and the whistle of the wind whipping around the edge of the building brought back other memories. Erica lying on a makeshift bed under the canopy of oilskin, so sweet, yet seductive.

Dirk shook his head to clear it of the unbidden images. *Damn her,* he brooded, *for taking the easy way out.* His hands squeezed the rough boards of the crude bench underneath him until his knuckles turned bloodless. *I should have protected her better. I should have gotten her to safety. Then she wouldn't have been forced to turn to Treacher for her own* protection. No, there had been no regret in her eyes. The son of a bitch was right, she was where she wanted to be. She has chosen her path. Now, I have to think of myself. Escape alone won't be as difficult as dragging a woman along.

He pushed up from the shaky bench. It clattered to the ground. He kicked it, and the act made him feel better, so he kicked it again. "May she rot in hell for all I care!"

He turned to enter the barnlike structure, determined to work out the details of escape. A dank smell—a mixture of odors the multitude of people who had been forced to stay there had left behind, ranging from the sweetness of expensive perfume and cologne to the sour odors of rum and burnt tobacco—greeted him as he entered the dark prisoners' shelter. A lone candle, flickering with the breeze following him in, threatened to go out and die as his compassion had died at the sight of Treacher's hand caressing her flesh.

Joshua rose from the squat, irregularly shaped table in the middle of the room and shot his hand out to curl around the finger of light to protect it, just as he would protect Erica. Dirk shoved the door closed, and the flame steadied to point straight up to the rafters above the two men's heads.

A look of hopeful impatience encompassed Joshua's face. "Did you see her?"

He studied the other man a moment. How he wished he didn't have to face him. Like a father, Erica had described him. What would he say to the man? "I saw her," he replied as he walked toward one of the beds placed in the old horse stalls to lend an air of privacy to them.

"Damn it, man," Joshua pressed, following him. "How is she?"

He refused to look at the older man's demanding eyes. "She's fine."

Joshua grabbed his shoulder and forced him around. "You don't appear too pleased about it."

His fist itched to smash into Joshua's jaw. *No, he's just another man she has managed to fool.* He pivoted in silence and pulled the blanket off the bed to expose a bare mattress.

"Dirk, what's going on?" Joshua persisted.

He attempted to swallow the temper heating his blood. *Maybe Joshua needs to know the truth.* Dark eyes whirled to meet inquiring blue ones. "You want to know what's happening? Then I'll tell you." All his frustrations and feelings of inadequacy rushed to the surface. "Your precious Erica is over there rutting with that damned bastard, and she doesn't care who knows."

Joshua reacted as if he had hit him. "No. You must be wrong. Erica's too young to know . . . Damn it, man, she's still a . . ."

Dirk turned away to avoid Joshua's questioning eyes.

"She is, isn't she?" Joshua demanded.

Their gazes locked and fenced for supremacy.

"No," he answered without a blink. He caught a glimpse of the pain in the older man's eyes before Joshua spun away.

"Damn you to hell for what you've done to her." Joshua walked back to the table, sat, and buried his face in his hands.

Dirk followed him across the room. "Look. I'm not sorry for what I've done, and I admit it was my doing. But I loved her and . . ."

"But not anymore."

"You didn't see what I just saw." He turned back toward the bed, all emotion draining from him.

"Perhaps, but you don't know Erica like I do. You're wrong about her, and by damn, I'll prove it to you some day." Joshua's fist smashed against the table, tossing the candle to its side. The flame sputtered and died.

"I wish to God you were right," Dirk whispered in the darkness. But his mind was made up. He would escape the first chance he got.

Erica pressed her fingers into her eyesockets, her mind wheeling with the hate and vengeance tainting her every breath. The only thing that mattered now was revenge against Wesley Treacher; not her love for Dirk, or the vows to succeed that she had made to her father, not even her life. She would see to it the pirate suffered for every pain he had caused her, for everything in her life she had lost because of him.

She crossed to the table and chair, seeking some kind of weapon. Her hands skimmed over the furniture, looking for a loose joint, a leg she could use as a club. She lifted the chair. It was light enough. If she pulled the bed next to the door, she could stand on it. When Treacher entered the hut, she would smash the chair over his head. Excitement sent the blood rushing through her veins. Using her shoulder muscles, she inched the bed away from the wall and close enough to the door to serve her purpose.

Now she would demand that the guard find Treacher and bring him to her. If he refused, she would scream bloody hell until he cooperated.

Reaching out for the door, she pushed against it. It didn't budge. A bolt on the outside held it firmly shut.

Lightning shattered the darkness as she crossed the room, bringing the chair with her. The window, maybe she could get out the window. Placing the chair beneath the small opening, she stood on tiptoe to test it. The sturdy barred frame wouldn't move.

She plumped down in the chair and forced her thoughts to remain calm. She would wait until Treacher returned on his own. He would come back, she had no doubt.

She crossed to the bed and pulled the chair with her, strategically placing it so she could grab it the minute someone opened the door. She waited, calmly. She could wait all night if she had to.

The door rattled on its hinges. She gasped and jumped up into position, the chair raised high above her head. She would smash Wesley Treacher to hell! Her arms shook with the weight of her weapon. It hadn't seemed so heavy earlier.

A flash of lightning illuminated the face entering the door. The chair crashed down, hit the floor, and spun wildly.

"Erica," Angela squealed in surprise. "What are you doing?"

She teetered on the edge of the bed. What was she doing? Had she really thought she could overpower Wesley Treacher with a chair?

She sank to her knees, her vow of vengeance still pounding strongly in the blood coursing through her temples. She glanced behind Angela's figure blocking the door. *I'll escape and find Dirk and explain.* She pushed up from the bed.

Angela's rough, dry fingers clasped her upper arm. "Don't even consider it, Erica. Wesley has three guards posted around this hut. You wouldn't get far."

Her shoulders slumped in defeat as the door closed softly behind Angela's back.

The blonde pulled a candle from the deep pocket in the front of her dress. She lit the wick and set the light on the table.

The flame danced in solitude. Alone, just as she was.

Righting the chair from the floor, Angela shook her head. "I should be angry with you, you know." The chair scraped against the floor as she sat in it. "Wesley was furious when he found out you were gone."

"Did he beat you?"

Angela nodded her head. "But nothing worse than what he's done to you."

Her hand flew to her face. Did she look as bad as Angela, with the bruises surrounding her eyes and mouth?

"Actually I was glad to find you gone. I hoped Wesley would forget about you." She looked down at her hands. "I was wrong. He's obsessed with you, Erica. He thinks you're the solution to his problem."

"I don't want to be the solution to his problem."

Angela rose to her feet and walked to the bed, testing it with her hand. "Hawkyns must love you a lot to come here and try to rescue you the way he did."

"Yes, he must have."

Angela swung around to face her. "Toby told me what Wesley did this afternoon. I'm sorry, Erica, truly I am. He has a lot of hurt inside. . . . I wish you could understand."

She chewed her bottom lip. Maybe, just maybe. "Angela, help me escape."

The woman shook her head in silence. "It's hopeless. You'd never get away. I'm sorry. I love Wesley, no matter what he is. I couldn't do something like that to hurt him."

"At least talk to Dirk for me," she persisted. "Please, Angela, tell him what happened."

Angela covered her ears. "No, don't ask me to be unloyal to my husband. I can't do that. No matter what he did to me."

Erica looked down at her hands. *Time. All I need is time. She'll help me, eventually. I know it.*

Erica dipped another dirty bowl into the pan of even dirtier water. *Washing dishes. I've been reduced to washing the dirty plates of filthy pirates.* She ran her roughened hand around the interior of the trencher to scrape off as much of the crusted food as she could. She wished it were Wesley Treacher's face she clawed at instead of dried potatoes.

She lifted her face when the feeling someone watched her overshadowed her vengeful thoughts.

Treacher leaned against a rickety table, studying her.

259

"Come here, Erica," he demanded in a bitter tone.

"Go to hell." She dropped the bowl on top of the other ones she had cleaned, pushed her hair out of her eyes, and picked up another.

In three steps he crossed the expanse between them, and jerked her to her feet. "Watch your foul mouth, my dear. It's not becoming."

"And washing dirty dishes for your stinking crew is?" She shoved the strands of tangled hair out of her face again.

His hand snaked around her arm and pulled her down the path leading to the harbor.

"Where are you taking me?"

He tossed an angry gaze over his shoulder. "We're going on a little trip."

She reacted without second thoughts. Planting her heels firmly in the sand, she stiffened her legs to keep him from dragging her any farther. She would go nowhere with Wesley Treacher.

He pivoted, picked her up—swinging her twisting body over his shoulder—and continued down the pathway.

"Put me down—" The impact of her midriff hitting solid flesh and bone knocked the air from her lungs, cutting off her words.

She swung her legs, trying to kick him in the chest. He wrapped his arm around her flying appendages. Balling her fists, she slammed them into the only spot she could hit, his lower back. His free hand retaliated with a stinging slap on her airborne backside. She punched his back again. His open palm landed solidly on her rump, bringing undesired tears to her eyes. She swung again, and his hand smacked her unprotected bottom so hard she gasped. Tears ran freely down her face. She couldn't stand the pain any longer. She fell limp against him, a giant groan tumbling over her lips.

He chuckled and patted her stinging rear as if it were the head of a faithful dog that had pleased its master. "Good girl."

Her fist balled again. His arm clutched her tightly around the knees. "Is it really worth it, my dear?"

Her hand remained clenched, but she held it in check.

From her upside-down position she could see the *Freedom* riding anchor in the harbor when the path converged with the shoreline. She searched frantically for a means to escape, but there was nothing and no one. Joshua. Dirk. Her heart cried soundlessly. Where were they? Where was Treacher taking her?

Running feet slapped against the well-worn track. She lifted her head, hope swelling in her chest. Through the jostling motion she recognized Angela racing to catch up with them.

The woman slipped and fell, crying out. "Wesley, you got to wait."

His feet slid to a halt, and he spun to face his pursuer, swinging Erica so she could no longer see what happened.

"Wesley, please." Angela's voice grew closer.

Taking advantage of the distraction, Erica tensed and bucked, trying to escape his clutch. His encircling arm tightened. "Keep still, Erica," he growled. His free hand came down solidly, enforcing his words.

"Wesley," Angela pleaded in a breathless voice. "Are you leaving again so soon?"

"Go away, Angela." He presented his back to his wife, throwing Erica's face inches from Angela's. The woman sprawled in the pathway, her arms reaching out to grab hold of the pirate's leg and stop him from walking away.

Erica watched the woman grovel, pity swelling in her heart, as she hung like a sack of flour from his shoulder between them. Angela's arms clung like the tendrils of a vine to his pants, and Treacher lifted his leg and shook her off.

Weeping, Angela dragged outstretched fingers across his boot. His foot tore loose and came down in her open palm, and he ground his heel into her flesh. Angela's scream ripped through Erica, and her balled fists slammed into Treacher's exposed kidney again and again.

His hand reached behind him, twisting her arms around his waist, and he held them firmly in front of him. His foot swung, striking his wife's prone body. With a groan Angela's breath gasped out.

"Leave me alone, you stupid bitch, and go back to the compound." Treacher spun on his heels to continue toward the harbor.

Angela's curled form lay in the dirt of the trail. She convulsed with racking sobs. Her face lifted from the ground, dirt and sand sticking to it.

Their eyes met. "Please, Angela," she mouthed. "Please help me."

Angela turned her face away, a negative reply in her eyes.

Her dropped head bumped against Treacher's back

262

as he carried her toward the ship, leaving her heart and hope behind in the trampled path beside the pirate's wife.

Dirk scanned the thin, dirty face of the woman handing him the bucket of stew through the opening in the fence gate. *She was pretty once,* he thought. But the bruises around her red-rimmed eyes gave her a haunted look, destroying the fleeting image.

Normally one of the guards brought them their two meals a day, and the sight of the strange woman made him wary.

"I got to talk to you," she said, her lips barely moving. She glanced back at the two guards behind her.

"Why?" He eyed her suspiciously.

"Please," she whispered. "I'll come back in an hour so we can talk." Without waiting for his reply, she tossed her stringy blonde hair and headed back down the path leading to the main compound.

Joshua's hand touched his shoulder. "What do you think she wants?"

"I'm not sure, but somebody beat her up. I'm willing to listen to what she has to say."

Sharing the food between them, they sat on benches in the yard to eat.

Mindlessly he chewed the nourishment.

Joshua set his half-eaten bowl of stew on the seat beside him and crossed his arms over his chest. "I bet you fifty to one Treacher's behind this."

He stood, set his trencher on the seat, and paced back and forth in front of Joshua. "Maybe, but there's no harm done by listening to her."

Sensing Joshua's eyes following him as he moved, he refused to acknowledge the other man. He knew the exact expression he would see written there: a look of accusation and betrayal. Why couldn't the man see Erica for what she was? To listen to Joshua, she was a saint who could do no wrong. Damn it, he knew what he had seen with his own two eyes. The strange woman might offer a means to escape. And escape he would. He glanced at the older man. Joshua could come with him or stay here; the choice would be his.

His gaze switched to the gate. Where was she? An hour passed and still no sign of her. Ready to forget the entire affair, he turned in disgust and headed inside the building. Anywhere to get away from Joshua Reynolds.

A rustling outside the fence caught his attention. A soft feminine voice hissed. "Hawkyns."

He whirled and approached the barrier, catching a glimpse of the woman standing on the other side. Watery blue eyes studied him through the boards. "Who are you?"

"Angela Treacher." The blue eyes held his dark ones in a steady gaze.

"And what would a pirate's . . . ?"

"Wife," she offered.

"Wife want with me?" he asked, bemused. Footsteps sounded behind him as Joshua joined him at the fence. Angela's eyes darted nervously toward the older man. "You can trust him," he assured her.

"We can help each other get what we want."

Joshua broke in. "This is another one of Treacher's

tricks. I wouldn't trust her."

"Listen," Angela pleaded, "Erica told me to talk to you and explain. . . ."

"Erica asked you to come here?" Dirk snapped. She nodded vigorously.

"Then you have nothing to say I want to hear." He turned to walk away.

Angela forced her hand and arm through the fencing. "No, wait. You don't understand."

Dirk pulled away from her fingers, but Joshua grabbed his arm. "Damn it, give her a chance," the gray-haired man implored.

He scowled at Joshua. "Quick enough to change your mind about her the minute you hear the name of your precious Erica. No, you were right the first time. This *is* a trick."

"If you don't listen to what she says, you're a fool."

His hands clenched at his side. Silently he turned back. He would listen, nothing more.

Angela's eyes darted from Dirk's closed face to Joshua's which offered encouragement, and back to Dirk's. She swallowed hard and took a deep breath. "Wesley set you up." Dirk's eyes narrowed, examining her. "He threatened her. He promised he'd kill *you* if she didn't cooperate." Pain roughened her voice. "He would have, too."

Dirk kitted his eyebrows with doubt. "You expect me to believe that? Brave little Erica. She slept with him to save me. Is that supposed to make me feel better about it?"

Joshua's grip crushed down on his arm. "She did what she thought she had to do," he said softly.

Angrily he shook the hand away. "No, I don't need

265

her to prostitute herself for me. I can take care of myself. Sparks danced between the two men.

"But she didn't." Angela's voice cracked in the static air.

He whirled back to face her. "Is that what Treacher told you? What do you expect him to say? You're his wife, for Christ sake."

"No, you don't understand. He couldn't have even if he wanted to. Erica knew that. He can't bed *any* woman."

He studied the woman through the fence. Did she really expect him to believe her words? Husbands told their wives all kinds of wild stories as an excuse not to have to sleep with them.

"I know what you're thinking. You're wrong," she whispered. "Wesley was injured in a knife fight ten years ago. I nursed him through it. I know what I'm talking about."

Dirk searched the woman's face for signs that she lied. She told the truth. His hand slapped against the fencing. "Damn my stupidity." His hand closed around Angela's wrist. "Tell Erica—"

"I can't tell her anything. Wesley took her off."

"Where?" he demanded.

"I don't know. He took her aboard the *Freedom* two days ago. I think they might have headed to Mexico, 'cause Toby ran around pretending to be a bullfighter before they left."

"Damn you, woman, why didn't you come to me two days ago?"

She hung her head. "I don't know. You've got to understand, I love Wesley." She raised her head proudly. "It's hard to betray him. But I want him back, and I'll do whatever I have to do to get him."

Mexico, he thought. *How would they get there?* "Are there any ships in the harbor now?"

Hesitation filled her eyes. Her lashes fluttered down to cover the emotion shining from them. Taking a deep breath, she nodded. "There's one ship, an old one, but it will sail. What will you do for a crew?"

"I don't know yet. I have to think this through. Come back in the morning." His dark gaze demanded she obey him. "Be prepared to let us out."

She nodded her head in agreement. He pushed his arm through the barrier and grabbed her wrist as she turned to leave. "You're doing the right thing, Angela. Thank you."

She tore away from his hand and raced down the path, not once looking back.

"I hope to God she comes back." Joshua's voice cut into silence.

"So do I."

Dirk lifted his head from the table at the thundering boom. "Damn," he mumbled under his breath. "Another storm."

With the senses of a man used to waking early, he knew dawn was no more than an hour away. He thrust his fingers through his hair and shook his head.

He and Joshua had spent the majority of the night discussing possible plans of escape. Discussion that had turned to arguments. There was no way for two men and possibly Angela to sail a ship alone. They would have to convince her to help recruit a crew. Even a few men would be better than none. There had to be others on the island who would jump at the chance to leave. Damn, escape had become complicated. Complicated by the need to get to Mexico and find Erica.

"Erica," he muttered. "How could I have been so blind? I did exactly what Treacher wanted me to do. Oh, Mermaid, forgive me for being so stupid."

A second boom reverberated in the air. He jumped up from the table and glanced at Joshua, sprawled across one of the beds. The older man lifted and shook his head.

"Cannon," Joshua announced. "I'd swear on my mother's grave, that was a cannon."

Dirk held his breath, praying the sound would come again. The ominous silence was so complete he could hear his heart pounding against his rib cage as if it wanted to escape. The seconds ticked by so slowly he almost gave up listening.

The third explosion brought a welter of discordant sounds, the crack of splintering wood and the screams of people in pain or terror, he wasn't sure which.

The two men crowded out the door and halted, heads raised, trying to decipher what was happening.

A gunpowder flash and a roar came from the harbor, followed by a lone, whining wail. Trees trembled and twisted in rhythm with the sound of the cannonball impacting two hundred yards from where they stood.

In unspoken communication they threw their combined weight against the gate. The wood shuddered and moaned but stubbornly refused to break. The clinking of the chain as it was released brought them to a halt. Dirk pulled Joshua back so the gate could swing open. Angela stood on the other side, staring at her hand holding the key as if it were a traitor. He clasped his warm hand around her icy one. She looked up at him with amazement on her face.

The ear-shattering explosion of another launched cannonball urged him into action. Grabbing her limp wrist, he started across the compound, glancing back once to make sure Joshua followed.

The whistle of the spinning cannonball came closer. Pushing her to the ground none too gently, he covered his head with his hands. "That one's too close."

Joshua hit the ground with a grunt, inches from his boot heel.

Tiny slivers of wood pelted them. He rolled to his back, checking to make sure they were in no danger of something larger falling on them. Already in the process of rising, Joshua pointed toward the harbor. Dirk pulled Angela up and followed the older man.

"What's going on?" he shouted to her over the constant din of noise filling the air.

"I think it's the United States Navy," she answered. "I'm not sure how they found us, but they're determined to blow the island. . . ."

The roar of cannon fire covered her words. He pulled her along behind him. They had to get to the harbor to see for themselves who bombarded the island. If it was the navy, their problems would be solved. He and Joshua could recruit enough men from the island to take the abandoned ship to Mexico to find Erica.

A stream of humanity heading away from the harbor slowed their progress down. Angela snapped out of her daze and began pulling back to escape Dirk's fingers clamped around her wrist.

"We can't go to the harbor. We'll be killed," she screamed. "Let go of me, please, let me go."

He turned to confront the fear etched in her water blue eyes. "You're going to have to trust me, Angela," he demanded, leaving no room for argument. "I need you to help me find Erica. I have no intentions of letting anything happen to you."

He pushed forward, Angela following docilely behind him. He stopped as they rounded the finger of trees blocking their view of the harbor. He strained forward to take in the magnificent sight greeting them.

Joshua paused beside him, his panting breath revealing his excitement as well. Two stately naval brigs swooped back and forth like alert soldiers. They dipped and bowed to each other as their paths crossed. The one lone pirate ship left in harbor was a glowing red ball of flames against the eerie morning light beginning to break behind it. The hapless vessel whined and snapped as if in agony. Bits of unfurled, burning sails dripped into the water like firework sparks. Dirk's exhilaration died in his chest. The navy had unknowingly destroyed his only means to Erica.

They watched in silence as the sun peeped over the watery horizon. The new day brought no new hope. How would he get to Erica without a ship?

He loosened his grip on Angela's wrist. She remained quietly beside him. He glanced at her. She shivered with what he could only assume was uncertainty.

Finding no resistance to their attack, the naval ships dropped anchor. Several dinghies slipped over the sides of one.

He stepped forward with Angela in tow. Joshua's boots crunched in the gravel behind him. They headed toward the place where the first boatload of sailors would land.

The craft bobbed toward the shoreline and eased onto the beach. Dirk reached the waterline as the officer in the boat stepped over the side, signaling the sailors with him to disembark as well.

The naval men stood with feet braced wide apart, still unused to the motionless earth. Alert, they cocked their pistols and aimed them at the three.

The officer walked toward them and lifted his hat from his head in a kind of salute. "Captain Hawkyns?"

Taken aback that the man knew his name, Dirk answered, "Yes, I'm Captain Hawkyns."

"I'm glad to see you well and alive." A broad grin split the naval officer's face as he stuck out his right hand. "Captain Edward Lane at your service, sir."

He grasped the offered hand. This man would help him find Erica. Hope flared and expanded at the warmth radiating from the handshake.

The rigid sailors relaxed and lowered their pistols to their sides as Captain Lane barked orders to them. "Gentlemen, give the signal." Pistols were raised skyward and a single volley fired. In answer a pennant flag was hoisted to flap beneath the American

Stars and Stripes on the flagship.

What was the man doing? Dirk's patience wore thin. He needed to talk to the officer and explain the situation. He had to convince this man to go to Mexico and find Erica. He sighed. He needed so much more than the U.S. Navy could provide.

"Captain Hawkyns? I believe this is a sight you won't want to miss."

His head whipped up to take in the harbor. The *Sea Hawk* glided into the bay, dipping her elegant prow into the undulating water to join the naval ships.

Joy and excitement set his pulse racing. He turned to Joshua, who still wore confusion on his face. "It's the *Sea Hawk,* man. We'll be on our way to Mexico in no time."

Joshua's face broke into a wide smile. "And the *Anna McKyle* right behind her."

He snapped his head back around. The long, exquisite bow of the clipper followed behind his brig.

"I'll be damned," he shouted and turned to question Captain Lane. "How did you manage to get the two of them together?"

Captain Lane grinned. "It's quite a story. Rob Taylor of the *Anna McKyle* came to the naval base in Bethesda and convinced the admiral the situation down here needed attending to. I got the assignment. Knowing Treacher was based somewhere in these parts, we went to Key West to get information and a guide who knew these islands. That's where we ran into your man, Captain Hawkyns. Apparently he had brought the *Sea Hawk* to Key West to do the same thing. He said he would have sailed these waters until he found you."

Lane turned toward Joshua and stuck out his hand. "You, sir, must be Joshua Reynolds."

"Aye, that I am."

The captain's stare touched Angela. "And is this the notorious Captain Armstrong I've heard so much about? Somehow I pictured you a bit different."

Angela blushed and looked down, unable to meet the warm brown eyes of Captain Lane. "No," she answered softly, I'm afraid not. I'm. . . ."

"She's someone who helped us," Dirk broke in. "Without her we'd still be in the prisoners' pen."

Angela smiled gratefully. He squeezed her hand in friendship.

"Where is Captain Armstrong?"

Dirk's dark brows pressed together with a smoldering look. "I think Treacher took her off to Mexico."

A second and a third boat filled with sailors landed, cutting his answer short. Lane turned to his men and pointed them in different directions.

"Your men won't find too many of the pirates. Unfortunately most are out to sea. They'll find scared women and children and a handful of men at the most."

Captain Lane frowned. "I was afraid of that when we had so little resistance." He tapped his finger on his chin in thought. "Well, then, I guess we'll have to devise an ambush for the returning pirates, won't we?"

"I hope you don't mind, Captain Lane, but I want to go after Treacher personally. I have to debt to settle with the man."

"I believe I'll go with him on the *Anna McKyle*."

Joshua took a step toward Dirk as he spoke.

"I understand, gentlemen. I hope you understand I have no jurisdiction in Mexican waters, so I can't go with you. If you don't find them, be assured I'll get them once they return home.

"One word of advice," Lane offered as he turned to leave. "Mexico is in the midst of rebellion, and Americans aren't popular there right now. Please be cautious."

"Don't worry, Captain. There's only one thing I want in Mexico, and as soon as I have her, I don't plan on staying."

The three men shook hands, and Captain Lane started up the beach as sporadic gunshots filled the air.

Dirk turned to Joshua. The older man answered the unspoken question. "Don't worry," he said, "I'll be right behind you."

Dirk nodded and surveyed the two ships proudly riding the waves side by side. Just as he and Erica would as soon as he found her—if he found her.

Chapter Fourteen

Vera Cruz, Mexico
June 20, 1835

Erica leaned against the smooth brass railing of the *Freedom,* watching the tropical landscape before her grow larger as the pirate ship approached it. She couldn't be sure where they were landing, but if she'd estimated accurately, they should be somewhere along the southern coastline of Mexico.

The Spanish-looking city they neared had low adobe buildings with bright red roofs. The tall bell tower of a cathedral stood proudly above the town like a guardian angel in its silent regality.

Her fingers squeezed the cool metal beneath them as her gray eyes swept over the clean white sand of the beaches lying like a carelessly tossed ribbon between the water and the many shades of green crowding down to the edge of the sand. She hadn't realized green came in so many variations.

Her pulse pounded with the force of a drum. Why did Treacher bring her here? Now that they had arrived, what did he have planned for her?

The pirate hadn't come near her during the entire voyage, but she had felt his gaze piercing her back every time she came on deck. Awake in the darkness of the cabin at night, she'd feared he would invade her room, but he had left her to the horror of her imagination.

She spun, presenting her back to the scenery, and stretched her arms down the railing. She arched her stiff spine, and one hand came up to touch her temple, throbbing with a pain caused by anxiety, pulsating with the fear of what the future held for her, as well as for Dirk and Joshua, left behind on the pirate's island.

Her head dropped, and her lashes squeezed together to block out the pain behind her eyes, to block out the images of the last time she had seen Dirk with a look of disgust and hatred slashed across his features, to block out the resigned look of trust on Aunt Constance's face when she and Joshua had left Baltimore. She had failed in everything that meant anything to her.

By now Edmund Bennett's greedy fingers would be itching to take control of Armstrong Shipping. How had she managed to make such a mess of things? Wesley Treacher. He was the reason.

Her chin lifted with determination. She would not lie down like a dying dog and give up. Once the ship docked, she would be back on land. There was a better chance of escaping from the city than from a ship. Her brows furrowed in a deep frown, and her mouth curled down with a sneer. But first, Wesley Treacher would pay.

"Thinking of me again, my dear?"

Her stare riveted across the deck, locking with Treacher's one good eye. A battle of wills began, to see who would look away first. Even when her vision blurred with moisture, she refused to give in to the need to blink.

"Excuse me, Captain."

Treacher glanced away, giving the sailor standing before him his attention. His eyes darted back to Erica, and an evil smiled creased his face.

She swung around to stare out over the rail. *I'll ignore him. I'll just pretend he isn't here.* Closing her eyes, the gentle peals of the cathedral bell washed over her, a voice offering strength to her flagging spirit.

Fingers brushing her shoulder sent a chill through her. *Not Treacher. Please, not Treacher.* She whirled to confront the enemy.

Toby's gentle eyes asked for approval. "We got to go below now, Miss Erica. Wesley don't want nobody to see you."

"Wesley Treacher can go to hell!" She pushed off from the rail and followed the big man across the deck. Her time would come once on land. Of that she had no doubt.

Erica tossed the gaily wrapped package in the corner with the rest that had arrived day after day for the last three days. Her loyalty and obedience couldn't be bought with frills and frippery.

The room she occupied didn't look like a prison, with the pastel walls complementing the ruffles and lace on the bed and one lone window. She crossed to the window and pulled the curtain away, revealing the iron bars encasing it, making her a prisoner.

"Damn you, Treacher. What is your game, now?"
The curtain dropped back down.

"Señorita?"

She brought her head up with a snap at the sound of the voice.

The serving girl, Juanita, waddled across the room, her nut brown face hidden behind a vase of long-stemmed red roses. Their scent wafted on the air, and Erica inhaled deeply the familiar smell, so like home.

Home. Would she ever see Baltimore again? God, what she wouldn't give for a few moments with Aunt Constance or just a chance to curl in her own bed and sleep — forever — safely.

Juanita placed the vase on a small, scrolled wicker table near the window, the door behind the girl's figure gaping open with temptation. Should she try to dart out the opening? A guard reached in, firmly shutting the barrier before she had a chance to react.

The servant whirled and gave her a smile speaking of innocence and contentment. As an afterthought, she slipped her brown hand into a large pocket and pulled out a small linen envelope as white as her starched apron. Carefully she propped the paper against the base of the flowers, then turned back, the smile still splashed across her wide face.

Erica slanted her brows in a frown. Another bribe. Just another bribe.

"Please, *señorita*. At least look at the card. It is from the *señor*."

"The owner of the villa?"

The girl nodded her head eagerly.

She sighed. Who was this man who held her here?

278

And why? Not once had she caught a glimpse of the mysterious *Señor* Rodriguez de Valdivia. But then, neither had she seen Treacher. The only person she had contact with was Juanita, besides the guards outside her door, of whom she caught only an occasional glimpse.

She stuck her hand out in acceptance, and Juanita slipped the note into her outstretched palm.

Neatly penned across the front in a flowing script was her name, *Señorita* Armstrong. She ripped open the envelope with her finger, and a carefully folded sheet of paper fell into her hand. Written in the same flourishing handwriting was an invitation:

I would be honored by your presence this evening for dinner in the formal dining room. Please accept my humble invitation, as I look forward to meeting such a lovely houseguest.
                    Señor Rodriguez de Valdivia

"Houseguest," she mumbled under her breath. Should she accept or refuse to go? She tapped her finger against her lips. It would be a chance to meet her jailer face to face.

Her heart beat with wild excitement. If she could confront him, she could convince him to let her go free. She would tell him all the things Treacher had done to her before leaving her in his care.

If he was any kind of gentleman, and she prayed to God he would be, he would have no choice but to see her returned home safely.

Turning to the dainty writing table next to the bed, she lifted the pen to her lips, chewing the end as she decided on the exact words to use in a reply.

"Until this evening," she jotted down on the piece of paper. Placing her answer in an envelope, she spun and offered it to the maid.

"You are going, *señorita?*"

"Yes, Juanita, I'm going. Now, deliver my reply and return here as fast as you can. We have a lot to do before this evening."

Her entire life hinged on this one night, and she would give it her best.

Erica stared at the image eyeing her back from the mirror, a gray-eyed, tawny-haired woman, not Erica Armstrong. She tilted her head; so did the image. There was no way to deny that she looked at herself now as a mature woman of the world. Her spirits soared. She would get this Señor Valdivia's attention and hold it. Surely he could deny her nothing.

The black silk gown fit her form to perfection, as if the Spaniard had known exactly what she looked like before he had ever seen her. How had he known? It didn't matter. All that mattered was that she convince the man that honor demanded she be sent home. She would use her feminine wiles to their best advantage. She smiled to herself.

A soft knock at her door brought her head around as the key turned in the lock. Nothing further happened. Had she only imagined the sound?

She cleared her throat and piped out, "Come in."

Not sure what she expected, the soft-eyed, older gentleman who entered the doorway wasn't it. Was this the mysterious Valdivia?

"*Señor* Valdivia awaits you, *señorita*."

Of course, the man would send his servant to escort her down. She swallowed hard and stepped forward, her chin tilted up. The evening began. She desperately hoped she was ready.

The man stood back from the doorway respectfully as she walked through it. His immaculate, white-gloved hand pointed down the empty hallway. Where were the guards?

She lifted her gown just enough that she wouldn't step on it and preceded him down the dimly lit corridor. At the stairway spiraling down into the yawning blackness below, she paused.

The servant cleared his throat, indicating courteous impatience. She stepped out, her foot testing the first descent. Dropping one side of her skirts, she ran her fingers down the smooth, highly polished banister as she took the stairs in a slow rhythm.

Her heart fluttered in a spot between her collarbone and throat with a feeling akin to fear. *What's wrong with me?* she chided inwardly. *I feel like a child going down to face punishment. All I'm going to meet is a man. Just another man. He will see things my way. He will send me home.*

She had stopped her downward motion as she thought. Her escort touched her shoulder, and an ominous chill slithered down her spine. She gathered up her gown and her courage and continued down the spiral to the blackness coming up to meet her.

Once she reached the bottom her eyes adjusted to the darkness. She could faintly see the outline of a foyer she recognized from when she had first entered the house three days ago. Funny. The steps then hadn't seemed so steep and eerie, but it had been daylight. Things always appeared different at night.

The servant brushed in front of her. His white-gloved hand, illuminated in the faint light filtering into the foyer, reached out, turning the knob of the door to her left. With an ear-piercing squeal the barrier swung on its hinges to reveal an even blacker abyss.

Her courage caught in her throat; she couldn't swallow. What kind of man was this *Señor* Valdivia? What kind of man lived in darkness?

A match flared. Her heart jumped as the small flame hissed when it touched the three wicks of a heavy gold candelabra midway in the room. "Come in, *señorita*," a voice rasped softly.

She took one step forward. The door clicked loudly right behind her. She jumped and caught her breath with a gasp. The urge to spin around and pound her fists against the solid structure blocking her escape overpowered her. *No*, she thought, *I am here for a reason. I will leave this room a free woman, not a frightened child.*

"You are as lovely as I knew you would be." The masculine voice, touched with a slight, aristocratic Spanish lisp, filled the room.

"Thank you, *señor*," she answered boldly, feeling foolish talking to the dark, feeling foolish carrying on such a mundane conversation when so much was at stake.

Her eyes scanned the room, picking out images as her vision adjusted to the candlelight coming from the middle of a long, top-heavy dining table with a dozen thronelike chairs encircling it. Two places were set in delicate, white bone china, contrasting with the Spanish walnut wood of the furniture.

The chair at the far end of the table scraped against the floor. "Please, be seated, *Señorita* Armstrong." Her name sounded so foreign in the man's Spanish accent.

Her hand skimmed the back of the chair nearest to her. It was positioned in an invitation to sit. Settling into the seat, she slid the chair forward under the table.

The chair at the far side of the table groaned softly as her host lowered his weight into it. *Only a large man would make a chair groan so*, she thought.

The circle of candlelight unfairly encompassed her and illuminated only the place setting and edge of the table where the man sat. In frustration she leaned as far forward as she could, attempting to catch a glimpse of the mysterious *Señor* Valdivia. Faintly she could make out the slight outline of one shoulder.

Two large hands, perfectly manicured, fell from the darkness to rest in a relaxed fashion in the flickering candlelight between them. They were long and slender, with a ring of immeasurable value on each finger. If his hands were any indication, he was wealthy beyond her imagination, and she considered herself a good judge of material riches.

"I hope you like breast of dove." His voice caressed each word as if he tried to touch her across the expanse of table separating them.

"I'm sorry, *señor*, but I have never tasted it," she answered, her words sounding too loud in her ears. "However, I'm sure I can trust your good taste."

He chuckled low in his throat. "Your words please

me, just as you do, *querida mía.*"

Good, she thought. *I must make him care what happens to me.*

The pop of a cork leaving a wine bottle quelled the words sitting on the tip of her tongue. She closed her lips tightly and watched white-gloved hands pour a splash of wine into the tall, long-stemmed glass before Valdivia. One ringed hand raised the glass, and it disappeared from the circle of light. With a small gulp he tasted the liquid, and the glass reappeared to settle on the table.

"Perfect, Diego." The jeweled hand waved vaguely.

Diego approached her, bottle in hand. The light revealed the face of the man who had escorted her to the dining room. She smiled and thanked him as he filled her glass. Without comment he returned to the other end of the table to pour the golden liquid into his master's glass.

She raised the glass and took a tentative sip of the wine. It was smooth and sweet and left a glow as she swallowed. The warmth radiated from deep inside, renewing her courage. She took another sip and placed her glass back on the table. "*Señor* Valdivia, why am I here?" Her calm, confident voice pleased her.

The aristocratic fingers drummed lightly against the polished wood of the table, making a softly clicking noise, then abruptly stopped. "You were left in payment of an old debt, *querida mía.*"

The hairs on her arms and the back of her neck bristled with a mixture of foreboding and indignation. She was not a prize mare to be traded or sold. She forced her emotions to remain calm. She couldn't allow her temper to spoil the effect she created.

Valdivia's warm laughter filled the room. She glanced up, eyes still blazing. "I was told you were spirited. I like that in both my women and my horseflesh. I am pleased."

Dishes clattered to the right of her, stopping the retort threatening to spill from her lips. *His words don't matter. What matters is the final result. I will convince him to let me go.*

A hand placed a steaming bowl before her, and a few moments later, a similar one sat before Valdivia, little fingers of steam curling toward the darkness where he sat. She toyed with her spoon, dipping it in and out of the seafood bisque as she formulated the question she wanted to ask. Pointedly placing the utensil before the plate, she brought her hands up to rest her chin and mouth against her clasped fingers.

"*Señor* Valdivia?"

His spoon clinked to a rest on the table.

"How long do you plan on keeping me prisoner here?"

"You are not a prisoner, merely my honored guest."

"Where I come from, *señor*, guests aren't locked in their rooms," she replied slowly and deliberately.

"Is there something you need that I have not provided for you?"

The man was impossible! "Yes, *señor*," she answered, keeping her voice as calm and steady as she could. "My freedom!"

The ringed fingers beat a patient rhythm against the table. "I'm sorry, *querida mía*, you have as much freedom as any woman could desire or need."

"I'm not an animal to be placed in a cage." She seethed with frustration. "With a guard at my locked door." Was there no getting through to this man?

A condescending sigh floated across the darkness to grate against her ears, burning with humiliation.

"I will see to it you have access to the downstairs and the courtyard in the future."

"You don't understand. . . ."

"Do not push me, *señorita*. I will do nothing more."

She lowered her head and bit her lip to keep from telling him what a conceited bastard he was. *How could any man be so thickheaded? My approach is wrong. I'm not using the right words.*

Diego removed the bisque bowl and replaced it with a plate holding two small dove breasts smothered in a tomato sauce. All she could picture were two cooing mourning doves, so innocent and beautiful, at the mercy of Valdivia. Sacrifices to his ego, just as she would become if she didn't get through to him.

She couldn't bring herself to eat the food in front of her. She laid her fork beside the untouched food.

"Is something wrong, *señorita?*"

"I seem to have lost my appetite."

As if from nowhere Diego appeared to remove the plate. The servant stood quietly behind her chair. No, she didn't want to leave yet. She still had things to say to Valdivia.

"Thank you, *querida mía*, for joining me." His words were a dismissal.

"No, you must listen to me." She stood in her place

and pushed back her chair. With a mad dash she tried to skirt the table and cross the room to where Valdivia sat in darkness.

Diego's hand shot out and gripped her upper arm with more strength than she imagined he possessed. "Let go of me," she demanded, slapping at the offending hand.

"Remove her, Diego, and see she is made calm." Valdivia's voice held no more emotion than if she were a frightened animal.

"Damn you to hell, Valdivia. You can't treat me like this." The servant dragged her toward the door by the arm. Her fingers clutched everything she passed — a chair, the edge of the table — but nothing slowed him down. "I'm Erica Armstrong, an American citizen. You can't do this to me."

His chair scraped against the floor as he rose. Hoping he would step into the light, she held her eyes glued to the spot where he stood in the shadows. She clung to the edge of the sideboard as they passed it. The lace cloth covering the furniture came with her as Diego pulled her from the room. Plates and dishes smashed to the carpet and bumped across the floor as she pulled the scrap of lace with her.

"You are only a woman. I will continue to treat you as such." Valdivia's final words rang out from the all-encompassing dark as he blew out the flickering candles.

"No, damn you, no." Her screaming sobs echoed in the blackness all around her.

Erica's fists hit the hard oak of the door as it

slammed in her face. The click of the lock brought renewed strength to her pounding, and the door rattled on its hinges. Little fingers of pain shot through her wrists, intensifying each time her hands made contact with the barrier. Her head lowered to the door, and her attack stilled. Her pounding was useless. No one would hear, or if they did, no one would care.

She turned and placed her slumped shoulders against the rough wood and pressed her open palms hard against it. Resting her head on the door, she closed her eyes. What a fool she had been to lose control in the dining room. She should have eaten and played the game he wanted her to play. But how could any man be so obnoxious? Did he really expect her to be thankful for his little tidbits? Did he think she would lick his hand in gratitude? Or had he been baiting her, drawing the angry reaction from her on purpose?

She pushed away from the door and began pacing the floor. Where was Juanita? She should be here to help her get undressed. She tried to reach behind her back and undo the offending buttons holding the dress closed. Starting at the lowest point, she released a dozen of the little pearls. The gown gaped, exposing her back. Her fingers strained to reach the no-man's-land between her shoulder blades. She wiggled and twisted, but nothing she did helped. Giving up on the bottom approach, she reached over her head hoping to snag the remaining pearls. She managed one, then another, and finally a third, but the rest remained out of her grasp.

"Damn," she swore, bringing her hands back in

front of her.

She kicked off the black satin slippers. One slid under the bed, and the other flew across the room. Crossing her arms under her bosom, she tapped her shoeless toes against the polished floor.

One minute, five minutes, at least ten minutes passed. The girl wasn't coming.

"If he thinks I need a maid . . . Oh, I will get undressed by myself," she muttered.

She reached behind her back, grasping the black silk of the bodice in each hand. She gave the material a hard yank, and the remaining pearl buttons splattered to the floor with little pings. She ignored them. "It's a waste of his money, not mine."

The elegant, ruined gown fell in a heap around her ankles, and she stepped away to leave it where it landed. She stopped, listening to the silence around her. Had she heard a noise? She turned expectantly toward the door. It was about time Juanita got here. The door remained stationary.

She must have been mistaken. She whirled back to the dress and ground her heel into the material as if it were Valdivia's face, not his gift, she ruined. As a final insult, she kicked the black pile into a corner.

The corset she wore was another matter all together. She picked at the lacing in the rear, and after twenty minutes, she squeezed the undergarment down over her hips. Covered only by her thin, filmy chemise, she stopped, her breath caught in her throat. Someone watched her. She knew it. The feeling creeped down her spine, leaving chill bumps in its wake. She glanced in the darkened corners of the room. Stepping to the other side of the bed, she checked for a hidden intruder. Nothing. The only thing with eyes in the entire room was an ethereal picture of Madonna and child hanging over the bed. Running her fingers over the angelic face, she found nothing. The picture was solid.

She shook her shoulders to rid herself of the ridiculous feeling. How could anyone be watching her?

She approached the dresser and opened the drawer to retrieve one of the nightgowns she wore. They weren't there. Riffling through the other garments in the drawer, she came up empty-handed. She opened the drawer above the first one. The gowns weren't there either. She checked the one below; it was empty as well. In frustration she slammed the drawer back into its recess and stood from her bent position.

Someone has taken them. I know they were there last night. It doesn't make any sense. She touched her fingers to her temples. *Why would someone steal the gowns?*

What difference does it make? There's no law that says I have to sleep in a nightgown.

She removed the remaining garments and shivered in the night air, enjoying the feeling of freedom. Freedom. The need to be free engulfed her. Tomorrow she would demand another interview with the Spaniard. This time she would be prepared for him. She couldn't stand another day of captivity. Her sanity hinged on finding a way out of the clutches of the madman. And mad he must be.

The sensation that someone watched her swept over her again. She crossed her arms over her breasts and dived into the waiting bed, pulling the soft cotton sheet up to her chin as protection.

A candle burned brightly on the night table beside the bed. She sat up to blow the flickering light out. As her hand circled the flame, her fingers brushed against a chilled glass with sweat trickling down the sides. A glass of cool wine. Just what she needed to calm her shattered nerves. In two long gulps she downed the sweet liquid, anticipating the warm glow that would radiate from her stomach.

The flickering light became two. She blinked to clear her vision. The flames multiplied to four and then eight. Her tongue stuck to the roof of her dry mouth. Swallowing became a conscious effort. She pushed at the pulsating candles, and her flying hand struck the long-stemmed wine glass, which rocked precariously and then it crashed to its side. A dark stain spread across the doily on the table as tiny shards of glass reflected the candlelight in a multitude of sparks.

A light, airy feeling sent her head spinning. She fell back against the pillows, unable to remain sitting a moment longer.

A blackness seeped in around her, leaving her mind muddled and disoriented. Voices invaded her nightmarish visions. Voices that shouldn't be there. She struggled to open her eyes, but the lids were so heavy they refused to budge. A dream nipped at her consciousness, or was it a dream? Reality and illusion intermingled, leaving her confused. The mumble of voices and other noises in the bedroom were real. The shuffle of shoes. Quiet, steady breathing. But she couldn't pull herself out of the sleeping state to investigate.

The soft sheet covering her lifted and drifted down around her knees. She should reach out and pull the covers back up, but she couldn't remember why. Her leaden arms refused to obey the nudge her mind gave them.

A cool breeze caressed her perspiring body, leaving a tingle in its path. She ceased her mental battle to regain control. It didn't matter anymore.

An odor assaulted her senses. A smell somehow familiar. She inhaled deeply. What did the scent remind her of?

A finger traced a burning trail down the flesh between her breasts. Her breath caught in her lungs. Bewildered, she could only think of one man who had touched her in that fiery fashion.

"Dirk," she whispered, reaching out to grasp him. Again her hands would not obey her mind's command. No, her eyes were still closed; his face could only be a phantom of her imagination. Yet the wandering finger still sparked against her aching flesh. She groaned.

"She is beautiful," a faraway voice lisped. "She will be the one."

Chapter Fifteen

The dark, seedy tavern looked no different from the others Dirk had entered since reaching Mexico. Mexico. He had forgotten just how many miles of coast that one word meant. Erica could be here in Tampico or as far away as the Yucatán Peninsula: almost a thousand miles of coastline, and at least a half-dozen ports. It was like looking for one particular fish in the ocean, an impossible task. But he refused to admit the possibility that they might not be successful. He would search for her as long as he must. He would find her.

Even with his back to a solid wall, as now, he still felt ill at ease. Catching the eye of the sloe-eyed barmaid, he gave her a disarming grin, which she returned, flashing teeth so white her olive skin looked even darker.

Definitely pretty, he decided, *as lovely as one could find in this type of surroundings*. A few months ago he would have pursued the wench, but now he had no interest. She didn't hold a candle to his lovely, gray-eyed Mermaid.

The girl approached him, hips swaying with an invitation readable in any language.

"*Sí, señor.*" Her eyes caressed his body. "What do you want?"

He leaned back in the chair, one arm thrown over the back in a casual manner. "A little information."

She placed one hand on her hip and swished provocatively. "Why is it the handsome ones only want information?" She crossed her arms under her bosom, which threatened to spill from the neckline of her blouse. "It will cost you the price of a tequila. Maybe more, if the information you want is hard to come by."

He stacked a handful of coins on the table and pushed them toward the Spanish girl. "I'm looking for some friends. A tall man with flaming red hair and a patch over one eye and a woman with gray eyes and golden hair. She might be dressed as a man, in britches."

The woman studied him with lifted eyebrows. "I'm sorry, *señor*, no one like that has been in here." She scooped up the coins and slipped them in her bodice. "And for you," she whispered huskily, "I would remember."

Some primeval instinct warned him to duck as a steel blade swooshed just inches from his ear. He pushed the table before him like a barricade, knocking the girl down in the shuffle. Peering over the rim of the overturned table, he pulled back again and looked behind his head. A second glistening knife quivered in the wall directly behind him.

He took a quick survey around the room. The only

way in to the tavern was the only way out. The large, squat Mexican guarding the door with feet braced wide apart couldn't be dealt with lightly. Neither could the two knives he held, one in his fist, the other between his teeth.

He drew his pistol but hesitated to use it. All he needed was an international incident. He'd been in more trouble since he'd met Erica Armstrong than he ever thought he'd see in a lifetime. As soon as he found her he would marry her and lock her in the house for the rest of her life.

The gravelly voice of his opponent brought him back to the present problem. "Hey, *gringo*, why you messin' with my woman?"

"I only asked her some questions, *amigo*."

"What kind of questions? Maybe you ask me, and I will know the answers?" A twitter of laughter circled the room, and the squat Mexican acknowledged it with a grin.

"I'm looking for some friends. I thought the girl might have seen them."

"Elana sees nobody but me," the Mexican growled. He glanced at the rising girl. "Is it true, Elana, the *gringo* only asked questions?"

The barmaid shot Dirk a look, then faced the man. "*Sí*, Antonio. He only asked me a couple of questions about a red-haired man and a woman in britches." She grinned.

The big Mexican relaxed and slipped the knives into the folds of his clothes. "Go on, *gringo*, get out of here."

Dirk rose to his feet, his pistol still held tightly in his hand. He and the Mexican warily circled each other until he reached the door. Without turning he backed out the opening and into the street.

"Gringo," the man called, the girl's arm clutched in his grip. "Tell him, Elana." He pushed the barmaid forward. "He paid for information, now tell him what you know."

Dirk stood straight, his senses alerted.

"The man with red hair and a patch. Is he a friend of yours?"

He hesitated in answering. "No," he said slowly, "only the woman."

She nodded and rubbed her arm where Antonio had held it so tightly. "He could only be one man. *El Muerto Rojo.*"

His pulse pounded erratically. The Red Death. What was Treacher up to? "Do you know where I can find him?"

"Vera Cruz. All young girls know about him. Fathers threaten to turn disobedient daughters over to him. Once you enter *La Casa Sin Salida*, you don't come out. If your lady friend is there, don't expect to find her. At least, not alive."

Dirk's heart lurched. The House Without Exit. No. He would find Erica. He couldn't lose her now, not like this.

The bright sunlight pouring through the uncovered window contrasted with the way Erica felt. Throbbing pain shot through her temples every time she moved. Even the automatic blinking of her eyes created agony. She dug the heels of her palms into her eye sockets. The pressure gave her some relief, but the throbbing in her head caused nausea to build in her stomach.

Memories of what had transpired the night before engulfed her. Had someone been in the room with her, or had she only imagined it? She honestly didn't know. The events stood out sharply in her mind, yet they were surrounded with a filmy, dreamlike haze.

She shook her head to clear the cobwebs from her mind. Instantly sorry for her actions, a groan of anguish escaped her lips.

The door rattled, and she pulled the sheet wrapped around her nudity tightly against her. Her feet slipped from underneath her thighs where she curled on the floor. Ready or not, she would face the invader.

"Good morning, *señorita.*" Juanita's sunny voice reverberated through her head. She covered her ears to keep out further sounds, so loud and unbearable. How could the girl be so bubbly on such a terrible morning?

After such a disastrous evening. Where had the girl been last night? Keeping her eyes scrunched closed, she made words come out of her mouth. "Where were you last night when I got back from dinner?"

The silence reflected the girl's hesitation to answer. "I'm sorry, *señorita*, something I ate earlier upset my stomach. I was ill."

Erica popped one eye open to search the maid's face. Her guilt appeared to be sincere. "My night-gowns? Where are they?"

The Mexican girl turned away and whirled back with a stack of clothing between her outstretched hands. "Here they are. I took them yesterday to launder and stitch. I would have returned them last night before you got back. . . ." The girl hung her dark head. "I'm sorry."

She mulled over the girl's answer. If what she said was true, she would have no knowledge of anyone being in the room last night.

"Please, *señorita*." Juanita's eyes implored. "Don't punish me. It won't happen again."

She closed her throbbing eyes and nodded reassuringly at the maid.

"*Señorita?*"

She looked up to find Juanita standing in front of her with a glass filled with a rose-colored liquid. The girl offered her the drink. "I think you'll find this will make you feel better."

She hesitated. "Wine?"

"No, no. *Señor* Valdivia thought you looked unwell last night. I thought this potion, one passed down generations in my family, might make you feel better."

"No, thank you, Juanita."

The maid looked down, hurt on her face. "As you wish, but I made it special, just for you."

She suppressed a sigh. "All right. Give it here. Nothing could make me feel worse than I already do."

The drink tasted bitter, but cool and soothing. She dropped her head back. At least it no longer ached. In fact, her mind was clear and alert, as if the rusty gears of her brain had been greased.

Memories of the disastrous dinner flooded over her. How could she have lost control so easily? Her purpose to convince Valdivia to release her had been lost in her flare of temper and exasperation.

She must see him again. This time she would be ready.

"Juanita." She pushed up from the floor. "I need to see Valdivia again. Today—as soon as possible."

The servant's eyes widened with disbelief. "No, *señorita*, you can only see *Señor* Valdivia when he summons you."

"Then take him the message I would like to see him."

Fear clouded the girl's eyes. "Oh, no. I would never be allowed to see the *señor.*"

"If I write a note," she persisted, "you could give it to someone who would see him."

"No, *señorita*, that can't happen. You don't understand." Juanita backed away from her towering figure.

"Why, Juanita? Why is that so impossible?" She took a threatening step toward the frightened girl.

The maid stubbornly shook her head and refused to look at her.

"Then, by damn, I'll figure out some other way to get to him. I refuse to sit here day after day and be somebody's puppet. Nobody," she turned her back, "is going to continue to pull my strings. Maybe you can see that your precious *señor* gets that message."

She waved her hand in dismissal. Without a word Juanita slipped through the door, leaving Erica to her anger and plans.

Quickly she dressed and stalked the door with determination. Her fists, still raw from battering the door last night, contacted the wood. She beat a loud rhythm against the oak barrier, refusing to give up her assault for any reason short of the door opening.

"Damn you, Valdivia, hear me!" she demanded in tempo to her pounding.

The doorknob rattled and twisted against her hip pressed against the cool metal. She stepped back, her mouth dry with expectation. Smoothing the soft gray cotton of the day dress she wore, she waited, hands on hips.

The door swung wide, admitting the staunch, dignified figure of Diego. He eyed her distastefully before he closed the door behind him.

"*Señorita*, you must cease your loud tantrum."

She steamed at his choice of words and his haughty manner. "I'll stop as soon as I see Valdivia."

"No one sees the master without him requesting it." He gave her a look of pity.

"I don't give a damn about his decorum. I'll see him now at *my* request."

"*Señor* Valdivia's message to you is to cease this nonsense, immediately," he informed her as he turned his back to leave.

"So my efforts have attracted his attention." She chuckled hopefully. "I won't stop until I see him."

Diego ignored her and opened the door. Some insane impulse gave her an imaginary shove, and she darted past Diego and out the door. The unprepared guard grabbed at her shoulder as she passed him, but by some miracle her feet continued down the corridor.

She paused momentarily to get her bearings and grabbed her skirts, hiking them up to an unladylike height. Going as fast as her slippered feet could take her, she headed toward the stairway.

"Stop," came Diego's angry cry. It didn't faze her; she sped down the hall.

Reaching the steps, her breath coming in uneven gulps, she descended them at a run. Her foot slipped, throwing her off balance, and she slowed down enough to maintain her equilibrium.

Near the bottom her hopes soared. Should she look for Valdivia or head for the front door beckoning her from the foyer? Freedom, her heart cried.

Her flying feet twisted out from underneath her. She hit the bottom step with one hip and winced as pain shot through the connected leg.

Her skirts billowed up to entangle her arms and face as she crashed to the floor at the foot of the stairway, the breath knocked from her. Fighting to escape the suffocating material of her dress and petticoats, she crawled in the direction of the front door.

A booted foot pressed against her rump, fueling her desire to reach freedom. She renewed her efforts to get to the door. No matter how ridiculous she looked, she had to reach the door. She pushed on frantically, pulling herself across the floor.

The passage to freedom, only a few feet away, tantalized her to continue her struggle. The boot came down cruelly on her outstretched fingers. A scream ripped from her throat as she halted. She rolled to see whose foot tortured her hand, but her skirts blocked her vision. She was panting heavily, and moans of pain and frustration seeped from her parted lips.

Strong hands encircled her wrists, and the booted foot released her crushed fingers. Soft thuds echoed on the floor next to her ear as the wearer walked away from her.

"Valdivia!" she shrieked.

The soft click of an opening door came from behind her as her captors lifted her from the floor and placed her back on her feet. Her injured leg buckled, and a hand reached out to steady her.

She twisted and kicked at whoever held her from the rear. Her head swung around enough to catch a glimpse of a trailing hand covered with rings slide around the closing door.

The guard shoved her back up the stairs she had just descended. She clung to the banister until he grabbed her around the waist and tore her fingers away.

At the top of the stairs, he dragged her down the corridor and unceremoniously tossed her through the waiting door of her prison.

The ominous crash of the closing barrier shuddered through her. Rolling over to stare at the ceiling, she caught her breath. An eye glared back at her from the far corner of the wall next to the ceiling. She blinked to clear her vision. The eye was no longer there. But she had seen it; it was real. Someone watched her every move. There could no longer be any doubt.

The late sun bounced golden rays off the red tile roofs of the buildings sitting like helmeted soldiers behind a line of defense. With his spyglass Dirk studied the houses of Vera Cruz dotting the hillside, not sure what he looked for. *"La Casa Sin Salida."*

His mouth went dry as he whispered the name. How easy would it be to find the villa of Rodriguez de Valdivia? He didn't have time for a search of the city. Two days had already passed since he had left Tampico. Two precious days he couldn't spare. Erica's life might depend on how quickly he found her.

His gaze moved to the harbor where the *Freedom* rode the tide at anchor. Treacher was here. *El Muerte Rojo.* He clamped his jaws down hard. The bastard would suffer for any harm Erica came to.

"Now what?"

Dirk swung his head to study the older man standing next to him. Joshua Reynolds. The man was a pillar of dependability. He had watched the gray-haired man suffer with self-recrimination, feelings that Erica wouldn't be in danger now if he had insisted she stay home. *You're no more at fault than I am, my friend*, he thought. "I'm not sure," he answered Joshua's question.

"We'd better do something soon, Dirk. Her life may depend on . . ."

"I know. Even if we find the house and get her out, we'll never get by the *Freedom* without someone recognizing her. The pirates can't know we're here. That's why I insisted the *Anna McKyle* stay out of the harbor. We can't afford for anyone to recognize the clipper's distinctive lines."

"We could use that fact to our advantage. You forget I was on the *Freedom* as a crew member. Treacher thinks some of his men took her for themselves. There's a standing order to pursue and destroy the clipper if she's sighted."

"Use the clipper as a decoy to get the pirates out of

the harbor?"

"Aye." Joshua nodded solemnly.

"No, I won't put Erica's ship in jeopardy."

"Better her ship than her life. Do you have another plan?"

"No, but the *Anna McKyle* means too much to Erica."

"Aye, she means a lot. Listen, man. Technically I'm in charge of her now. It's my decision to make, not yours. With the clipper's speed, I can keep well ahead of the pirates. Just lead them a merry chase until you find Erica and get out of Vera Cruz."

Dirk considered Joshua's words. "No heroics? You'll stay well out of their gun range?"

Joshua nodded.

"All right." Dirk snapped the spyglass shut. "I'll take one man with me. As soon as I locate Valdivia's house I'll send the sailor back with a message." He stuck out his hand in farewell. "Have the *Sea Hawk* take you to the clipper, then send her back to wait for us. Good luck, Joshua. We'll see you in port, and hopefully, we won't be far behind you."

"Dirk," Joshua called as he turned to walk away. "Take care of her. She's the daughter I never had."

He knitted his brows. "She's more precious to me than life itself."

The darkness gathered around Erica, huddled on the sofa in the small sitting room off the bedroom. She would never enter that room again, no matter what.

If someone watched as she had been shoved back

into the room yesterday, when else had she been observed? Sleeping—bathing—dressing? Oh, God, how humiliating. Someone had spied on her during her most private moments. The only person it could be was Valdivia.

Valdivia. What kind of monster was he? She rubbed her bare arms, erasing the chill bumps puckering her skin. Why did he do this to her?

Snatches of images of the nocturnal intruder brought the rush of chills again. The hand had touched her possessively. Had that been Valdivia as well?

Why were the images so hazy? Had the maid been right? Had she been sick? Or had it been something else? It was more like she had been drugged. Yes, of course. She had heard of that happening to people. But how?

She hugged her arms across her chest as she relived the details of that evening. She had barely touched the food, in fact she had only picked at the meals she had been offered since she had arrived in Vera Cruz. But the wine, she had willingly drunk the wine. Of course, how could she be so stupid. Valdivia had drugged the wine.

Excitement from her conclusion tingled down her spine as a plan formulated in her mind. If he thought she had drunk the wine, if he thought she were drugged, maybe she could catch him by surprise. Freedom could be hers. But she must convince the watching eye she suspected nothing. She took a deep breath. That meant going back to the bedroom. But then, going in there could be no worse than the performance Treacher had forced her to give for

Dirk. If she had survived that, she could survive anything, including another act.

Her decision made, she rose from the sofa. The locked door of the bedroom squealed open. Juanita's familiar steps came into the room. She moved toward the bedroom, her slippered feet crushing the soft carpet beneath them.

Strategically placed lamps illuminated the bath the maid prepared in the middle of the room. She would have to wash and get ready for bed in full view of the peephole.

She took a deep breath as her eyes strained to glance up in that direction. No, she must act as if no one was there. Knowing full well Valdivia watched her every move, she slipped out of her dress. She presented her backside to the corner. She'd be damned if she'd strut before him. Observing Juanita from the corner of her eye, she watched the girl putter around the room unsuspiciously.

Once in the water she wanted to turn to the spot where the Spaniard's eye would be and give him the dirty hand sign she had seen used among the sailors on board the *Anna McKyle*. Instead she forced her eyes not to look in that direction, but bathed as quickly as she could.

Calmly she dressed in the most concealing nightgown in the dresser drawer, which wasn't modest by any means.

With relief she made her way to the sitting room to wait for the maid to bring her dinner. Her heart beat a furious tempo against her chest. Would she be able to feign being drugged? Her plan required courage and strength. She tried to remember what she had felt like that night she'd been drugged, but the images were hazy and partial.

The Mexican girl entered the sitting room with a dinner tray, interrupting her anxious musing. She took a deep breath and sat up straight. The evening began; she would be successful.

Smiling reassuringly at the girl, she took the outstretched tray and set it in the customary spot on the wicker table next to the sofa. She curled her legs underneath her and leaned forward to inspect the food.

Juanita remained, watching her. She frowned. She hadn't planned on the girl staying in the room. She swallowed hard. Was the maid suspicious? She glanced up, impatience on her face.

The girl cleared her throat at her hostile stare. "Is there anything else you want, *señorita?*" She shifted her weight from foot to foot.

Erica relaxed her features and gave the servant a brilliant smile. Tonight must be special. The girl was anxious that everything went as planned. "Oh, no, nothing. This looks delicious, and for once, I'm starving. I must be feeling better, thanks to your remedies."

Juanita gave a little curtsey and left the circle of light the lamps created in the dark room.

She waited until she heard the click of the outer bedroom door before she moved. Lifting the lids from the plates, she stirred the food with the fork beside them. Valdivia planned well. The rich, salty food guaranteed that if she ate it she would drink the wine without thinking.

She grabbed the offending glass and glanced

around the room, looking for a place to pour the contents. She apologized to the large rubber tree near the window as she dumped the liquid into the soil around the plant.

She inhaled deeply. She couldn't go back now. She must continue with the charade.

Leaning over the dinner tray, she grabbed the heavy silver fork from beside the plate and carefully wiped it clean. Then she pushed the piece of silverware into the wrist of her nightgown.

She entered the bedroom as if it were a stage. She blinked, glancing around the room with a look she hoped conveyed confusion. She swayed, took two steps, and fell across the bed face down.

Forcing her breathing to be slow and even, she waited in the silent room. What if she was wrong? What if no one came? The minutes passed so slowly her nerves frayed with apprehension.

The bedroom door squealed. Her heart leaped into her throat. The urge to jump up from the bed screaming became so strong that she pushed her weakening mouth as hard against the satin coverlet as she could.

The clickety-click of booted feet edged closer. The rhythm of the stride had a familiar ring. The fingers of her right hand underneath her stomach reassuringly touched the handle of the fork in her sleeve.

A cold hand traced her shoulder. She lay as still as she could, suppressing the shivers threatening to course through her body. Her ragged breathing sounded so loud in her ears she feared Valdivia would realize she was conscious.

Long fingers grasped the flesh of her arm tightly,

the metal rings on his fingers cutting into her skin. She clenched her eyes tight and relaxed as he flipped her over on her back.

The desire to peek a look at the mysterious face leaning above her overwhelmed her. Maybe if she glanced through slitted eyelids. No, she couldn't take the chance. He might notice.

The bed creaked as he lowered his body next to hers. The mattress sank with his weight, and she rolled to lie against his outstretched form. A familiar smell filled her nostrils. The same odor from the previous evening. A smell that made bile rise in her throat. A moan escaped her lips. She could feel his eyes watching her, waiting. Any minute now he would call her bluff.

"Good, good, *querida mía*. You know I am here." He laughed from deep in his throat.

Valdivia rolled to lie on top of her and placed wet kisses against her neck and upper chest. She couldn't stand his repulsive touch much longer.

Her fingers curled toward the weapon concealed in the sleeve of the nightgown as his hands began to unlace the ribbons holding the bodice of the gown together across her bosom. She waited, poised, the fork held firmly in her grip, until he began an earnest assault of her exposed breasts.

Her arm flew up in a wide arc, and she plunged the fork down into Valdivia's back. The force of the impact jarred her arm, and for a moment, she thought the fork wouldn't push its way through his bare skin. She continued her downward pressure. The fork sank deeply into his flesh as he screamed in pain. Warm, sticky blood coated her fingers still gripping the handle of the fork.

Taking advantage of his momentary weakness, she pushed at his offending weight still stretched across her body. Easily she shoved him away as he writhed in pain, one ringed hand reaching behind his back, clawing at the fork embedded there.

Without looking at the man, she took off for the door at a dead run. She didn't care what he looked like; she just wanted to escape. Gathering the laces of the front of her open nightgown as she ran, she clutched the two halves of the bodice tightly in her hand, the same hand that had stabbed Valdivia, coating the front of her gown with his blood.

She threw the door open. The writhing man on the bed came alive. "Damn you, Erica Armstrong," he shouted, his voice devoid of any Spanish accent. She didn't stop to think about that as she sprinted down the hallway in the darkness, trying to locate the stairway.

Flying through the darkness, her breath tumbled from her lungs as she impacted with a solid obstacle, hard as rock, yet warm, living flesh. The guards. She'd forgotten about the guards.

"No," she shrieked. "Let go of me."

"Miss Erica. I'm not going to hurt you."

She blinked in the darkness. She knew that voice and would remember it always. Toby. What was Toby doing here? Did Treacher wait for her downstairs?

"Please, let go of me, Toby," she insisted, but the slow man held her arm tightly.

Valdivia crashed from the bedroom into the hall. She screamed and clawed at Toby's fist wrapped around her arm as he dragged her down the hallway, back toward her enemy.

Valdivia swayed in the corridor, the lamp he held in his hand throwing eerie shadows on the walls around him. Coming to a halt, the Spaniard hunched against the wall and lifted the light even with his face.

She gasped in surprise. "It can't be," she whispered. "I should have known it was you all along."

Toby stopped at her words. His gentle face registered surprise as Treacher rocked back and forth in the semidarkness, the fork protruding from his back casting a giant shadow on the wall.

"Wesley, you all right?" The big man's fingers loosened their grip on her arm. She jerked from his hand and raced toward the stairs.

"Toby," Treacher groaned, "hold on to her. Don't let her get away."

The big man's arms flew out, capturing her flying hair.

"Please, Toby, you must let me go," she implored. Treacher took three steps closer, murder in his one good eye. "Toby, please," she begged. "He's going to kill me if you don't."

"Oh, no, Miss Erica," he reassured her. "Wesley always lets the women go after a while. He'll let you go, too."

Treacher stopped, pain glazing his eye, leaned against the nearest wall, and placed the lamp on the floor. "Bring her here to me, Toby."

Screams erupted from her throat as the big man pushed her forward to her death.

"That's right, Toby. I'll do with her exactly what I've done with the rest. She's no different than the others."

She twisted her head, trying to sink her teeth into Toby's big paw as she fought him with all her strength, but he anticipated her move and forced her arms high above her head. Then he thrust her toward the pirate like a hound offering retrieved game to its master.

Treacher's hands reached out like serpents, and his fingers coiled around her neck, his thumbs placed strategically at the pressure points pounding in her throat. She tried to scream, but no sound came out of her open mouth. She watched in horror the look of pure delight on his face as he squeezed the life out of her.

Her lungs pulled frantically at the nonexistent air. Flickers of light popped in front of her eyes. *I'm going to die*, she thought as her fingers clawed ineffectually at his.

Her chest screamed for air as she heaved, and her vision blurred. An animalistic growl of agony came from behind her. With a gasp her lungs billowed with vital air as the strangling pressure around her neck released. The room swayed, and she closed her eyes. Falling against the wall, she fought unconsciousness. Her hands flew to her throat, so raw and sore, her fingers tracing the bruises encircling it. She was alive. But why? Her head flew up as she gulped air, never getting enough to ease the pain in her chest.

"Toby?" Treacher choked hoarsely.

Toby's large hands wrapped viselike around his master's throat. "I won't let you kill her, Wesley," the big man cried as he squeezed tighter and tighter. "I can't let you hurt her that bad."

Treacher's fingers clawed at Toby's. His face turned

purple, and his uncovered eye protruded from the socket. The only sounds in the corridor were Toby's sobs and the gurgles emitting from Treacher's gaping mouth. The disbelief in the pirate's eye froze as his body relaxed and his tongue rolled out to fall limply to one side. His body dangled like a broken doll in Toby's still clutching hands.

A shudder ripped through Erica's body. Treacher was dead. Toby had killed him. *My God, that could have been me.* Her fingers curled around her throat in protection.

The roar of gunfire tore through the momentary silence. She opened her mouth to scream, but her tender throat refused to allow any sound to pass. Toby's eyes widened in childish disbelief as he crumpled, blood spurting from the gaping hole in his chest. As he slid to the floor, his frozen fingers took Treacher with him.

She turned her eyes away as bile rose in her throat, burning and bitter.

"Get out of here, *señorita.*" Diego's soft Spanish cracked like thunder. Her head jerked up in fear. He clutched the still-smoking gun in his hand.

She didn't hesitate. She raced down the dimly lit hallway to the stairs. Glancing down the spiral, she caught a glimpse of her bodice covered in blood. *My God, I've been shot.* She jerked open the material to discover the blood wasn't hers. Gripping the bodice together, she tore down the stairs. At the bottom she tied the loose ribbons as best her shaky fingers could to cover her nudity.

The front door loomed before her. She was free. Her slippered feet slapped the floor as she ran. As

313

her hand touched the knob her mind screamed, free to what? To roam the town of Vera Cruz without money or knowledge of the language? And worst of all, dressed in a sheer nightgown smeared with blood.

Where will I go? She stopped. *I have to think.* Her hand shot to her temple. The crash of furniture shattering against a wall echoed from above. Wild laughter followed close behind.

There was no turning back. She had to get out of this house. What she wouldn't give for a miracle now. What she wouldn't do to be able to open her eyes and find that the last few months of her life were only a dream. A nightmare she could erase from her memory.

Chapter Sixteen

The front door protested with a high-pitched whine as Erica tugged on it, almost as if the house didn't want to let her go, as if she had no right to leave its dark confines. She pulled against the door with all her might; the large oaken slab crashed against the wall, and she crossed over the threshold.

On the wide portico she stopped to get her bearings. The musical peal of cathedral bells washed over her. Of course, the bell tower, the one she had seen so many times from the window of her prison. If she could reach the cathedral, she would be safe. The Fathers would give her asylum until she could send word home. She was in need, and priests didn't turn away those in need, did they? All she had to do was figure out which way to go. Her chin dropped. All she had to do was get there before someone stopped and questioned her about the way she looked.

She raised her head. *One step at a time*, she thought. *I'll find the church if I take one step at a time.*

A stone walk led away from the house, cast in shadows with a few spots lit from the moonlight filtering through the leaves of the trees lining it. She stepped from the porch, her gown gathered in her hands. Gravel crunched. Footsteps approached her. She ducked behind a low line of hedges following the contour of the house. There she crouched, heart pounding in her throat, waiting to see who would appear from the side of the building.

An armed Mexican paced by, unconcerned. A guard. Her eyes darted around. How many more of them were there? He couldn't have heard the gunshot, or he wouldn't be so nonchalant.

She held her breath as he strolled past, whistling, inches from where she huddled. Not until his retreating footsteps had melted into silence for several minutes did she finally rise up to continue on her way. She must be careful. She couldn't be caught now. The guards would never believe Diego had let her go.

Easing from her hiding place behind the bushes, her sleeve caught on one of the spines covering the branches. She gave a tug to free it, but the hedge hooked its thorns in the gown, unwilling to release her. She gave the material a vicious yank. The sleeve tore, leaving a small swatch of lace still dangling in the twigs and adding to her disheveled appearance.

She glanced left, then right, and sprinted down the walkway. The path twisted and curved several times before coming to an end to meet with a road. Between her and freedom stood an obstacle she hadn't counted on.

The wrought-iron fence loomed at least three times

as high as her head, with sharp pointed spikes at the end of each bar fingering toward the starless sky. The twin gates arched as high as the fencing, with the spikes even closer together.

She ran to where the gates met and tried to pull them apart. They remained solidly unyielding. Like a caged animal, she followed the fence a few yards to the left, hoping to find a smaller gate or opening. Nothing. Grumbling, she reversed her direction, going back toward the front gates. The rhythmic thud of feet caught her attention. Another guard. Slipping into a deep shadow, she fell flat on the ground. Maybe she'd be lucky enough that the guard wouldn't see her.

She waited, listening hard, as a shadow flitted across the dark iron bars of the fence. The man patrolled on the outside of the barrier. It didn't make sense to have a guard there, but she didn't question anything Treacher's twisted mind would have conceived of.

The footsteps drifted past her and faded. She took a breath of much-needed air. She must get over the fence, now, before the guard returned.

She placed her foot in the iron bars and pulled herself up until she could slip her other foot one level higher. Halfway up the fence, the material of her nightgown entrapped her step, and she teetered, nearly falling back on the ground. If she fell the noise she made would undoubtedly give her away. She couldn't afford to go crashing to the ground. Hesitating only for a moment at the thought of exposing herself, she grabbed the billowing skirt and tied a bulky knot with it around her waist. What she wouldn't give to have on her shipboard britches. What she wouldn't do to be aboard the *Anna McKyle*, now, headed home.

She concentrated on each step higher. Keeping her eyes glued to the top of the fence, she was afraid to look down, knowing she would never continue her climb upward if she did. Heights had always scared her. Looking up was the only way to deal with climbing. She chastised herself. *Some sea captain I make, afraid to climb the rigging.*

With only a few feet to go, perspiration ran down her face as a combination of fear and exertion heated her pounding blood.

Her groping fingers stretched to clasp the top of the fence, and she wrapped her hand around one of the spearlike protrusions to steady herself. Her left foot curled around the crossbar. Placing her weight on it, she pushed up, and the thin slipper on her foot slid on the slimy moss coating spots of the iron bars. She hung there, shooting pain traveling up her straining arms from the shoulder sockets.

"Damn it," she muttered in sheer frustration. She had reached the top. She couldn't fall now. Swinging her feet like pendulums, one slipper dropped with a thump on the ground. She didn't follow its descent. It didn't matter. Her bare toes curved around the bar they sought so she could push her body up.

With a grunt she threw her leg over the fence, straddling the top bar between two pointed spears as if it were a horse. Her breathing came in short gasps as she clung to the top, trying to figure out how to get down the other side.

Look down. Her eyes refused to obey the command. *If I don't look at the ground, I won't know how far up I am. I have to determine that fact in order to decide how to get down there.* Clutching the spear before her tightly, she forced her head to tilt. She swayed with dizziness and gripped the bar until her fingers ached.

She caught her breath with a noisy intake. Had she come that far? It was too high to jump; she would probably break her legs. The ground lay in dark shadows. Who knew what she would land on if she tried.

Footsteps. The guard was coming back. She spied the top of his dark head as he walked toward the spot where she perched on the fence high above him.

He came closer. *Please don't look up*, she prayed. *What do I do? If he sees me I'm caught. But if I jump now and land on him, he'll break my fall, and, maybe, I'll knock him unconscious.*

She pushed her legs underneath her body and balanced like a tightrope walker to the top of the iron fence with her toes, her fingers still grasping the spear. The man stopped directly underneath her.

She must move now. She shoved away from the top of the fence. The fall took forever. Her bent knees struck the side of the man's head and one shoulder as they landed in a heap on the ground. A grunt of pain hissed near her ear. She hoped he would be dazed long enough for her to get away.

Rising to her feet, her untied skirt tangled around her legs. Down she went, striking the side of her head on the hard ground.

Strong fingers grabbed her flying ankles as she scrambled to get up. She landed in a sprawl on the ground. Little pieces of pebbles and twigs dug into her knees and elbows. A cool breeze caressed the back of her exposed legs and bare buttocks as she struggled to push down her gown riding up around her waist.

With a squeal, she pulled her captured leg, trying to kick the grasping fingers away.

"I'd know that sweet bottom anywhere." A familiar voice drowned out the sounds of her struggling.

"Dirk?" she breathed as she rolled over to throw her arms around the assailant, pushing him back down on the ground. "Is it really you?" She began to giggle. Tears of joy and relief blocked her throat, squelching the laughter and leaving broken sobs in its wake.

Dirk wrapped his warm arms around her shaking body as they sat awkwardly in the dirt. He rained soft kisses on her hair as he rocked her, cooing gently as if to an injured child. "It's all right, Erica. It's over. I'm here. I swear to God nothing else is going to happen to you."

She clung to him, unable to believe he was real. She glanced up to reconfirm what she had seen. Her fingers traced his lips and cheeks. Her crying softened to hiccups.

He dabbed at her wet eyes and nose with the sleeve of his shirt. He smiled and gave her a questioning look.

She sniffed aloud and wiped the back of her hand across her face.

"Good girl," he cooed as he patted her head gently. Easing her back while holding her shoulders between his hands, he eyed her with concern across his face.

"Are you injured somewhere?"

Her eyes followed his to the blood on her bodice. "No," she answered wearily, "the blood's not mine."

Thankful he didn't question her further, she rose obediently as he pulled her to her feet. Critically he eyed her from head to foot. "You aren't dressed for traveling, are you? Just how far did you think you would get in that?" he asked, indicating the torn, soiled nightgown.

She glanced down at her disheveled state. She gave him a crooked smile and a shrug of her shoulders. "I wasn't given much choice."

He slipped off his shirt and urged her to put it on over her gown. She remembered the last time he had offered his shirt to her, in the creek on Jamaica. Their relationship had come a long way since then. Shyly she looked up as she buttoned the front to read remembrance on his face.

"You sure are hell on my shirts, Mermaid."

Her eyes danced. "I just like to see you bare-chested."

"Come on," he growled, grabbing her by the hand. "I want to get out of here before anyone notices you're gone."

"No one will follow," she whispered. "Treacher and Toby are both dead. I . . . ." She choked on words that refused to be spoken.

He stopped and circled her shoulder. "Don't think about it now. I just thank God you're safe."

The quiet, dusty road they traveled circled down the side of the mountain at a steep incline. She followed, matching the pace he set. Sharp stones in the road battered the tender sole of her shoeless foot, and she slowed, limping slightly as she lagged behind.

He glanced back at her as she came to a halt. His dark eyes dipped down to take in the bare foot she had lifted from the ground to rest on top of her slippered one.

"Jesus Christ, Erica, I didn't realize you were barefoot."

She hung her head as if she were guilty of a crime. "I'm sorry," she choked, her nerves still raw and easily shattered.

He scooped her up in his arms. "Why didn't you say something sooner, silly girl?"

She didn't answer. Laying her aching head against his bare chest, she reveled in the familiar warmth and smell of him. She smiled in the darkness. She was glad now she'd lost her shoe. Being carried like this by him was wonderful. She rubbed her cheek against his furred chest. *Yes*, she decided. *This is definitely nice.*

She arched her neck so she could see his face. He walked with eyes staring straight ahead, not looking at her.

"Dirk," she asked with curiosity, remembering the last time she'd seen him, remembering the last words he'd spoken to her, "how did you find me?"

He glanced down, never breaking his stride, and gave her a piercing look.

"I mean," she continued, "the last time I saw you, you . . ." She looked away, placing her head back against his chest.

His shoulders lifted even with the weight of her body. "Erica, I was a fool."

322

"Oh, no, my darling. Just a man." Her fingers lightly covered his mouth, stopping the words he was going to say. "I know how it must have looked when you saw me with Treacher."

"Angela explained."

She buried her face in his neck, relieved she didn't have to elaborate.

"We followed the Mexican coastline looking for some sign of you." A strange look almost akin to horror passed over his face, but the look disappeared as quickly as it came. She didn't dwell on it.

"We found the *Freedom* anchored here in Vera Cruz. *El Muerto Rojo*. It's a name the people have given Treacher. The Red Death. Even little children know of him and dread the name. It wasn't hard to find *La Casa Sin Salida*."

She looked up expectantly, waiting for his interpretation of the Spanish. "The house . . . ?"

He cleared his throat as evidence of the debate raging inside him passed over his face. "The House Without Exit. You weren't the first woman he'd brought up here." He looked down to catch her reaction. "But you are the only one to have come out alive."

She gasped as realization washed over here. How lucky she'd been to escape with her life. But, most of all, how fortunate she was to have the love of a man like Dirk Hawkyns.

"My God, poor Angela," she whispered.

"She's aboard the *Sea Hawk* now, waiting for us."

"What will I tell her?"

"Perhaps the truth would be the best thing."

"And Joshua? Is he there, too?"

Dirk smiled down at her. "The old salt is on the *Anna McKyle* leading the pirate ship on a merry chase. We had to get the *Freedom* out of the harbor."

"The *Anna McKyle*, here?"

He chuckled. "She's been to Philadelphia and back." He glanced down. "Made your deadline in plenty of time. In fact, your man, Rob Taylor, brought the U.S. Navy back to find you."

"She made the delivery deadline?" Her heart pounded with excitement. That meant her letter of credit from the sale of her mother's plantation was safe. There might still be a chance to save Armstrong Shipping from Edmund Bennett. "Dirk," she asked breathlessly, "what is today?"

He stopped and stared down at her, puzzlement on his face. "Of all the questions I thought you might ask, the date wasn't even on the list."

"I'm serious. I have to know."

He shook his head and stepped forward. "June . . . twenty-fourth."

Six days. If we can get to Baltimore in six days, I can take care of Bennett. "How soon can the *Sea Hawk* get us home?"

"A week, more likely ten days, depending on the weather."

"No, we have to be back sooner."

"Erica, what's the rush? Trying to get rid of me as soon as you can?" Merriment danced in his eyes.

She studied him through lowered lashes. After she opened her mouth to tell him the entire story, her lips clamped back together, cutting off her words. *No, this is my problem.* As much as she loved him, she wasn't ready to turn her life over to him.

It was time she took control of her destiny again. She had to remember how important it was to remain strong and independent.

Dirk carried her over the gangplank and across the deck, stopping only once to give the orders to set sail. He crushed her to his chest as if he couldn't get close enough to her. She didn't resist. She could read the desire deepening his eyes into the dark, bottomless pools she knew so well. She allowed his feelings to wash over her. Wanting him as much as she knew he wanted her, she ached with an intensity she never thought could be possible.

He smiled with delight as her face softened with the need to be loved, his long strides taking them past knowing faces, his intentions clearly written across his strong features.

Rising sails snapping in the breeze and the groan of the anchor lifting so the *Sea Hawk* could leave the harbor faded as he carried her into a small but elegant cabin. His cabin.

The bed he lowered her on smelled clean and fresh, yet emitted an intoxicating scent uniquely his own. She took a deep breath, reveling in the feel of the soft bedding beneath her.

She smiled and touched her fingers to the space between his brows furrowed with lines. Deftly she smoothed them out, leaving tiny, unerasable creases. Then, tracing the worry lines around the corners of his eyes, a small frown bowed her mouth. She didn't remember them being there before. "Did I cause these lines of worry?"

He eased his weight over her, his hand reaching up to grasp her questioning fingers in his. He chuckled, and it sounded more like a growl. "Lady, I've done more worrying in the last month since I've met you than I ever planned on doing my entire lifetime."

"I'm sorry," she whispered. "I never meant to . . ."

His gently, seeking lips muffled the rest of what she tried to say. But somehow the words were no longer necessary. All that had meaning was the way his tongue lingered at the corner of her mouth, urging her to meet his bold thrusts with an equal amount of enthusiasm, the way his teeth grazed the soft mound of her bottom lip as he sucked it into his mouth only to move on down to the hill of her chin and claim the jetty of flesh and bone with passionate kisses. She savored the emotions and the tension rising from the very core of her; she shivered with anticipation.

As if from some secret recess of her mind, unbidden images of Treacher touching her crushed the rising desire. She stiffened with resistance as Dirk's hand traced a path down the column of her neck to rest on the button at her throat.

As if he understood what she remembered, his mouth moved up to her ear. "Please, my gentle Mermaid, make love to me. I need to know you're mine, and only mine."

Whether because of his request or his knowing touch, she relaxed and turned back to devour his lips with all the passion she possessed. When he pulled away, she opened her lashes to probe the fiery depths of desire his eyes had become.

Love guided their hands as each eagerly divested

the other of clothing. He lifted up and tried to scoop her underneath his body, which was eager to possess her.

Instead of following his lead, she giggled and scooted across the bed. He pursued her with his intense, ravenous eyes as if he sought just the right moment to pounce on her.

She rose to a kneeling position and placed her hands on her knees. Her breasts swayed provocatively as she laughed. She watched him stalk her, his eyes never leaving the tempting display her bare bosom made. She wiggled, knowing it made her uncovered flesh ripple, taunting him to throw caution to the wind.

"Damn you, Erica, come here," he demanded.

"Make up your mind, sir," she teased, again making her breasts quiver. "Do you wish to make love to me, or," she paused to slit her eyes seductively, "do you want *me* to make love to you?"

He lunged for her and missed as she scurried off the bed, squealing as she crossed the room.

Raising one eyebrow, a smirk lifted his mouth. He stretched out across the bed on his back, his hands placed behind his head in nonchalance. He lay there, unabashed, in his full glory. Her gaze traveled up and down the length of his firm, bronzed body. It was magnificent.

Their eyes locked for a short moment. Then, to her surprise, he lowered his lashes and stifled a deep, exaggerated yawn. Nestling down on the mattress as if to get comfortable, he crossed his ankles and sighed.

From across the room, she couldn't decide how to

handle the turn of events. She giggled nervously. Was he sleeping? She took a step closer to the bed. His chest rose and fell in a slow, steady rhythm. Two more steps. Still he didn't move.

"Dirk?" she whispered.

His arm snaked out and grabbed her around the waist, pulling her down on top of his waiting body. His eyes filled with laughter as he held her tight against his chest, their bodies touching intimately from head to toes. "You want to make love to me?"

She stared wide-eyed in hesitation, then nodded her head.

The arm crushing her to him relaxed as he drew spiraling circles in the small of her back. She placed little kisses and nibbles on his neck and ear; then, lowering her body, she traced the curves and dents of his heaving chest with her lips, marveling at the way her tongue entwined in the soft hair she found there. Enjoying the power she held over him, she grew bolder as her mouth inched lower, dipping into his navel. He quivered, and a groan bubbled from his throat as she worked her wiles, tasting all of him.

Placing his hands under her arms, he guided her back up to face him. He rolled, positioning her underneath him, and buried his manhood deep inside of her, worshipping her rising hips with powerful thrusts of his own.

Eyes opened wide, she watched in fascination as sweat from his body coated hers. His ragged breathing filled her ears as he whispered, "You're the only one who can make me lose control."

His words sent her crashing over the edge as the sweet pain of fulfillment washed over her. His cry of consummation followed closely on the echo of hers. Turning, he took her with him as they lay side by side, savoring the afterglow of love.

Bending his face, he placed a soft, loving kiss between her closed eyes, another between her pliant breasts. "Oh, Erica, how empty my life would be without you. I love you more than you could know."

Erica padded across the cabin and knelt before the sea chest pushed at an awkward angle against the wall. Her sea chest. Dirk must have had it brought aboard from the *Anna McKyle*. Alone in the room, she ignored her nudity and eagerly lifted the lid. Digging down through layers of clothes, she located what she sought. The letter of credit. She hugged it to her bosom as if it were a living thing and giggled. *Thank you, God, it's here.*

A soft knock pattered on the door. Hurriedly she stuffed the papers back into their hiding place and grabbed a pair of britches and a shirt.

"Just a minute," she called as she slipped into the pants and pushed her arms into the shirt. Still buttoning it, she stepped over to the door and opened it a crack to see who stood on the other side.

"Can I come in?" A soft, feminine voice broke the silence.

"Angela? Of course."

The sad-eyed blonde stepped into the funnel of light the lantern on the desk created. Her arms were wrapped protectively around her shoulders. "Thought you might like some female company."

"How did you know I was awake?"

329

"I'm just in the next cabin. I could hear you shuffling around in here."

Erica blushed deeply. If the woman could hear her walking, what else had she heard? She turned away to hide the embarrassment flushing her face.

Angela shifted from foot to foot behind her. "I need to know about Wesley. Dirk thought I should talk to you."

She whirled back around. *How selfish of me. Here I worried about who thought what about me while my friend suffers with real pain.*

She could understand love, though perhaps not blind love like what Angela felt for her pirate husband. But love made one do things quite out of character. She knew about that. Honest sorrow welled inside of her for Angela's loss. Lowering herself on the edge of the bed, she patted the spot next to her. How could she explain Treacher's death? Dirk had recommended truthfulness. She glanced down at her hands. "I'm sorry, Angela."

The woman studied her face. "He's dead, isn't he?" She sat stiffly, her throat and jaws working.

Erica slipped her arm around the quaking shoulders. Angela's tears came swiftly and heavy. She laid the blonde head against her shoulder and let her soak the front of her shirt with the storm of uncontrolled weeping. She rocked and patted the woman, letting her emotions run the full gamut. "There was nothing anyone could do for him. He wasn't the man you married. His mind had become so twisted with pain . . . I'm sorry."

Sorry for what? she thought. *Not because Treacher died. The man deserved his horrible end.* She rocked

330

the weeping woman in her arms. She was sorry her friend had to suffer so. Angela was just another of Treacher's victims, nothing more.

Angela sniffed aloud as she lifted her head from Erica's shoulder. "Tell me. How did he die?"

What do I say? The gruesome scene flashed across her eyelids, lowered to hide the conflict raging behind them. No matter what Dirk thought, she couldn't tell her the truth. It would hurt Angela too much.

"It was an accident. One of the servants shot him by mistake," she lied, watching the play of emotions flutter across her friend's face.

Angela looked away as she whispered, "And me? Did he mention me?"

What harm would there be in alleviating the woman's misery? "His last words were about you, Angela. He died asking for you."

Angela's face brightened. "I knew he would realize, someday, he still loved me."

Erica turned away so Angela wouldn't see the stark pity residing in her eyes. Stilling her emotions, she glanced back. "Have you thought about what you want to do now?"

The blonde smiled wistfully. "I figured I'd go home—to Cambridge—where my parents are. Dirk said it would be no problem to drop me off there."

"Are you sure? You're welcome to come home with me."

Angela eyed her curiously. "Erica, I know you come from a world I know nothing about. I wouldn't know how to behave among your rich friends." She patted her hand resting lightly on the bed. "Thank you, Erica . . . for everything. But mostly for being a

331

friend, even when the situation didn't warrant it."
Angela looked away in embarrassment. "I'm sorry
for the grief my husband brought you. I would
change it all if I could."

"I know that, but you don't owe me anything. You
aren't responsible for what Treacher did,"

A heavy hand pounded on the door, breaking the
mood in the cabin. She disengaged her arm from
around Angela to answer the insistent knock.

"Yes?" she asked the unfamiliar face.

"Miss Armstrong? Captain Hawkyns thinks you
should come on deck. There's something you ought
to see."

"Is something wrong?"

The sailor shrugged. "Captain just said to get
you."

Running feet slapped the deck over her head.
Something was wrong. She could tell. Hurriedly she
glanced back at Angela, who rose to follow. She
pushed the messenger out of the way, her bare feet
racing down the companionway.

An unearthly glow greeted Erica as she drew level
with the deck. Dirk stood at the railing, barking
orders as the sails were lowered, and the *Sea Hawk*
groaned in protest to drift toward the glowing flames.

She pushed her way through the seamen and rigging, unmindful of her uncovered feet, to stand
beside Dirk. The ocean was a mass of flames doubled by the reflection in the water. She shrieked in
disbelief.

The graceful lines of the *Anna McKyle* were outlined in fire, as if someone had covered her with a thousand candles for a Christmas display. The sails were illuminated as bits of burning canvas showered the deck, which burned brightly as well. The clipper's proud bow was buried deep in the side of the *Freedom*. The flames reaching out with flashing fingers to engulf the pirate ship.

she swayed, her breath coming in short gasps. A warm hand touched her arm, and she shrugged it away. Again the finger curled around her arm, and she turned to face their owner. "What happened?"

"I'm not sure." Concern filled Dirk's eyes.

"Where are Joshua and Rob?" she choked over the loud crackling of the fire.

"Erica, we're looking for them. I've got several boats already launched searching for survivors. I was just getting ready to join them."

"I want to go with you."

"Erica, don't be ridiculous."

"They're my men and my ship. Don't try to stop me." She scrambled over the side and down the rope ladder cutting into her bare feet to the dinghy waiting below. She settled on the seat as he descended to join her. Burning debris floated around them. The mainmast on the clipper cracked and groaned then fell with a crash onto the glowing deck.

"Joshua," she screamed until her throat was raw, hoping beyond reason for an answer.

The oarsman pulled the boat out into the water. A weak cry of pain came from the left of the boat. She pointed out the bobbing head and weakly lifting hand to Dirk. The head disappeared as they neared it. She stood to dive into the water.

"Damn it, Erica. Sit down. You'll only manage to drown yourself." He dove over the edge and headed toward the spot where they had seen the survivor.

She scanned the glowing water as Dirk jackknifed under the surface. A minute passed. Then another. "Dirk," she called. His head hit the surface a few feet from the boat, and he dragged something behind him.

"Give me the oars," she ordered the sailor. The man hesitated, not sure what to do. "Damn it, I can row this boat. Help Dirk get that man aboard."

The seaman pushed the oars toward her outstretched hands and bent to lift the still body from his captain's hands. The man coughed and sputtered as she bent over his body; she saw the face as the body slumped on the bottom of the boat. One of hers, but not Joshua or Rob.

Dirk clung to the side of the boat. "I think I saw someone else. I'm going after him."

"Be careful." Her hand grazed his. He smiled and twisted away, heading toward the burning ships, his wet hair glistening with the flames reflecting in it.

The man at her feet groaned softly. She pushed the oars back at the rower as she knelt beside the prone figure. "Where are Mr. Reynolds and Mr. Taylor?"

The man coughed. "Don't rightly know, Cap'n. They were both at the helm the last time I seen 'em."

She glanced at the burning, empty deck of the clipper. The helm box burned brightly, ghostly. She followed the line of the railing until her eyes reached the bow. The proud figurehead, the image of her mother, snapped and cracked as the flames licked at the golden hair.

334

Please, God, she prayed. *Let Joshua and Rob be alive.*

"Erica," Dirk's voice sounded across the water. "Over here. Hurry."

She caught a glimpse of his waving arm.

Without instruction, the seaman rowed the boat in the direction of Dirk's voice. His head bobbed toward them. She stood, ready to dive in the water to help.

"Please sit down, miss," the rower urged as he shoved the oars back at her. He rose and dove into the water to join Dirk struggling with a figure.

She rowed the boat until a hand clasped the edge. Setting the oars, she reached over the side to help hold the survivor up as Dirk pulled himself into the boat, followed by the seaman. The wet, still figure bumped over the side without protest. She knelt to push the burnt, blonde locks from Rob Taylor's ashen face.

"Rob," she whispered. His eyelids fluttered and relaxed.

"I didn't see anyone else. I think we'd better get him aboard the *Sea Hawk* as quickly as we can," Dirk offered softly.

She sank to sit on the bottom of the boat, Rob's head resting in her lap. Her fingers pushed at his matted hair. "He and Joshua were together." She looked up at Dirk. "Didn't you see any sign of Joshua."

Silently he shook his head. "There was no one left alive in the water. I searched until . . ."

The *Freedom* exploded with an earth-shattering roar drowning out Dirk's words. The two ships twisted as if in mortal combat, each trying to drag the other one down.

The pirate ship listed to one side, and the charred remains of the clipper ripped in half.

"Oh, Joshua," she faltered, "where are you?"

The only answer she received was a loud sucking sound as the ocean dragged the twisted remains of the *Freedom* and the *Anna McKyle* into its briny depths.

Chapter Seventeen

The scene greeting them on the deck of the *Sea Hawk* came straight from the bowels of hell. All around her lay prostrate bodies, most of whom moaned in pain or screamed in agony.

Erica's gaze ran over the survivors, her mind trying to take in the gravity of the situation. *My crew, my ship, my God, Joshua.*

She turned her eyes away. So much of her life was wrapped around the *Anna McKyle*. It represented the love between her mother and father, something she would never experience again. The ship stood for her break from social standards, her need to go against the dictates of society. But most of all, the clipper was a symbol of her personal freedom to be an individual.

She turned back as Dirk and the sailor lifted the figure of Rob Taylor over the side of the brig. She cleared a path for them. They laid him beside another sailor who groaned and threw his head back and forth. She glanced in concern at the man. Then stopped, her eyes hardening. She didn't recognize him. He wasn't one of hers, but one of the pirates. Her heart blackened. If this man lived and Joshua died . . . How could God be so unfair?

"Erica," Angela called her name, bringing her ugly thoughts to a halt. "How can I help?"

She rose to face the woman. "Rob. Please take care of Rob." She pointed to the still figure of her Second Officer. "I have to check the survivors. I've got to find Joshua."

Angela knelt before Rob, lifted her skirt to tear strips from the hem. "Go on, he'll be all right. I've seen men in worse condition live."

Erica stepped across the bodies littering the deck, searching each face, seeking a sign of Joshua. She found Dirk hunched over one body, his hands pumping at the unresisting chest. Her eyes followed his action. Woosh. Woosh. What was he doing? The man was surely dead. She continued to watch fascinated as his unbroken rhythm pushed air in and out of lungs. The man gasped and coughed, water pouring from his mouth. Dirk had saved him and brought him back to life. She had never seen such a thing.

"Captain Hawkyns," a voice called from the other end of the deck.

He rose as helping hands flipped the wheezing man on his stomach. One of the men began slapping the convulsing back.

"Over here," called the voice again.

She matched his long strides as he followed the beckoning hand. "Have you seen Joshua?" she asked.

Dirk pivoted and grasped her shoulders in his

hands, squeezing her until pain shot down her arms. "Damn it, Erica, either help those alive here on deck or go below."

"No, you don't understand. I have to find Joshua."

"If he's here, we'll get to him. If not . . . there's nothing we can do for him now."

"Captain Hawkyns, hurry," called the insistent voice.

She covered her ears, not wanting to hear the words Dirk spoke. "No, he's here. I have to find him."

He pushed her aside and crossed over to where the crewman stood pointing down.

Erica stumbled over a body, looking. "He's here. He's got to be here. Please, God, let him be here."

"Erica, over here," Dirk called. "It's Joshua."

She lifted her seeking eyes and blinked. Had she heard him right? She tore across the deck, falling to her knees beside the still form. So pale and . . . "No, he can't be dead," she groaned.

Dirk straddled Joshua's body, pumping against his chest.

"Breathe, Joshua, breathe," she mouthed in rhythm to Dirk's movement.

"He just stopped breathing, Captain. Just before I called you," the sailor informed them.

"Save him, Dirk. Please save him."

His arms pumped up and down, over and over. "Erica, tilt his head back. Each time I release, blow your breath in his mouth."

She hesitated. How could that help?

"Do it, damn it. I've seen it work."

339

She caught his rhythm, bent over, and placed her mouth against Joshua's cold lips. She blew gently as Dirk's hands came up.

"No. Harder. Now."

She obeyed. Each time he said, "Now," she emptied her lungs into Joshua.

"Please, Joshua," she whispered between gulps of air.

Joshua's chest rose with a wheeze. Dirk's hands halted, and one reached over to squeeze her shoulder. Again his ribs lifted and expanded on their own.

Stretching across Joshua, she placed her head against Dirk's shoulder. "We did it. He'll live, won't he?"

"I think so." Together they rolled Joshua's body over. He jerked with spasms as he gagged with the force of the water coming from his lungs. Twice Dirk slapped his back with the heel of his hand, and water gushed from his open mouth.

Silent tears of joy and relief trickled down her cheeks.

"Come on, Erica." Dirk lifted her as he stood. "I want to check the rest of the men. Most are cold and tired, but there are a few with burns and another with a bullet wound."

She scanned the huddled forms around her. *My God, is this all that's left of my crew?*

"Erica. Kitten."

She knelt beside Joshua.

"I'm sorry. I couldn't let the pirate ship turn around and head back to the harbor. I got too close. I took the only path open to me. I had to stop her

340

from going back to Vera Cruz. I had to. . . ."

"Ssh, Joshua. I understand. Just rest. I'm thankful you are all right."

"Aye, I couldn't go without seeing my Constance, now could I?"

She shivered in the cool sea air and wondered how much colder the survivors felt. She tucked the blanket up around his chin. "We're going home, Joshua. We're going home."

Joshua's blue eyes shone with gratitude as his leaden lids eased down in exhaustion.

"Erica," Dirk's understanding voice called softly behind her.

She twisted to stare up at his comforting figure. "Thank you," she mouthed to him.

"We're moving the injured below." He raised his hand, and at a flick of his finger, two crewmen picked up Joshua's body and laid him on a makeshift canvas stretcher.

Reluctantly she released the older man's cold fingers as he was carried toward the companionway stairs. Dirk gathered up her empty hands and drew them to his chest. "Don't worry, sweetheart. He'll be his old self in a matter of days."

She nodded and laid her aching head against his inviting chest. How warm he was, warm and secure.

"My God, woman, you're freezing." He pushed her back at arm's length and probed her eyes, which conveyed no emotions.

She swayed, and her knees would no longer support her. Gladly she pressed against the shelter of Dirk's sturdy body. The drying dampness of his shirt sent a tiny shiver through her, but the comfort of his heartbeat right next to her ear dominated everything she felt or heard. As if from far away he spoke, the resonance of his voice humming up through his breastbone. She strained to catch his words. They must be important, but no matter how hard she tried, they remained an unfathomable muffle.

Her feet left the ground, and she struggled in momentary panic until his warm breath caressed her temple and the soothing timbre of his voice penetrated her confused brain. *I am safe, always safe, as long as Dirk is here.* She surrendered to the security of his arms.

Gently Dirk placed her cold, numb body on the bed still mussed from their earlier lovemaking. How small and vulnerable she looked to him as she lay there so unmoving and pale, so unlike his Erica. He pushed back the golden wisps of hair netting her forehead like fine filigree, the coolness of her skin frightening him.

"Erica?" he whispered, willing her eyes to open.

Her albescent lids fluttered but remained drawn down over her soul's windows, and she sighed so plaintively that his heart twisted savagely in his chest.

His hand traveled down to the hollow below her cheek, seeking signs of warmth, but finding only tepid flesh, coated with a clammy sheen.

Recognizing the symptoms of shock, he took quick action. He stripped the clothing from her body, noting the perspiration beading her sweet curves and hollows. Damn, how could he have been so stupid not to recognize earlier that all was not right with her? She had been through so much in the last few hours: escape from Vera Cruz and a close call with death; then watching her ship blaze a fiery path into the depths of hell, taking many of her crew; and finally, suffering the near loss of the man who was like a father to her. She had remained so strong through it all, until the end when she had looked for Joshua, fearing she wouldn't find the older man. He had been so demanding of her, expecting her to hide her fears and emotions, and she had obeyed. He could still visualize her bending over Joshua, blowing her life's breath into cold blue lips.

He ripped his clothes from his torso and tossed them aside. If anything happened to her, it was his fault, and he would never forgive himself. Pulling the pillows from beneath her head, he stuffed them under her feet to elevate them, praying the blood would rush back to her colorless face. He joined her on the bed, gathering her up in his arms, and pulled the covers up over them. Holding her as close as he could, he willed her to absorb his warmth and vitality.

"Please, sweetheart, I can't lose you now." Briskly rubbing his roughened palms over her arms and chest to stimulate her circulation, he pressed his mouth to her cool cheeks and chin to warm them.

Without warning his veins began to sing, the blood rushing to his lower extremities and creating a hardness between his thighs he had not intended.

"Damn it," he mumbled, unable to resist the urge

343

to cup her exquisite breasts, which, to his surprise, responded, the nipple puckering like a button against his palm.

As if burned because of his shameful actions at a time like this, he jerked his fingers away. Before his fist could gain any distance, her hand lifted shakily and encircled his wrist to place his hand back on her breast.

"Why did you stop?" She whispered huskily.

"Erica?" he answered incredulously. "I thought you were . . ."

"I know what you thought," she breathed dreamily, "but how could I remain unfeeling when you were so obviously stirred?" Her other hand skimmed down his thigh to capture his rigid flesh.

"You little minx," he growled. "You scared me out of my wits."

He rolled to trap her body, now stirringly warm, beneath his weight. Taking her earlobe in his teeth, he pressed down none too gently on the tender pendant of flesh.

She squeaked in protest and reached up to push his face away. "What was that for?"

"That, Erica, was punishment for making me think you were so ill." His tongue soothed the reddened skin.

She giggled and returned the nip on his shoulder.

"Damn it, woman, you're asking for it."

She circled her arms around his neck and pulled his face down to meet hers. "Yes, I am. I'm asking that you make love to me. Make me feel complete, Dirk. Let me know I'll survive the agony twisting my heart. So many men lost so needlessly. Will I ever stop feeling responsible for what happened to my ship today?"

His thumbs brushed the hair away from the sides of her face and traced a line from her temples to her chin. "I would gladly shoulder your pain if I could, but life doesn't work that way. But in time, I promise, it will dull." He traced the curve of her lips and willed them to smile back. "What happened to the *Anna McKyle* is no more your responsibility than it was mine or Joshua's. I could have stopped him, but I didn't. I know what you're feeling. Losing a ship is like watching a friend die. I'm truly sorry, Erica. I would change places with you if I could."

His mouth pressed against the downward curve of hers, and he touched her lips with his tongue. Her mouth opened under his gentle urgings and allowed him access to the warmth of her orifice. He probed tentatively until her tongue curled around his, creating an exciting swordplay that stirred his ardor.

Love was such a confusing emotion. The more time he spent with Erica, the more passionately he wanted her. She was like an addiction; he was never sated. The rush of desire pounded in his pulse as she pressed her pelvis against his, begging him to hurry. As his hand skimmed down her narrow waist, he counted the gentle ridges of her ribs beneath his fingers. Her gasp of delight sent a surge of roaring blood through his body, and it took all of his willpower to keep from plunging into her inviting depths. He wanted more from their lovemaking, more than just the sating of their bodies. Their union must create a bond between them, one that would chain her heart and spirit to him in an inescapable way.

His fingers encased her round bottom, stilling the movement of her hips with a control to which she yielded. Her surrender accentuated his need to dominate her further. His mouth lifted from hers and seared a path across her face to her ear. Swirling his tongue in the pearly shell, he felt her shiver each time he blew gently. She moaned, an earthy, almost animal sound, and he savored the power he held over her, the ability to make her writhe beneath him in lusty anticipation.

The game they engaged in was a familiar one to him. He had played it many times with many women, but never before he'd met the lovely siren stirring in his arms did he care whether he won or lost. Now it was the challenge of maintaining his control that drove him forward. She could plead and beg all she wanted, but not until he had pushed himself to the limit of his endurance would he take her. Only then would both their fulfillments be total and complete, and her culmination was uppermost in his mind.

"All in time, sweet Mermaid," he crooned. "Just be patient."

He tasted the familiar trail leading to her breasts and sucked one and then the other into his mouth as if they housed a life-giving fount in their round softness. Never before had he felt the need to worship the woman he held in his arms, until now, and worship her he did, with his mouth and fingers and eyes.

One hand led the procession, exploring every nook and cranny she offered up to him; then his tongue followed, caressing every inch of her skin that rippled with gooseflesh against his cheek as he moved lower. His other hand followed his mouth, tracing patterns in the moistness his tongue left behind.

"Oh, Dirk, why do you torment me so?" she gasped in tortured delight.

He moaned in response, never once letting up his ransacking of her senses. His hand reached the triangle between her thighs, and without resistance, her knees drifted apart to allow him access. He stroked her womanhood until her breathless panting left no doubt in his mind she was at the pinnacle of release. Then his fingers stilled.

Crying out in frustration, she tangled her hands in his hair. "Oh, God, no," she pleaded.

A triumphant rush of mental satisfaction surged through him. She was his, totally his—heart, body, and soul. With a deep rumble of exultant laughter, his mouth replaced his hand, and pulling her to him as he clutched her curved buttocks, he brought her to a crashing climax. Her cries of satisfaction triggered an inevitable necessity to seek his own peak of pleasure, and he lifted her hips to meet his where he knelt between her thighs.

Greeting his thrusts with equal force, she took him inside her as if she couldn't get enough of him. Her blissful systole dominated all of his senses. With a mind-exploding rush, he cried out his zenith of ultimate pleasure that only she, his Erica, could bring him to.

Her fingers toyed with the knotted muscles of his shoulders as she guided him to rest across her stomach and chest. As if he were dearer to her than life, she stroked the wet tendril of hair splashed across his dark brow, whispering words of delight into his ear only inches from her mouth.

"Thank you, darling, for giving me so much of yourself."

In response he kissed her breast, rising and falling beneath his mouth. *One day, I'll make up for all your losses,* he vowed, as his sooty lashes drifted down over his eyes.

"Salted fish in a barrel. That's what we're like," Erica announced with a sigh.

Angela laughed. "I know what you mean. You can't turn around on this ship without stepping on someone else's toes."

"It's only been three days. By the time we reach Baltimore, I'll be ready to murder for a little privacy."

A warm arm slipped possessively around her shoulder. She leaned back against Dirk's familiar chest.

"Am I interrupting something?" His words rang out confidently.

Warm sun feathered her cheeks. She glanced around the deck as sailors, both his and hers, vied for a spot to soak up the sun. She smiled up at his dancing eyes. "No, just complaining."

"I thought as much."

She dropped her chin, and his intense gaze bore

into the top of her head.

"I think I'll go check on Rob," Angela said. "He gets so bored sitting in that bed all day." The blonde darted away before they had a chance to comment.

His hand toyed with her unbound golden hair, lifting strands and curling them around his finger.

From across the deck she could feel eyes watching them. She glanced around, and her gaze locked with Joshua's. A queer look crossed his face before he whirled away. Had it been disapproval she had read? She had seen that same look another time, when they had met in the companionway as she had left Dirk's cabin.

And then there were the knowing looks of the seamen when they thought she wasn't looking. Last night at the dinner table, one young officer had referred to her as "the captain's lady-love" just as she had entered the room.

Her hand reached up to remove the hair from around Dirk's finger. She shrugged away from him. Maybe she should move out of his cabin and in with Angela. It was wrong to stay with him. It was wrong to let him make love to her.

"Erica, what's bothering you?"

"Nothing. Please, I just need to be alone." She whirled and tore down the companionway steps to escape the knowing looks she would see if she glanced up.

The door opened with a squeak of hinges. She sat up on the bed. At last, he came to confront her. She didn't look in his direction. It was Dirk's cabin; he didn't need her permission to come in.

Erica crossed her ankles and folded her hands primly in her lap. She raised her head enough to see him, but not enough to stare boldly. He studied her from the darkened doorway. Self-consciously she stared at her hands to avoid looking at him. How could she tell him her decision to move out of his cabin had nothing to do with how she felt about him?

He shifted his weight, and his boots shuffled on the floor. Her confidence ebbed lower and lower the longer he scrutinized her, stripped her with his eyes glistening with spots of fire from the light of the lantern hanging by the door.

She crossed her arms over her breasts even though her shirt was buttoned modestly to a point at the base of her throat.

Silently he traversed the room, his eyes forcing hers to lock with his. So intense was his look it sucked the breath from her body.

"Feel better now, sweetheart? Figured you were tired. I left you alone so you could rest. I was tempted a dozen times to join you." He grinned knowingly. His fingers reached out and toyed with the top button of her shirt. She lowered her eyes, observing his finger manipulate the button from the loop holding it in place. Standing, she slipped from his grasp. Abruptly he pulled his hand back and placed it behind his back as if to control it. "I came to get you for dinner. You hungry?"

"Couldn't we just have something light here in the

cabin?" She didn't want to face a room full of snickering people.

He raised one eyebrow in question. "As captain, it's only proper I preside at my own table."

"Please."

"Erica, if I didn't know better, I would think you were unwilling to face your friends and my officers. Has someone offended you?"

She looked away and shrugged her shoulders. "It's just . . ."

Dirk's hands forced her around to face him. "You have nothing to be ashamed of."

She glanced down, confused by his words. He made her feelings seem so foolish. No, she wasn't wrong.

"Look at me," he demanded, and she obeyed. "Are you ashamed of us?"

"Dirk, you don't understand." Her hands lifted in a helpless gesture. "They all know what we've done."

"And what is that?"

"We've made . . . love out of wedlock."

"Are you sorry you love me, Mermaid?" He cupped his hand under her upraised chin.

"No, never," she answered so quickly there could be no doubt of her sincerity.

"Then the expression of our love isn't wrong. It's only natural. No one on this ship looks down at you, Erica. Believe me, they don't think anything at all about it, except to feel envy at what we have. You're my woman," he said matter-of-factly, "And that's all they need to understand."

Something clicked inside her mind. He didn't

mean anything offensive by calling her "his woman," she knew, but she didn't like the sound of the words. "I love you, Dirk," she said low and meaningfully, "but I'm nobody's woman except my own."

His hand dropped to his side. "Don't quibble words with me, Erica. You know what I mean."

"No, Dirk, tell me. I'm not sure what you meant when you called me 'your woman.'"

He snorted in exasperation. "I meant that I love you." Then he circled his arm around her. "And as soon as we reach home, I plan on marrying you."

"Are you asking me or telling me?" Her words carried a low threat.

He threw his arm back down to his side. "What in the hell do you want from me? If you expect me to get down on bended knee and plead with you to marry me, Erica, don't hold your breath."

"Look," she offered, trying to calm them both down. "I just feel you shouldn't assume things about us."

"I've not assumed anything," he protested.

"Damn it, you constantly make assumptions." She threw up her hands at his unreasonableness. "Everybody on this ship knows you plan to marry me, don't they? Did you just assume I did, too?"

He turned his back to her, his body stiff and unyielding. "Are you saying you don't want to marry me?"

Her hand reached out and touched his rigid shoulder. "I'm not saying anything one way or the other. Nobody's asked me," she answered softly.

He spun to face her, her hand sliding around to his shirt front. "I'm asking you now."

What had she done? She had pushed him into a proposal unintentionally. Marriage? Is that what she wanted? She didn't know. She swallowed hard. It would mean giving up so much. Giving up everything she had found important in her life, independence and the right to be what and who she wanted to be. "Please, Dirk," she offered lamely, "we hardly know each other."

His piercing gaze burned clear to her soul. "What in the hell is that supposed to mean?"

"Give us some time before you press me." Was that so unreasonable? All together they had spent a grand total of a week together. "Ask me again when we reach Baltimore."

He pushed away her hand resting feather-soft on his chest. "You, lady, can go straight to hell." Roughly he shoved her grasping hand from him. His long strides reached the door in two steps.

"Please, Dirk," she beseeched. "Don't leave like this."

His head whipped around, and he gave her a look that would have wilted a weaker woman. "What do you expect me to do? I won't follow behind you like a puppy waiting for you to throw me tidbits. All I know is that I've followed you halfway across the western hemisphere, and you can't make up your fickle mind whether you want me or not."

"I never asked you to follow me."

"You're right, Erica. You didn't. If I'd had any sense at all, I would have left Jamaica, gone back to Philadelphia, and forgotten I ever knew you." His hand grabbed the door, and he slammed it in her face before she could reply.

Placing her empty hands flat against the unyielding wood of the door, she pressed her cheek hard against it as well. *Why can't he understand how I feel? I'm not wrong. I have a right to make my own decisions.*

Dirk gripped the wheel of the *Sea Hawk* as if it were his worst enemy. He wished it were Erica's neck. He would enjoy watching her squirm a little right now as he applied pressure around that long, slender column.

He forced his hand to relax the powerful pressure. How had things turned out so disastrous? He had enough experience with women not to have totally muddled his first proposal of marriage. Even a ten-year-old boy could have done a better job.

But then, only she could have twisted what he said to make it sound like he tried to tell her what to do.

The lady had a lesson to learn. He smiled to himself. This time there would be no way for her to run off unless she planned to swim. She needed to learn how to deal with men — at least, *this* man. He would lower that proud little nose of hers a notch or two.

"Captain," a young officer offered, tipping his hat as he passed by, the same man who had asked after his bride-to-be at the dinner table a few moments ago. The same man he had told in no uncertain terms to mind his own business.

He acknowledged the officer with a curt nod of his

head.

He had barely managed to get through the meal with everyone eyeing him with curiosity. This ship was like a thin-shelled egg, everybody tripping over each other. Half the ship had probably heard their argument. Even Joshua had glared at him questioningly.

Gall rose in his throat when he thought about the way she had pressed him to propose, and then had had the nerve to say she wasn't sure. He hadn't followed her clear across the Gulf of Mexico to be dangled on a string. He wanted her. He wanted her now. As his wife.

What was she so afraid of? Every time they got close, she pulled back, that cool, aloof look on her face. She had accused him of being presumptuous. Was it wrong to think she cared as much for him as he did for her?

Maybe she was right. Maybe he pushed her too fast. Women liked to be wooed and petted. *If that's what she wants, then, by damn, I'll woo her stockings off. But first, I'll give her a few days to think about it.*

"Erica, are you sure this is what you want?"

"Angela, it's the only way. You don't mind, do you?" Erica hesitated in the door of Angela's cabin, two seamen standing beside her, her sea chest between them.

"No, of course not." The woman stepped away from the door to allow them to enter.

The only sounds in the room were the grunts and groans of the sailors dragging her trunk across the floor.

The door closed softly behind the two men as they left. Angela cleared her throat. The two women stared at each other. Erica turned and sat on one of the chairs at the small table.

"Does Dirk know you've moved out?"

Erica frowned. He assumed things so well, surely he could figure out she wouldn't stay in that cabin with him after he had suggested she go to hell. "He'll know soon enough."

She glanced up at her friend to see confusion and discomfort written across her features.

Angela scurried across the room to the door. "I think I'll check on Rob. I usually read to him about this time after dinner."

She smiled, the corners of her mouth barely lifting. The door closed with a click, leaving her to her disturbing thoughts.

She glanced around the empty room. What was she doing here? What did she want? Her fingers kneaded her temples. Why couldn't he give her time to decide? From the moment she had seen Dirk across that ballroom floor in Jamaica, he had pursued her relentlessly, trying to take control of her life. No, she had to admit honestly, trying to save her from her own self-destruction.

Booted feet echoed down the companionway outside the door. Her heart raced. He had come to apologize. She laughed. Dirk Hawkyns apologize? Never.

The feet stopped outside the door. It had to be Dirk. She held her breath tightly in her lungs. Would he come in or go on by? He must have discovered the fact that she had moved out by now.

A knock rapped confidently on the door. She stood, unable to make up her mind now that the decision was hers.

"Come in," she croaked hoarsely.

Relief flooded over her when Joshua's familiar face edged around the door. "Want some company, kitten?"

Kitten. She smiled. She liked him calling her that, better than Captain. She extended her head in a gesture of invitation. The tall man ducked into the room, closing the door softly behind him.

"Missed you at dinner tonight," he offered. "So did everyone else—including Dirk."

"I doubt that very seriously, Joshua."

He crossed his arms over his chest and gave her a knowing look. "Fighting?"

She looked away, refusing to answer the question.

"I didn't think the two of you could find something to argue about so soon."

"He's thickheaded, arrogant and . . . Oh." She threw her hands up in exasperation.

"I won't argue the point with you." He studied her face, which was rigid with anger. "Right now I would say his opinion of you isn't much better."

"Damn him, Joshua. He had the nerve to come in here and *tell* me we were going to get married."

He looked at her blankly.

"Don't you see. He didn't bother to ask; he just

357

assumed."

He shook his head and shrugged his shoulders. "You women are all the same. You expect everything to be couched in flowery words, all wrapped up in tissue paper, with a big bow on top."

"That's not true, Joshua. I just believe I should be consulted on such a major decision regarding my life."

"Erica, think about what you're saying. Do you think he would sweep you up and carry you off to a justice of the peace without consulting you first?"

She paced the room, thinking about what he said. She stopped and hung her head. "No," she whispered softly. "Oh, Joshua, I've been such a fool."

He swung her to face his large chest, so like her father's. In fact, he even smelled warm and paternal to her. His large hand reached up to pat her head in a consolatory gesture. "Lord, child, what did you say to him?"

"We don't know each other that well. I asked him to wait until we reached Baltimore to press me for an answer."

"He didn't like that, did he?" he finished the thought for her as he stroked her hair.

She shook her head, her face still muffled against his shirt.

"Words of advice, kitten. A man like Dirk Hawkyns won't wait forever. You're willing to share pleasure with him, but not commitment."

She raised her head to protest.

"I know what I've seen," he said, placing his finger over her open mouth. "Don't try to deny it. You're a woman now. His woman, and only his. It's just a man's nature to take over and protect. He does it because he loves you."

"Please, Joshua. Talk to him and try to explain how I feel."

His hand encircled her chin. She thought he would agree to help her, but his eyes hardened, and he shook his head. "Like I said, you're a grown woman, Erica. It's time you handle your love affairs like one."

He released her and stepped back. How she wanted to remain in the circle of his arms. Instead, she lowered her head, unable to accept the pity lingering in his eyes.

The door closed, and she glanced up to find she was alone. *This is up to me. I have to make things right between us. I know I'm strong enough to do that.*

Chapter Eighteen

Erica felt so silly as Angela clucked and cooed over her like a mother hen. She wore the same pale lavender gown she had worn the night she and Dirk had met at Vanessa Metcalfe's ball in Jamaica. She hoped it would stir memories in his mind when he saw her.

She was out to seduce him, she freely admitted to herself. She hoped her plans would be successful.

For two days he had not once approached her, but left her to her own misery. She had made it a point to go up on deck whenever he was there. Answering her questions with polite but distant words, he had treated her as if she were a stranger. His perfect gentleman's attitude drove her wild. Nothing she did broke through the barrier of propriety he placed between them.

The entire ship had helped with her plan. Dinner tonight would be a joint effort on all of their parts to get the lovers back together. She had no idea that they all cared so much. Dirk had been right. No one thought badly of her because she loved him or because she expressed her love in a perfectly natural way.

She smiled. Tonight Dirk would arrive as usual at his table, but she would be the only person to join him. She hoped he wouldn't get up and leave when he discovered what she had planned for him. She hoped—and she swallowed hard—that she had the courage to go through with her plans.

The ship's bells chimed the hour of the officers' dinner. She quickly gathered her shawl and her bravery to face the evening.

Angela stepped back and grinned. "Perfect. He won't be able to resist you." She gave Erica the little push she needed to take the first step out of the door.

"Good luck," Angela giggled. "I promise to make an effort not to listen through the walls tonight."

"I hope to God there's something for you to listen to," she chuckled nervously. "You'll remember to see to it my trunk is put back in his cabin?"

"Of course. It's all arranged. Now, go on. Everything will go fine."

She rolled her eyes. "I hope you're right."

The narrowness of the companionway was something she hadn't counted on. She found it hard to maneuver in the ballgown, and finally turned sideways to inch like a crab toward the galley and the small room off to the side serving as the officers' mess.

She couldn't get over how differently things were done aboard the *Sea Hawk*. On the *Anna McKyle* the line of distinction between common sailor and officer had been ignored when it came to meals. She sighed. As usual, she was the one who did things against the book. Maybe that was why he still had a ship, and she didn't.

She crossed the galley, several pairs of curious eyes inspecting her as she headed toward the small, private dining room where she would find Dirk.

"Good luck, Miss Armstrong."

She looked up and smiled.

"Hope you sleep well," called another voice.

She blushed.

The sailor grunted as someone poked him in the ribs. "Well, I didn't mean nothin' by it," he grumbled.

The door to the dining room was closed, as usual. She hesitated before it, almost losing her courage to continue. *No, I must do this*. She stiffened her resolve and her spine and firmly grasped the knob in her hand. The door opened easily, and she stepped over the threshold, head down, not daring to glance at the head of the table where Dirk would be sitting.

His chair scraped back, and he rose to formally welcome her to his table. "Miss Armstrong."

Both hands clasped the doorknob, her back to her future. *Damn him, for being so correct.*

Squaring her shoulders, she turned, putting on the sweetest smile she could muster. Dirk stared at her with his mouth gaping open, wide enough for a herd of wild horses to plunge through.

"Captain Hawkyns." She dipped him a curtsey her mother would have been proud of.

He clamped his mouth shut and gave her an

awkward bow from the waist in reply. Gliding across the room as if she had wings, she waited at her designated chair at the far end of the table.

The amazement on his face melted into realization that she waited for him to properly pull out her chair before she sat. He moved away from the table and nearly stumbled over the chair next to him as he came around to assist her in being seated.

"Why thank you, Captain." She flashed him a seductive smile and flipped open the fan in her hand as she sat. As she watched him round the table to resume his own seat, her lips, hidden behind the fluttering fan, curved in a smile.

Recovering, he sat back down and gave her a dashing smile that almost took her breath away. "You look lovely tonight, Miss Armstrong."

The fan stilled and fell to her lap. She forced the smile to stay plastered on her face as she dipped her head in answer to his compliment. *Damn him, for being so cool.*

Awkward moments passed as they waited for the others. Knowing they would never show, she forced herself to keep an innocent look on her face.

Impatiently he began drumming his fingers on the solid oak table. She waved her fan gently, nervously. He cleared his throat to say something, changed his mind, then stared at her in a most ungentlemanly fashion. Her knees shook under the table.

"Perhaps they didn't hear the bell," she offered.

"Perhaps," he answered, setting his templed fingers in front of his face.

She squirmed in her chair. "Or perhaps no one else

363

is hungry."

"Possibly," he said, sitting forward in his chair. "But it seems rather odd that they all lost their appetites at the same time."

"Nonetheless," she said, ignoring the smirk on his face, "don't you think we should proceed with the meal?"

"By all means. I'm sure you've planned this well."

His hand lifted and rang the summons bell. The cabin boy entered, his arms laden down with a tray.

Without a word, the boy set a large candle in the middle of the table, and lighting it, he approached the two sconces on the wall and carefully smothered out the flames burning brightly beneath the glass.

In the semidarkness he served the meal: Erica first, giving her a conspiratory smile, and finally, Dirk. He eyed the boy with a dark look.

The cabin boy lifted the lid from the plate before him, and Dirk's black eyes shot her a look of amazement. "Oysters?" he asked, nearly choking on the word.

Patiently she waited for the lad to leave the room before she answered. She peered at him and said as seriously as she could, "I understand they're an aphrodisiac. I thought they might make for a pleasant evening."

"It's a good thing no one else showed up. It could have been a real fiasco."

She blushed at his crass suggestion. Stabbing one of the baked delicacies with her fork, she slipped it into her mouth. Through lowered lashes she watched him place one of the cooked shellfish in his mouth, his eyebrows rising in delight. "Be damned. Smithy never cooked anything this delicious for me before."

"If that's so, sir," she countered, "it seems to me you're in need of a wife to handle your servants for you."

He stopped chewing to stare at her. "Perhaps. Do you know anyone who might like the position?"

"I might have a few prospects, if the benefits are good."

With ill-timed accuracy the door swung open. The cabin boy entered with a dusty bottle of wine and two unmatched glasses.

"Sorry," the boy mumbled under his breath as he passed her. "We did the best we could."

Dirk set down his fork and burst out with laughter. "Is the whole damn ship involved in your scheme?"

"Why, sir," she answered innocently, "I have no idea what you're talking about."

The boy scampered from the room when Dirk rose from the table and stalked her where she remained frozen in her chair.

She dropped her fork, which clattered to the floor, and she examined his face, afraid to move, almost afraid to breathe.

Pulling her chair across the floor, he scooped her up before she had a chance to say a word. "Candlelight and oysters," he growled. "I'm surprised you didn't have a violinist."

She wound her arms around his neck. "I would have if I could have found someone on board who played one."

"You never cease to amaze me," he mumbled in

her soft hair.

"Just think how boring your life would be, if I was predictable."

"Boring or normal?" he queried, grinning down at her. His soft lips descended on hers, and she kissed him back with all the fervor she possessed.

He pushed open the door to the galley with his foot and crossed the room in purposeful strides. A round of cheers filled the crowded room, but he didn't stop. She waved gaily over his shoulder to all those who had helped her win back her man and had shown her how foolish her immature fears had been.

How right it felt being back in Dirk's cabin. Erica glanced to the far corner; her sea chest sat in its makeshift place, crowding Dirk's against the wall. She smiled to herself, satisfied that her plans had gone well—in fact, better than she had dared to hope. She was where she belonged, in the arms of the man who meant the world to her.

The door closed behind his back, shutting out the universe existing beyond it. The yards of petticoats and skirts flowed around them, and he held her in such a way that her bosom pressed high against the décolletage of the dress like alabaster half-moons.

"Damn you, sweetheart, first you feed me potent food, then display yourself so enticingly I couldn't possibly resist." He swung her slippered feet to the floor and whirled her so she faced away. "And if that isn't bad enough"—his fingers tugged at the row of tiny pearl buttons holding the gown together along

366

her spine—"you encase yourself in clothing that could drive a sane man to murder. There must be at least a hundred of these to contend with before I reach my just reward. I'm sorely tempted to throw your skirts above your head and take you against the wall."

She giggled and twisted away from his eager fingers, leaving one of the buttons in question in his grasp. "Dirk, so impatient. Aren't you the one who usually tells me to show a little self-control?"

Pressing his shoulders against the wall he had only seconds before threatened to use, he crossed his arms over his chest and eyed her up and down. "Then soothe the savage breast, my winsome Mermaid. Make waiting worth my while." He arched one of his dark brows at her.

Entertain him? The thought was most titillating. She would give him a show he'd never forget. The lovely dress she wore became unimportant. The gown had served its purpose and served it well. She reached behind her back, gathering the silken material of the bodice in her hands, and jerked, the precious pearls snapping like the castanets of a Spanish dancer she had once seen long ago.

His eyebrows lifted higher in amusement, then dipped back in place, accenting the hungry gleam filling his eyes as she slowly lowered the satin from her shoulders.

The gown fell in a shimmering lavender pool around her ankles and knees. She stood before him like a newly risen phoenix, her breasts spilling forth from the lace-trimmed whiteness of her chemise. The stays encompassing her waist fit snugly under her soft swells, pushing them up and out as she drew slow, expanding breaths of air.

"I think I like you best in womanly frippery," Dirk declared as his gaze burned where it fell on her bosom.

"Are you sure?" she asked, taking the small cap sleeves of the garment and pushing them off her shoulders. Reaching behind her back, she untied the latticed ribbon of her corset, proud that her slim waist barely expanded as she eased the bindings out of their eyelets. At that moment she saw herself through Dirk's eyes. She was a woman of grace and beauty, and until now it had never been important to her how others perceived her. His adoration sent a thrill coursing through her.

The stays fell away from her body, and she inhaled deeply. Her nipples peeked like shy children through the lace of her undergarment. She chuckled huskily as the front of his trousers swelled in response.

"You want to take your last statement back?"

"What?" he replied, his gaze sweeping up, perplexed.

"About liking me best covered in womanly clothes."

"Did I say that?" His arms unfolded from his chest, and he pushed away from the wall. He reached out to capture her barely concealed breasts, she stepped back and away.

"Stay where you are. I'm not done yet," she insisted.

"How long do you plan to torture me?"

"Not torture, soothe, remember?" Bringing the chemise up around her waist, she reached underneath and loosened the ties of her pantalettes. Pushing the lace-covered tubes down her legs, she stepped out of them, exposing her long, silk-encased limbs. Shrugging off the loose linen shift, she remained standing where she was, clad only in stockings and garters as she slipped her feet from her shoes.

There was no longer any chance of holding him back. Sweeping her up with one arm, his fingers tore at the fastening of his pants. He turned her so she straddled him, and as he had threatened earlier to do, he pressed her against the cabin wall, impaling his manhood deep inside her. Wrapping her legs around his hips, she rode the waves of passion like a small boat in a storm, clinging to him with all of her strength. He was aroused beyond endurance, yet she could feel him holding back, waiting for her to join him on the crest of fulfillment as they rocked in unison to a shared rhythm.

The tremor built in her midsection, sending out warm rays to every point of her body. She soared to heights she never dreamed reachable. Even the roughness of the paneling behind her back became pleasureable as the tension ignited every nerve in her body. As release washed over her, she cried out Dirk's name again and again. Her words worked like a control switch, and he responded with a tremendous shudder.

He dropped his head against the pillow of her breasts, his rasps of exhaustion heating her skin. "You're a witch, Erica. No matter how hard I try, I never get enough of you."

Holding her firmly, still joined to him, he turned and knelt down on the bed, letting her fall gently back against the mattress. Then he stretched out beside her, winding his arms possessively around her to hold her close.

She nestled in the hollow spot below his collarbone, reveling in the afterglow of making love. She listened to his breathing become slow and even. Did he sleep? It wasn't important as long as they were together.

It's grand being in love, she thought dreamily. *Even the fighting isn't so terrible when making up is so much fun.* Fondly she placed her lips on the point where his pulse jumped in his neck, and she enjoyed the taste of his sun-kissed skin.

Sleepily he moaned, his hand reaching across to run his fingers through her golden hair. He pulled her closer and rubbed his chin on the top of her silky head. "Unless you plan on seeing this through, Erica, don't get me started again." One of his dark eyes popped open, and he grinned at her. "It wouldn't take much urging on your part, you know."

"Marry me," she stated simply, not believing she had actually had the courage to say the words.

He pushed up on one elbow, forcing her to lift up, too. Their eyes met in the darkness and held for an eternal moment. He raised one eyebrow and taunted, "Are you telling me or asking me?"

She playfully shoved his face away and rose to her knees on the bed, the moonlight casting provocative shadows across her nakedness, highlighting the stockings and garters she still wore. "I'm asking," she whispered huskily.

His hands reached out to fondle her bare breasts, swaying tantalizingly before him. "Then I accept."

Stretching toward him, she laid a light, loving kiss on his receptive lips. "I love you," she said with childish simplicity.

Her heart pounded like a bass drum against her rib cage. The words of her father's letter ran through her mind. "A prenuptial agreement. If he loves you, he won't object to signing it." She swallowed, her throat refusing to make the necessary movements. How will he accept what she was about to say?

She curled one finger in the soft mat of hair covering his chest. She hoped his heart would be as pliable. "Dirk," she began sweetly, twisting the dark thatch round and round, "there's one more thing."

He rolled them over to lie on top of her. "Don't ask me to make decisions regarding the wedding. Whatever you want will be fine with me." He planted kisses across her neck and chest.

Her mind reeled, and she nearly forgot what she was going to say. "No, Dirk," she gasped as his tongue curled around one breast, "this is important." She tried to push his head away and cleared her throat to bring her spinning head back down to earth. *Just say it and get it over with.* "I want us to sign an agreement."

"An agreement?" His mouth stopped the assault on her bosom, and he lifted his head. "What kind of agreement?"

"A prenuptial agreement saying what you own

stays yours, and what is mine remains so."

Gently he pulled her to him. "That's not necessary, sweetheart. What I have I freely give to you." He looked at her; the seriousness played across her face. "If this is your way of retaining your independence, then I'll sign whatever you want me to." His mouth descended to reclaim one beckoning breast.

She arched up to meet his lips. Should she tell him the truth? Should she tell him about Armstrong Shipping? *Armstrong Shipping,* she groaned inwardly. By the time she reached Baltimore, Edmund Bennett would more than likely own fifty-one percent of it. No, she couldn't think about that now. If he loved her the agreement wouldn't matter.

He answered her groan with a growl of his own as he misunderstood the reason for it. His mouth continued to descend, drawing a flaming trail along the arc of her ribs. "The only things you have I want are your love, your heart, and your body. Those items aren't included in this agreement, are they?" His tongue traced a line to her navel, leaving a moist, fiery path. "If it's that important to you, I'll agree. Just remember what I told you on that island in the Florida Keys, honesty between us."

She stopped breathing. She wasn't being dishonest. He had to be aware of who she was and what she owned. At some point Joshua must have told him. Of course he knew. His easy acceptance of her request meant that he loved her. She reached down and traced the line of his shoulder and neck. Finding his ear, she followed the contour with her finger. She sighed as he moved lower to savor her womanly charms. She was so lucky to have a perfect, caring man like Dirk. Fantasies of them together, giving parties, maybe touring the Continent, filled her mind—pleasant images of her running Armstrong Shipping and coming home to her loving husband.

"Oh, Dirk," she gasped as he pushed her senses to the abyss of gratification. The skyrockets of love burst around her and sent her swirling over the edge.

The need to give him as much as he offered her overwhelmed her. Reaching down, she led him up to lie between her thighs. Her hand felt between them, finding his staff warm and willing. Slowly she stroked him, then guided him to her portal of love. How perfectly they fit, like lock and key. She arched up to meet his building rhythm, seeking to please him without reserve. Losing all sense of the world around her, she was rocked by another crescendo at the same moment he tumbled over the edge.

As he sank, exhausted, to melt against her, she wrapped her arms tightly around him and drew him as close as she could. She was happy, so totally blissful. In fact, her head was in the clouds.

The morning sun peeked into the cabin. Dirk's eyes traced the perfect curves of Erica's body, rolled seductively in the sheet. He wanted to touch her, but at the same time he didn't wish to wake her. She looked so peaceful. She deserved some peace. He held his eager hand in check.

What an unusual woman she was. So gentle, yet so fierily independent. But he had to know she was different the first time he'd met her, so long ago in the lagoon, when she was still a budding child. She'd had fire even then.

He put his free arm under his head and thought about the strange request she had made last night after proposing to him. He chuckled under his breath. What a woman. A prenuptial agreement. Only Erica could have thought of something like that. So determined to remain her own woman, she needed his reassurance he wouldn't try to put her behind needlework and petticoats. No, he loved her for what she was. Wild, innocent, and honest.

A small frown creased his brows. She did trust him, didn't she? He had never given her any reason not to. No, she just had a need to be self-sufficient. What had happened in her life to make her so cynical? He couldn't imagine. What secrets did she clutch to her bosom that frightened her so? He glanced down at the twin orbs peeking up at him from the covers. It made no difference just as long as she never denied him her sweet bosom.

Carefully he lifted her head and slipped his arm from underneath her. She moaned and turned on her side, still fast asleep.

"No," she mumbled. "You can't have it, Bennett. It belongs to me." She sighed. "Dirk, you'll be waiting for me. Always waiting for me."

As he dressed to start his day, he listened to her words, the creation of her dreams.

"Sleep, sweet Mermaid," he said, pushing the tangle of hair from her face. "I'll be here for you, always."

374

July first. The day felt like any other. The *Sea Hawk* dipped and rose below her feet. The sails snapped over her head as if it were any ordinary day. Somehow she had expected the world to come crashing down on her. But no. She was still here and breathing. She groaned. And at least three days from reaching Baltimore, if all went well.

Damn you, Edmund Bennett. She raised her fist to the horizon of water before her; then she pressed her shaking fingers into her aching eye sockets.

She wouldn't turn the stock certificates over to him. He could take his blood money when she got to Baltimore, or he could go to hell. Her lips clamped in determination. No matter what her father had signed, she would never give Edmund Bennett controlling interest in her company.

What if he demands the certificates from Aunt Connie? Would she turned them over to him? No, there was no way she could. Only she, Erica, had the combination to the safe that held the certificates. She was the only one who could get to them. She was safe and so was Armstrong Shipping, at least until she got to Baltimore.

The days were idyllic, and the nights full of warm loving. Erica wished the journey would never come to an end. Heaven couldn't be better than being here with Dirk. The entire world was a shadow of the life she led aboard the *Sea Hawk*. She didn't want to face the mundane rhythm of existence outside the security the ship offered.

However, the afternoon the lookout announced the entrance to the Chesapeake Bay, excitement coursed through her like electric shocks.

"Home," she breathed as the twin capes of Charles and Henry came into view. "So close."

She glanced up at Dirk as she stood beside him at the helm. She liked it there, beside him, sharing his life. "There were times I thought I might never see these sights again."

He circled her shoulder and drew her close to his warmth.

Angela's hand whipping in the breeze caught her attention, and she waved back. She pulled from Dirk's embrace to join her friend, but Rob Taylor, his arm still in a sling, moved faster to join the woman. Angela had been waving to Rob, not her. She blinked in surprise as the two heads bent close together intimately. They were in love. But when had this shipboard romance begun? She'd never noticed them together that much. She glanced up at Dirk. She didn't notice much these days that didn't include the man she loved.

Rob had been bedridden for days. Of course. She smiled, Angela had nursed him with the devotion of a woman in love. How could she have been so blind?

Dirk's arm refolded around her shoulder as he pulled her closed beside him. "Surprised?"

"Am I that transparent?"

"Only to me," he answered as he placed a kiss on top of her head. "Love seems to be contagious these days."

She flashed him a glowing smile. "Actually, I think they look nice together."

"Good," he answered, grinning. "I wasn't ready to do battle for you again."

"What do you mean?"

He shrugged. "I've always suspected Rob Taylor felt something more for you than an officer should feel for his captain."

"Oh, Dirk, no." She slapped his arm playfully. "You really think so?" She looked up eagerly. Her hand squeezed the muscle of his arm. "Would you have really fought for me, again?"

"I'd fight Satan himself for you, if I had to. Don't you know that yet?"

She laid her head back against his soft shirt. "Things will be different now, my darling."

"What do you mean by that? Are you going to do battle for me?"

She giggled. "Just wait, you'll see. Everything is going to be so good for us."

He lifted an eyebrow. "I'm happy with the way things are now."

The next morning they reached the Choptank River, leading to Cambridge, Maryland. Erica watched Angela pace the deck beside her with anxious eyes.

"My God, Erica. We'll be there in a couple of hours. I hope I've made the right decision."

She squeezed the woman's hand reassuringly.

"Don't worry, Angela; everything will be fine. We won't leave you until we know it is. My offer's still open. You can always come home with me."

Angela hugged her lightly. "Thank you, Erica. But this is my home, regardless of my reception."

She nodded; she understood how her friend felt. *Home,* she thought. Only a day or two more and she would be home, too. She couldn't wait to see Aunt Constance's smiling face and the docks and buildings of Armstrong Shipping. What a wonderful sight that would be.

She glanced across the deck at Dirk. How proud she would be to show him her domain. Life would be perfect with her ruling the Armstrong empire, and Dirk leading the life of a gentleman. *Yes,* she decided, *our marriage will be the perfect one.*

The shoreline whipped by, and her gaze caressed each tree and rock they passed. Dirk's voice broke through her musing as he issued familiar orders to his crew to prepare for docking. She watched, fascinated, as he maneuvered the brig with a light, expert hand into the Cambridge harbor. The quiet water lapped at the sides of the ship. With only one other craft at anchor, they were soon solidly moored at the wharf.

To her left, Angela looked ready to cry as she clutched the one pitiful bag holding her few possessions. A hand tapped Erica's shoulder, and she jumped. She whirled to face Rob Taylor, his seabag at his feet.

"Captain, I've come to tell you good-bye."

Her head swung back to stare at Angela, who still

watched the town of Cambridge unaware that Rob stood there ready to go with her.

She whirled back, stuck out her hand, and offered it to Rob. "Good luck. She needs you."

He grinned sheepishly. "I think I need her, too."

Pulling the tall, lanky man to her, she hugged him like a brother. "If the two of you ever need me, you know where I am. I owe you my life, both of you."

He pulled back and shrugged his shoulders. Bending, he picked up his seabag and started across the deck to where Angela anxiously shifted from foot to foot.

Joy surged through her as he folded his long arm around the blonde and pulled her to him. Angela slumped against his chest. She fervently hoped life treated her friends well. They deserved the best.

She sniffed, holding back the tears of departure threatening to escape her eyes, as the couple stepped onto the lowered gangplank. Angela spun as the two reached the dock, waved enthusiastically at her, and blew her a kiss.

Dirk's hand slipped into hers, and she glanced up at his face, tears of joy running freely down her cheeks.

"They'll be fine, Erica. Don't worry about them."

She pressed her face into his chest. How glad she was he was there. But most of all, how lucky she was he loved her so.

The eastern horizon was still a faint, pink line when the *Sea Hawk* passed Bodkin Point and entered the Patapsco River, leading to Baltimore. Erica had stood vigil for the past few hours waiting for this moment. From this point on she knew every twist and turn the shore made. Soon she would be home.

Dirk's eyes brushed the nape of her neck, and she reveled in the sensation his gaze created. She whipped around, her hair flying wildly in the wind, and flashed him a loving smile, which he acknowledged with a lazy salute of his hand and a wink suggesting more than words could have.

She whirled back to catch every detail of the Maryland coastline as it passed by, not wanting to miss a moment of it. Like a six-year-old child impatiently awaiting Christmas, she thought the hour would never come.

The river was crowded with ships and smaller, personal craft even at this early hour. As if in a parade, she waved and shouted words of enthusiasm to every vessel passing within hearing distance.

She clapped with glee as the first wharfside buildings on the edge of the city appeared. Baltimore was exactly as she remembered it. Nothing had changed in the few months she had been gone. Excitement bubbled inside her, threatening to burst if she didn't share her feelings with someone. Pushing away from the rail, she sprinted across the deck to join Dirk where he stood behind the massive wheel of the brig.

"We're home," she blurted with zeal as she curled her arms around one of his and laid her head on his shoulder.

Playfully his hand reached out to tousle her windblown hair seeking out her mouth like a magnet. For the hundredth time she pushed the tawny tresses out of her face and held them back with the flat of her hand.

The docks appeared as a mass of spars and rigging bobbing up and down in rhythm with the gently rolling river. The brig strained forward like a spirited steed looking for the comfort of its stable after a long, hard race.

Glancing down at her, he wrapped an arm around her shoulder. "Where's the best place for us to dock?"

"It's a ways yet," she answered. "You can put in at the *Anna McKyle's* berth. I'll show you when we get there."

His brows slid down in a fleeting frown of puzzlement, but he said nothing. His arm dropped to his side. She gave him a quick smile, knowing he needed his concentration to keep the ship in line in the crowded harbor.

The public wharves turned into private ones, and eventually they reached the area devoted to the larger shipping lines of Baltimore. Dirk held his lips in a tight, thin line, and the frown returned to furrow between his eyes. She studied his profile in the bright morning sun. Was there something wrong? Had she missed something? No, he just concentrated on maneuvering the brig through the unfamiliar channel.

The docks of Armstrong Shipping sat off by themselves, the stenciled letters proclaiming their ownership standing out proudly on the two piers.

She pointed to an empty berth near the end of the wharf that could easily accommodate two ships the size of the *Sea Hawk*. Instead of watching where she pointed, his eyes skimmed over the docks and shipyard of Armstrong Shipping.

He's impressed, she thought proudly. "Dirk?" She tapped his arm to get his attention. "The dock is over there." Again she indicated the empty space at the pier.

"I see it," he snapped.

"Dirk, what's wrong?"

"Nothing, Erica." His words were short and clipped.

She blinked. He wasn't telling the truth. Perhaps she'd interrupted his train of thought. She let the conversation drop.

Squeals of protest filled the air as the smooth, finished planks of the brig rubbed against the rough, weatherworn boards of the dock. The Armstrong stevedores stood on the pier not sure what to make of the strange ship. She realized they had no idea why the *Sea Hawk* had chosen that particular wharf to anchor at.

She giggled when she saw the round, spectacled face of Mr. Kerr scurrying down from the office building. It was good to be home.

"Ahoy there, sir," the little man said, the words completely out of character for him. "I'm afraid this is a private dock. You can't stay here."

She ran to the side rail closest to Mr. Kerr and gave him a quick wave of her hand. "It's all right, Mr. Kerr. The *Sea Hawk* is here with my permission."

"Miss Armstrong?" His funny face turned red with disbelief. He took off his glasses and cleaned them

382

with the fresh white handkerchief he took from his pocket. Perching the wire rims back on his nose, he took another squinting look at her grinning face. "Is it really you?"

"Of course, Mr. Kerr. Who else would berth here?"

The little man came to life, directing the dockworkers to take the lines the seamen tossed from the ship. In no time the brig was secured to the pier, and the gangplanks were lowered.

She studied Dirk's face during the process. Not once did he look in her direction. What had she said to him to upset him so? There was no doubt he was angry. But why?

She stretched her arm to touch his shoulder, but he roughly shook her hand away and marched across the deck of his ship to see to the final details of the docking. Why did he shrug her off? Her hand drifted to her side as she searched her flustered mind for the answers to her questions.

His path brought him directly back in front of her. Still he refused to look at her. His jaws worked in anger, and his eyes were thin slits below his knitted brows.

"Please, Dirk," she implored, "what have I done?"

He riveted his black, smoldering eyes on her, a smirk flashed across his taut mouth. Sweeping his arm in a wide arc indicating the dock and shipyard surrounding them, he asked, "All this belongs to your family?"

"Oh, no," she answered innocently. "It belongs to me."

"Just as I thought," he mocked. "This is why you

383

wanted that damned agreement, isn't it?"

"But you knew," she defended her actions. "Joshua told you, didn't he?" She pushed back her flying hair.

His boots thudded like thunder as he walked away, leaving her with her mouth hanging open. She ran after him and grasped his arm to stop him, but her grip was like a fly in the wind. She didn't even slow him down as he ripped his arm from her fingers.

"Wait, Dirk, it's not like you think," she choked out of her throat, raw with unshed tears.

"And what in the hell am I suppose to think?"

His words cut like a razor through her heart. She glanced at all the gawking faces: crewmen, dock-workers, Mr. Kerr, and Joshua. "Please, can't we discuss this later?"

"No! We'll discuss this now, or not at all."

Her temper rose like mercury. "I will not stand here and discuss our private life in front of an audience." Her voice quaked with suppressed anger as she crossed her arms defiantly over her chest.

She didn't resist as his iron grip clamped painfully around her upper arm. Quietly she followed as he led her across the deck and down the companionway to their cabin.

The door whined in agony when his fist struck it open and then slammed it behind her before she had barely entered the room. Looming over her, he placed his hands on each side of her head, pinning her to the door. She swallowed hard, remembering the only other time she had seen him this angry. The night he had discovered she was the one who had usurped his cargo. That night her femininity had protected her.

Now it meant nothing to him.

"Explain," he growled, his black eyes boring holes into her brain.

She opened her mouth, but all that came out was a pitiful squeak. She managed to shake her head. Why did he act this way? He loved her; she knew he loved her. He couldn't be upset about the agreement. Her father had said if he loved her, he wouldn't mind.

"You think I want your damned money, don't you?"

Her head wobbled back and forth on the column of her neck as he pressed her back into the door against which he held her prisoner. No, she didn't think that. Why wouldn't her mouth work so she could tell him?

"Just what did you have in mind for me, Erica? Did you plan on running Armstrong Shipping during the day, and then coming home to your dear little husband at night?"

Somehow her dreams sounded all wrong coming from his mouth.

"I guess you planned on me running your household of servants and playing your stud at night. Did you really think I would lie down and allow you to emasculate me while you ran around pretending to be the man of the house? Wearing pants doesn't make you a man, Erica." He glanced down to take in the clothing she wore.

Placing both of her hands against her chest crushing her into the grain of the wood behind her back, she pushed. He had no right to distort her dreams. "You stupid, thickheaded prig. It wasn't to be like

385

that, at all." She struggled to escape him.

Amusement lit his face as he watched her useless efforts. "I won't sign your agreement." He stepped back, surprising her, and she almost fell against his heaving chest.

"Then I can't marry you, Dirk," she whispered.

His eyes traveled the full length of her, then back to her face. "Then get off my ship and get out of my life," he demanded in a low voice.

She blinked, unable to believe what he said. *No, he doesn't mean that. He's only angry.* Blindly she reached behind her and twisted the knob of the door. *God, please let the door be jammed so we will be forced to work this problem out here and now.* The door opened easily against her palm. She opened her mouth to say something, but the black look on his face quelled the words as righteous anger filled her mind.

Closing the door with a slam behind her, she stumbled down the companionway. *In a few hours he'll cool down. I can reason with him then. I'll explain the promise I made my father. Dirk will understand and forgive me. He has to. I love him.*

Lifting her shoulders, she took the steps to the deck. This evening they'd work the entire problem out.

Chapter Nineteen

At the top of the stairs Erica drew a deep breath and collected her wits about her. Dirk's final words to her still stung her ears. *No, he didn't mean those harsh things he said.* She pushed all thoughts of the fight out of her mind.

Joshua caught her eye from the wharf and lifted his hand in greeting. Pasting a bright smile across her face, she crossed the gangplank to join him.

"You two all right, kitten?"

"Of course," she reassured him. "Just a slight misunderstanding."

His eyes skimmed over her face briefly; then he said, "I've sent word to Constance to let her know we're home. I figured she didn't need to be shocked by our storming the house without warning."

"Sounds good." Mr. Kerr caught her eye and held it, concern flitting across his face. "Excuse me a minute, Joshua. There's a couple of things I need to discuss with Mr. Kerr."

He patted her shoulder and sent her on her way.

She gave the little man directions to see that her sea chest and other personal items were removed from the ship.

Mr. Kerr nodded. "Anything else, ma'am?"

She studied his anxious face. Was there something he wasn't telling her? "No, not now, but I'll be back later this afternoon to go over things with you. Will that be soon enough?"

"Yes, of course. Whatever you think. It's just good to have you back." His shoulders dropped in relief.

"Good. Could you see that a public conveyance is located to take us to the house. I don't feel like waiting for the Armstrong carriage to be sent for." She smiled. "Right now all I want to do is go home and take a hot bath in fresh water." She rolled her eyes in anticipated delight.

Turning back to Joshua, she took his arm. "I'm ready to go home. How about you?"

Joshua glanced around. "Isn't Dirk going to join us?"

She looked longingly at the ship. "Maybe later. He has a few things he wants to take care of first." She studied Joshua from the corner of her eye. Did he believe what she told him? He gave no reaction to her words. Should she tell him they were still fighting? No, there was no need. By this afternoon the entire matter would be solved. As Joshua had told her before, she had to handle her own love affairs.

She searched the *Sea Hawk* one last time, hoping Dirk would come on deck, but there was no sign of him. She swung her head back around and watched her steps as the two of them headed up the walk leading to the back entrance of the office building.

She couldn't wait to be home.

The public carriage was nothing spectacular, and the poor, tired horse pulling it did well to clippity-clop along. What should have taken a half an hour, at best, ended up being an hour ride in the slow vehicle.

She chewed her bottom lip and then the skin around her fingers in frustration. Why couldn't Dirk have been more understanding? Why did he have to be so unreasonable? She sighed, leaned back against the leather seat, and closed her eyes. She would make him understand this afternoon when she returned, and they could be alone.

Joshua bent forward from the other seat facing her to pat her hand affectionately. "You know, when we started this trip, I had no idea so many changes would take place."

She opened her eyes to stare up at him from her slouched position in the seat. "Neither did I, but I wouldn't change anything. I never would've met Dirk. I can't imagine life without him, now."

Joshua smiled wistfully. "I know, kitten. That's exactly how I feel about your aunt."

The vehicle stopped with a lurch. She leaned forward in her seat to see home. The house beckoned to her tired body and mind with windows that had curtains and drapes thrown wide in welcome. The front door opened, and Constance's slim figure raced down the front steps, her skirts flying wildly about her.

Joshua pushed the cab door open and started to

leap out, but remembering his manners, he turned back to help her from the carriage.

Grinning, she shoved his hand away and waved him out the door. "Good lord, Joshua, go to her. I can manage by myself."

He smiled back and didn't hesitate. His large frame unfolded from the cab, and Constance met him at the bottom of the marble steps, swinging her arms around his neck, oblivious to anyone who might be watching.

From the steps of the carriage, she heard the sobs of joy and relief escaping her aunt's lips as the woman wept openly in the arms of her man.

A small smile playing across her lips, Erica turned to pay the cabbie. He doffed his worn hat to her in appreciation of the tip she gave him.

She lingered on the curb as the carriage pulled away, not wanting to interrupt the sweet reunion taking place before her. Joshua had lifted Constance from her feet while her attention had been distracted with the cabdriver. Unwillingly the tall man released the slim form in his arms, and Constance slid back down on the walk.

Constance's face beamed as she whirled to face Erica. Stretching out her arms, she rushed to her aunt like a lost child. She didn't resist as her aunt held her tightly to her motherly breasts.

"Thank God, you're home," Constance babbled, not bothering to try to hold back the tears coursing down her face.

Joshua guided them affectionately toward the front door. The two women stumbled up the walk arm in arm.

Once through the door, Constance held Erica's face in her hands and straightened her arms so she could look at her niece. "I believe you've become more beautiful than I remember." She turned a smiling face to Joshua. "You took good care of her for me."

"Don't thank me, thank Erica's fiancé."

Constance caught her breath and looked at her for confirmation.

She nodded her head, laughing. "He's wonderful, Aunt Connie. I can't wait until you meet him. He's still down at the docks, but I imagine he'll be here for dinner this evening."

Constance squeezed her gently. "I'm so happy for you, dear." She giggled as she added, "Maybe we can make it a double wedding."

"That sounds wonderful, Aunt Connie. But right now all I want is a nice hot bath and a change of clothes."

She turned and headed up the stairs. Her stairs. Glancing back to tell her aunt she loved her, she kept her silence when she saw the passionate kiss the two were involved in. She lifted her eyes heavenward and breathed in a whisper, "Thank you, God, for bringing us home safely."

Dirk watched in self-imposed silence as the Armstrong Shipping stevedores toted the sea chest from his cabin. Anger churned like a tight fist in his chest. That damned woman was quick to see that what was hers was removed from his ship. What's hers is hers, and what's his is his. He grunted. That's no damned way to start a marriage. He had been a fool, a blind fool, to agree to her terms to begin with.

He paced the deck, his temper sitting precariously on the surface, his hands clasped tightly behind his back. He wanted nothing to do with her money. Why didn't she trust him enough to realize that on her own? Why couldn't she have been honest with him in the first place? The idea that she insisted he sign a legally binding paper stating he had no right to what she owned was degrading. Either she loved him enough to accept his word he didn't want her wealth, or she could go straight to hell. It was the principle of the thing!

"Captain?" a voice behind him asked reluctantly.

"What?" he snapped at the intruder, refusing to turn around or stop his pacing.

"Everything designated to be unloaded is off the ship. Shall I give the crew leave?"

"No," he commanded, refusing to speak in anything but monosyllables.

"Then, what are your orders, sir?" the voice persisted.

"Damn it, I'll let you know when I'm ready, mister."

"Aye, aye, sir."

He listened in fuming silence as the footsteps faded away. What *did* he want to do?

He knew what he *should* do. He'd like to wring the bitch's lovely neck and force her to see a little sense.

What he *would* do was a different matter altogether. His mind made up, he headed across the deck barking orders to prepare to get underway. It was time to put the entire affair behind him. It was time to go back where he belonged. Philadelphia.

Feeling refreshed after her bath, Erica dressed in a smart, sky blue day dress, complementing her figure well. Taking one last look in the tall cheval mirror in her bedroom, she slipped out the door and headed downstairs.

There was no sign of Constance or Joshua. She chuckled inwardly. She could imagine they were spending a few quiet hours together. The last time she was home, she would have never considered such a possibility. But then, she had still been an innocent girl.

She couldn't wait to get back to Armstrong Shipping. Once she explained the matter to Dirk, he would understand. As her father had told her, if he loved her there would be no hesitation on his part to sign an agreement. Dirk did love her.

Her carriage waited at the front entrance. Regally she headed down the front steps and slipped into the carriage door the driver held open for her.

"Afternoon, Miss Armstrong. It's good to have you home again."

"Thank you." She smiled as the man closed the door. She sat back on the soft leather seat. She had definitely missed the luxuries of life. It was good to be back in civilization.

Well past three o'clock, she reached the offices of Armstrong Shipping. Not bothering to go in the building, she skirted around the side to the docking area, determined to talk to Dirk before tackling whatever Mr. Kerr had waiting for her.

Her eyes raced ahead of her feet, following the line of the wharf to the berth where she had left the *Sea Hawk* anchored.

She stopped; her heart skipped a beat. "No," she choked. "This is impossible."

The empty berth mocked her.

Her feet carried her down the walk, refusing to accept what her eyes saw. She didn't stop until she stood in front of the slip where his ship should be. Her heart beat erratically, causing a pain so intense she thought she would die. He was gone. Dirk had left without explanation and without bothering to say good-bye.

His final words raced through her mind. "Get off my ship, and get out of my life." She slipped to her knees, the skirt of her gown spilling around her. He had meant what he had said. He didn't love her after all. He had gone and taken her very existence with him.

Tears forced their way out of her tightly closed lids. Why? He couldn't care so little for her. He had pursued her relentlessly. He wanted her, he loved her. She had wounded him beyond forgiveness. Childish wails escaped her white, taut lips. She didn't care who saw her. Her entire life had come to an end. Nothing was important to her, except that Dirk had deserted her.

Her knees grew stiff and numb, yet she still knelt before the empty berth. The sobs turned to hiccups and faded. Rising slowly, her head bent in defeat, she headed toward the office building.

Her thoughts came in crowded confusion. What did she have to do now? Mr. Kerr. She had promised him she would give him some time this afternoon. *I can't let my employees see me this way.* She brushed off her gown and pushed the hair from her face. She dabbed at her eyes to erase any signs of her crying.

The back door opened with an echoing squeal, and as it closed behind her, the slam reverberated in her ears. The clerks moved into her line of narrowed vision in slow motion, their voices distorted and unclear. One cocked his head at her, a question on his face. He had asked her something. But all she could hear was the name she had called in her mind. Dirk. She nodded her head to the waiting employee, fearing that if she opened her mouth the tears would start all over again.

She reached the safety of her office and closed the door behind her. Pressing her back against the barrier protecting her from the outside world, she muttered, "I've lost him." She stumbled across the room and sank in the desk chair. Laying her face in her open palms, she dug the heel of her hands into her eyes trying to make the nightmarish reality go away.

A timid knock made a woodpecker sound on the door. She raised her head and wiped the back of her hand over her puffy eyes.

"Come in," she croaked, not meaning the words as she said them, hoping whoever stood on the other side of the door would go away.

Mr. Kerr's worried face slid around the barrier as he pushed it open to enter. She lifted her chin and forced a shaky smile on her lips.

"Miss Armstrong, I'm so relieved you decided to come back today." His words barely penetrated the fog in her brain.

"Yes, of course," she answered automatically.

"Miss Armstrong." He cleared his throat. "There are some things that have happened since you've been gone you need to know about."

"What do you mean?" she asked, trying to show an interest in what he said.

"Edmund Bennett has been around here. . . ."

The vile name washed over her like cold water. Her mind swam up through the protective haze surrounding it. "Edmund Bennett has no right to be here under any circumstances."

Mr. Kerr's head dropped to his chest, his glasses sliding down his nose. "It seems he does now, ma'am."

She blinked. "What do you mean?" Fear invaded her heart.

"He came in here four days ago flaunting stock certificates of Armstrong Shipping, claiming he now owns controlling interest in the company. I checked with Miss McKyle, your aunt"—he paused to take a breath—"and she confirms his story. Apparently he now owns fifty-one percent of the stocks."

Her mind became a swinging kaleidoscope of colors, angry red, frightened yellow, devastated blue. First Dirk, and now the company. In a matter of minutes her entire life had fallen into ruins.

She blinked, trying to fully comprehend the current disaster. How had Bennett gotten hold of the certificates? They had been in the safe; only she knew the combination. There had to be some mistake.

"Miss Armstrong, did you understand what I said?"

A numbness coursed through her, her emotions put on hold by her protective brain. Dirk she could do nothing about, but Edmund Bennett — that was a totally different story. She'd be damned if she'd let that man ruin her life. She jerked open the top drawer of the desk, hunting for a blank piece of paper to write a terse note to the man, demanding he meet with her. Instead of paper, her hand circled around the pocket pistol her father had kept hidden there.

Undecided, her fingers squeezed and released, squeezed and released the ornate handle of the gun. Finally her hand tightened one last time around the pistol. "Thank you, Mr. Kerr," she dismissed him. "I'll handle things from here on."

He pushed his glasses back up his nose and peered at her with a concentrated squint. "Miss Armstrong, are you all right?"

Her hand caressed the butt of the gun. Edmund Bennett would be sorry he had ever tried to make trouble for her. She glanced up at the man in front of her. "Yes, Mr. Kerr," she answered, her voice sparked with life, "I've never felt better. Please, I'd like to be alone."

"Yes, ma'am," he said, dipping his head as he rose to leave the room.

"Mr. Kerr," she stopped him as the door was about to close, "please see that my carriage is brought around. I have an errand to run."

The little man nodded and closed the door.

Rising, she took the pistol from the drawer. She spun the barrels to check and see if it was loaded. Each chamber held a bullet. A determined smile

397

lifted her lips as she slipped the small gun into the deep recess of her reticule. She hesitated. Did she do the right thing? She pulled the drawstrings with a yank. She did the only thing she could. Lifting her chin, she started for the door.

By damn, Bennett would return those stocks to her, or she'd see to it he never had a chance to use them. She'd not allow him to push her another step back. She would show him who controlled her life and Armstrong Shipping.

The rooming house where Edmund Bennett lived was seedier than Erica expected. Its symmetric, Georgian lines needed repair, and the white trimming ached for a coat of paint.

She signaled for the driver to stop. Her hand reached inside her reticule, confirming that the pistol was still there. She closed her eyes for a moment, thoughts of what she intended to do overwhelming her. Either Bennett would turn the stock certificates back over to her willingly, or she would force him at gunpoint to do so. She would shoot him if he gave her no other choice. She had shot a man before to protect what was hers. She would do it again without hesitation.

Descending from the carriage, she instructed the driver, "Wait for me. I shouldn't be long."

The man nodded his understanding and crawled back up in the driver's seat, hunkering down into a slumped position as if he expected to wait for hours.

She stepped toward the white picket fence surrounding the house. The gate swung on loose hinges as she opened it. Marble steps that had once been white, but now were badly stained by the weather, led to the front door. A man living here had no right to tell her what to do. How dare he try to step out of his class.

Raising her clenched fist, she knocked on the door with sound determination. A middle-aged woman opened it and gave her a welcoming smile.

"Yes, deary, can I help you?"

She clutched the reticule tightly to her side. "I would like to talk to Edmund Bennett, please."

The woman's brown eyes gave her a quick looking over. It was unseemly for a woman to come to a man's place of residence and insist on seeing him. She could read the disapproval on the woman's face.

"I'm sorry, but Mr. Bennett isn't at home just now."

"May I come in and wait for him to return?" she demanded more than requested.

"No, I'm sorry. He won't be back for at least a week. However, if you would like, you may come in and write him a message."

"Yes, I believe I'll do that."

The door swung wide in the woman's hand, and she stepped into the foyer to follow the lady into a large sitting room, surprisingly neat and clean compared to the outside of the building. She waited patiently as the woman brought her pen and paper and indicated a small writing table in one corner for her use.

Starting a spiteful note demanding he come to the office immediately, she stopped in midword. *No*, she thought, *this is not how I want to handle him*. She crumpled the letter in her hand and spun to face the startled look of the landlady.

"I have no message," she instructed. "In fact, I would prefer it if you didn't mention I was here."

Pushing past the surprised woman, she let herself out the door, still clutching the aborted note in her hand.

The coachman sat up, startled to see her returning so soon. Without a word or a backward glance she climbed into the carriage.

In the security of the vehicle, she sat barely breathing as it lurched forward. Her hand unfolded from around the crumpled note, and the ball of paper rolled from her hand onto the floor.

I have made a total mess of my life, and there is no one but myself to blame. She closed her eyes and tried not to think as the carriage took her home.

Dirk perused the face of the man sitting across the table from him. "No, I'll toss them in the harbor before I'll sell them for that price." The crates of Cuban cigars were worth twice what the broker offered him. He'd be damned if he'd allow the man to cheat him out of one penny due him. He'd sat on the cargo for two weeks; he'd sit on them another two, if he had to.

The broker sighed and lifted his shoulders in resignation. "I'll do the best I can."

"You'll do what I want, or I'll take my business elsewhere," he corrected.

"Captain Hawkyns, you're being a bit unreasonable," the agent blurted in a voice grating on his nerves. But then, everything lately annoyed him.

"Those are my terms, Mr. Jackson. You can take them or leave them. The choice is yours."

The agent gave him a disappointed smile. "Then I guess I'll have to keep looking for a buyer, won't I?"

He pushed back his chair and rose, ending the meeting. "You know where to find me when you have a proper offer." Spinning, he walked away without waiting for the agent to acknowledge his statement.

Heading toward the wharf where the *Sea Hawk* rode anchor, he dwelled on the pain surrounding his heart. Of all the disasters he thought might befall him, he had never considered he might become the victim of a coldhearted woman. Erica Armstrong had used him from the beginning. He laughed bitterly to himself. She had taken the cargo intended for him and had fought like a banshee to keep it. Like a fool he had fallen in love with the chit instead of beating the devil out of her, which was what she'd deserved.

Worst of all, she'd ruined him for other women. Sexually he had no trouble performing, but it was just that—a performance. He obtained no pleasure from the act. It wasn't from lack of trying a variety of different women. Somehow they all fell short when compared with his sleek, sensual Mermaid. *Damn her to hell,* he vowed.

He had even tried to wash her out of his memory by drinking himself into a state of oblivion. Still she hid in the recesses of his mind and came out to haunt him when he least expected it. Was there nothing he could do to rid himself of the spell she had cast over him?

As he wandered the dusty, wharfside street, the night grew later. His actions were foolish, as he increased his chances of someone mugging him. But, in a way, he wished someone would try. It would give him the opportunity to pound his fists into living flesh, something he'd been itching to do since leaving Baltimore. He clenched his fists and snorted in disgust. No matter how long he roamed the streets of Philadelphia, no one ever took him up on his brazen offer.

With the *Sea Hawk* only a few minutes away, he dragged his feet, unwilling to face the ghosts residing aboard. But he had nowhere else to go. Even Dolly Monet had grown impatient with him, telling him to not return to her gaming house until he stopped his reckless, self-destructive ways. "You can't find an answer between every woman's thighs. Go away, Dirk, until you're ready to continue the good life God bestowed on you," she'd told him.

Dirk threw his hands up in frustration as he continued down the cobbled street to the ship. What good life? Everywhere he looked he saw Erica. His cabin had become a haunt of memories bombarding him when he entered it. He had been forced to sleep in the common sailor's quarters to avoid the womanly smells lingering in his domain. What he wouldn't give for a night of restful sleep without images of her siren's body leaving him in a cold sweat.

Maybe he should take the pitiful offer the agent had given him tonight for the crates of Cuban cigars. He could then leave port, head to someplace like China, and lose himself in a crowd of strange people and smells.

No, he wasn't ready for that yet. Dolly was right. First he had to cut the strings binding Erica to his heart. Then he could escape to an unfamiliar port.

The *Sea Hawk* loomed before him, and slumping his wide shoulders forward, he went / aboard. He paced the deck, refusing to go below until his eyes closed from pure exhaustion. He stumbled down to his cabin, grumbling all the way, and grabbed a bottle of rum from the case that had been full a few days ago. There were only a few bottles left. He didn't bother to get a glass, just poured the sweet, burning liquor down his throat as if it were a bitter medicine, a cure-all for his ills, a remedy for pain. He sputtered and gagged, then tossed the half-full bottle at the distant wall in total disgust with himself. His life had gone to hell all because of an ungrateful woman, and there wasn't a damn thing he could do about it.

Erica couldn't believe only three weeks had passed since the day her life had fallen apart. That was how she saw the fifth of July. It felt as if years had gone by.

Not sure how, she managed to maintain a calm façade around her aunt and Joshua. Even though Constance followed her with guilty eyes, she refused to allow either of them to know how devastated she was. She didn't blame her aunt for turning the certificates over to Edmund Bennett. The man was a monster and a sadistic devil. On the day of the deadline he had shown up and demanded what he claimed was his property. Constance had explained they were in a safe, and she didn't know the combination. The next day he had arrived with a court order, a policeman, and a locksmith. The safe had been opened, and the certificates turned over to him.

The lawyers Erica had approached had frowned and been evasive. What he had done had been completely legal, even if somewhat unethical. A thief had entered her life and taken what he wanted, and there was nothing she could do about it. At least, not according to the attorneys. She smiled. The day and night surveillants she had hired to watch Bennett's boardinghouse would inform her as soon as he returned to town. When he did, she would take care of him personally.

Constance and Joshua had gently prodded her about Dirk's sudden disappearance. She had explained by saying that he'd had business to take care of in Philadelphia, and that he would be back in a few weeks. What would she say when those few weeks turned into months? That day was coming up soon.

Her life had become an automatic existence. She ate, slept at the proper times, and spent her days in the shipping office doing whatever was necessary. But none of her actions meant a thing to her. If there was such a place as a living hell, she was in the middle of it.

Joshua's penetrating voice brought her around to the present. She sat with a forkful of food poised at her mouth. How had she gotten to the table? What meal was she eating?

She studied the morsel of beef dripping juices into

her plate below. It must be supper.

"Erica?" Joshua's questions jolted her brain.

"Yes, I'm sorry," she mumbled. "I didn't catch what you said."

"I asked you when you expected Dirk to return."

"It shouldn't be too much longer," she answered evasively, dropping her fork, which clattered against the china.

Joshua set his utensils down at a precise angle to his plate and clasped his hands in front of his face. His eyes roved over her blank face. "Damn it, Erica. I've listened to that weak story for two weeks now. I personally think you're lying."

"Joshua," Constance choked. "I don't think you need to be so harsh with her."

"Constance," he warned, "let me handle this my way. I know what I'm doing."

Erica blinked at the conversation taking place before her. What she had dreaded for weeks had finally arrived. She would have to explain. Pushing back her chair from the table, she rose to escape the room. *I can't handle this. I don't know how to tell them.*

Undaunted, Joshua rose right behind her and followed her as she attempted to dart from the room. His strong grip circled her arm and forced her to turn around and acknowledge his presence.

"Damn it, Erica," he pressed. "I think it's time you tell us what's going on."

"Nothing," she protested in an irritated voice. With strength she didn't know she possessed, she jerked her arm out of his grasp. Running for the stairs, she hiked her skirts up to take the steps two at a time.

Tears blinded her vision.

His longer strides helped him to catch up. Halfway up the long staircase his grip found her arm again. Swaying together, they nearly toppled back to the bottom. *Let me fall*, she prayed. *Let me escape the misery my life has become.*

His muscled arm shot out and steadied them on their high perch. Constance's scream of terror resounded in Erica's ears. She crumbled where she stood to land in a heap on the step, tears streaming down her face.

His broad chest braced her, and he swung her into his arms like a small, fragile doll to carry her back down the stairs.

"Oh, Joshua, what have I done?" she sobbed.

"Come on, Erica," he cooed. "We'll figure it out. Things can't be all that bad."

Constance's hysterics added to the confusion as she sank on the bottom step. "I'm sorry, Erica. I didn't mean to do it. Please forgive me."

"It's all right, Aunt Connie. It doesn't matter anymore."

Joshua carried her limp form into the nearest room, her father's study, and carefully laid her on the sofa. She twisted to bury her face in the soft damask covering the cushions. Joshua's determined strides echoed back across the room.

Constance's sobbing reached a crescendo as Joshua comforted her. "There, there, Constance, my girl. No need to cry. You're not at fault." The sobs became muffled as her aunt buried her face in Joshua's shoulder.

Erica ached with the need to feel a similar love, but

from Dirk. Only Dirk.

She had no idea how much time passed before she heard the door of the room click as Joshua closed it behind him. She rolled over to face him as he crossed the room with purposeful strides. She swallowed. What would she tell him?

Standing over her, he studied her face. "Now," he demanded quietly, "what is going on between you and Dirk?"

She considered putting up her defenses again and swearing nothing was wrong. No. She was tired of carrying her burden alone. Maybe confession would let her escape the agony surrounding her heart.

Rising from the sofa, she walked to the desk to locate the letter her father had left her so long ago. Her hand closed around the smooth linen paper in the drawer, and she unfolded it with care before handing it to Joshua without saying a word.

He questioned her with his eyes before he glanced down at the paper in his hand.

"Go ahead, read it. I think it will explain everything." He smoothed the edges as he read what his friend had written to his daughter, and she watched the emotions play across his face. "Jesus Christ, Erica," he whispered without looking up as he finished reading. "You didn't ask Dirk to sign an agreement like this, did you?"

She nodded dumbly. "It was what father wanted."

"Do you know where he went?"

She stared at the floor as she shook her head, her eyes misting over with self-pity.

He slowly folded the letter in the original creases. With an abrupt movement he sat on the sofa and tapped the paper against his knee. She watched him between wet lashes. She could almost see the wheels of his brain working as he thought.

"Kitten," he began, taking a deep breath, "your father was a good man, my best friend, and he only wanted the best for you. But he wasn't infallible. This letter," he declared in a fatherly voice, "was a mistake."

She presented her rigid back to him. "No, Joshua, you're wrong."

The sofa groaned as he rose behind her. He touched her shoulder with a gentleness that spoke of pity. "Your father imagined a more traditional courting when he wrote this letter, of that I am positive. He had no idea his daughter would turn out to be an independent hellion with her lover chasing her halfway around the world to save her from her own self-created disasters."

She winced at his words as they struck home.

"Dirk had proven himself beyond a shadow of a doubt, girl. He never even knew you had money." His hands gripped her stiff shoulders and turned her around to face him. "Believe me, Erica, your father would agree with me if he were here now."

"Joshua, what do I do? He's gone, and I don't know where to find him."

"And you're going to give up like that?" He snapped his fingers and shook his head in disbelief. "If I were you, I would start in Philadelphia, and I wouldn't stop until I found him. It's nothing more than what he's done for you."

"What if he refuses to see me?"

He threw his head back and laughed. "Woman,

that's never stopped you before."

She chewed her bottom lip and blurted out, "Will you go with me?"

He shook his head firmly. "Nay, kitten. Like I told you once before, you have to handle your own love affairs. I'm to marry your aunt in two week's time. I won't leave her again."

She dropped her hopeful gaze. He was right. This was something she had to do on her own. She had lost sight of her strength for too long. She would find him. She wouldn't give up until she did.

Chapter Twenty

Philadelphia, Pennsylvania
August 3, 1835

The man's a classless bastard, Dirk decided, *but his money will spend as well as anybody else's.* Flashing Jackson, the agent who had arranged the meeting, a broad grin, he sat back in the solid captain's chair, making it rear on its two hind legs. The offer for the crates of cigars was a damn good one, in fact, more than he had hoped to get. After three weeks of waiting, he was pleased.

"I believe, Mr. Bennett," he said with confidence, "we'll be able to do business together."

Edmund Bennett had a look about him that reminded Dirk of a cold, wet fish, something he would hesitate to reach out and shake hands with unless he had no other choice. The man's uninviting hand jutted out at him, and he tried to appear enthusiastic as he gripped it in a gentleman's agreement.

Had it been his choice, he would have gotten up from the table and left at that moment, but business wasn't conducted that way. There was a dinner to get through in the company of the man. He might as well make the best of the situation.

"Where are you from, sir?" he asked, a fixed smile on his face.

Bennett sat back, his chest puffing up like a strutting turkey's. "I'm from Baltimore, Captain Hawkyns. In fact, I'm in the shipping business myself. I'm the major stockholder in one of the largest companies down there."

His black slash of an eyebrow lifted in curiosity. Must everything be a reminder of Erica Armstrong? "Really, Mr. Bennett. So what do you want with my cigars?"

Bennett grinned boastfully. "I admit to having a weakness for fine cigars. They're hard to come by these days with the problems in Cuba. And since taking over Armstrong Shipping, I figured I deserved a reward for my hard work." He thumped his chest with a finger.

Dirk forced his face to remain calm and impassive when he heard the name Armstrong Shipping. What did this man have to do with Erica? Tension stiffened every muscle in his body.

"You wouldn't believe the little chit I had to deal with," Bennett continued in a conspiratory tone. "I'm so sick of women who don't know their place. They should either be in the kitchen or in the bedroom, if you know what I mean." He cast a leering grin at the two men at the table.

411

Dirk's fist clenched in a ball under the table. His hand itched to plant itself in the middle of the baying jackass's face. The smile pasted on his face was anything but friendly.

"Anyway, the bitch tried to run me out of the business, but I evened the score. When she was out of town, and out of my hair, I managed to gain control of the company."

His eyes narrowed with a look akin to a dangerous animal as Bennett prattled on, boasting about how he had treated Erica. *The son of a bitch,* he seethed, *no wonder she was so scared of marriage and felt she needed to protect herself from men.*

"I can't wait to see the look on her face when she finds out *I'm* in control now." Bennett ended with a chuckle.

The only thing keeping him from jerking the other man out of his chair and beating him to a pulp was the appearance of the waiter, who began serving the meal. His hands clasped the knife and fork in a death grip as he wished they were vital parts of Bennett's body. The food tasted like ashes in his mouth, and only through sheer strength of mind did he manage to smile and act as if he found the other man's story amusing.

"Yes," he commented with complete honesty, watching Bennett's face with his dark, devil eyes, "women can be quite unpredictable."

Bennett smiled in agreement.

"Edmund?" he asked as his finger played with the stem of his wineglass. "You don't mind if I call you that, do you?" He gave the man a disarming smile.

"Of course not. I'd be honored, sir."

"Is this your first trip to Philadelphia?"

Bennett's eyes lit with curiosity. "Why, yes, it is."

"Well, then, perhaps I can show you some of the highlights of our City of Liberty you might not find unless you knew about them." Dirk gave him a knowing, wicked grin.

Bennett slammed the flat of his hand against the table. "You sound like my kind of man. I would be pleased to join you for a tour of the more interesting places." Bennett's leering laugh echoed through the room.

He had played his man right. Now that he had his interest, what was he going to do with him? "Good," he answered, pushing back his half-finished meal. "Mr. Jackson, we'll leave you to draw up the bill of sale. We'll meet you in your office tomorrow morning, but not too early, as I have a feeling we're in for a long but pleasant night."

The agent's mouth dropped wide at his unusual behavior. "Yes, of course, Captain Hawkyns," he agreed with confusion. "Until tomorrow then."

Dirk's mind worked furiously as he led his prey out of the hotel dining room and into the street to flag down a cab. He wasn't yet sure how, but he had to play on the man's inflated ego and his obvious greed.

What I wouldn't do to have those stock certificates in my possession, he mused. *What I wouldn't give to see the look on Erica's face when I handed them to her.*

There was only one person who could help him with the plan formulating in his mind. Dolly Monet,

413

the one true friend he had in Philadelphia, the one person who wouldn't question his motivation for taking advantage of scum like Edmund Bennett. He frowned slightly as he remembered the last time he'd seen her; she had sternly sent him away from her sporting house. With the right phrasing of words, she would understand that he was there for important reasons, and she would help him with every resource she had available. He smiled in the darkness of the cab. The one thing he could depend on was Dolly's resourcefulness.

Edmund Bennett giggled when they stopped in front of the ornate, red brick building. Music and laughter overflowed from the doors and windows thrown open in invitation. Like a child in a candy shop, Bennett scrambled from the cab and impatiently waited for Dirk to join him on the walk.

With a sigh of disgust he stepped down and turned to pay the driver for their fare.

The woman who met them at the door had a regal beauty belonging in an aristocratic salon. She carried her ripe, full body with pride. He still found Dolly as fascinating as when he was a lad.

"Dirk Hawkyns," she said with a naughty grin. "I thought I wouldn't see you again so soon. Still looking to lose your sorrows between one of my ladies' creamy thighs?"

He laughed and chucked her under the chin. Dolly knew all about Erica and what had happened to their relationship. Yes, Dolly meant a lot to him. "Perhaps, Dolly. But tonight I brought along a *special* friend with me."

414

The madam crooked an eyebrow at him with questions.

He watched Bennett from the corner of his eye and gave Dolly a solemn nod. The man had no style. Bennett rubbed his hands together in lusty anticipation.

Dirk tapped his shoulder and pointed the way to a back room. "Perhaps you'd like a drink and a glance at the gaming room. I think you'll find Dolly's lovelier girls to be back there."

Bennett didn't hesitate, but jumped ahead of him, following Dolly's swaying figure. The woman pushed open a brightly painted door to show them a room less crowded than the common room. Smoke curled in little fingers, beckoning the men to enter. Bennett nearly stumbled over his own feet as he rushed in, eager to see the sights.

Dolly showed them around the room, taking them from gaming table to gaming table. She introduced each dealer, who was always an exquisite woman dressed as regally as a duchess. Dirk marveled at the madam's ability to obtain such refined, beautiful women to work for her. Not one displayed crass or common manners. His companion practically drooled down the front of his shirt at the opulent display of feminine charms.

Bennett's eyes settled on an angel of a girl dealing faro. Dolly noticed where his look fell and discreetly ushered them in the girl's direction.

The dealer's lovely, almond-shaped eyes followed their movement toward her table. As if by magic a deck of playing cards appeared in her long, perfect fingers. Dolly placed a possessive hand on the girl's soft, bare shoulder as she spoke. "Carla, you remember Captain Hawkyns."

The girl nodded with the manners of a highbred lady.

"He has brought a *special* friend with him tonight. Please see to their needs for me, will you?" Dolly flashed an all-encompassing smile and turned, giving Dirk a wink only he could see. "I think you'll find Carla very obliging."

Dolly melted into the crowd. She had done all she could. Now the rest was up to him and the slim girl before him.

"Well, my friend, shall we buck the tiger?" he asked Bennett, indicating a seat before the exotic dealer.

Bennett sank into the seat, his eyes glued to the deep cleavage displayed before him.

Carla's magician's hands flipped the deck of cards in an intricate, shuffling pattern. She smiled knowingly at Dirk and then seductively at Bennett. Placing the cards in the dealing box, she spread the betting layout before the two men. "Place your bets, gentlemen," she breathed in a husky voice.

Studying the thirteen emblems emblazoned on the green cloth, Dirk stacked his chips in a neat pile before him, then placed his bets. Bennett's chips lay in a scatter as he absentmindedly placed a few chips on two of the ranks on the layout.

Carla lifted the top card from the deck. "Two of clubs, loses."

The next card appeared. "Six of diamonds, wins."

Bennett grinned as he boasted, "See, my friend, this is easy." He scooped the two piles of chips toward him. With careless confidence he covered several more of the ranks.

Dirk smiled as he placed his bet, knowing what he did at this point wouldn't make a difference. The play was in the dealer's control.

The deck of cards dwindled in front of the dealer. Bennett's pile of chips steadily grew larger. Dirk's rose and fell like the ocean tide. In the end it wouldn't matter. "Doesn't seem to be your night, does it?" Bennett smirked.

He gave him a shrug of his shoulders and continued to watch the play.

Bennett grew bolder and bolder with his reckless betting. He cursed proficiently when the dealer swept away a large chunk of his chips. Carla soothed his restlessness with a smile promising much. He settled down to do some serious gambling.

Dirk watched, fascinated, as the lovely Carla played a cat-and-mouse game with Bennett. His chips rose to tantalizing heights; then, just as quickly, she would reduce his winnings to nothing. Each time he lost she would woo him with a provocative display of her lush, ripe body and a glance offering a reward if he stayed at the table. The first debt marker he signed with a confident flourish. At the second one a small frown furrowed between his greedy eyes. By the third one the man owed a small fortune. Desperation shone brightly on his face sheened with sweat.

Dolly came to the table each time to approve the markers as he signed them. Dirk would hold his lips

417

tightly together to keep the laughter from bursting forth as she skillfully mulled over each one, giving it careful consideration. Then she'd remark with a smile that would have put Satan himself at ease, "If you're a friend of Captain Hawkyns, I know you must be good for any amount you sign for."

The stack of markers grew higher, and the sweat on Bennett's face popped out in bold drops, threatening to soak the collar of his shirt.

Dirk hid his amusement behind hooded eyes. "You're getting in rather steep, aren't you, my friend? Don't you think it would be wise to stop?"

His words had the exact effect he hoped for. Bennett turned cold, angry eyes on him and snapped, "This is none of your damn business, Hawkyns. So just keep your nose out of it. If the game is too rich for your blood, then keep your mouth shut."

Under different circumstances, Dirk would have reacted with violence to the man's cutting words. But Bennett had taken the bait and was running pell-mell with it. Dirk's eyes flashed dangerously, but he clamped his lips tight and gave the man a noncommittal shrug of his shoulders. His conscience was at ease; he had given the man plenty of warning.

The faro game proceeded with the pattern of winning and losing cards, leaving only three remaining in the dealing box. Carla's hands paused dramatically as Bennett's frazzled appearance told of the money he had lost so far that night.

Carla's eyes rested with a deceiving, sleepy-eyed effect. "Care to call the turn, Mr. Bennett?" Her palm covered the king of diamonds lying face up in the box.

"Damn it, you know I have nothing more to bet."

Carla shrugged as her fingers grasped the royal face card.

"Perhaps you'd care for a side bet, Edmund?" Dirk spoke low and evenly.

Bennett glanced up, startled. "Side bets aren't permitted."

His eyes danced over Carla's figure. "I personally don't think the lady is listening to what we are saying."

Bennett's eyes slid to Carla's blank face, and then back to Dirk hopefully. "Just what did you have in mind?"

His eyes flickered over Bennett's unsteady gaze, which darted around the room. "I can call the last three cards in exact order. I have one chance in six to call them right." He paused to let the impact of his words sink in. "If I lose, I'll cover your markers, and the Cuban cigars are yours as well."

Bennett's eyes glistened with greed. "And if you guess right?"

"Then I want your controlling interest in Armstrong Shipping."

Bennett's face registered disbelief. A sly smile crept across his face. "And if by chance you should win, my friend, I'll lose everything, and still I'll owe the lovely Miss Monet fifty thousand dollars. I can't risk that."

Dirk gave an exaggerated sigh. "You drive a hard bargain." He lifted his hand and motioned to Dolly.

The madam glided across the floor to their table,

giving him a questioning look. "Is there something I can do for you, Captain Hawkyns?"

"Mr. Bennett and I have come to an agreement. I would like his markers signed over to me."

"You are very generous to your friend," she said with a sweetness betraying nothing. She lifted her shoulders in unconcern. "As you wish, Captain. It makes no difference to me as long as I am paid."

He cast his dark eyes at Edmund Bennett for consent.

"I honestly don't think you can call them, Hawkyns." Bennett nodded his head in agreement to the bet.

He closed his eyes in concentration. The dark orbs opened to glance at the gathering crowd, then slid over Carla's waiting hand. "Ten of diamonds, six of clubs, jack of hearts."

His eyes turned cold and bore into Bennett. He waited for the man to call for the play to begin.

With little concern Bennett's thin hand lifted and signaled to the dealer to lift the top card.

The king of diamonds slide down to reveal a red card dotted with more diamonds. "Ten of diamonds," Carla whispered.

Bennett stared confused. Then he grinned. "Only luck, Captain Hawkyns," But his mouth worked nervously along with the Adam's apple in his throat.

Carla's long hand fingered the corner of the revealed card. She looked to Bennett, waiting for him.

Bennett's gaze explored the sea of strange faces surrounding the table. He lifted his finger, and Carla's hand removed the ten of diamonds.

The crowd gasped in unison. Dirk raised his eyes to Dolly, standing in the crowd, then skimmed over Carla. The woman's skill with cards never ceased to amaze him. The six of clubs sat uncovered in the dealing box.

Bennett let out a defeated roar. "You sorry sons of bitches, you've cheated me."

Dirk reached out and lifted him from his chair until his toes barely swept the floor. "Those are strong words, my friend. You'd better be ready to prove them or shut your whining mouth."

The other man swallowed hard, his eyes revealing a hatred and contempt hard to ignore. A look of glee swept across Dirk's face.

"Why?" Bennett croaked.

"Let's just say I delight in matching my wits with strong-willed women. The difference between you and me is that I succeed where you managed to fail."

Bennett tried to wrench from Dirk's strangling grip on his collar. "Well, I hope you have more luck controlling the obstinate bitch than I did."

He threw his head back and laughed. "I think you'll find I already have. Now, Bennett, I would like my stock certificates." Slowly he released the other man.

Bennett straightened his twisted clothes. "Meet me at the First Bank of Baltimore in two weeks. I'll turn them over to you then."

He sneered. "I believe we'll just head there to-gether, and I won't even charge you passage on the *Sea Hawk*." He glanced around and caught the eye of one of the big men Dolly kept discreetly positioned around the room to maintain order. He shoved Bennett's unwilling form toward the guard, pushing him almost to his knees. "Keep an eye on him until I settle with Dolly."

Without a word the large man nodded. Bennett would be standing in exactly the same spot when he returned.

He crossed the room to an unnoticeable door in the far corner, leading to Dolly's private office. With the door firmly closed behind him, he grabbed her in a hug of sincere affection.

"We make a good team." Her laughter was deep and warm, and she tousled his black hair the way she had when he was a boy. "If I ever decide to turn crooked on a permanent basis, I think I should hire you."

"You're a vixen, Dolly. If I didn't know you better, I might think you were serious."

"Fifty thousand dollars," she giggled. Playfully she twisted from his bearlike hug and whirled to pick up the stack of markers Bennett had signed. "I think you'll owe me for the rest of your natural life."

"Ah, Dolly, I already am in debt to you up to my gills," he teased.

With a flare she lifted the glass from the lamp on her desk and carefully placed a corner of the markers in the flame. "I always wanted to know what it would feel like to burn fifty thousand dollars." She set the burning papers in a pewter dish on the edge of the desk. Fascinated, they watched in silence as the papers became a black, charred shadow of what they had once been.

He slipped a hundred-dollar bill from his coat pocket and handed it to Dolly. "For Carla. A reward for her time and skillful effort."

Dolly tucked the bill in the sleeve of her gown. She touched his cheek with true affection. "You're a good man, Dirk Hawkyns. I hope this woman in Baltimore is worth all of your trouble. I hope she deserves someone as wonderful as you. If I was only twenty years younger, I'd give her a run for her money."

"Let's just say the lady and I are made for each other. She's as strong-willed as I am."

She wrapped her long, lovely arms around his broad shoulders as she whispered in his ear, "May God take good care of you."

He placed a peck of affection on the top of her head. "Those are strange words to come from you, Dolly. But then you never did do things the way everyone expected. Thank you. I couldn't have done this without you."

He turned away almost sorry to leave, but Erica waited in Baltimore for him. At least he hoped she did.

Erica glanced at her maid's hunched form molding to the contours of the carriage seat. Her eyes moved away from Larissa to survey the scenery outside the window. The sights of Philadelphia greeted her as famous buildings and historical spots flew in then out of her line of vision.

Her heart pounded with loud thumps of anticipation. Within minutes they would be at the docks where she hoped to find the *Sea Hawk* and Dirk. "Please let him be here," she whispered.

Larissa's aged face lifted. "Are we there yet?" the maid asked with a note of impatience in her voice.

She chuckled. Larissa had been her nursemaid for as long as she could remember. They had left Baltimore three days ago, and the trip had been long and hard. The old woman had grumbled and complained the entire way, not wanting to come in the first place. But Erica had had no choice except to bring her along for the sake of social dictates. Not that she couldn't do this alone. She could. Joshua had been right. She must find Dirk and work the problems out with him for herself.

The road took a sharp turn, and she swayed in unison with Larissa as the carriage lurched around the curve. The spectacular view of the port facilities on the Delaware River came into view. Her heart began a thumpity-thump against her chest, and she gasped for breath. Dirk was here in the crowd of spars and rigging. She could feel his presence like a tangible object tightly grasped in her hand.

The driver pulled the horses to a stop and twisted around so his voice carried to where she sat. "Any particular wharf you lookin' for, miss?" he asked.

Her head swung from window to window to get her bearings. The never-ending docks were a blurred jumbled no matter which way she looked. Hours would be needed to search out every pier. She lifted her slumped shoulders. If that was what she had to do, then she'd better get started.

"May I suggest you try the wharfmaster's office,"

the driver offered as he studied her confused face. "Maybe he can help you."

She smiled her gratitude and nodded approval of the man's idea. With a click of the reins the horses started forward, the vehicle jerking unevenly to the animals' rhythm.

They stopped in front of a small, weather-beaten building with windows so smudged with dirt she couldn't see through them. The carriage door opened in the driver's hand, and she descended to the cobbled street.

"Wait for me, Larissa. I won't be long."

"Humph," the old woman grumbled.

Gathering her skirts around her, she stepped toward the front door of the building. Dirk would be easy to find. She prayed she was right.

The opened door revealed a dimly lit interior with a long counter running down the length of the room. A dusty smudge covered everything, and a smell of stale cigar smoke and stagnant sea odors assaulted her nostrils. Overwhelmed with the desire to leave before talking to anyone, she turned back to the door.

As if from nowhere a reed-thin man popped up from behind the counter. His sullen face and grimy spectacles reflected the mood of the building he worked in. The urge to reach out and wipe the dirt from his glasses so she could see his eyes surged through her. She held her hands firmly down by her side.

"Yes, ma'am," the stick of a man muttered. "Can I help you?"

Her mouth lifted in an automatic smile. "Yes, I was hoping to talk to the wharfmaster, if I could."

"Sorry, ain't here right now. Gone to lunch."

It couldn't be much past eleven o'clock. Odd that someone would be gone for lunch so soon. Maybe that was the reason for the sour disposition on the clerk's face. She pressed sweetly, "Well, then, maybe you can help me."

He screwed his beady eyes up as tightly as he could. "What can I do for you?"

She took a deep breath. "I'm looking for a particular ship that is hopefully here in your harbor."

The clerk glanced back down at his stack of papers. "What ship you lookin' for?"

"The *Sea Hawk,*" she said, pausing. "Captain Dirk Hawkyns?"

He nodded and turned to a large registry on a desk behind him. Flipping a few pages of the already-opened book, he took his long index finger and skimmed lightly down the page. "She was here. Pier seven, berth twenty-three."

"Thank God," she whispered and pivoted to leave.

"I said she *was* here." The clerk's words bombarded her back. She stopped, fearing what his next sentence would be. "She was reported to have sailed early this morning."

She spun around, her eyes holding a plea. "Can you tell me where the ship was headed?"

Briskly he shook his head. "Her hold was empty. The captain wasn't required to give destination."

Her chin slumped to her chest.

"But word has it," he continued, "Captain

Hawkyns might be headed to California or maybe even China."

She dipped her head in thanks. No, he couldn't have left. Not today. His destination might as well be the moon. She would never find him now, no matter how long she looked. She backed away from the counter and stumbled out the door.

"Sorry, ma'am, I couldn't be more help. Look, why don't you go on down to the pier. Maybe they didn't leave as expected. It's always worth a try," the clerk offered in a kindly voice.

"I'll do that." Hurrying out the door, she choked back the fear threatening to burst forth in the form of tears. *No. He's still here. I know it.* Frantically she signaled the driver as she leaped into the carriage. "Pier seven," she ordered, "and fast." She would catch him before he left.

The vehicle strained against the speed of the horses, nearly throwing the two women from their seats. The driver had taken her seriously and raced down the street to the designated location.

"Erica, why ae we rushing?" Larissa gasped as her shoulder pounded into the side of the coach.

"It's important, Larissa. Stop complaining."

The carriage came to a grinding halt, throwing the maid into her outstretched arms. She hoped they had reached the wharf.

She stuck her head out the window. A small, insignificant sign with a faded red seven on it flapped in the light sea breeze over the pier. She stumbled from the carriage before the driver could help her.

"Erica, wait," Larissa called.

Picking up her skirts, she started down the pier in an unladylike sprint. *Please,* she prayed silently, *let him still be here.*

Her eyes skimmed over the ships in the berths as she passed them. A few of the slips were empty, and her eyes jumped several ships ahead of her feet. She didn't bother to count as she went. She would know the *Sea Hawk* the moment her eyes found it.

The pier went on endlessly, her heart sinking lower and lower with each step she took. Panic took hold of her chest and squeezed so tight she thought the pain would suck the breath from her body. *What do I do if he's not here?* Her fear grew to mammoth heights.

She didn't stop until she ran out of pier. Then she reversed her direction, running back down the wharf checking each berth. *I missed it. I just missed it.*

Silent tears came first, and then sobs ripped through her very soul. Refusing to believe what her eyes told her, she again turned and raced up the wooden planks creaking doom with each step she took.

Her foot stepped into nothingness, and she stared down into the murky water slapping at the pilings. The swoosh of the water called her name as the breakers curled into beckoning fingers. She teetered on the edge of the pier, ready to answer the summons of the Delaware River.

Arms encircled her shoulders, and she strained to pull away from them. *Have I lost my mind?* Her hand clutched Larissa, and she slumped back against the maid. Without resisting she turned and let the old

428

woman lead her back to where the carriage waited.

"What's happened, can't be helped," Larissa murmured as she patted the bent, golden head. "You're not doing any good here. It's time to go home, Miss Erica. It's time to call off this wild-goose chase."

She knew the woman was right, but at the same moment her heart stopped being a living thing. It was just an organ pumping blood to her body, nothing more.

Chapter Twenty-one

Baltimore, Maryland
September 12, 1835

Early autumn leaves touched with yellow and gold cascaded from the giant sycamore tree in the garden Erica could see through the French doors of the study.

Where had the summer gone? She shivered in the cool darkness of the room. Now she had nothing to look forward to except the cold, dismal winter lying ahead.

Setting down her pen, she sat back in the desk chair, contemplating the scrubbed, unused fireplace. Maybe she should order a fire be laid to warm up the room. No, Aunt Connie would hear and fly in the room to tell her again how pale and sick she looked. Besides, the chill was in her unfeeling heart, and there was nothing she could do to eliminate the ice residing there. Nothing, that is, within her grasp. She sighed so deeply the sound startled her in the ghostly silence of the room.

She didn't bother to look up at the soft tap of her aunt's heels clicking against the floor as the woman came into the room.

"Goodness, Erica. It's rather chilly in here, don't you think? Shall I have a fire made for you?"

Bitter humor coursed through her. How nice to know the cold was real and not a product of her broken heart. Circling her shoulders with her arms, she nodded her agreement.

Glancing up at Constance's figure poised before the desk she sat behind, she decided marriage definitely agreed with her aunt. She and Joshua had wed almost a month ago. She envied them their marital bliss. No, she was truly happy for them. She raised a questioning eyebrow at the look of concern on Constance's face.

"Joshua and I have plans to go out this evening. I don't expect to be back until late."

She nodded in silence and looked back down at the papers in front of her.

Constance cleared her throat.

She shot her gaze back up at her aunt.

"I hate leaving you here alone, dear."

She slammed the pen down on the desk top. "Good lord, Aunt Connie. I'm not a child. I'll be just fine."

"I'll have cook send a tray in here for you at dinner time."

"Fine, Aunt Connie." She picked up her pen.

"You'll eat it, won't you, dear?" Constance persisted.

Resigned to her aunt's annoying concern, she pushed the papers away. She hadn't read them anyway. The desire to throw them on the floor bubbled to the surface. No, an outburst of anger would only upset her aunt further, and then she wouldn't go out. "Don't worry about me. I promise I'll eat. Now, will you go and have a good time?"

Constance nodded her head and turned to go.

She rose and circled the desk. Placing her arms around her aunt's yielding figure, she kissed the woman affectionately. "I love you, Aunt Connie. Thank you for caring about me."

Two large tears slipped down the older woman's face as she clutched her. "I just worry about you, dear. Nothing seems important to you anymore. It's like you're in a trance, and you don't care what happens around you."

"I promise, I'll do better, if only to make you happy." She loved her aunt too much to see her in so much pain, especially because of her.

She whirled away from the door as it clicked softly behind Constance's retreating figure. Her aunt had no idea how right she was. She didn't care any longer what happened to her.

Like Edmund Bennett. Her surveillant had informed her he had returned to Baltimore over a month ago, but she made no attempt to confront him. Why didn't he come down to the shipping office and demand his share of the profits? She buried her fingers in her temples and rubbed. His reasons didn't matter. All that mattered was that he stayed away from her. She wouldn't bother him as long as he left her alone. She would cling to Armstrong Shipping as long as she could. It was all she had left.

A soft knock on the door brought her musing to

an end.

"Come in."

The manservant who walked in with an armload of firewood gave her a perfunctory nod of his head and crossed the room to the hearth. Removing the silk flower arrangement from the deep cavern of the fireplace, he placed the logs in a symmetric fashion on the andirons, then strategically placed kindling to light the fire.

A curling flame caught the dry wood with pops and snaps as it licked hungrily at the logs as if it had a ferocious appetite to fill.

She turned back to the desk and resumed her seat. Has my life come down to being fascinated with the building of a fire? With a groan she buried her face back into the papers demanding attention.

Once the servant left, she gave up all pretense of working, and pushed the papers away. She would never read them. Stepping toward the fire, she placed her icy hands in front of her. The warmth tingled in the tips of her outstretched fingers, then slowly traveled up her hands to encompass her arms. How wonderful the warmth felt. Like a cold, lonely child she crept closer and closer to the flames until the heat hitting her face made it impossible to breathe. Then she turned and roasted her backside, enjoying the sting pulsating from every nerve in her body. It was good to feel something, even if it was pain.

The staccato rap on the door annoyed her. Whoever it was could go away. It sounded again. Damn, why didnt' everyone leave her alone.

"Come in," she snapped.

The smartly dressed butler pushed through the

433

door. He offered a small, stiff bow from the waist.

"There's a gentleman here to see you, miss."

Her mind whirled dizzily. Who could it be? She had no men friends. It could only be one person. How dare Edmund Bennett come here to her house. Anger simmered on the surface, warming her chilled blood. "Give me ten minutes and show the gentleman in." The word gentleman came out in a sneer.

He nodded and stepped back, closing the door with a brisk motion.

Her mind raced. Bennett was here to demand his share of the profits and his rights as the major stockholder of Armstrong Shipping. She would never give him either one. She must be prepared to confront him. Circling the desk, she pulled out the top drawer. Her hand brushed against the pocket pistol she had placed there weeks ago after her aborted effort to face the man at his boardinghouse. Her father's gun. Justice would be served when the man died from a bullet from Eric Armstrong's gun. Her hand glided over the mechanics of the pistol, checking it carefully. Then she loaded it and sat down on the chair, the gun grasped tightly in her hands.

The lazy wall clock swung its pendulum back and forth, ticking away the minutes, announcing her emotions swinging from fear of what she was about to do to desire for revenge. Revenge won the struggle. She was ready. She wouldn't hesitate to do what she had to do.

The door swung silently on its hinges. She glanced down readying the pistol to be fired. The weapon trembled in her hands as she raised it, her arms stiffly extended in front of her, the desk between her and the intruder.

"Erica." The voice speaking her name came from a dream. Her head froze, unable to look up and confirm what her ears told her.

A warm hand wrapped around hers and gently took the gun from her hands, sending electric shocks jolting through her body. Her gaze touched on the darkly clad figure of a man. She followed the lines of the jacket covering the broad chest.

Her breaths came in short pants as her emotions seesawed back and forth from anticipation of what her eyes would see to fear that her mind had crumbled and played tricks on her.

When her gray eyes, blurred with tears, found the dark, liquid pools she prayed would be there, an animalistic moan slipped out from between her lips. A thousand words formed in her mind, pushing and crowding each other to be the first to reach her mouth. As a result of her vacillating emotions she was speechless. She held her position, her arms still outstretched as if her hands held the gun.

With a click, Dirk uncocked the pistol and placed it on the far end of the desk, out of her reach. His penetrating gaze skimmed over her slim figure. Casually his stare rose to rest on her trembling lips.

Then their eyes locked, dancing, fencing, each trying to make the other look away. From the corner of her eyes, she saw his hand ease into his jacket. What did he reach for? A gun to shoot her, a knife to stab her, a pretty package with a bright ribbon on it to appease her? She held her breath until her lungs felt ready to burst as she read the conflict in his eyes.

Pain jabbed at her gray orbs as they misted with

the need to blink. Her lids flickered down over her vision to clear it. She concentrated on his hand, forgetting the battle between their looks. His fist slipped out of the front of his jacket, clutching a neat stack of papers slightly dog-eared at the corners. With calculated slowness he set the papers on the desk in front of her.

Skimming over the written words, she knew them by heart. Fifty-one shares of Armstrong Shipping.

"Where did you get these?" she blurted, not believing what she saw.

"Where doesn't matter. The point is, they belong to me."

She backed away from the desk and turned to the painting of the *Anna McKyle* gracing the study wall behind her head. She pulled the picture toward her, and it swung on hinges to reveal a small wall safe. Her eyes darted back to find him watching her with amused cocksureness on his face. Placing her body between him and the safe lock, she opened the metal door. She reached her hand inside and pulled out a leather satchel, which she tucked under her arm as she slammed the safe shut.

With as much poise as she possessed she whirled back to the desk and placed the leather bag face up before her. Wordlessly she picked up one of the certificates he had laid before her and reached in the satchel to pull out an identical paper.

Her eyes flew back and forth between the two certificates. They were exactly the same. His were authentic. Dirk Hawkyns now owned fifty-one percent of her company.

Her gaze shot up in accusation. He was now the

enemy. She threw out her hand to grab the pile of papers, but he moved faster and held them up just out of her reach.

Forgetting her dignity, she had to get them back. Racing around the desk, she struggled to retrieve what was rightfully hers. All the feelings she thought had died weeks ago surged back: love, hate, vengeance, and desire. They bubbled up from the pit of her stomach fully armed and ready to do battle to gain supremacy over her heart.

"Give them back to me," she demanded, panting from her open mouth. "They're mine." She didn't care what he thought of her.

"Are they, sweetheart?" he taunted. "Seems to me you were careless to let them get away from you in the first place. Wouldn't Bennett sign your agreement either?"

Like a hellborn fury she lunged at him, her fingers curled to do battle. He sidestepped her, and she staggered. His arm encircled her waist, stopping her from falling on her face. Clutching her tightly to his heaving chest, her arms caught in the crush, he maneuvered her back to the desk. Her eyes followed the movement of his hand. The certificates slapped on the desk's flat top.

"Now, sweetheart," he mocked. "I'll sign your damn agreement."

Her head swiveled around to face him. His words were like a bucket of freezing water thrown into her face. This wasn't how she meant to act. She choked on unswallowed saliva as she mumbled, "No, you don't understand. It's not necessary anymore."

His wild laughter echoed through the room and

through her head. "You're damned right. A prenuptial agreement wouldn't be necessary anymore, would it." His eyes shot hot flames of anger, scorching everywhere they touched her. "Now, I own more than you do."

She closed her eyes to shut out the hate and digust that seemed to pour out of his devil eyes. "No, Dirk. It's not like that," she whispered. "I never meant to hurt you. I was only doing what my father requested at his death."

He released her from his crushing grip without warning. She swayed, trembling like a lone pine at the mercy of a tempest, expecting thunder and lightning to strike her down at any moment.

"Damn you, woman, for the way you make me feel." His booted feet clicked across the wooden floor as he walked away.

Her eyes flew open to study the rigid back he presented to her. Then her eyes darted down to the unprotected stock certificates. Should she grab them and run?

As if he read her thoughts in the vibrant air, he spun to watch her actions. "If they're that important to you, then take them."

He offered her the return of her company. He offered her everything except what she wanted. Him. She shook her head slowly. The motion picked up speed, and her head whirled dizzily. "No, Dirk, you are more important to me."

Looking down at the floor buckling in her swirling vision, she stuffed the back of her hand in her mouth. *What have I done? What have I said? He will laugh at me and make a mockery of my feelings.*

He crossed back to stand in front of her. Fearing she would see pity, or worse, disgust on his face, she dared not look up. The warmth of his body reached out to caress her, to tease her body aching for him to touch her. Whether in love or hate, she needed to feel him pressed against her. Her wanton body threatened to betray her dignity and strength.

She didn't care. She wanted him. She needed him to take her in his arms. She needed . . .

A ripping sound destroyed the silence in the study. She lifted her eyes to investigate.

With his hip perched on the edge of the desk, he held both sets of certificates in his hands, his and hers. She was positive she heard the papers scream in protest as he tore them asunder, ripped them into two even halves. He drew his left hand holding one half of the destroyed stocks to his chest. The other hand reached out, offering her an equal share.

"Now, they're even. Yours and mine. And they aren't worth a damn without the other half."

She stepped forward, unable to resist the magnetic pull of his eyes. Her hand extended to accept his gift. "Why did you do this?" she breathed so lightly she wasn't sure he had heard her.

"Because I love you, and not what you have."

Her arms lifted humbly, begging him to love her. Forcefully his arms surrounded her waist, molding her body against his. She dropped her head back to meet his questing lips, her hunger matching his. As they kissed, their tongues dueled for superiority.

Needing to clutch him closer, she released the shreds of paper she held in her hand. She didn't care about them anymore. She had Dirk. That was all she needed.

His warm, empty hands tore at the tiny pearl buttons on the back of her gown. She glanced at the floor as papers floated down around them, dotting the darkness like quaint flakes of snow, drifting on top of the ones she had released seconds before.

"Love me," she pleaded, unabashed.

"Ah, Mermaid, I've loved you since I first saw you on that island in the middle of nowhere." He gathered her up in his arms and carried her toward the door. "Marry me."

She nodded eagerly.

"Now," he demanded.

Her head stopped, still lifted high in a nod. "But Dirk, it's late."

His finger came down to rest lightly against her open lips, stilling her protests before she spoke them. "Just say yes; don't argue with me."

He dropped her back on her feet, turned her around, and buttoned up the back of her gaping gown.

"You're serious," she shrieked.

"Of course I'm serious." He whirled her back to face him. "Now get a wrap. It's chilly outside."

"But Aunt Connie and Joshua . . ."

"Will understand in the morning when we see them," he interrupted. Possessively he drew her to him as he whispered huskily, "I want to make love to you, Erica. But I want to make love to my wife."

"You may kiss the bride." The words floated around her like soft down. Dirk's lips claimed hers in a feathery kiss promising more, much more. She strained forward to maintain the contact between them for as long as she could.

"Now," he said as his mouth blazed a trail across her jaw to her ear. "I have a wedding present for you."

"Present?" she mumbled softly, wanting only one thing from him — his love colored with desire. She circled his neck.

"That's right, Mrs. Hawkyns. Aren't you even curious?"

The loud "humph" of the justice of the peace brought them both back to reality.

His arms released her, but only briefly. She leaned back as he scooped her up to carry her out the door.

"It's customary, young man, to carry the bride over the threshold *into* the house, not out the door." The justice's voice followed them down the steps.

"Perhaps, sir," Dirk said over his shoulder. "We don't do things the customary way. Do we, sweetheart?"

She giggled into his jacket. Then he swung her into the carriage and joined her on the seat.

The vehicle started with a jolt, taking them in the opposite direction from the house.

"Dirk, where are we going?"

"I told you I had a wedding gift for you."

"You planned this entire evening, didn't you?"

He lifted his wide shoulders. "I had hopes things would work out like they did. But then, I'm not the only one guilty of planning elaborate evenings, if I recall right."

She blushed, remembering the night she had proposed to him aboard the *Sea Hawk*. Her eyes skimmed the scenery outside the coach window. They were headed for the docks.

"Dirk, why are we going to the harbor?"

"Hush, Erica. Don't ask questions."

In front of Armstrong Shipping the driver pulled to a stop. She opened her mouth to ask why. Dirk placed his hand against her lips and lifted his eyebrow in a silent order.

Taking her hand, he helped her from the carriage. She looked up at the sign in front of the building. Armstrong Shipping. "I guess we'll have to do something about the name. I'm a Hawkyns now, not an Armstrong."

He didn't reply as he led her around the building and toward the wharf. What did he have planned? A wedding present, he had said. Her heart beat with childish anticipation. Would she feel like this every time he bought her a gift? She hoped so. If she had to give up her freedom now that she was his wife, she hoped their life would always be thrilling and exciting.

He led her down the pier toward the *Anna McKyle*'s empty berth. She stopped. The slip wasn't empty. What had he gotten her? She lifted her skirts and sprinted down the creaking boards. He matched her strides and laughed. "Slow down, woman."

In front of the slip, she stopped. The moonlight dotted the undulating water, rippling like a white ribbon, then cast a silver light over the bow of a ship unlike any she had seen before. The figurehead danced with the movement of the ship, a mermaid with golden hair flowing in curls to hide the upthrust

442

breasts as it wrapped its tail around the ship's stem.

"Dirk, she's beautiful, but I've never seen anything like her before. She's not a clipper. . . ."

"A steamer. The newest thing. She'll make all other ships obsolete. Wind or not, she'll make good time." His hand reached inside his jacket and pulled out a piece of paper. He placed it in her hand.

Her fingers shook as she opened the folded document. The *Mermaid*, the ownership papers proclaimed. The owner—Erica Hawkyns.

She gasped. "Dirk, she's mine? She's beautiful. But I don't understand."

"Do you think I'd do to you what I wouldn't allow you to do to me?"

Her eyes widened in disbelief.

"She's yours, Erica. Do with her as you want. My gift to you for the loss of the *Anna McKyle*."

"You mean I can captain her, if I want?"

"If that's what you want." His eyes held hers, the love he felt for her as a person shining through.

How could she have ever doubted him? She had assumed he expected her to stay home and do wifely things. But instead he offered her a choice and would love her no matter what she chose to do. Could she be a wife, a good wife, and still be her own person? She didn't know. She did know she was willing to give it a try.

She swung about and threw her arms around his neck. "I love you, husband," she cried.

"I love you, too, wife. I won't tie you down to a life you don't want to lead."

Indecision danced across her face. What did she want? She wanted it all. Her eyes flew to the *Mer-*

maid and then to his face—a face demanding nothing but that she choose for herself.

"Can't we share the *Mermaid?*"

"How do you mean?" he replied. "There can't be two captains."

"I know, but can't the captain take his wife along?"

"Do you mean that?" His eyes smiled down on her.

She took the ownership papers and tore them in half, slipping his share into his hand. "I mean it."

He swung her up and whirled her there on the dock.

All her life she had sought the way to release her soul to the freedom of the universe. At last she had found what she looked for. Their shared love was all she needed to be an independent individual. A woman of strength.

<u>FREE</u> Preview Each Month and $ave

Zebra has made arrangements for you to preview 4 brand new HEARTFIRE novels each month...FREE for 10 days. You'll get them as soon as they are published. If you are not delighted with any of them, just return them with no questions asked. But if you decide these are everything we said they are, you'll pay just $3.25 each—a total of $13.00 (a $15.00 value). **That's a $2.00 saving each month off the regular price.** Plus there is NO shipping or handling charge. These are delivered right to your door absolutely free! There is no obligation and there is no minimum number of books to buy.

TO GET YOUR FIRST MONTH'S PREVIEW... Mail the Coupon Below!

Mail to:

HEARTFIRE Home Subscription Service, Inc.
120 Brighton Road
P.O. Box 5214
Clifton, NJ 07015-5214

YES! I want to subscribe to Zebra's HEARTFIRE Home Subscription Service. Please send me my first month's books to preview free for ten days. I understand that if I am not pleased I may return them and owe nothing, but if I keep them I will pay just $3.25 each; a total of $13.00. That is a savings of $2.00 each month off the cover price. There are no shipping, handling or other hidden charges and there is no minimum number of books I must buy. I can cancel this subscription at any time with no questions asked.

NAME _____

ADDRESS _____ APT. NO. _____

CITY _____ STATE _____ ZIP _____

SIGNATURE   (if under 18, parent or guardian must sign)   *2200*
Terms and prices are subject to change.